STONEWALL INN EDITIONS
Keith Kahla, General Editor

SOME
MEN
ARE
LOOKERS

ETHAN MORDDEN

 ST. MARTIN'S GRIFFIN NEW YORK

"The Hunt for Red October" originally appeared in slightly different form in *Waves: An Anthology of New Gay Fiction*.

Design by *Bryanna Millis*

Library of Congress Cataloging-in-Publication Data

Mordden, Ethan.
    Some men are lookers / by Ethan Mordden.—1st ed.
      p. cm.
    ISBN 0-312-19336-x
    1. Gay men—New York (State)—Social life and customs—Fiction.
    2. Manhattan (New York, N.Y.)—Social Life and customs—Fiction.   3. City and town life—New York (State)—New York—Fiction.   I. Title.
    PS3563.07717S65   1997
    813'.54—dc21   96-53928
                                                                                          CIP

First St. Martin's Griffin Edition: October 1998

10 9 8 7 6 5 4 3 2 1

To the memory of
ROBERT JAMES TRENT
April 27, 1945–February 25, 1995

ACKNOWLEDGMENTS

To my always excellent copy editor, Benjamin Dreyer; to my diplomatic agent, Joe Spieler; to my editor, Keith Kahla, with whom I gladly reunite after a perilous intermission. It's a jungle out there.

CONTENTS

The action begins in 1988.

The setting is mainly New York City, in and around the apartments of Dennis Savage and Bud, in a high-rise on East Fifty-third Street.

The players include:

DENNIS SAVAGE, a schoolteacher in his late thirties.

VIRGIL, his live-in, in his late twenties. Creative, whimsical, increasingly restless. Formerly known as Little Kiwi.

BAUHAUS, Virgil's crafty, sinister, demented dog.

CARLO, né Smith, given name Ripley, a constant visitor to East Fifty-third. Ageless and all-conquering, the hottest cowboy in town.

PETER KEENE, an editor in book publishing, just coming out and a little cock-crazy. More than a little.

VIC ASTARCHOS, a porn model and hustler, big-time.

CASH WESTMAN, a vile seducer with S&M interests.

MISS FAYE, a drag queen. Style: thuggish pixie. Life's Hope: to win Oscar for her fabulous Teacup Scene, thereby ranking out that meddling Dominique Sanda, with her incessant Lesbian Dance Sequence. Age: advanced, though a tidy exercise program makes her feel like a twenty-year-old. Unfortunately, the twenty-year-old usually isn't interested.

KONSTANTIN, a Russian émigré construction worker, married and a father; also, to his bewilderment, Peter Keene's lover.

TOM DRIGGERS, a mostly offstage character. Once a champion party boy, now dying in the hospital.

ZULIAN, nicknamed Zuleto, an episode in Bud's past, today the operator of a motorboat fleet catering to tourists in Venice.

CANDIO, Zuleto's son. Devastating, with—as they put it in Venice—occhi assassini: killer eyes.

BILLY, a street kid given a second chance. Wiry, trashy, appealing.

BERT HICKS, a good guy gone lurid on Stonewall heat. But is he telling the fatal truth?

ROY AND NICKY, a typical best-friend couple: One is content with the contract as it reads, while the other wants to amend it with an all-the-way love clause.

FATTY DE PINERO, a shadowy character.

BABY FRUMKIN, an imaginary character.

COSGROVE, a changeling with dreams of revenge and an arsenal of whoopee cushions, Virgil's inseparable buddy and the live-in of

BUD: who narrates.

EXORCIS

Virgil and Cosgrove have a new sport they call the Commercial Game. They cruise the television with the mute button on, seeking commercial breaks for which they provide their own extemporaneous soundovers. It's hectic but simple. All car pitches are for Subaru. All horror movie trailers are for something Cosgrove has entitled *Exorcis*—"You can run, you can hide," he gloats, "but it's coming to get you"—and all cereal spots are for Sugar Boy Pops, a brand I am unfamiliar with.

They were playing the Commercial Game one evening when Lionel dropped by Dennis Savage's to tell us that Tom Driggers was back in the hospital for what was almost certainly the last time, and had asked to see Dennis Savage. Tom and he had been very close once—very, *very* close was my impression. But they hadn't spoken in quite some time now.

"Subaru!" Virgil cried. "The car in a million!"

"With hatchback and full accessories!" Cosgrove added. "Radio, tape deck, mascara tray."

"He's really bought the farm," Lionel was telling us. "All that money and power, and down he goes to nothing."

"You'll ride like a king!" Virgil announced. "It's Subaru!"

"See how it goes!" said Cosgrove, as a Pontiac sailed by.

"You should be there," Lionel went on. "He's got a roomful of . . . of toadies and pimps and comparable phantasmagoria of the bad old days. That's what he's dying to. There's nobody *human* in that room."

Virgil, Dennis Savage's live-in, is, like Cosgrove, considerably younger than most of our circle. So he isn't as well informed as we are and, again like Cosgrove, often keeps one ear on our conversations, sifting through the terms and concepts for material he can use in the act: his life. I saw him sifting now, losing touch with the television as he took in this new thing about toadies and death and power.

"Tom had everything and now he has nothing," Lionel continued. "I'm afraid to have to admit that this is a very gay story.

What ups and what downs, I mean? He looks like a beanbag sculpture. So, if we could only not maximize his failure . . ."

Dennis Savage looked at him.

"Okay?" said Lionel.

Dennis Savage looked at me.

"As a kind of restabilizing act of mercy?" Lionel added. "For me? Okay?"

Dennis Savage said, "Not okay."

"Ladies, aren't you tired of your derodeant?" Cosgrove declaimed, smoothy-announcer-style. "Don't you want Mamzelle Hint O'Spring instead?"

"That's not deodorant, Cosgrove, that's laundry de—"

"I think a man deserves something better than to die with all his would-be heirs drooling over him," Lionel went on.

"What about that carpenter Tom was living with?" I asked. "With all the tattoos? I thought that was supposed to be love for life."

Lionel sighed. He gestured then, resolute but resigned, one of those things hands do in the air when words can't tell. "It sort of was, actually. Love. Which was very unusual for Tom. Tuffy, his name is. He isn't around all that often. Tom won't talk about it, but apparently Tuffy has developed a prodigious case of plague necrophobia. He's a simple guy, you know, very basic, and he just doesn't get it, or anything. He is very desperately threatened."

Cosgrove heard that. I saw him whisper "He is very desperately threatened" to himself.

"What kind of man," said Dennis Savage, "has a lover named Tuffy? What's his *morality,* if you gay commissars will pardon me for asking?"

"Whose name is Tuffy?" asked Virgil, switching off the television. "Is he some rough boy of the streets?"

"Is he?" I asked Lionel. "He certainly puts on a hard act, as I recall. Ferocious triceps."

"Tom always liked it down and dirty, you know."

"I could be Tuffy," Virgil ventured.

"And I could be Tuffy on weekends," said Cosgrove.

"Look," said Dennis Savage with his famous weary patience. "Tuffy and his like are for people who cannot live in reality. People who go through their time on earth like a teenager at his first fuck. People who have no sense of responsibility or fairness or loyalty. Tom Driggers is the Circuit personified—drug up, dance, screw, sleep it off, and do it again. He got rich organizing service industries for other people like himself. He ran buses to the beach, he ran whores to the closeted rich, he ran discos till you drop. He *had,* and he *had,* and he *had*—and when the rest of us appetitive sexboys looked around and saw that our appetites could kill us and backed away, Tom Driggers went right on having. That's why he is on the verge of defunct. I'm sorry to say so, but if someone has to die of this cursed poison, it ought to be Tom Driggers. Because he took his choice, and this is his consequence."

Somewhere in all that, Dennis Savage had left Virgil and Cosgrove and had resumed addressing Lionel, not gently.

"And you can stop begging me to visit that disgusting, putrid piece of Texas redneck trash, because he's going to die with his kind around him, not with me!"

"For pity's sake—"

Dennis Savage chopped out the following words: *"He has what he created!"*

There was silence.

"Someone," said Virgil, finally, "is rather snarky today."

"He is very desperately threatened," Cosgrove quickly added.

"I'll quit while I'm behind," said Lionel, getting up to go. Virgil saw him to the door, where Lionel turned to Dennis Savage, regarding him mildly but holding it out into a stare.

Dennis Savage faced him down.

Virgil was watching them, and Cosgrove was watching Virgil.

"Maybe you could think about it," Virgil said suddenly to Dennis Savage, "and maybe you would change your mind."

"And maybe I won't."

Lionel nodded and left.

After closing the door, Virgil stood in thought, his back to us; Dennis Savage nudged me with a glance, indicating his lover. We all know one another so well that we sometimes operate like a mime troupe, entirely in visuals.

"Can I show my movie now?" Cosgrove asked. "It's the first videotape that I really made myself."

"I helped him," said Virgil, still at the door.

"Virgil always helps me."

"I'm not sitting through another *Friday the 13th* sequel," said Dennis Savage, "I'll tell you that."

"It's *The Lost Boys*."

"Are you undergoing a mystical out-of-life experience with that door," Dennis Savage asked Virgil, who hadn't yet moved, "or would you like to join us on the couch?"

Virgil coolly came over, sitting on the far side of the couch from Dennis Savage.

"Hey!"

"Easy," I said.

"Well, what's he supposed to be, my eighth cousin thrice removed? Come over here, you."

"Cosgrove," said Virgil, staying put, "it's movie time."

"Were they misunderstood cuties," Cosgrove cried, jumping up to make his presentation, "or mean ghouls? A magical club, or killers on the loose?"

"Let's skip the trailer," said Dennis Savage. "Just run the film."

"This is becoming a very snarky apartment," said Virgil.

Dennis Savage leaned over me and asked Virgil, "How come I don't know what that word means?"

"Virgil and Cosgrove Productions present," Cosgrove began, with a—at any rate trying to—flourish, and onto the television screen came the credits of *Pee-wee's Big Adventure*.

"Sure," said Dennis Savage. "The three things I most wanted to do tonight were go to the dentist for an emergency root canal, trade fashion tips with Prince, and see *Pee-wee's Big Adventure*. That's one down."

"I mixed up the boxes," said Cosgrove, wrestling with his software. "We have so many now."

"And if Jerry Lewis isn't them, the Ritz Brothers are," said Dennis Savage. "An elite collection."

"We have *The Fruits of Worth*," said Cosgrove. "It's an art classic from the black-and-white days."

"*The Grapes of Wrath*, Cosgrove," said Virgil.

Cosgrove had *The Lost Boys* cued up at last, and on it came, to his cheers. Actually, this was Cosgrove's big night in another way, for he was just two hours short of getting anything he wanted (within reason). This started when it occurred to me that it would make everyone's life easier if he had some incentive to behave himself. This would comprise, for instance, not muttering "He was touched by the ugly stick" in a voodoo accent when passing one of God's unfortunates in the street; and, when asked to prepare dinner, not presenting one's live-in with a plate of baked-bean sandwiches and potato chips. If Cosgrove could stay innocent for a month, I told him, he could choose his prize—and if nothing more than *The Lost Boys* happened in the next two hours, he was a shoo-in.

Early in the movie, there is a scene in an amusement park at night, where a restless montage brings together images of the seedy and the erotic. This worrisome marriage of what repels and what appeals is then epitomized in a song called "I Still Believe," performed by an oiled, shirtless bodybuilder, dancing, singing, and playing the saxophone. This is, in fact, Tim Cappello, one of Tina Turner's sidemen, a versatile musician who was also, at the time of filming, a titanic devotee of the gym. He isn't handsome, and his slicked-back ponytail hairdo strikes an alarming note. (Studies have revealed that 84 percent of men with ponytails are paint-sniffers, serial killers, or Axl Rose.) Nevertheless, as he grinds his hips and blows his horn, Cappello is a very hot package. He's magnificent. Watching his act, I kept trying to place him culturally, for he seems to fuse the self-presentational imperatives of the gay avatar with the reckless abandon of hetero trash. What is this picture telling us? I wondered. It's not familiar yet it's instantly recognizable. Or it's not likable but it's irresistible. Or it's not pretty: It's straight.

Suddenly Dennis Savage, pointing at Tim Cappello, cried, "That's Tom Driggers. I mean, that's his echelon, his kind. Am I wrong?" he asked me. "He was always pulling in these bizarrely sexy characters off the street—like that one, there—and that was—"

"So who can blame him?" I asked.

"*You* didn't live like that!"

"I never got the chance to. Tom Driggers had the luck to find these guys. He'd walk into a straight bar, order a scotch, and smile at the man next to him, who would almost invariably turn out to be a horny fireman in a crossover frame of mind. Wherever *I* went, there was Arnold Stang."

"So, ontologically speaking, the whole gay world represents a sequence of hot encounters with, if possible, the enemy. Is that it?"

"No talking in the theatre," said Virgil.

"This isn't a theatre," Dennis Savage told him. "This is an apartment where real people live. This is where dreams of infinite sexual exaltation come to die. Where things are a little dull but everyone talks sense. This isn't one big bedroom."

"He is very desperately threatened," Cosgrove whispered.

Virgil took the remote from Cosgrove and put the movie on hold.

"Are you just mad at that guy because of the way he lived?" he asked Dennis Savage. "Or did he do something to you?"

"He did something to me, and put the movie back on."

"Maybe you would talk about it. Otherwise you might seem very fanatic to us."

Dennis Savage, Napoléon on St. Helena, sighed profoundly. "I put that incident and Tom Driggers behind me long ago, and I have no intention of dealing with either again."

Virgil looked at Dennis Savage, then at me.

"Don't try this door," I told him. "I don't know the story."

"It was one of the few things I managed to keep from you," said Dennis Savage. "Thank God for something, I'm safe."

"You're never safe," I said. "It's Exorcis the storyteller, coming to get you. You can run, you can—"

"Children, put the movie on."

"All right," said Virgil. "But you're being horribly snarky tonight."

"You know what I think?" said Cosgrove.

I put my hand on his mouth. "You're on the verge of losing your reward for a month's good behavior," I warned him.

"Please be nice," he pleaded.

"Put on the movie!" Dennis Savage roared.

The rest of the screening passed in silence, a genuinely absorbed one. Virgil and Cosgrove love horror films, especially the *Exorcis* ones with supernatural menace in which the forces of humanity rout the forces of evil. Yes, it's coming to get you, but you can stonewall it for a time and, at the last, destroy it. *The Lost Boys* is conceptually bewitching—the boys themselves are punk-style vampires, which makes sexiness a metaphor for aggression. I was amused. But Dennis Savage watched with one eye, lost in recollection.

So deep in thought was he that when the movie ended our clapping startled him. He almost jumped.

"Hooray for Cosgrove," said Virgil.

"My first tape," Cosgrove preened.

"And now," Virgil went on, "Cosgrove gets to choose his prize for being a good boy."

"Oh, yes?" Cosgrove said. "Suddenly it's now, sometimes." He jumped to his feet and surveyed us all. "I want a suit. The kind with a vest and a tie."

"Done deal," I said.

"How come I don't get a suit?" Virgil asked Dennis Savage.

"What do you want from me? You have a job. You're earning money of your own—go buy yourself a suit."

Virgil looked away. "I wouldn't know what to say."

"Virgil," said Cosgrove, "would you help me pick out my suit? I can't decide between pin-stripe and burnt umber."

"Cosgrove, we have to figure out where you will *wear* your suit for the first time!"

"It could be somewhere important," said Cosgrove.

"I know just the place," said Virgil, getting excited. "We could all go to *A Chorus Line*!"

"You've seen it seven times," said Dennis Savage.

"Cosgrove has never been there!"

"It's like this," said Dennis Savage, doing his Slow and Careful. "We have three more months till school's out. I *think* if I can just husband my crumbling sanity till then, I can use the summer to recover in. I say I *think* I can. But every little squeeze and assault that I suffer from now till then is going to threaten the equation."

(Virgil was rolling his eyes and Cosgrove was making farting noises.)

"Yes," Dennis Savage went on. "Yes, I knew I'd immediately win the sympathy of the room."

"I don't think *A Chorus Line* is important enough for my suit," said Cosgrove.

"How about the opera?" Dennis Savage asked me.

"All I have left is *Götterdämmerung* next Friday," I said. "That's a little epic for Cosgrove."

"Cosgrove is a little epic himself," Dennis Savage shot back with a grin. "They ought to get along just fine."

"Cosgrove at the opera!" Virgil breathed out, in awe.

Elated at being the center of attention, Cosgrove suddenly turned apprehensive. "They won't make me sing, will they?"

"Most of them just sit there," Virgil assured him.

"I thought you liked to sing," said Dennis Savage.

"Only my famous personal medleys."

"Look," I began.

"Can I please go to the opera with you?" Cosgrove asked me, most winningly. "I just think I need to, in my suit."

"Of course you can," I replied, already dreading it; but Cosgrove hadn't quite placed himself among us emotionally then, and he needed encouragement.

"Cosgrove meets Wagner," said Dennis Savage, as if pronouncing the title of a porn loop.

"Would you lighten up?" I said.

"Yes, as you have lightened up on me because I won't see Tom Driggers."

"Did I say a word?"

"But what are you *thinking*?"

"You are so mean," said Virgil.

"Don't you judge me," said Dennis Savage. "Because you don't know what happened."

Bauhaus, Virgil's pet, a Gila monster disguised (not well) as a dog, crawled out from under the couch, growling at phantoms he visualized somewhere between the television and the bookcase. He froze. He pointed. He rolled over. He went to sleep.

"And," Virgil continued, to Dennis Savage, "you're entirely snarky."

"What does that word mean?"

"It means," Cosgrove cut in, "that he says bad things about me, and makes me cry."

This was an allusion to old times, when we were still collecting and integrating our odd little family: when Dennis Savage thought Cosgrove might undermine his relationship with Virgil. When everyone we knew was still alive except our great-grandfathers. When it never occurred to us that maybe you don't *have* to spend the summer in the Pines.

Things are so different now that Dennis Savage and I speak of Before and After. Before was, you used up a weekend prowling for partners, no limit as to how many or what you'd do. After is, you spent a weekend ministering to your live-in, Cosgrove, because while amusing himself at a street fair he ate twelve coconut Sno-Kones in a row and came home in vast distress—in fact, diarrhetic—and had to be not only cared for but euphemized. (We settled on a diagnosis of Compulsive Bathroom Manifestation, in the style of the trendy affliction, such as your Decreased Intelligence Clarity, your Unenhanced Attention Commitment.)

You become so aware of age. I remember my epiphany, when I was playing a tape of Barbra Streisand's last night on Broadway in *Funny Girl* for my young friend Allan the Actor, a *Funny Girl* buff. "The Music That Makes Me Dance" is the key cut; he was duly blown away, and I was thrust back to my long-gone days of innocence and youthful thrill. Everything was possible then, though so little was permitted, except for Saturday matinées in New York. But theatre would lead to liberation. "Did you actually see the show?" I asked Allan. He said, "I wasn't born then."

Oh, you become so *aware* of age, boys and girls!

If Cosgrove was going to sit through *Götterdämmerung,* he'd better familiarize himself with the action; so I parked him with a German-English libretto booklet and went off to visit Tom Driggers in the hospital.

I expected to greet a pride of his hot mondo trasho monsters, but he was alone, packed in bed in a silent room. He looked like a dirty, broken thimble.

"Well, is he going to make his entrance?" Tom asked me. "I want to shake hands with him and say goodbye. Does he know that I miss him? Some folks don't especially know a thing like that."

"I brought you some strawberries. I even washed them." I put them on the table by the bed. "They're all set to go."

"Oh, hey."

As we made our fitful conversation, I kept thinking back to Tom Driggers in his youth as an upstart entrepreneur of Free Stonewall. He was something to see in those days, a kid striking it rich, betting each new dollar against the last, double or nothing and never losing. He owned the world, because everything that matters is for sale, or so, for some, it seemed. Tom Driggers was a happy man. His hungers were satisfied, yet he could stay hungry. Unlike most of the men who ran the gay service industries, he was easy to work for—in fact, a pushover. And unlike most of the men with the money to concoct their sex lives at will, he was young and arrestingly nice-looking. He virtually ran sex in New York. He decided when and where and who would do what and to whom, as the old limerick goes. He had a very potent sense of free choice.

What I mean is: Do you remember the 1970s?

I wondered what Tom Driggers was remembering. He was floating in that end-of-term hospital haze that says, There is no time, place, world. There is only the end of my life, very soon.

"What happened between you and Dennis Savage?" I asked.

I could see him trying to think back to it, but people like Tom Driggers don't absorb much, even at their best. Ten years later, on his deathbed, he had as much recall as Siegfried after drinking Hagen's potion.

"He sort of . . . he just got mad at me suddenly. And he wouldn't speak to me ever again, and he wouldn't explain. Is he always like that?"

"No, he usually explains. At length."

Tom lay quiet for some time. Then: "We were very close, you know. He was a different kind of friend than everyone else. See, he never asked me for money or wangled into staying at my Pines place." He pulled his blanket more tightly around himself, as if tucking himself in, a child without parents. "He really . . . he really liked me, I know that much. He was so . . . well, serious about things. You're always saying the wrong thing with someone like that. No one comes much anymore. They did the first times. Would you ask him to come see me? I won't say the wrong thing. I'll say anything he wants."

When I got home, I went right to Dennis Savage's, where another visit was just ending. An older man of our acquaintance had dropped by, a man from Very Before. When we were in our early twenties, he had hit fifty—a presentable, even an attractive fifty: But all the same, he was an Old Queen standing on the border of invisibility. (Don't blame me. I didn't make the world; I don't even forgive it.)

Now this gentleman was even more senior, yet he was looking back to the sexy seventies, pleading with Dennis Savage to make a certain limited peace with our communal past by paying respects to Tom Driggers on his deathbed.

Dennis Savage was taking it all in a good mood, till Virgil came home from work and, introduced to the visitor, said, "They call me Tuffy."

"Who calls you Tuffy?" asked Dennis Savage. "Name three."

Virgil looked at him. "My gang. The Lost Boys." His upper lip went up and his teeth peered out.

"What is that mouth doing?"

"If you don't call me Tuffy, I'll swoop down on you and drink your blood."

"Nobody calls you Tuffy," Dennis Savage began, but just then Cosgrove came in, and he called Virgil Tuffy, and luckily Carlo arrived at the same moment, because the two of us had to help Dennis Savage over to the couch and pacify him. Lately his nerves have been like nails scratching slate.

The older man of our acquaintance made his departure, pausing only to meet Cosgrove. Virgil introduced them. "This is Tuffy."

"I thought *you* were Tuffy," the man said, smiling.

"Somehow we're both Tuffy," Cosgrove told him.

"Are you one of the Lost Boys, too?"

"I'm the Lostest Boy of all."

The man turned to Dennis Savage. "Maybe tomorrow?" he said. "He hasn't much longer,"

Dennis Savage, dazed, made no reply.

"They come at me from every side," he said as the door closed. "On the left it's Tom Driggers and guilt, and on the right it's a legion of Lost Boys swooping down to drink my blood, but guess what? We absolutely *can't* have two people named Tuffy. We shouldn't even have one."

"I'll be Tuffy," said Virgil, "and Cosgrove can be Tuffy-boy."

"Hold me down," Dennis Savage feebly begged. "Make them stop."

Virgil took Cosgrove into the kitchen to get dinner started—spaghetti and salad—and once Dennis Savage got a few sighs out of his system, the room went calm. He even got a little buoyant.

"What a *refreshment*," he exclaimed. "Imagine: socializing with someone who's older than I! They said it couldn't be done," he concluded, in song, echoing an ancient television commercial. Cigarettes?

Carlo decided to marvel. "How old is he?"

I said, "He's so old, he'd have to be carbon-dated."

But Dennis Savage topped me: "He's so old, he remembers the Great Vowel Shift."

"He was dressed real swank," said Carlo.

"It's generic," Dennis Savage replied. "T-shirts for the beautiful boys on the streets of New York. Jacket and tie for the mature male. I love old men. 'They make me feel so young,'" he sang. "You know, Club MTV should run a special edition for people over fifty-five. Methuselah Disco." He froze. "I hear whispering. The gremlins are up to something."

"That guy used to own the Witch's Hat house," said Carlo. "Remember? On the Island? Way to the east, on the last walk. How come he was here?"

"Oh, everyone's after me about Tom Driggers. But the more they hack at me, the more resolute I become. Even unto death. No for an answer is what it is. I, Dennis Savage, tell you this. You may bury me in a plain coffin in potter's field. Oh, and let my tombstone read—"

"'I was a big silly queen who flamed up and down the patios of the world,'" I helpfully put in.

Carlo said, "I want my tombstone to say, 'He was free.'"

Dennis Savage paused, reflecting on that. He nodded. "We were all free, weren't we?"

We other two nodded.

"We made our choice, right? Each of us. We were gay and free."

Nods.

"I mean, there's social heritage, genetics, and the breaks, but otherwise we made our own arrangements, each according to his desire. No?"

Yes.

Dennis Savage broke into a grin and said that the old man who had just left had recalled working with me on a charity variety show at the theatre in the Grove in the late 1970s. "I asked him what you were like to work with, and he described you as 'difficult but worth it.'"

"*You're* a bargain, you ruthless pixie?"

"How would you describe yourself, Bud?" asked Carlo.

"Fun but worth it."

"I need a nap," said Dennis Savage. "Go downstairs. I'll call you when dinner's ready."

"Spaghetti and salad? That could be five minutes."

"It'll take Cosgrove two hours just to identify a green pepper. Trust me."

He went into the bedroom, and Carlo and I went downstairs to my place.

"That Dennis Savage is all busted up about Tom Driggers, huh?" said Carlo.

"Not precisely. But out among the gay population there is a general need for him to be, so there's this war going on."

I poured myself a drink and gave Carlo a tangerine, his latest passion.

"Well, you know," he began, pulling the fruit apart. "I guess if Tom Driggers is passing on, then the whole thing really is over. Because Tom was the center of this here gay life, I do believe."

"More than you?"

"I was on the sidelines of a lot of it, as I recall. But Tom always had such incredible men around him. They weren't just lookers, they came fully equipped with a *scene*. Remember that body-builder who was half back? Raymond? God, he was heavy. Some demon with all the parts you wanted, remember? White man's talk and black man's size. Really *dense* rap. You didn't know *what* he was, there. For a pair of bills—or for free, if Tom wanted to oblige you—Raymond would come over as the moving man who forgot his dolly or something when he was moving you in that day. Remember? He'd be kind of sticking around, and then he'd say he thinks he's got a heavy case of the sex tingles. And there's only one cure for that. And first you have to test him for the tingles, test these various bodily sectors, you know. Like are you picking up sex crackle in his cock hairs if you stroke them. You remember that? And the only cure? Snap, crackle, pop was the cure. Raymond. Jesus. Tom Driggers made the one-night stand into like . . . like an opera, you know?"

"What went wrong between him and Dennis Savage, do you recall?"

He shook his head. "So long ago, now. You visit Tom?"

"Just today."

"I paid my respects last time. I don't want to go again and see him like that. He was so handsome. That dreamy way he had of moving, like he'd just got up from a night of fabulous sex. Eyes half-closed. He had it, Tom Driggers. He could've walked right into his own movie, now, couldn't he?"

"He came about as close as anyone does, I'll say that."

"They had to shut him down," Carlo said. "He had a client list like with cardinals and mayors in it. He was creating too much hotness. Going on like that, he would have exploded the whole city. You know this entire life is based on people lying about their dreams. Especially cardinals and mayors."

Dennis Savage stormed in. "This coterie has become too in-grown and decadent," he cried. "It delights in nonsense. It's virulent. It's insane. It's like that English family that was devouring the population."

"The Thatchers?" I asked.

"No, centuries ago. They lived in a cave, and it was all incest and cannibalism. They would raid the neighboring towns or drag people off the road. You notice how long it takes the kids to set up a simple spaghetti-and-salad dinner? They're still at it! First they had to go to the store for black olives for the sauce. Then they had to go to the store for garlic. *Then* they noticed that we're out of lettuce! So they get back from the store with lettuce, and lo, we're out of *spaghetti*!"

He collapsed on the couch.

"Play some music?" he asked. "To calm my nerves."

"*The Phantom of the Opera*?"

"Yes, please. The love duet."

I cued it up on the CD player.

"Everything's out of control," he continued, as the music began. "We've got to get with a more soothing program. We've . . . What's wrong with your record? That isn't English."

"It's the Japanese cast. I thought a cosmopolitan boy like you would—"

"That's *exactly* the game they're playing upstairs! Is everyone *crazy*? The Japanese cast of *The Phantom of the Opera*? What, you don't have it in Hebrew?"

"I've *Les Mis* in Hebrew, with the incomparable Dudu Fisher."

"Saint Michael, Saint Timothy, Saint Acteon!" he cried out. "Shield me! Preserve me!"

"Is there really a Saint Acteon?"

Carlo rubbed Dennis Savage's neck, and Dennis Savage buried his head in Carlo's shoulder. "If you knew what they're doing up there. They called me out of the kitchen into the bedroom. 'Cooking break,' they call it. And Virgil leaped off the bed and threw me on the floor and pretended to bite my neck. And our bewitching little Cosgrove was laughing insanely the whole time."

"Guess we have a vampire in the family," I said.

"It happens," said Carlo.

"And Virgil keeps calling me 'snarky.' Where'd that word come from?"

"Sounds like L.A.," said Carlo. *"Snarky."*

Cosgrove came in just then, went into the bedroom, and called for me.

"What's going on with his teeth?" Carlo asked. "How come they're sticking out?"

"Don't go in there," said Dennis Savage. "He's going to swoop down and drink your blood. There's one just like that in my place." He ruefully shook his head. "First it was juice-in-a-box—now this!"

I opened the bedroom door and peered in. Cosgrove, still doing the teeth, was standing on the bed.

"Are you a vampire?" I asked.

He slowly nodded.

"Are you going to swoop down and drink my blood?"

He slowly nodded.

I closed the door.

"Well," I told the others. "I've got one, too."

"Please come in," Cosgrove called through the door. "It's very important."

"I'll go," said Carlo.

"Is it okay if Carlo comes instead?" I yelled.

"Better!"

So Carlo went into the bedroom and there was some noise and laughter and Carlo came out bearing Cosgrove in the fireman's carry and they flopped down together on the couch.

"Now Mr. Smith is a vampire, too! We're the Lost Boys!"

"I'm going to have Roast Cosgrove for dinner," said Carlo.

"No," said Cosgrove, in delighted alarm.

Carlo stroked Cosgrove's hair and looked at him a long time, and said, "I'm going to spank you to make you tender, and then I'll eat you up, as slow as can be."

Whereupon Virgil joined us.

"Dinner's almost ready. All I have to do is wet the macaroni product."

"Why don't you just call it spaghetti?" asked Dennis Savage. "Why is everything in this family done in high-tech?"

"That's what they call it on the box, you snarky man who won't visit your friend in his dying hour."

"He's not my friend," Dennis Savage replied, in earnest.

"You could go there and say, 'I'm still mad at you but I'm sorry that you're a wounded warrior.'"

"Or," Cosgrove put in, "you could say, 'I want you to die, you gob of spit!'"

"Cosgrove, that's not nice," said Virgil.

Cosgrove, aghast and penitent, scrambled out of Carlo's grasp and went up to Virgil. "I didn't mean it. It was my worst joke ever. Please be nice."

Virgil put his arms around Cosgrove and held on real tight, boy-close, and Carlo didn't say anything but his eyes were hot slits and I believe that had he been nude we would have seen steam rising from the end of his cock, and Dennis Savage turned away, blushing, and I asked him, "Aren't you used to us yet?"

Dennis Savage always remarks that although he's never bored, nothing ever seems to happen. So Cosgrove's suit was an event, as was his study of *Götterdämmerung* in preparation for his debut at the opera. And I must admit that for someone who in terms of intelligence and education is utter riffraff, he certainly did survey Wagner's apocalyptic faerie with an eye for the logical paradox.

It was our most restful period together since he moved in. As I worked at my desk, Cosgrove sat listening to the Fonit-Cetra CDs of the Furtwängler-Flagstad recording through my headphones, wearing one of my old pairs of eyeglasses with the lenses pushed out, for that omniscient look—essential when dealing with the end of the world—and occasionally stopping the music to question an inherent contradiction.

"If the Ring makes you all-powerful," he asked, "how come Siegfried takes it from Brünnhilde so easily?" And: "If Brünnhilde loves Siegfried so much, how come she wants him dead? Maybe he was mean to her, but he didn't know what he was doing."

Scholars have been debating these points for a century; I did my best. But on the subject of Tom Driggers, Dennis Savage wasn't doing half as well with Virgil, whose questions were searching and reproachful and, no matter how much Dennis Savage ordered him to stop, relentless. Dennis Savage would come downstairs in the refugee's irate despair and warn me not to answer the door in case he was being pursued. Useless; by now our lives have stretched so intimately beyond the norm that we all hold keys to one another's living quarters, and feelings, and fears. But then, everything in gay life stretches beyond what the world recognizes as normal. We shape our own norms: and violate them.

Tom Driggers held on, waiting to reconcile with Dennis Savage, and Dennis Savage wouldn't budge. Carlo went back to the hospital, and he said there was no one in the room,

"Including Tom Driggers," said Dennis Savage.

"No," I replied. "Tom is very much a presence even at this moment of his dimming out. Because he's still hungry."

"Is there sex after AIDS?"

"He's hungry for friendship."

Dennis Savage looked at me, estimating the possibilities. "You're the last person I expected to hit on me about this. Or anything."

"I'm not hitting. I'm observing."

Dennis Savage turned to Carlo. "You think I should go to him, don't you?"

Carlo smiled. "I think you should do what you want."

Dennis Savage threw himself across my couch and lay there brooding.

"Where are the Tuffys?" I asked.

"They decided to make a meat loaf. Dinner should be ready in about eight years."

A good, long silence.

"Okay," said Dennis Savage.

Another silence, this one pregnant.

"Okay, I'll tell you. Because that's what this is, isn't it? We're waiting for the tale to spill out, aren't we? Oh, and you"—me, this is—"get your tape recorder on."

"Electronic belts running through the walls of this apartment are activated by the sound of the human voice," I told him. "It's all automatically fed into a word processor and shipped directly to the typesetter. Editors, binders, and artists converge. Presto, the book is in the stores, and your blood flows before the world's eyes."

"I had such a case on him," said Dennis Savage. "Such a damn case. And he was available, you understand. Unlimited sexual access. But I could never get in touch with him *personally,* somehow. That was so strange to me. We all know about that time when the guy you've been fucking throws himself into your arms and bleats about how wonderful you are to him. You're reaching someone, not just pleasuring him but . . . or when they try to toss it off and they gulp, and some even start weeping. I like that the best." He turned to Carlo. "Right?"

"That will truly be known to happen here and there."

"Well, not with Tom Driggers, try as I might. It was just Grrr, whirr, thank you, sir, every time. Oh, he liked me. He just didn't . . ."

Carlo nodded.

"Are your tape belts running?" Dennis Savage asked me. "Am I on?"

"Every word."

"I'd hate to be misquoted. So we were like that for years. Years of that, can you imagine? Flesh on flesh, and I cannot do better than that smooth, taut, overgrown boy; and maybe he can do better than me, but he likes it so much he starts to howl, and when he gushes he creams maybe a quart, quart and a half. I mean, what . . . what more is there than . . . what?"

He looked at us.

"Sometimes I ask myself, Why doesn't he want to know me better? Why is it only the Night Before? I would see men having breakfast together Saturday and Sunday mornings. I used to go out for brunch just to watch them! Okay, I let down the sexual revolution. I wanted something . . ."

"Something stable?" I asked.

"Something more than cum," he said. "We flash forward. Tom has money and power, and we have remained in touch. He opens Weasel's. Remember? Down near where the Triangle used to be? It was the first dance club after the Tenth Floor. Big. Rich. Hot. Right?"

Carlo and I nodded.

"Spartan decor. The usual menorah lighting and waiters to die—the Tom Driggers waiters, homo straights. God, he had an eye for that type. Tattoos and no underwear and 'C'mon, I'll *pay* ya next week!' What are we supposed to derive from that? Tell me."

We couldn't.

"Look, I like it hot, same as anyone. But what I always wanted was somewhere there would be a door that I could walk through, any day of the week, and the person in the room behind the door would know how I felt just by the face I had on. On the back side of the door would be all the assholes and schmucks and idiots who fuck your day up. But on *this* side I'd get a human being instead of an android.

"That's all those beauties turn out to be, after a good long while. Fabulous androids. Blond boy in black T-shirt and khaki shorts. Or dark hair, jaw for years, sculpted soft mouth that gives out with irresistible 'Yeah.' Classic gym hunk dancing in a tank top, arching his back by the water cooler. You want it, they have it. Order now—they do everything. Except feel. Put your arms around them sometime, try them for warmth. There's nothing *in* them!

"So. Enter Little Virgil. I know he seems unaware, but it may be that all his amateur theatricals are his defense against what he sees. It's not that he doesn't know what's real: It's that he *does*. He and Cosgrove have reduced the cosmos to nice and mean. 'Please be nice' means Affirm me. 'You're being mean' means You won't give me what I need. Virgil has his job and Cosgrove has his chores, followed by endless playtime. Life is a weekend. So they make videotapes, they cook, they sing, they giggle, and every now and then, when no one's looking, they fuck each other."

He extended a hand in the air as if balancing, weighing something. "You thought I didn't know, right? What am I, the gay King Arthur? So what? This is how I wanted it, behind the door in the room. I don't need to startle myself with drive-by icons. I thought I did, once—I was wrong. There's nothing better than high-concept sex except a high-concept lover. That's what I wanted. Someone . . ."

"A fruit of worth," I put in.

"I'm wandering. . . . Weasel's. Oh. That night . . . Yes. I was in an awful mood, something like the tenth night in a row of a very heavy case of no-lover blues. The last place in the world I wanted to go to was a disco. But I'm not going to improve the quality of my social-romantic life in an empty room, am I? And Tom had been nagging me to come down there. He intimated that he'd set me up with one of his people. Terrific, but I wanted a *person* for once. I'd *had* people. Had them up to . . . Don't you ever offer your guests coffee or something?"

"Who wants what?" I said, heading for the kitchen.

"Tangerines all round," said Carlo.

"I want black coffee," Dennis Savage grumped.

As I ground the beans, I said, "Cosgrove calls this 'fresh-squoze style.'"

"Well, isn't he the phrasemaker."

"Why be snide about it? You used to find them endlessly amusing."

"Having one little rascal on hand is amusing. Having two of them, ganging up on you and calling you strange names and conspiring and spooking, is not amusing. That's Dien Bien Phu for life."

Carlo said, "I truly think those two are getting sweeter and more secret every day."

"Why secret?" I asked.

"I'm not all the way sure. But I believe it has to do with how guys who don't know them just see two tasty morsels there while we see something else. Something with more in it."

"More what?"

He shook his head. "Haven't figured that part out yet. But it's something we know that nobody else ever will. Something in how we see each other, I believe."

Everyone served, we settled back down for the rest of the tale.

Dennis Savage took a sip of coffee for dramatic emphasis and plunged in. "I got through the door of Weasel's, and I wasn't in a great mood but I looked fine. You don't enter a disco showing your feelings; you show the feelings of the guy you want to get."

"Or the guy you want to be," I said.

"Same thing."

"No," said Carlo. "It truly isn't."

"Before we open *that* can of worms, can I close up *this* one?" said Dennis Savage. "Weasel's took up the ground floor of one of those long, deep buildings, and I was heading for the room at the back, looking for Tom. I saw him, just as I made the doorway. But I also saw one of his employees—you know that job, where they're always hustling through the place lugging cases of beer? So here's this guy heading right for me with a case, a classic android—golden-blond, rippled up, and a face in a million, on the short side but horribly wide-shouldered and tight-waisted. *Horribly*. A colored tattoo on his left biceps—the Tom Driggers touch, of course. This boy is roaring through the room, and as he reaches me, instead of leaving us both maneuvering space, he edges me tightly between his case of beer and the wall—I mean, he's *pressing* me with this thing! And as he moves on, he calls over his shoulder, 'Get the fuck out of the way, asshole!'"

Dennis Savage immediately turned to me and said, "What would you have done if that had happened to you?"

"The appropriate response—the classy and valiant response—would be to grab him by the hair, jerk him back so that he'd drop his box of beer, and give him a solid kick in the shin. Down he goes, and that would feel great. On the other hand, you would be surrounded by bouncers and bartenders and physically thrown out of the place, which is one of the least egosyntonic experiences I know of."

"Exactly."

"Besides, you're connected to the owner, right? It's a little like I'll Tell Teacher, but you could have gone right to Tom Driggers and said—"

" 'Did you see that?' Of course he hadn't. Tom misses whatever he can't use. I told him what happened; I was so mad I was shaking. And he just stood there. He didn't get it and he didn't want to, and now I can't tell you how angry I was. I'm a *customer* in this joint and this guy is an *employee*. He's supposed to make things *pleasant*, not *assault* me!"

He turned to Carlo. "What would you have done?"

"Well, you're right about all the staff guys falling on top of you. What you *could* do is offer the culprit guy fifty bucks for a blow job, and go to a stairwell or a back alley, and *then* let him have it. A little no-risk retribution there."

Dennis Savage nodded, visualizing it. "I felt so . . . diminished. So *helplessly* furious. It was as if *nothing* I did for myself could ever really make a difference—all those evenings at the gym, all the worrying about my haircut and my clothes, the psyching up before a big weekend at the beach. No matter how hard I worked, there was going to be some piece of hot stuff locking me out, and Tom was aligning himself with it. Okay. One side of me knew it was his nature never to admonish an android for anything. But the other side hated him for holding me hostage to his upside-down world in which nothing matters—but *nothing* and *nothing*!—except the clarity of hot. You *hear* me? That's what it was. I never spoke to Tom again. He sent me flowers. He kept calling, and I kept hanging up. He even wrote me a letter, which was quite an event for him."

"Did he deal with the episode itself?" I asked.

"No. That would have been to admit that it had occurred."

Smiling his thorny wry smile, Dennis Savage shook his head. "The funny part of it is, years later the blond kid turned up on *Ryan's Hope*, tattoo and all." He laughed. "I was so glad when it went off the air. I hope to pass him, a year or so from now, under-going meltdown in some gutter."

"I always thought the most beautiful men would be the nicest," I said.

"But what if there's nothing special inside of them," said Carlo, "to live up to this special picture they show on the *outside*? They think they should be a movie star, or someone on a yacht. But all they're good for is hotting up the sheets. A few days later the money's gone and they're back where they were. No yacht, no movies. It makes them mean.

"I truly say *that's* what you ran into that night in Weasel's. Here's this guy—young, handsome, build. And what's he doing? Sipping one of those cocktail drinks with fruit and a little paper umbrella by a Hollywood pool while producers do the seven-year-contract shuffle? He's hauling those damnhell stacks of beer! Running them upstairs, downstairs, hurting his back and making him sore, and where's it getting him? Sure, now and then some fat cat'll take him to Key West for a weekend. But he's got to put out for it, doesn't he? Or he'll bunk up with someone like himself, an-other guy just as sore as he is. Two of them together can't even make the rent on a little room in the slums. And right in the mid-dle of this, here comes this guy who hasn't got a worry uptown or down, strolling into Weasel's with all his bills paid, and the blond beauty lugging his beers is thinking, What's *he* so glad about? It's like in Vietnam, sometimes, when American soldiers would capture a village, and instead of cowering the villagers would be giggling. So the soldiers would get mad and shoot at them, and now they'd be crying and screaming, and the soldiers would feel righteous about it."

"How do you know about that?" I asked.

"You remember my buddy Daniel Johnson? He's a vet."

"So how come you're not like that?" Dennis Savage asked Carlo. "What makes you so pleasant and easygoing and, resent it though you may, caring? When they were sorting out the gifts, who gave you what?"

Carlo was silent for a bit. Then: "Can I say something about Tom Driggers? If you don't go see him off, and you come to regret it, you will never be able to undo it, and you'll hurt real tough. But if you do go, and come to regret that, it won't matter. Because giving too much never feels as bad as giving too little."

"What do you say?" Dennis Savage asked me.

"I think there's some pathos in this man hanging around waiting to be forgiven. But he is in fact partly responsible for the incredible growth of Attitude in gay New York. It's unfair to exculpate him just because he's dying. One thing has nothing to do with the other."

"Listen to this," said Dennis Savage. "It was something like three months after the Weasel's disaster. Tom had finally given up on me. I was feeling low that whole year. As if I'd already got everything that was coming to me and it would be downhill from there. Remember?" he asked me. "You must have noticed."

"It's hard to tell with you. Your depressed is rather like your playful."

He sighed. "So the night was young and I had to do *something*, so I just went out walking and there I was, passing the Forty-sixth Street Theatre, where *The Best Little Whorehouse in Texas* was playing. It had been running for a year and I hadn't seen it, and I was looking at the people waiting to go in, and checking out the pictures, and feeling utterly miserable and left out, and then I saw this big blowup of the chorus boys doing what looked like a striptease—that number where they change from football uniforms into cowboy drag?"

I nodded; Carlo hadn't the faintest idea what we were talking about.

"Well, you know chorus boys. There was one in the center of the shot who must have been the sexiest hunk ever photographed. I mean, he was just . . . vast truth. Two hundred pounds of original sin."

"Sounds like one of Tom Driggers's boys," said Carlo.

"Exactly. I hadn't taken much money with me, and all I could afford was standing room. In I go. Two minutes before curtain, this astonishing kid takes the place next to me. Black hair, pure white skin, wide eyes, and slim, slim, slim. He looks like Walt Disney's Pinocchio just after he turns into a real boy. Well, we start talking, and he's bashful, which only adds to the attraction. And he's so busy trying to sound grown-up that he makes himself even younger. He said, 'I heard this play has a country-western score, so I'm a little skeptical.' *Skeptical,* coming out of that little-boy mouth."

Smiling, he shook his head.

"He's new in town, so I offer to take him around. And we have a few dates, but he keeps dodging my come-on. He was so fucking sweet I was going crazy. Anyway, I finally got him to Bud's for dinner, and then I took him upstairs. We spent the weekend together—boating in the Park, bicycling to Brooklyn. Sunday he made breakfast, and everything was burned. The toast was burned, the eggs were burned, the plates and napkins were burned. And he talked in his sleep. I held him in my arms and he held on to me, and out came these confidential non sequiturs about his family. Just strings of . . . of what?"

"Feelings," said Carlo.

"He said, 'Pop is so nice to me.' Or 'Anne will take me to her dance.' One night he started a story about I don't know what, something with 'the anonymous Greeks.' *Anonymous Greeks.*"

"What does that mean?" Carlo asked.

Dennis Savage began to weep.

"Oh, no," I said, "not another crying story."

"Everyone cries around you," said Carlo.

"Anyway," said Dennis Savage, wiping his eyes, "I knew he wasn't an android, didn't I?"

The following afternoon, Cosgrove and I picked up his suit, and that evening we went to *Götterdämmerung.* Cosgrove fretted because he didn't have the chance to show himself off to Virgil in his virtuous new chic—curtain was at six P.M.— but he brightened when I told him how much more effective he'd appear to his buddy's eyes after he had absorbed the grandeur of a Night at the Opera. And, in the event, I have to say that Cosgrove acclimatized himself beautifully. *Ring* audiences tend to be stationary and strictly attentive; and so was Cosgrove. Except for a frantic five minutes during the second intermission, when he insisted that he saw Mr. Popyucork, the Sheriff of Hangtown, "gleaming" at us from the top gallery, Cosgrove moved among the cognoscenti as a native.

(There are a number of Misters in Cosgrove's world. Mr. Popyucork inhabits only his nightmares, but Carlo is Mr. Smith and Dennis Savage, not to his knowledge, is Mr. Fee Fo Fum.)

I have introduced many an associate to a work of art. I took Lionel to *Salò,* and he was so dazzled we sat through it twice; and I took Dennis Savage to *La Strada.* He didn't care for it, for which he got a slap upside of the head. Till now my protégés have always been coevals—never before had I squired anyone younger than myself to anything. It felt somewhere, I would guess, between going to Weasel's and listening to someone talk in his sleep: being in charge of an uncontrollable adventure.

Cosgrove was so eager to exhibit himself to Virgil that after we cabbed home, racing like the wind, Cosgrove went on up to Dennis Savage's while I got out at the sixth floor to rustle up something from the fridge. Thank God for peanut butter and jelly.

When I made it upstairs, in mid-sandwich, despair was in season. Cosgrove was crushed, Carlo worried, and Dennis Savage agitated: Virgil had not come home from work, and it was past midnight.

"I wanted to show him how I could look," wailed Cosgrove.

Dennis Savage asked, "Should I call the police?"

Nobody wanted to. Cosgrove took off his jacket and showed Carlo how the vest could be worn inside-out for a sporty checkered look. Suddenly he seemed exhausted, dazed by a long day and a long opera. He sat next to Carlo, and Carlo slowly unfastened Cosgrove's tie.

"I wonder if I should ever wear a tie," said Carlo.

"You'd have to," I observed, "at *Götterdämmerung.*"

"I'd best stick with *Friday Night Wrestling.*"

I went down for another sandwich. Up again: no Virgil.

"I'm getting really concerned," said Cosgrove.

"He never, never does this," said Dennis Savage. "He always comes straight—"

Key in the lock.

Virgil walks in, and everyone is invisible to him but Dennis Savage.

"I was at the hospital," said Virgil. "You wouldn't go, so I did. I saw him die. I had to tell lies. I gave him messages from you that you should have said yourself. I made them up."

He was advancing on Dennis Savage.

"There was everyone there, and all he wanted was you. He held my hand and asked me, 'When will he come?' That's what he said. Are you so proud now? He died away, and you did nothing. That's how you treat your best friends."

Chénier on oath, Dennis Savage said, "You know it isn't."

"I know what I see. Everyone asked you to go, and no, no, you wouldn't."

They were face to face. Dennis Savage tried to put his arm around Virgil's shoulder; the boy threw him off.

"Who was in that hospital?" Virgil cried. "Who would it take to get you there? If you don't care about everybody, you don't care about anybody!"

"That's not—"

Virgil gave him a shove, and another shove.

"Who's going to come when *you're* in there?" he said, his voice rising. "Who should care about *you?*"

Dennis Savage grabbed Virgil, but he broke free again.

"Shouldn't you see this death?" he shouted. "It's *blood* and *shit*! That's how you go, because I saw it *happen*! And no one even to say, 'I'm sorry you're dead today.' That's what *you* gave him!"

Virgil shoved him again, this time so hard that he went down; but Carlo was up, Cosgrove's tie in his hand. He reached for Virgil, and Virgil leaped away, shouting, "This is not with you!"; but Carlo is a one-man crowd when he wants to be, and he surrounded Virgil and snapped the tie around his skull at eye level and tied it up and spun him around, all this so fast we others scarcely saw it happen. Virgil was sobbing and Carlo was spinning him; none of this made sense. Bauhaus gaped. It was some sort of picture, an action yet to be reckoned, sketchy, snarky, who knows? Dennis Savage was getting up and Carlo had pulled Virgil close, gripping him around the torso and arms so he couldn't move, whispering in his ear. Blinded and immobilized, Virgil bore it as Carlo carefully loosened his hold and gently pushed him toward Dennis Savage. Virgil stumbled. Dennis Savage caught him, and took care of him, and all was still in the room.

After a long while, Dennis Savage unfastened the tie and took Virgil into the bedroom. Carlo went with them; I don't know why.

"Tuffy didn't see my suit," said Cosgrove.

We were sitting on the couch.

"Aren't you hungry?" I asked.

He was silent.

"How did you like the opera?" I asked.

"Thank you for taking me there. It was really nice."

His voice caught on something, and I held him for a while. True: Everyone around me does cry. To distract him, I talked about *The Ring*. I answered his questions—Brünnhilde loses the Ring to Siegfried because it wants to be with the more powerful person; and Brünnhilde wants Siegfried dead, even though she loves him, because he hurt her and her love has magnified the hurt. She was very desperately threatened. Androids may be dead fish, but they shield us from our passions.

Carlo came out of the bedroom, looking a bit pale.

"Is he all right?" Cosgrove asked.

"It's quiet now. They're talking."

"You know what I would like?" said Cosgrove, mildly brightening. "A chicken breast and some nice baked beans. And then seven-layer cake. And I would like a little blue car of my own size to ride in. I wouldn't have to park it, because it would come inside with me. And I would like the Ring, to rule the world. Everyone who was mean to me dies horribly. They're screaming as they die, and I would laugh."

"Don't say that," said Carlo, stroking his hair. "You don't know what you're talking about."

Then his voice caught, too.

"Why is Mr. Smith crying?" Cosgrove asked me.

I said, "He is very desperately threatened. See, we're the Lost Boys," I said. "The anonymous Greeks, a hill of unknown dead. We have been abandoned," I said. "But you know what? I still believe."

Wonderingly, Cosgrove touched Carlo's moistened cheeks.

"You don't have to be a vampire," he told Carlo. "See, how I break the spell, and your eyes are now clear?"

"Exorcis," I said.

Carlo shook his head; the tears kept flowing. "Can I please stay with you tonight?" he said.

THE MUSIC OF
THE NIGHT

Have I ever mentioned that I play the banjo?

Quite some years ago, in my days as an off-Broadway music director, I coached the teenage son of a producer and an actress I worked with, in preparation for some music exam that he had to pass to get into Dublin University. In return, he gave me banjo lessons and helped me find an ax of my own—a Fender, no less, secondhand, in splendid condition.

The producer was wealthy, with a gigantic apartment on Central Park West; each of his kids had not only his own room but his own terrace, and the boy and I would sit outside of an afternoon and trade jokes as I mastered "Go Tell Aunt Rhody" and "The Groundhog Hunt."

I'm rusty now, but every so often I haul out the banjo and take it for a spin. Cosgrove, who found it fascinating from day one, kept trying to sing along, improvising lyrics when the folklore failed him. He hit some sort of apex with "Camptown Races":

> Cosgrove's tired 'cause he slept too late.
> Doo-dah, doo-dah.
> Chicks with dicks are a heavy date—

and I immediately put the banjo in his lap and taught him some chords. If he's busy playing, maybe he won't sing.

(When neither Virgil nor I am around to stop him, Cosgrove parks himself in front of the erotic cable channel, where he incubates an obsession for "chicks with dicks"—preoperative transsexuals—waiting hours, if necessary, for a glimpse of this ultra-contemporary phenomenon.)

Oddly, Cosgrove, who usually can't find anything he can do without fumbling, is a decent rudimentary banjo artist. With the instrument tuned to G Major, Cosgrove can muster a worthy D^7 and a quite competent "bar 5" (for which one places the finger flat across the fretwork at the fifth bar, lining the strings up in C Major), all together giving him the wherewithal for at times quite lengthy concerts.

Of course, Virgil will not be left at the hitching post when the latest Pony Express is mounting up, so I had to show *him* some chords, too. Then you get the Bremen Town Musicians in residence on your sofa.

Virgil and Cosgrove were down here all the time, because Dennis Savage was trying to become a writer and he needed a silence, a room of his own, to create in. I didn't mind; I wasn't working much. After publishing twenty-one books in fourteen years, I was discovering the joys of CD liner notes and magazine work: You write a few pages, announce, This is finished, and take the rest of the month off.

Anyway, the kids had also taken up the pleasures of the CD, especially my portable Sony D-10, a tiny box that hums with Beethoven, Wagner, and show tunes. You juice up the machine in the wall, plug in two headsets, plant Virgil and Cosgrove with the player between them, and enjoy the peace—broken, at intervals, when they suddenly join in on a line they like, such as "In the *tea*, my Lord," and "Don't ask me how at my age one still can grow," and, in *Show Boat* (which they adore because it has a prominent banjo part), "Maybe that's because you *love* me." They stare off into space when singing out these lines; it's quite bizarre.

Actually, many things in my apartment have long delighted and attracted them: the wind-up Victrola, my high school yearbooks, my old French Meccano building set (which they love to take out and examine but never literally *play* with). Still, the jewel in the crown is always the banjo. When I played, they would hover, watching my fingers and singing along. They even danced, an improvisational combination of do-si-do and the finale of *A Chorus Line,* Virgil's favorite musical. For novelty, I showed them how to turn the banjo into the Japanese koto by stopping the fretwork way at the bottom of the fingerboard, where the strings sound high and diffuse.

This they *loved.*

"The *koto!*" Virgil breathed out.

"Teach me, now," said Cosgrove.

I did teach them; and Virgil decided to buy his own banjo, so

I took him down to Matt Umanov's on Bleecker Street and helped him pick one out. That night, Dennis Savage banged at my door, shouting, *"I'm going to kill you!"*

He was coming down a lot, too, to show me his pages and take criticism, resisting all the way. Usually the kids are deep in their CDs when he arrives, but one evening they got out the banjos to show him what they could do.

"Play some Sondheim," he suggested, probably figuring that of all composers, Sondheim is the least banjo-friendly.

He underestimated the possibilities. Virgil plunged into the first bars of *Pacific Overtures* (on the koto) and stamped on the floor.

"Nippon!" Cosgrove howled. "The froating kingdom!"

"No," Dennis Savage suddenly begged in a poignant manner. "No."

"We froat," Cosgrove concluded, cutting to the last line of the number.

Dennis Savage was floored. "I didn't think you could play show music on the banjo."

"We can play anything," said Virgil.

"How about 'Over the Hills and Far Away'?"

"Actually," I said, "you *can* play show tunes on the banjo. For instance, harp effect." I ran through the chords of "(Everything is beautiful) At the Ballet."

Virgil was humming; he knows his art. Cosgrove tried a line: "Raise your arms, and there's a dying swan!" This is not pure Kleban. And Dennis Savage was contemplating all of us, and our past and future. He does this pretty often now; time has made his melancholy avid.

" 'I was pretty,' " he sang.

" 'I was happy,' " Virgil sang.

"I was Cosgrove," Cosgrove sang; but someone was banging on my door.

"Guess who I saw in the gym today!" Carlo cried as I let him in.

"Give us a hint," said Dennis Savage.

"Someone you've met. Incredible-looking. Redhead's complexion with hair half-blond and half-brown at the one time. You keep looking at it, want to smooth that hair. *Beautiful* strange, everything tight and trim, thighs, tips, abs, mustache. Clone of death. Especially how he carries himself, swaggering around like he invented rimming."

Dennis Savage was stumped.

Cosgrove said to Virgil, "I bet it's one of those chicks with dicks."

Virgil said, "Cosgrove"; and Cosgrove was abashed.

"Clone of death," I put in. "Are people like that still around?"

"This one is," Carlo answered. "That whole weight room was in a hypnotic state. He was taking turns at the weight bench with some cute little mud puppy who wanted to do some innocent flirting. But our man suddenly starts feeling the kid up. *Everybody's* watching. And the guy tells the kid, 'I could get high on your cream. I want to fuck you like crack.'"

"Jeepers," I said.

"Someone we've met?" Dennis Savage repeated.

"We all knew him. Some time ago."

"And he's still—"

"He's *stiller*. He was never like this before, he's new! He's tough and he's tight and he'll take no prisoners."

"I insist upon guessing this," said Dennis Savage.

"Look at it this way," said Carlo. "He could also be one of your maybe B or B-plus hunks, junior slim grade, always having boy friend fights with Scott Hellman."

"That's Bert Hicks," said Dennis Savage. "I mean, half of the description is Bert Hicks. The other half is . . . who?"

"*He* says he's all Bert Hicks. But he's surely got someone else's eyes. You know? Like he's been having nothing but the most evil sex for ten years. And like where did Bert Hicks get that shithouse build on him?"

"Gyms are public places," I said. "Anyone may enter."

"Builds like this don't happen in public."

"Not to Bert Hicks," Dennis Savage agreed. "And where'd he get the heavy eyes from? No one knew that about him before."

"No one knew *anything* about him before," said Carlo. "He wasn't the kind of guy you needed to know about."

That isn't true. Bert Hicks wasn't the kind of guy *Carlo* needed to know about—not a heavy traveler along the Circuit, a craftsman of cruising. A quite good-looking but also nice, funny, intelligent guy in his early twenties at the time, the very early 1980s, Bert respected Stonewall style, but up to a point, meaning he did *some* of the gym and wore *some* of the clothes and went to *some* of the Places. Stonewall was competitive; Bert half tried. What are you supposed to do, kill yourself? Some of the men of that era had but one thing in their lives beyond work, food, and sleep: cruising. Bert had one thing, too: Scott Hellman.

Another of my villains, Scott did *all* of the gym, the clothes, the Places, the orgy in Room 213. He was everywhere, celebrated. *Too* handsome, *very* built, *so* hot. He and Bert were something between best friends and lovers, constantly quarreling, mostly over Scott's incredibly shabby treatment of Bert. Like some—not all— really dazzling men who do it because they can, Scott drove Bert berserk with frustration. Scott would set up a dinner date, then B.I. (for "Better Invitation," meaning you cancel at the last minute because someone more attractive beckoned) or simply not show up at all. Scott would "borrow" money. He'd exploit Bert in creative ways, such as inveigling him into taking Scott's visiting mother to the Brasserie while Scott went on the town.

But Scott got away with it because Bert was in love with Scott, and because Bert knew he could never get Scott to treat him fairly but he *could get Scott.* That price was worth Bert's paying. So Bert thought.

I didn't. "You're much better-looking than you think you are," I once told him. "Dennis Savage recently remarked that you're a walking ad for the not too muscly but nicely chiseled look. You're good company. You're punctual. You return phone calls. I've also noticed that you trouble to keep up with major cultural things. You don't let your mind go bad."

"So?" he asked, grinning at all this nonsense.

"So you can do better than Scott Hellman."

His opinion, of course, was that better than Scott Hellman Rock Hudson couldn't do, but he played it politic with me and made one of those "Oh, I suppose" gestures.

"For instance," I continued, "I can't imagine having a conversation with Scott. All I ever hear him say is 'Boy, what a fuck *that* was!' about somebody or other. Sure, he's a knockout, but he lacks content. What do you two do after sex?"

"Lie there. Dream. Be happy. Or that's what I *would* do if Scott didn't jump up and grab a shower and race off somewhere."

"To cruise?"

"He does other things. He and some friends are running a pool championship. They meet someplace downtown."

"*Gack.* What a gringo."

"Gringo?"

"Carlo's term for a thuggishly macho intolerant straight. He means it as a compliment, unfortunately."

"Scott has his junky side, okay, but who doesn't?"

"He cheats on you like crazy."

"We both cheat. Everybody cheats."

A silence as we ponder that. I think it's always true of some people, sometimes true of some other people, and never true of the three or four people left over.

"Tell me," I said, "what do you guys do when you're alone besides fuck?"

He shrugged. "What does anyone do? We . . . Well . . ."

"How come everyone I respect finds Scott stupid and boring and you don't? Because they all respect you. Kern Loften told me he spent a goodly portion of the Dress to Kill Party discussing Chinese literature with you."

"Well, we both majored in—"

"I'll bet I could name a half dozen of the most imposing novels of the postwar era and you'll have read them all."

"What does that have to do with anything?" he protested; but he was a gambling man, and insisted I proceed.

"*Pictures from an Institution.*"

"Yes."

"Well, that's easy. *The Naive and Sentimental Lover.*"

"Yes."

I was impressed—it's John Le Carré's only novel that isn't about spies, and it's intensely homoerotic, and thus not renowned, especially among the fluttery Le Carré academics.

"Okay. *Cities of the Red Night.*"

"Yes," he said, but uneasily. Did he *want* to lose?

"*The Once and Future King.*"

"No. Well, it was read to me, as a child, but I didn't actually—"

"That's a yes. Anyway, that was all cinch stuff. Now I roll out the cannon. It's 1976, and everyone's opening—but how many finish?—the extraordinarily colloquial *JR,* William Gaddis's genius work, the novel of conversations."

"Yes," he said, turning white—*why?*—"but only to pass the afternoons while Scott was off meatracking. Besides, you're wrong, Gaddis's genius work is *The Recognitions.*"

Jesus, he *was* well-read. I tightened the survey. Something international, epic, too intrepid for the riffraff . . . Ah! "Elsa Morante," I said. "*History: A Novel.*"

"*Yes,*" he cried, in despair. "It was the greatest novel of the last ten years. But I do more than read. Scott isn't the only—"

"I think Scott is sapping your confidence, if you'll forgive my forwardness. In fact, I think Scott *needs* to sap your confidence. It may be that you're what Scott wishes he were, if only he could—"

"Are you *crazy*? He's the only man I know who's totally content with what he has. Every time I look at him, I just wish . . . I wish . . ."

"You know, Carlo's opinion is that half of looks is how you carry yourself."

"That's fine for him to say. The most startling forearms and the longest torso and the biggest dick in the city, and his opinion is, It's all in the walk."

"If you moved like a winner instead of like Scott Hellman's victim, you could get any guy in—"

"*Goddamn it!*" he shouted, throwing himself on my couch.

"What? What? What? What?"

"Well, he did it again, didn't he?, is what!" Bert crossed his arms tightly against his sides, as if, unleashed, his vital organs would come crashing out. "I told him if he stands me up *one more time* . . . and of course he did. I mean, I've asked him and I've lectured him and I've stood him up myself and I've humored him and I've not returned his phone calls and guess what I finally figured out? *Nothing* takes!"

"Of course it doesn't," I joined in, warming to my subject. I've loathed Scott Hellman ever since he picked Dennis Savage up in the Eagle, then, as they were going out the door, saw someone cuter, picked *him* up with a smile, and ditched Dennis Savage without a word. "Scott lives to betray and betrays to live."

"Well, brace yourself for the news, because I made a stand and he thinks it's a bluff, so naturally he . . . But it isn't a bluff this time. I'm moving to San Francisco."

"What?"

He nodded dramatically. "Surprised, aren't you? *Great!* Wait till *Scott* finds out! See, I only just happened to meet this kind of valiant guy at the baths. What a *hero!*" Bert shook his head gently at the fond memory. "He's going to put me up till I can find a place—and, hang on, his firm is looking for someone with a background in Chinese. Me."

"What's the job?"

"Who cares? It's a chance to—"

"Bert? Just tell me what the job is, okay?"

"Why should I?"

"Why won't you?"

I waited.

"Bank teller," he said, his hands over his ears.

"Bert, it's so *sketchy*!"

"What's so great about being a librarian? Anyway, this San Francisco guy told me I really stand to score out there."

"You can score here. That's—"

"No, *Scott* is here!"

"Dump him!"

"I *can't*! Don't you see that? Don't you see how *amazing* he is? He's so . . . Scott. No one who sees him can . . . I mean, no one can know anything. It's all Scott. It's all love. It's all me. Everything . . . all mixed up. That's *why* San Francisco. It's not . . . Listen, okay? Will you listen? San Francisco is not mixed up."

That was the last we heard of Bert Hicks. As for Scott, he hit thirty-seven or so and began to slow up. Less gym, fewer parties. He decided to let his body find its natural condition, and he got some light reading done. He thought rain was reason to stay in. He gave up on *GQ*: all that young. He stopped having brunch with people he admired but didn't like. He ceased to matter, except to himself.

The interesting thing was, Did he ever miss Bert? But when I asked, people told me I was being ridiculous.

End of flashback. "Carlo," Virgil was saying, "you're just in time to hear Cosgrove and me on the koto."

"Do what?"

They played a selection.

"Dueling banjos, huh?" Carlo said when they had done.

"That was 'Finishing the Hat,'" Cosgrove said. "In a way."

"I always wondered what was meant by 'hammer and tongs,'" Dennis Savage told us. "Now I know."

"Why discourage them?" I asked. "Music blesses any house."

"Oh, look who's playing supportive and benign, with his bunny rabbit ways."

"Last night he spanked me," Cosgrove put in.

"Oh, for heaven's sake!" I said.

"We see the truth," Dennis Savage announced. "We take in the world. We learn of corruption."

"First of all," I said, "it was a very light spanking; and, second, he asked me to."

Virgil froze Cosgrove with an accusing look.

"I was depressed," Cosgrove pleaded.

"If you're depressed, you should come to me," Virgil advised him.

"Yeah," said Carlo, imagining who knows what unspeakable filth. "Can you see that?"

Dennis Savage said, "I may have to write about this."

A mild alarm went off in my head.

"Hold your horses, buster," I told him. "I patrol this territory."

"He thinks he's so Peter Rabbit," Cosgrove grumbled, about me. He was annoyed because he'd got in trouble with Virgil.

"So what do you call that stuff you play?" Carlo asked the kids.

"Music," said Cosgrove.

"No, what's your outfit? Got to have a name there, for the theatre signs."

"The Koto Brothers?" Cosgrove offered.

"Seems like you should be some kind of *ensemble*," said Carlo. "Listen, first you got your Symphony Orchestra. Hear that? Then comes your Philharmonic. That's fancy. But hottest of all is your Ensemble. Like a Baroque Something Ensemble, or the Something Van Beethoven Liquid Ensemble. See?"

"Oh!" said Cosgrove, seeing it. "The Von Sondheim Koto Ensemble!"

"Of Manhattan Isle," I added, as Dennis Savage's eyes shot darts of molten lead, arrows exquisitely poisoned so your brain jellies as you live, and assorted impatient shrapnel.

And Virgil said, "Yes!"

"Why *Von*?" Dennis Savage asked.

"It sounds like us," Cosgrove answered.

Carlo agreed: "It'll look dandy on the marquee."

"For our succeeding selection," Virgil began; but Dennis Savage took the banjo from him and laid it on the couch.

"Intermission," he explained.

"What I'm thinking," said Carlo, "is what's next about Bert Hicks?"

"That's easy," said Dennis Savage. "Invite him to dinner."

Well, it *was* Bert Hicks and it *wasn't*. Or, like, it *was* Bert Hicks. But never in all Stonewall had you seen a man so reinvent himself by going clone. It was as if you had left Gloversville and come back ten years later to find Tacitus's Rome where Gloversville had been. This guy was built and torrid, a sinful package of afternoon delight. Jesus, what confidence good looks give you!—not to mention the red-gold hair. Yet it was the same face, the same (one presumes) insides. Whatever hurt him originally and led him into a no-win relationship with Scott Hellman must still shimmer, with an elated ache, within him. Yet his eyes shone.

You devil, I kept thinking. You *devil*! as he sat in Dennis Savage's living room, sopping up the host's Hundred Ingredients Beef Stew, one of the spectacular taste treats in the Western world (though I always crinkle up my mouth and pretend it's garlicky, to keep the cook from becoming content and aging too quickly—getting indignant keeps him fresh). You devil: You pulled it off. You upped and moved and changed and now you're some kind of absolutely winning man. But Dennis Savage, after motioning me into the kitchen, could only shake his head.

"This is uncanny," he said. "This is danger."

The kids were rather intrigued by Bert, until Cosgrove asked him, "Do you know many of these chicks with dicks I've been hearing so much about?"

Bert smiled. "I only know bods with rods."

There was a pause.

"I know some really hot tanks," Bert went on, "who spread out for you like they've been trimmed a thousand times. But they still have that first-time tightness. I know heavy street trash, sexy blond boys who'd snuff you for a twenty, but they love to be fucked coco-style, on their back like a chick. I know Bill Congdon, a man of the world with the biggest tattooed dick in San Francisco, an eagle with veins. I know Wesley Tusan and Bob McCrack, first-floor-front apartment in a building in which there lives a very handsome and innocent boy who walks on crutches and has highly developed abdominals which excite Wesley and Bob. Their idea of a party is you all come over and drink a few cold ones with the door open till this boy passes by on his crutches, and Wes and Bob pull him into their place and they take his crutch away so he's helpless, and then we all strip him and stretch him out on the bed and everyone takes a turn whipping the kid's ass. He's so beautiful like that, and I kiss his tears just then. I know Paul Nestling, a real hairy fucker, whose idea is if you can think of some sex thing and he isn't willing to do it, he'll give you ten straight cash dollars. I know Pete Puleo, he won the South of Market rimming contest three years running. Some of the judges haven't waked yet. I know amputees and ex-cons and shit freaks and killers. But I can't say that I know any chicks with dicks."

There he paused, grinning and positive about himself and without a shred—not a shred—of self-mockery. He had passed into the looking glass. Boys and girls, he wasn't one of us anymore.

Cosgrove phrased it well. "I don't like this guy," he whispered to Virgil, and they went into the bedroom to practice their new Von Sondheim Koto Ensemble *Me and My Girl* medley.

"How's Scott?" I asked Bert.

"I was about to ask *you*." He was still grinning. "I haven't seen him."

"Excuse me for remembering, but wasn't he the love of your life?"

Bert laughed. "Those are juvenile infatuations. Oh, I am going to see him real soon. Scott. Yes. That'll be happening. But I thought I'd . . . I'd land here, you see. I'd make my presence known. Gym talk really travels. And then . . . yes, my old Scott Hellman. Scott will get what he wants."

Dennis Savage took away Bert's empty plate.

"Great dinner," Bert said, surveying us. "God, you guys are still the same. Still holed up in this enclave, huh?"

"Huh," I said.

"Those kids are really right little numbers. Jesus, I'd love to tie their hands at the wrist and cane them. First one, then the . . . What's that noise?"

"The kotos are messing up on their Gay," I said. "Noel Gay," clarifying. "*Me and My Girl*?"

"That's some theatre show?"

"Right," I said, trying to remember what musicals he and I had seen together. *Ballroom*? *King of Hearts*? *One Night Stand*?

"So, Rip," Bert very heartily continued, turning to Carlo. "You're as titanic as ever. So fucking *buff*! They remember you back in San."

"There were some good times then," said Carlo quietly.

"Good times?" Bert echoed. "It's Cum City."

Dennis Savage beckoned me into the kitchen. "What on *earth* does that think it's doing?" he said.

"Talk about the San Francisco Earthquake."

"He doesn't deserve my stew."

"I can see why he wanted to redecorate his outside, but why is he playing this role? He was nice before, and now he's—"

"Shit freaks and killers, did you hear that?"

I was thinking about it, and took too long to respond, so he said, "What are you getting so *inner* about?"

"Well . . . that was the feeling of the seventies, wasn't it? That the best men were the ones who had the most sex? Hot was the first virtue. Is there any stew in the pot for me to take home?"

"I'm bringing it to school for lunch tomorrow."

I struck a pathetic pose and begged shamelessly. *"Please."*

"You chiseler," he muttered, shoveling leftover stew into a plastic container for me.

"Thanks awfully. Do we have to go into the living room again?"

"Foolish man," he said. "We haven't asked the fifty-dollar question yet."

So back we went. Bert was exhorting Carlo about some frantically devious sex practice and Carlo was shrugging; in the bedroom, the koto group was exercising "Once You Lose Your Heart."

"Cock," Bert is going. "Fuck," he insists. "The allness of it," he invokes. "Come on, Rip."

"Where did it get me?" Carlo laughed.

"Man, you are a legend. Guys are dreaming about you, wondering what you could be like. And *where did it get you?* What does that mean, coming from you?"

"Who could believe what something *means*?" Carlo replied.

"Like that's such heavy trim."

"I just don't—"

"Morbid stuff, you know?"

"I'm asking—"

"I know a guy, pro wrestler, just this side of three hundred pounds, big crusher kind of man, and when he stretches you out on his—"

"Why did you come back to New York, Bert?" Dennis Savage asked.

Bert paused, smiled—real slow and certain—and then he said, with an air of Surely You Knew This All Along, "Revenge."

Bert looked up his old pal Scott Hellman in due course, and they started in right where they had left off. Except now Bert was the cynosure who got everything God can give, and Scott was the guy who gets stood up. Oddly, seeing his former boy friend walking around like Mr. New York energized Scott, recalled him to his days of note. He began, almost, to compete. He reinstated himself in the weight room and retrieved his sense of style, dressing down with the abandon of a disco teen. He was calling up old friends, running with a crowd, bumping into you on the street clearly on his way to where.

Actually, he wasn't bumping into *us* because we didn't seem to get out on the Circuit anymore. Dennis Savage and Virgil had their day jobs, I had my daily walk or bike ride, Cosgrove had two households' worth of chores to do, and who knows what Carlo's up to when he's out and about? But by the evening, barring the odd dinner date or theatre trip, we were all in either of these two apartments, cutting our capers.

Dennis Savage complained about it: "No one ever wants to go anywhere. Are we waiting for Godot or something? I remember a time when we were heading somewhere *every night*—parties and dancing and crazing around in the Village." He became keen. "I remember it *vastly*."

"How about I treat us all to *Grand Hotel*?"

"This already is *Grand Hotel*! Everyone's all checked in, and no one's checking out! Every night the kids are *in the house*, rehearsing the Yokohama Harakiri Dozo Band, or whatever it is. And you are *in the house*, playing records. Carlo—who, as I recall, has his own place—is *in the house*, mooching dinner."

"You're in the house, too," I said.

"I can't go out by myself. I've forgotten where everything is."

"Have you some more pages for me? Of your stories?"

He did. But no sooner had they landed on my desk than I spotted familiar names in his text, places I intimately knew, things I'd said. Three sentences in, I realized that he had viciously purloined a recherché episode in my past and proposed to bandy it in his fiction. I thought it best to deter him.

But deftly, deftly. "You know," I said, "I think the plot slips up a bit here, with the intrusion of these subsidiary—"

"Down, Rover," he said. "You're not finessing me out of my rightful rebuttal."

At least I was able to devastate his confidence in the semicolon, pour boiling oil upon his tender ablatives. He was groaning soon.

"Please," he begged. "Please."

"The price of education," I observed, "is to see ourselves as we are seen," as my pencil marked away. I even found a spelling error.

"What's the latest on Bert and Scott?" he asked, to throw me off my game.

"Why don't you write them into your story?" I replied, chiding a tautology and relishing a failure to follow through with the subject-verb agreement on *neither-nor* constructions.

"I'll leave them to you," he said. "You always love the direst tales. I know how you'll end it, too—Bert finally hypnotizes the love of his life and finds it a shallow thing after all in this world of vanities. Right?"

"Too pat. It needs a twist."

"Speaking of twists, how are you and Cosgrove doing?"

I had to think about that one, and put down the pencil. "Well, he knows that Virgil is the side of the bread with the butter on it. But he has to eat the other side, too, doesn't he?"

Then Carlo came in with the latest on Bert and Scott. Carlo always knows these things; he keeps up with what's left of the Life. Like: Bert wore a mesh jock to the Black and Red Party. *Nothing* but a mesh jock. (Dennis Savage said, "Are they still holding Black and Red Parties?") Or like: Bert and Scott had their hands in each other's pants during the last twenty minutes of *Labyrinth of Passion*. Rick Conradi was one row behind them and saw the whole thing. (Dennis Savage said, "Why can't *we* go out to the movies instead of having them in?") And even: Bert and Scott are starting to look alike. Scott just bought a motorcycle jacket and cut his hair down to but *nothing*. (Dennis Savage said, "Maybe I should get a new haircut," to which I replied, "What hair?," only trying to be symmetrical in this screwball comedy sort of way; but you know how huffy he gets.)

Anyway, the latest was that Bert had moved in with Scott, and Carlo thought there was something wrong with that but he couldn't figure out what. Dennis Savage said, "No, it's true love after all these years." And they were looking at me because they knew I didn't buy the story as it stood.

"It needs a twist," I insisted.

Then the door opened and in poured the rest of us: Virgil and Cosgrove, grinning with their banjos and the Saddam Hussein of dogs, Bauhaus.

Dennis Savage said, "Just what I need, the Von Suppé Glockenspiel Terrorists."

"Here comes movie night!" Cosgrove gloated.

"What's the selection for us, pal?" Carlo asked.

"*The Widow Keebler.*"

"No, Cosgrove," said Virgil. "*Lady Keaton.*"

Carlo and I glanced at Dennis Savage.

"*Mrs. Soffel,*" he said. "And if it's movie night, why do I see those five-string dishpans?"

"Well, first it's the Von Sondheim Koto Ensemble of Manhattan Isle," Virgil explained, "with their tasty new medley from *Company.*"

So that's what we did that night. It's funny how life went on like that around here. It missed the appeal of the unexpected—the dangerous, even—that life had at times in the 1970s. But I can't say it was ever boring. It must be a little like those intricate three-geisha massages they perform in certain Japanese bordellos. By the end, you're utterly exhausted, yet you didn't precisely *do* anything. It kind of got done to you.

Maybe we *should* have been getting out more. My friends were grumbling that anytime they phoned, day or night, I always answered, so instead of being able to tape a message and rush on with their day, they had to blow half an hour chatting with me. And Carlo observed that whenever he dropped in, *somebody* was around.

We were all around when he dragged Bert in from the gym. I mean *dragged*: Carlo had hauled Bert all the way across town to make him tell us something—and Carlo was angry, a rare state for him.

"Go on now and tell them," he growled at Bert, pretty much throwing him onto the couch.

Well, you can kidnap Bert, especially if you had been, like Carlo, a brief era before, the most apparent man in gay New York. Status has its privilege. But you can't make Bert blow his suave.

"A cold one?" he asked me, resettling himself on the couch as heftily as possible, the cowboy at tea. "Yeah, thank you. Saint Pauli Girl, if you've got it."

"Beer?" I said, suddenly realizing that this was my apartment and I was the host. "All I have is water, coffee, and Absolut. That's all I drink."

"We've got Hershey's chocolate Super Shake upstairs," said Virgil. "And grapefruit juice."

"Just tell them!" Carlo shouted. "Who cares what you drink?"

The rest of us stood there, amazed.

"Yes," said Bert. "Well." He's letting it out slowly, smiling as at some private joke, enjoying the attention. "You know, Scott was always such an aggressive kind of guy. What Scott wanted was what Scott got." He laughed. "Well, that's cool. That's what sex is for, right? You'd be strolling the avenue on a fine spring day, you and Scott. Cruising the avenue. And something cute passes by, and that's the last you see of Scott on that fine spring day."

He paused, nodding at us all, his hands extended, as if to ask, Look, aren't we all the same human under all our dodges and façades? Who are we to judge, right?

"So now it's years later and the story is, Who's cute and what does Scott want *today*? What does Scott want?"

He grinned.

"Scott wants me."

He nodded some more.

"Would I let an old buddy down?"

He pointed rhetorically.

"'What do you like to do?' Remember that question? 'What do you like to do?' You have to get what you need. Now, Scott used to need to top his boys. He basically liked them leaning over, braced against the wall, legs wide, a good fast pump. Back in San they call that a creamdown."

"I'm not wild about this," said Cosgrove.

"But now it seems that our Scott here likes to be creamed himself. Any style you want. And that's fine with me, because what I like to do is screw my boys coco-style, when they're on their back and you start on them standing and then get yourself onto the bed and really sizzle them up with your arms around them, slow-stroking them to the sky. You know how beautiful it is to hear a really sexy guy moaning with hot while your cock works him to and fro?"

"Listen to this," Dennis Savage murmured, really alarmed.

"What Scott wants, I shall have to give him. That was always the case with me and Scott. Always. And Scott wanted to spend a fine spring day on his back, going all the way, none of that paranoid safe-sex stuff, over and over and more and again. In between, he took rest breaks to slurp on my joint. You know, to catch his breath. And finally we were lying there all brained out, our bodies slick and our sticks running with cum. After all those terrible aching years of wanting him and wanting him, right up there so close and never, never, never, never, never being allowed to feel that warmth. Well, almost never. Not . . . *really.*"

Here was a flash of the old Bert, the man who needed instead of the man who had.

"Now I'd felt it. Can you *imagine*? Lying next to him in the darkness, listening to him breathe, knowing what it was like at long last. Leaning over him and watching him smile. I've seen plenty of those smiles. But never on him. He was smiling for me today. Scott smiled with *love* for *me*. So he reached up to touch me, and I told him I have AIDS."

Glance around the room at such a moment; see what your friends are like. Carlo, calm now, looked like Jean Valjean near the end of *Les Misérables*. Virgil was staggered, trying to figure out why this would happen. Dennis Savage put his hand on my shoulder, which meant, I think, If you want to toss this thing out of your apartment, let me help. Cosgrove simply took up his koto and diddled out "The Music of the Night."

"I told him I have AIDS," Bert repeated, "because when I have something, I need to share it with my buddy Scott. He always shared with me, didn't he? I'm talking about years and years of sharing, such terribly *painful* years of that Scott-style sharing, such love-is-punishment sharing and *slavery* sharing, and sharing *hurts*. It *hurts*, dudes!" He turned to me. "*You* know this, right?"

I said, and this is quotation, "'Oh, 'tis an earth defiled, whereon we live.'"

"What Scott put me through with his sharing you will never know, with your gang here in your fun-filled apartments. You think books and music saves you? You think they make you special, or is it invulnerable you are? Well, Scott is not invulnerable, so I told him I have AIDS, and now Scott has what Scott wanted."

"You said your say," Carlo told him. "Get the fuck out of my friend's house."

Now Bert, suddenly, was affable and assured, reconstructed again. Bert, the clone of death. He got up and went to the door, smiling—but Virgil followed him and said, "You told him that. But is it *true*?"

"Don't spoil the story, sweetheart," Bert replied. And off he went.

Exhalations and exclamations ensued. Had we been old biddies, we might have gone in on one great gust of *Well!* Then we put it behind us. We're home. Dennis Savage returned to studying his new story. Virgil remarked on how angry Carlo had been, and Carlo, who had turned on the television to catch up on *Monday Night Football,* laughed and gave Virgil a pat on the rump. Then the koto kids demonstrated how to get to Carnegie Hall ("Prectice! Prectice!," as the old joke runs), and I decided to get some retyping done. It sounds noisy—hell, it *is* noisy—but I can work through it.

When Dennis Savage brought me his latest emendations, he was in a good mood.

" 'I was pretty,' " he sang as my pencil flew. " 'I was happy.' "

"I love Cosgrove," I sang.

He thought that over and gave it a soigné but sympathetic nod. Surprise. You never thought that I was going to admit it, did you?

That's the twist.

We froat.

THE HUNT FOR
RED OCTOBER

N o, I *like* Roy," Dennis Savage was saying. "Look, he's spirited and friendly and youthful and even smart, and those are useful qualities in a neighbor. I just don't understand why he's always going on about cock, and big-hung, and giant meat, and so on."

"Ask him yourself," I said. "He's coming up for a coffee date in about ten minutes."

"Well, haven't you noticed? I swear, he can turn any conversation over to his favorite—indeed, dare I suggest?, *only*—topic within three exchanges, *without a single non sequitur.* How does he do it?"

Roy is one of the new young gay guys who are starting to take over our building. When Dennis Savage and (shortly after) I moved in, sometime before the Spanish-American War, the entire apartment house was straight but for us and the closeted old grouch in 11-I. But during the last few years a striking number of gays have joined us, including a few lookers and one out-and-out hunk who seems to have sparked fantasies in Virgil and Cosgrove. He has become known to them as Presto.

"Then there's Roy's wistful little pal," Dennis Savage went on. "So polite, so yearning, so resigned. He's like a scream of agony too well brought up to let itself be heard."

"Well, Nicky's got a case on Roy," I said, getting out the cheese-and-crackers tray.

"A *case*? Like Israel had on Eichmann. He's up to his ears in the love of his life, and Roy doesn't notice and couldn't care less."

"What happened to all the cheeses I bought?" I called out from the fridge. "There was a Brie, a Gruyère, and a Stilton."

"I ate the little pie one," Cosgrove answered from the living room. "And Bauhaus was starting in on the Stilton."

"Who invited Bauhaus down here?" I asked Dennis Savage while examining what was left of the Stilton. "He's *your* dog."

"You're not going to offer that to Roy, are you?" asked Dennis Savage. "God knows where those jaws have been."

"I'll just trim off the——"

"Nicky," said Dennis Savage, shaking his head. "If there was ever someone *born* to doom and gloom." He followed me and the cheese tray into the living room. "He reminds me of that pathetic little drudge in *Les Mis,* what's-her-name, who dies in the rain."

"Funette," Cosgrove put in.

"Yes, Funette. And such an *apt* name, because in fact she . . ." No, that didn't seem right, did it? "Funette?"

"I think you mean Eponine," I said.

"Of *course,* Eponine!" Dennis Savage whirled on Cosgrove, who was reviewing his CD collection. "So who's Funette supposed to be?"

"Now you'll never be sure," Cosgrove coolly replied, rearranging the CDs in the wooden display case he insisted I buy him—four feet tall, two feet wide, and I have no idea where we'll put it. Besides, Cosgrove owns only five CDs as yet—a Skinny Puppy single, the 8½ soundtrack, the Swedish cast of *The Phantom of the Opera,* the Riccardo Muti *Symphonie Fantastique,* and a Kate Bush album that Cosgrove swears he found lying on a sidewalk somewhere. He is very earnest about his CDs. He wants to become an aficionado, to be known for his taste, his energy in unearthing the arcane and wondrous. Having folded himself into my manner of living unquestioningly, he now wants to break out and discover something of his own. So he has refused to let me give him CDs or suggest key titles. He probes my expertise, yes, but mostly he consults reviews and catalogs and spends hours in stores and (his venue of choice) flea markets, examining, weighing, wondering.

I like this. I am sympathetic to anyone who surrenders his independence in worship of the unjust and vindictive god Demento, who rules over all obsessed collectors. Gods, of course, are the mythological idealization of fathers, and all known mythologies are heterosexually man-made. But Demento has his campy side. He likes to be thought of as dread, yet he'll materialize in a Sabu take-a-peek loincloth and Rochelle Hudson fuck-me-or-I'll-scream-the-place-down wedgies. Cosgrove fears and serves him. "Is it *rare* enough?" he worried when he considered buying the Swedish *Phantom* on a visit to the show buff's specialty shop, Footlight Records. I told him, "It's outlandishly expensive, it's incomprehensible, and it's available in only two places in the entire world: this store and Sweden." Still Cosgrove pondered. Then I said, "Just think, no more than five or six Americans will own that album. This is unique."

"I'm coming, Demento!" cried Cosgrove. He blew his bank account on it—double-disc CDs imported from Sweden run to fifty bucks or so. But Demento was content.

So was I, because collecting is building Cosgrove's confidence. When he and I first crossed paths, he had no façade, no protection. The slightest challenge dismayed him. Now, when I tell him that the Klondike people package their ice-cream sandwiches in boxes of four so that we can enjoy a treat on four different occasions— as opposed to eating right through the box in a single sitting, then testing one's bedmate by groaning and holding one's stomach all night—he says, "Demento lured me on." He says, "Too much is never enough." He says, "I suffered, you didn't."

Then there's his going-to-the-showers gambit—and, while we're at it, his "Great Moments from Movie Cinema" (as he terms it) act. Looking innocent, Cosgrove will approach the uninitiated, then suddenly wobble his hands about his ears as he writhes and screams, in the James Dean manner, " 'You're *tear*ing me a*part!*' "

I've told him how disconcerting this can be; but when he feels too deeply chided he marches into the bathroom and turns on the shower. The noise locks out a reproachful world, and he actually gets under the water, washing the difficulty away. Fresh and clean, he comes out as if nothing had happened.

"Funette," Dennis Savage muttered, one eye on Cosgrove. "He slips in Funette, and I bought it."

Doorbell; enter Roy. Roy merrily says, "Did anyone see the gay porn clips on the sex channel last night? The guy with the whopper dick in the living-room scene? Did you *scope* that?"

Dennis Savage made a helpless gesture: See what I mean? Cosgrove pointed out his CD display case, Roy called it "nifty," and within twenty seconds he was going on about veins and how much they add to a "truly elegant dick structure."

"Cosgrove already scarfed up the Brie," I said, presenting the cheese, "but there's Gruyère and—"

"Watch out for the Stilton," Dennis Savage stage-whispered.

"Now, here's the true thing," said Cosgrove. "Should my next purchase be a complete opera, the kind that comes in this box with a booklet like a whole portfolio? Or should I catch up on my rock classics?"

"There's so much life here," Roy observed, as he crackered up some Gruyère. "That's what I like about you guys."

"For instance," Cosgrove continued. "Should I lay in some Wagner? is the question."

"Yes, laying in. The feel of some tightboy's enormous, jizz-spurting cucumber as it very slowly plays into you," said Roy, in the serenely reckless tone of the New Waver for whom sex talk, no matter how lurid, is to be taken as a formal element of liberation. "You're stretched out and ready. Psyched for it. Then . . . first, that delicious trembling as the head presses against your rim. People don't think of this, but it's all geometry. The line of your body diagrammed on the bed, the triangular head and its tubular mass generating a logic of—"

"Where's Nicky?" Cosgrove asked.

Well, that stopped him. "How should I know?"

"You're always together."

"Are we? I hadn't noticed."

Dennis Savage cleared his throat. "You're more or less insep-arable," he said. "At least, to the naked eye."

Roy laughed—a touch nervously, I thought. "Or to two naked cowboys," he said. "They were dozing, but then they get up and find a pair of thin white-linen drawstring pants. So one of them tries them on, and the other helps him, you know, adjusting the waistband, admiring the jut of his buddy's behind. So the guy in the pants gets hot, while his cowboy friend rubs his neck to loosen him up. Then his hands steal around and pull the string, and the pants immediately sag to the floor, revealing—"

"How can you tell they're cowboys," said Cosgrove, "if they're naked?"

"They'd still have their Stetsons on."

"I," Dennis Savage began, in his careful mode, "always think these fetishist fantasies are like the haikus that fourteen-year-old girls write. For your eyes only."

"No, it can be very everyday as well," Roy replied. "Just your standard date. He says, 'Let's get naked.' And his zipper pulls down on a whopper, big-time. Instantly, the mind clears of its trash. The *truth* of the partnership is . . . Figure it." He paused, eyes half-closed, savoring the moment. "This prince, this tyrant. This wolfling about to . . . to stuff your cream tunnel with—"

Roy halted as Cosgrove jumped up, went into the bathroom, and turned on the shower.

"Did I say something?"

"Try the Stilton," Dennis Savage urged.

The doorbell again. Now Virgil joined us, waving a brown paper bag like Churchill flashing victory fingers.

"Look at this contest I'm entering!" he crowed. "I could win fifty dollars!"

Out of the bag came a romance comic book; the contest, flourished on the cover and detailed on the last page, called for a brief essay on the theme of "My Dream Man."

"It's surely open only to pubescent girls," I put in.

"It doesn't say so."

"It assumes so, because that's who the readership is."

"I'm entering anyway. I even bought a composition book and an extra-fine-tipped pen. Hi, Roy. Where's Nicky?"

Flopping onto the couch, Virgil fished a spiral notebook and pen out of the paper bag, murmured, "My dream man . . ." and dug in.

"I wish people didn't lump me with Nicky all the time," Roy grumbled. "He's one friend out of many that I have. And he's so . . . you know."

Dennis Savage said, "No, tell."

"Well, sure, I'm fond of him in his way, but he's this kind of asexual, isn't he? Try standing around in a bar with him sometime. He never wants to talk about the guys and scope them out. You'll spot some really fly number and speculate as to the size and weight of the junk he carries, and Nicky just . . . he just . . ."

"Doesn't really care?" Dennis Savage asked. "Do you find that aberrant?"

"Oh, please. There are only two kinds of gays—size queens and liars."

"I'm not a liar," said Dennis Savage, "and I'm also not a size queen—although I can be impressed. I don't know how many kinds of gays there are, but even the four males in this room are completely different from each other."

"And wait till Cosgrove comes in," Virgil added, looking up from his notebook.

"Kinds of gays?" Dennis Savage went on. "I don't know if there are kinds of gays any more than there are kinds of people."

"I've offended you, haven't I?" said Roy.

"I'm always offended when someone assumes that his taste is my taste. I also find this romanticizing of size questionable in an age in which fucking and sucking are fatally risky. This is seventies material. It suits coming out and beginning to comprehend the expanse of male sexuality. But that was an experimental age. This is an embattled age. Today, your icon is poison."

I asked, "Who wants more coffee?," and Cosgrove rejoined us, prompting Virgil to do a little number on the Dream Man contest. Cosgrove expressed a thrill or two and we talked of any old thing till Roy blurted out, "Look, everybody, I'm sorry. I didn't mean to expose you all to my . . . I thought you . . . I mean, who doesn't feel this way? Isn't cock the center of male sexuality?"

Dennis Savage and I were silent, Virgil was deep in composition, and Cosgrove was reshelving his CDs, to study the effect from different parts of the room.

"I'm sorry," Roy repeated. "I should be more low-key about it, I guess." He shrugged. "Everybody's got something."

"That much is true," said Dennis Savage. "I gay-bashed a classmate on Halloween when I was a teenager."

Virgil came to life with "I hid my sister Anne's Barbie Goes Camping accessories in the Victrola in the garage and didn't tell her where they were for seven years."

"I peed off the roof last Tuesday," said Cosgrove.

I was lying low in the kitchen, safe from Truth or Dare. By the time I returned, with a bowl of miniature pears and Rome apples, the air had cleared and Roy was about to go.

"I'll have to give a dinner," he said. "Because you guys were so helpful when I moved in and all." As he shook our hands, he said, "It's a gay thing, right? Support group and like that."

"Make sure Nicky's there," Virgil called out from the sofa, and Roy said, "Oh, count on it, because he'll do the cooking. He's very handy for those things the rest of us . . . you know, can't be bothered with."

Cosgrove was holding the door and Roy gave him a pat on the butt as he passed. Suddenly Cosgrove grew wary, enigmatic. " 'Is it safe?' " he asked, almost whispering to himself.

Now listen to Cosgrove's question: "Do we see it as valuable because it's rare, or is it rare because it's valuable?"

"Rarity is everything," I told him. "We don't want what we can have."

"How do we know what is rare?"

"The hard-core enthusiast figures it out. It's partly word of mouth from other collectors and sheer experience, and of course there are the catalogs and discographies, but it's mainly the innate expertise of the fanatic. The children of Demento live for what is rare, so they *have* to know about it. They find a way, burrow in deep."

"Hmmm," says Cosgrove. "Which is more important—when you find a certain rarity you had been searching for forever and ever, or when you crash into a rarity that you didn't know there could be?"

"That's up to the individual collector to decide. But one thing you must never do is pass up a rarity when you find it."

"Why?"

"You may never happen upon it again, for one thing. But there is also Demento to consider. Those under his fierce tutelage are not free to select their own personal assortment of rarities. *They must have them all.*"

Cosgrove loves these talks. It's totally risk-free sport, like getting into mischief so inventive that your parents never thought to forbid it and thus cannot punish you.

"And of course," I went on, "when Demento learns that you have scoffed at him by passing up some treasure, he will be revenged."

"He's everywhere," Cosgrove gloated.

"Once, I happened upon the original Brunswick *Show Boat* 78s in a thrift shop, in excellent condition, for forty cents! Remember, this is not only a super-rarity but, for its first half century, the only *Show Boat* album with *logo cover*!"

"You snapped it up?"

I shook my head. "I already owned the LP re-release. Two copies of the same album? Ridiculous. Then, two blocks from the store, panic set in. I raced back—the album was gone! Another collector had seized it. And, late that night, Demento paid me a call."

" 'They're coming to get you, Barbara!' "

"With a wave of his hand, Demento studded my Capitol *Pal Joey* with cracks, hisses, and skips, mildewed the cover of my Ann Sothern *Lady in the Dark,* and slit the binding of my mint copy of *The Saint of Bleecker Street.*"

A knock at the door. It was Virgil, to announce that he had finished his essay on "My Dream Man" and sent it off.

"I still say they can't let a male win this contest," I told him.

"No, I outsmarted them. I signed it Kiwi Brown—that could be anybody. Anyway, I happened to browse through that comic book, and all the romances ended happily. So the guys who put it together must be very naïve."

"Virgil," said Cosgrove, "will you read us your composition, 'My Dream Man'?"

Virgil seemed a little startled; apparently, he hadn't been planning to share his vision with the rest of us.

"It's just this little contest piece," he said.

"Why don't you read it at Roy's dinner on Friday?" I asked.

"Yes," Cosgrove agreed. "A star-intensive event!"

"No," Virgil replied, with immense conviction. "No, I'll read it only if I win the contest." I could see him thinking, That could be twenty years from now, and they'll forget all about it.

I won't.

Roy was right: Nicky did cook the dinner: prosciutto, melon, and watercress salad followed by London broil with wild rice and mushrooms, and, for dessert, Grand Marnier over raspberries and sherbet.

"Primo!" Dennis Savage cried, as the salad appeared.

"Nicky always produces," said Roy.

"I want extra-well-done meat," Virgil warned us.

"Me, too," Dennis Savage added.

This is, for some, a problem in our group: We all like it more or less burned to death. "Yes," Nicky promised. "Yes, I will." But it clearly threw his timing off to put the beef back in the oven. Cooks assume that there will be a well-done zealot or two, not a house full of them. It wilted the mushrooms and dried out the rice, but Nicky was happy if Roy was happy, and Roy was happy.

"A toast to the kitchen," he said, raising his glass.

"Everybody likes Nicky," said Virgil, joining in.

"Let's not get carried away," Roy joked.

Cosgrove pulled in with a bag of CDs and his catalogs, breathless and brisk and in charge.

"Just hold on," he told us, "because I got British dance bands and a very suspicious-looking opera by Berlioz and look at this weird thing." He held up Lucia Popp's *Slavonic Opera Arias*. "That's sure to be rare, because who knows what 'Slavonic' is? Then I got Rachmaninoff's *Second* Symphony, not just his First."

"Who's conducting?" I asked.

Cosgrove examined the box. "André Previn."

"Victor, EMI, or Telarc?"

"One guy did all those? How am I supposed to know which—"

"I told you, the devotee commands the trivia."

"Quick, what are the differences?"

"Victor is incomplete, with shallow sonics. Telarc is excellent. But the EMI is one of the classic performances of Russian music— and it's out of print as we speak."

For a terrible moment, Cosgrove checked the box, then flourished it aloft—it was the EMI—for all to savor the cover shot of Previn conducting batonless, his hands floating and his features dim, lost to the rapture.

"You really scored," I said. "This is something no one else can have."

"And all for three dollars a disc!" Cosgrove exulted. "Yes, there I am, crossing West Tenth Street, innocent as a clam, when . . . What are they serving?"

"London broil," said Virgil.

"Very well done, my portion," Cosgrove sang out; in the kitchen, Nicky sighed.

"Take no notice," said Roy. "Nicky's always making little noises."

"Anyway, there was this street fair. So I saw a booth of used CDs and scooped them up!"

"I don't see what's so great about those little mouse records," said Virgil, who can understand any fetish except someone else's. "Bud's got a million records—why don't you tape some of his?"

"It only counts if you own them in the true format. Listening to tapes is like kissing your uncle instead of some nice friend."

"My uncles were okay," Virgil airily recalled. "Though one had this sort of ruthless streak."

"Still," said Cosgrove, admiring the jewel boxes spread out before him, "it's a giant haul in the Western world. A whopper haul for me, Cosgrove."

"I hope no one's all opposed to gravy," Nicky called out from the kitchen. "Or forks. Or plates."

"How come you sound so warlike?" asked Virgil, proceeding into the kitchen.

Their voices lowered, and I pretended to admire a Mucha reprint hanging in the vicinity, hoping to tune in on the conversation in my harmless yet resolute writer's way. As I had suspected, Nicky was feeling unloved and exploited and Virgil was comforting him. When Nicky said, "Sometimes I want to curl up and die," Virgil answered, "Dying is easy—*comedy* is hard," a phrase he picked up somewhere. I thought, No: Comedy is easy—*friendship* is hard. There's so much there there.

"So, Virgil," said Roy, as Virgil parked himself next to Cosgrove and his CDs, "how's that Dream Man thing coming? Bet you've got some major boner in mind, long and fat, with one of those pointed heads I love."

Virgil just looked at him.

"Yeah," Roy went on. "Some call them donkeys and some thumpers, but I—"

"No," said Dennis Savage. "No, if it's the taxonomy of cock size that we're addressing, can we please get our terms straight? The heavy endowments are called, in ascending order: exploso cock . . ."

Roy was intrigued.

". . . raw, long and quivering, suitable for any occasion—"

"Veined and pulsing, with a mushroom cap?" Roy asked. "So cream-filled, and bouncing high?"

"No, that would be the next larger size, the bazooka cock."

Roy was silent, pensive and shivering in his dream. Virgil, eyeing him, whispered something unkind—or so I guessed—to Cosgrove. Cosgrove nodded.

"Bazooka cock," Dennis Savage went on, warming to his subject as a Classics scholar fields questions from the floor on Beauty and Truth in Petronius Arbiter, "is neither rare nor common. Certain connoisseurs claim the ability to detect the bazooka by a man's walk or the set of his shoulders, perhaps by his pronunciation of the word 'often.'"

"Bazookas pronounce the *t*?" Roy asked, hopeful, eager for a code.

Dennis Savage shook his head. "A legend," he pronounced. "The true bazooka is deceptive, elusive. You know the phrase 'a grower, not a shower'? The bazooka is like a strange and fearsome rumor that courses through the public ear, not only showing but then—so *implausibly!*—growing in power and purity till it must be revealed to one and all as an official proclamation."

"It is real," Roy intoned. "It is near us." He could have been in a trance.

"Someone in this room is a sleazoid," Virgil observed.

"And his initials," Cosgrove added, "are Roy."

"Exploso," Roy reviewed. "Bazooka. Yes, and then?"

"And then," Dennis Savage replied. I have to tell you, he had not looked this quietly yet consummately joyful since Hamilton College invited him up for an autumn alumni panel on "The Four Best Years of Your Life."

"Well, *what's* then?" cried Roy.

"What's then is last, and hugest, and perhaps more a magic than a reality. Yet it is truer than truth."

"Oh, Lord," Roy murmured, looking at me now. But this was Dennis Savage's scene, and I kept still.

"What's then is the Godhead, before which all humankind—the intelligentsia, the clerisy, the military, the press—make their solemnly frenzied kowtow . . ."

"Say it!"

"... the seldom-seen but oh-so-devoutly-to-be-wished-for ... Red October."

"*Yes!*" Roy cried. "Oh, *yes!*"

"Although," Dennis Savage concluded, with a wry chuckle, "I still wonder how appropriate such talk is in an age of epidemic."

"True, but it's all fantasy," Roy assured us, as Nicky began parceling out the laden platters. "I dream to the bitter end, but I don't do anything with anyone. Besides, who knows where the heroes are?

"Well, given your field of interest, you must frequent Folly City."

"I've never been," said Roy, accepting his plate. "A strip joint is just a little too downtown for ... Thanks, Nicky, the dinner looks fabou."

"It was kind of hard keeping everything together with so many demands for—"

"Right." Then, to Dennis Savage: "How far do they go? To the nude?"

"Each dancer does two numbers. First, a strip to the almost, then a dance in the, uh, full truth, entering—as tradition and the management demand—with a hard-on, as the crowd goes more or less wild."

"No!"

"Well, yes, actually."

"But are any of them ... exploso? Bazooka?"

Dennis Savage nodded. "And, once in a blue moon, one glimpses Red October."

Roy let out a squeal.

"There's seconds on everything," said Nicky, joining us at last with his own plate. Nicky: average in every respect, pleasant, undemonstrative, resigned. Does he remind you of Bert Hicks? No—Bert was a player, quite formidable in his tactful way even when Scott Hellman was exploiting him. Nicky was no player. Nicky was a hopeless adherent: Being treated as subsidiary by the man you love is preferable to not being treated at all.

"Of course," Dennis Savage went on, "the special feature of Folly City is that the dancers are available, at the going rate, for private shows."

"A show?" said Roy. He seemed pensive. "They dance for you at home?"

"If somebody wants to hire me," said Cosgrove, "I do the Russian kazatski."

"A private *show*?" Roy repeated.

"Well," Dennis Savage replied, "sex. That's where the dancers really make their money. I gather they've closed the back room where this used to take place, so now you take them home or to their hotel or whatever."

"You gather? You aren't a regular?"

"Oh, most gay men in New York know about Folly City. You don't actually have to go there."

"But do you?"

"I've never been."

"A likely story," Cosgrove whispered to Virgil—whispered, I should add, as Olivier might have whispered "Never came a poison from so sweet a place" to the top balcony of the Old Vic. "He probably dances there himself, when no one's looking."

"He'd have to," I observed.

"Why don't we . . ." Roy began, then halted, probably hoping somebody would help him. I did: "Plan a trip to Folly City and see it for ourselves?"

"Well, don't you think we should?"

Nicky said, "Count me out."

"I'll be listening to Slavonic opera arias," said Cosgrove, showing Virgil the wondrous libretto booklet, with critical introduction and texts in four languages.

"I think it would be fun," said Dennis Savage. "Refreshing and so on. Like a field trip when you get to miss a day of school."

"How much do these private shows cost a guy?" Roy asked.

"It greatly varies. A full-fledged date would run you upwards of a hundred, but a quickie around the corner in a peep-show booth could fall as low as—"

"A peep-show booth?" said Nicky. "Is this a life?"

"They print all the words to the arias, see?" Cosgrove told Virgil. "So you can sing along at the significant moments."

"What's a good night for this trip?" asked Roy.

Dennis Savage wasn't sure. "I'll confer with certain sages of my acquaintance and we'll set a date."

Nicky sighed and Roy let out a tiny thrill.

"But I warn you," Dennis Savage went on, "there are cases of innocent and even noble men who blundered into Folly City on a dare and, overnight, became addicts, slaves to a passion that cannot be named among decent people. Can you risk that?"

"You mean, it's like crack or something?"

"I mean, it's like truth. It becomes its own Red October."

Roy was so intrigued he was virtually squirming in his seat. He said, "I think we should go and make our visit."

It took a few weeks to get everyone's free nights aligned, and by then Dennis Savage had bought himself one of those trendy haircuts where they shear off the sides but leave it extra full on top. I thought he might be just the tiniest bit Cretaceous for this essentially youthful look, though I said nothing; and Virgil wasn't sure how he felt about it. As so often, it was Cosgrove who tendered the most direct opinion: Whenever Dennis Savage appeared, Cosgrove would cry, "Here comes Ragmop!"

It was Saturday afternoon, and I was hoping to get a little work done before we went to Folly City, for Cosgrove had gone upstairs with his Gameboy to finish off his and Virgil's Tetris championship. I once thought that video games might become Cosgrove's fascination—we have three hand-held systems, plus the Super Nintendo hooked up to the television—but, as Demento's lifelong adherent, I should have realized that something as street-corner as video games could never tempt Cosgrove's need to assert his individuality. Anyone can play video games. Collectors seek the arcane—the fantasy, really. We're not talking of an accumulation of matchbooks or butterflies. We're talking about encircling something that most people do not know is there.

(Sometimes I think that's all that writers ever do. We get so deep into our perceptions and analyses: But is anybody listening?)

Anyway, I wasn't getting any work done, because Nicky had arrived, early, fretting and loquacious. He had been absolutely opposed to this trip and absolutely determined to come along—"Because," he explained, "sometimes you have to humor Roy or he gets all intense about everything."

So I said, "I resent this derogatory nuance that has been creeping in on that word lately. *Intense,* as if that were the nth of bad style. As if we're not supposed to cultivate passions anymore."

"You think Roy treats me like sludge, don't you?" said Nicky.

Okay. I like directness. "He does seem to take you for granted."

Nicky nodded. "I embarrass him. Because I've never figured out the, like, dress codes. I'm in black sneakers, everyone else is in white. I still wear Lacoste shirts. Or the I-put-too-much-honey-in-my-tea kind of thing. Roy's all concerned about how people are judging him, always. And I . . ." He shrugged. "I gave up a long time ago. But here's what you don't know. He's very nice to me when we're alone. He gets all roughhouse with me, like frat brothers or something. He's affectionate. We take naps together, listening to music. We're dressed at the time, like schoolboys in a Victorian story. That's what I love."

Nicky was staring at me, as if expecting a question.

"Of course I have a crush on him," he finally said, filling in for me. "But Roy wants a boy friend his gang can all respect. See, they have categories of—"

"Please don't say any more," I told him.

"Yes, there *are* certain categories of hotness which tell what people want in life." He leaned forward. "Don't you think everyone really knows what category they're in? Or do some guys try to fool themselves up somehow?"

"Gosh, I'm late for habañera class," I said, rising; and Nicky got up, too, but he kept on talking: "Now, me, I know what category I'm in. But what I mean to tell you is, Roy is all inclined to promote me to a higher category as long as no one else is around to see. And what I mean to *ask* you is—"

Just then Cosgrove came in, and he and I got very involved in discussing Cosgrove's Tetris scores, and the significance of sound wrist coordination in the mastering of Tetris, and the overall history of Tetris from the age of Nebuchadnezzar to our own times. And by then Dennis Savage and Virgil and Roy had joined us. So off we went.

Now, Folly City may be many different things to different people. But it reminded me of that moment in *A Christmas Carol* when the ghost shows you a terrible vision of what you will become. In fact, once we had climbed the stairs, paid our way through the turnstile, and edged through a dank hall into the long, narrow "lounge" where mirthless aficionados schemed and lurked, Cosgrove took one look, vastly feared, and made a run for it. I had to pull him back up the front stairs by the belt of his pants.

There's something odd here. When you mention Folly City, no one says, "Who?" The place is *very* known. Yet where was our generation? Why was the operating concept that of degenerate age woefully fastening upon youthful beauty?

"And now," came the announcement over the speaker system, "let's welcome our next handsome dancer, Pietro."

We duly entered the auditorium, and out stepped a man of about twenty-three, trim and confident, throwing himself around to Frankie Goes to Hollywood's "Krisco Kisses." He got down to a vest and a jockstrap. Then he walked off through the backdrop of dark Mylar strips. The deejay put on "Dancing with Myself," and after a bit of a wait the same performer reentered, naked, with his dick turned on to full. There was applause, and some of the rows of seats began to shake.

"Those guys are beating off!" Dennis Savage hissed to me.

"Where are the kids?"

"They're in the back row, holding a Tetris championship."

"In this darkness?"

"Cosgrove brought that lighting thing that fits over the top. You could put them in the Black Hole of Calcutta, and they'd play Tetris. Where's Roy?"

"In the lounge. Where's Nicky?"

"With the kids."

"Now," said the announcer, "let's welcome Theobald."

The men hanging out in the lounge came to life at this; to a man, they hastened into the auditorium. I took a break in the lounge; Cosgrove wandered in after me to say, "This place is horrible."

"Did you see the Tetris machine?" I asked.

It was the full-size arcade version, of course, with colors and music well beyond Gameboy technology. It's a friendly machine, so eager to be played that it runs through a sample game as you stand there; and Cosgrove drew near. But how could you make contact with this great hulking monster of a Tetris? Why are the falling shapes so different from the ones in the Gameboy version? Even the music is alien, vicious. This Tetris was unsafe, and Cosgrove declined to play.

"Well, you seem to be new here," said some old guy.

Cosgrove, grim and tight-lipped, replied, " 'I tell you, that thing upstairs is not my daughter!' "

The old guy mulled this over and decided to drift away—wise move—just as thunderous applause broke out in the auditorium.

"Theobald must be quite some package," I told Cosgrove, who said, "When can we—" I'm sure that "leave?" would have been the rest of it, but just then Roy came running out, grabbing us and saying, "*Theobald* is the one!" and "What a *panther*!" and "Did you see the *whopper* on him? It must be . . . hmmm, not *quite* Red October. But surely a major bazooka! Now, how do I arrange for . . . well . . ."

"Stand there, by the telephone," I said. "He'll come through that door and voilà."

"Please don't French at me now, what do I—"

"Pounce."

"What's he excited about?" Cosgrove asked. "It's just people."

"Theobald!" Roy cooed, inching up, as the dancer entered the lounge looking wet, warm, and debauched.

"Hey, folks," said Virgil, joining us with the Gameboy. "I broke a hundred thousand. Nicky didn't do so well."

In fact, Nicky was doing quite badly, coming in to look on miserably as Roy negotiated with the amenable Theobald.

"He isn't really going to take him home, is he?" Nicky asked me. "Wasn't this whole deal some joke or other? Some silly nonsense?"

"Not to Roy."

The two of us watched as Roy spoke with Theobald. Lucky Roy to have snapped him up, for other gentlemen were crowding around, their eyes on Theobald, ready to leap the second that his present conversation showed signs of evaporating.

"Why did he bring me along if this is what it was?" Nicky asked me. "Should I have to know about this?"

"This place has the worst potato chips," said Cosgrove, passing by with a napkinful and a glass of punch.

"I told you not to touch the refreshments," I reminded him. "Who knows where whose hands have been around here?"

"Bartering for that guy!" Nicky went on. "As if nobody had any feelings."

"Hey, Cosgrove," Virgil called out. "They just set out the bread sticks!"

"Save some for me!" cried Cosgrove, avoiding my outthrust arm as he charged through the lounge.

"I don't mind what he does, but why when I'm right *there*?" Nicky pleaded. "Why, to *torture* me?"

An employee came in bearing the refilled punch bowl, and Cosgrove asked if he was planning to bring out any chocolate-covered macaroons. "It's my favorite dessert," Cosgrove explained.

"That's my third favorite," said Virgil. "My second favorite is lime Frozfruit and my all-time is tiramisù, which is probably not available here, I would imagine."

"You got that right," said the guy, as Dennis Savage came into the lounge, noting it all in a single look. Roy's presentations to Theobald appeared to have reached the bottom line: The two were head to head, whispering the intimate details that marry love and money on the fringes of the gay world. Theobald nodded thoughtfully, Roy made a gesture, and away they went without a glance behind them.

Nicky dropped onto the banquette that lines a wall of the lounge, distraught, beaten, the lover who dared not speak his name—an archetype as basic to gay life as any Theobald in full bloom. Dennis Savage and I flanked him, trying to soothe his pain, reason through it, and, perhaps, find some hope in it somewhere.

"I'm okay," Nicky kept saying. "It's not as if he signed a contract with me."

Munching a bread stick, Virgil came up and said, "If he's mean to you, just throw him away like tomorrow's sawdust."

"Theobald," Nicky mused. "Turns it on, turns it off." He shrugged. "Well, that's the style. They make sex the way a musician makes music."

"This ridiculous *collecting* mania of the randy gay male," Dennis Savage said.

Now Cosgrove horned in, with a new idea: "Why don't *you* take someone home, too, Nicky?"

"Oh, never," said Nicky. "This revolting trash."

"I don't mean Ragmop. Take home one of the dancers."

"You can't buy love, Cosgrove."

"But what if you can't *have* love? At least you can buy some nice company and not give way to secret tears that all can see."

"Oh, was I so . . . I'm sorry for all embarrassing you."

"Not at all," I said.

"Only a few people saw," said Virgil.

"And would you please," Dennis Savage asked me, "tell that thing to stop calling me Ragmop?"

"He's not a thing," said Virgil.

"Well, I'm not Ragmop."

"I'm not a thing," Cosgrove mused, "but somehow you are Ragmop."

Which got a giggle out of Nicky, at any rate.

"Let's get this boy home," I said.

"No, I . . . Can I come with you guys? Please?"

One could hardly have said no. Back on our own turf, as we piled into the elevator, a virile voice called out, "Hold that, please," and Presto joined us, with a stalwart grin.

"Could you push fourteen?" he asked.

Virgil and Cosgrove were very subdued, taking turns gazing up at their mystery love. Presto was not unamused by the attention; he held up his fingers to put donkey ears on the pair. Just then, Nicky burst into tears.

We all tried to comfort him as Virgil told Presto, "We're rehearsing a play."

"Looks like a real Greek tragedy" was Presto's opinion.

"No, *Close Encounters of the Third World*," said Cosgrove, master of the *fallacia consequentis*.

Well, we took Nicky to Dennis Savage's and calmed him down with a V-8. We said all the useless cheer-up things. We pointed out Bauhaus, who appeared at the bathroom door with one of his "Oh, them" looks, raced into the living room, dropped a little treasure upon the carpet, and sauntered into the kitchen. We cast aspersions upon Theobald, though most of us don't even know what he looks like. Then Roy came in to brag.

Oh, that Theobald! So wicked, so eager, his whopper flopping hard and ready out of his pants. His power, his readiness to do!

"This is an entirely different class of people," Roy told us. "They're not like, you know, the guys you meet in bars, guys you could have gone to high school with. They're . . . sex people. There's something inside them, like a motor. I see it now—these dancers and porn stars and so on, they're not doing it because you and I aren't available. It's because they're so hot that fucking is their vocation. Of course, I made sure we took the precautions. But can you imagine telling this . . . *monolithic* guy that you want to get pleasure-fucked, and he doesn't say, But do I like you?, or, Is it Thursday? No, he just sets you right up on the bed and proceeds to slide his big, fat, cream-filled joint right up your—"

Virgil, Cosgrove, Nicky, and Bauhaus dashed into the bathroom; the sound of the running shower directly followed.

"I blew it again," said Roy. "Speech is not free here."

I said, "The problem is that, in actuating a fantasy, you're threatening everybody's sense of stability. We all dream of encounters with the holy Lucifers of the sensual world, okay. But that's all they are. Dreams. Didn't you notice that all the men in the audience tonight were dreary old losers?"

"*We* aren't, are we? I'm not even thirty yet."

"But where were our coevals? I'll tell you. They're out seeking some more earthly version of the dream in socially reputable places. Because the only fit partner for Lucifer is another Lucifer. Anyone less total must feel inadequate. Threatened. Humiliated. Tell your friends where you went tonight and what you got. Tell them about Theobald. You think they'll be glad and plan their own trip to Folly City? On the contrary, they'll—"

"Good Lord!" cried Roy at something behind me; Dennis Savage and I turned to look. It was Nicky, nude and erect, walking in like a strip dancer launching his second number. And—I swear to God and all Her angels—he had a raging bazooka. Maybe even a bazooka plus.

"What's . . . what's going on?" asked Roy, as Nicky planted himself before his friend.

"Here's what you like, right?" said Nicky. "This gadget? You don't care about people, you just want a thing! Fine, now somebody put on Frankie Goes to Hollywood and I'll prance for you!"

"Has he been drinking?" Roy asked.

"He was swigging the V-8 like a man possessed," I said.

"Nicky," said Roy, as Dennis Savage went into the bedroom

for something, "our friends will become alienated if you carry on like this."

"You don't like my boner?" replied Nicky, falsely coy.

"You're offending our hosts," Roy insisted, though I noticed that he couldn't take his eyes off Nicky's erection. "You've virtually cleared the room with this . . . this outrageous stunt."

"No, I approve of this," I said. "It's mildly eerie yet presented in a farcical naturalism that gives the whole thing a deceptively quotidian feel. A *Symphonic Fantastique* or so."

Dennis Savage came back with a bathrobe, which he tossed to Nicky.

"No," Nicky said, shaking his head slowly. "No, because if I don't show a big dick, Roy won't like me."

"He *must* be drunk," said Roy. "He's never like this."

"You don't *know* what I'm like! You never listen to me, or ask me how I feel, or do anything except take me for granted!"

"Come on," said Roy, helping Nicky into the bathrobe. "I do, too, listen to you." He patted Nicky's shoulder. "Boy, and I thought you were this quiet type."

From the bathroom, Cosgrove shouted, "We're not coming out till everybody's dressed!"

"All clear," I announced; and even Bauhaus joined us.

"In all the fuss," said Virgil, "I never got to make my surprise revelation, which is, Guess who won the Dream Man contest?"

"Virgil, we're rich!" Cosgrove exulted.

"Actually, I only got third prize. Fifteen dollars."

"That's still enough for one brand-new CD."

"So let's hear the award-winning piece," said Dennis Savage.

"It's weird how you can know someone for so long," said Roy, regarding Nicky, "and be ignorant of the most basic things about them."

"It's not basic, I tell you," said Nicky, almost pleading. "It's just a device. The real me is more than something that goes up and down upon the application of erotic stimuli."

"Woo," said Cosgrove.

"It's college," Virgil agreed.

"We have to talk," Roy told Nicky, patting him again. "Come on, let's get you dressed."

"Now you like me in public, is that it?"

"What, I always liked you, you silly . . . big . . . boy . . ."

"Let's hear your piece," Dennis Savage urged Virgil, and Cosgrove and I clapped expectantly. Nicky gave us all a weary grieving look, but he let Roy lead him back to the bathroom. On the way, Roy whispered, "Is it really big when it's flaccid, too? Because I think I love that effect most of all . . ."

"I must admit, I was not planning to read my essay," Virgil told us, looking after Roy and Nicky with some disapproval. "Of course, upon publication, copies were to be circulated." He took a bow, to Cosgrove's "Bravossimo!," to which Dennis Savage (no doubt still grudging the "Funette" episode) replied, "I wonder if you mean 'Bravissimo.'"

"Sure, Ragmop."

Dennis Savage was patient, elegant, so *comme ça*. "Didn't I ask you," he asked me, "to arrange for our delightful little Cosgrove to stop—"

"Let's go out for haircuts," said Cosgrove. "'Barber, I'll take the Ragmop trim, please.'"

Dennis Savage rose, saying, "Now I'm going to mow you down."

"Stop fighting," said Virgil, heading for the bedroom, "and I'll read my piece."

Dennis Savage poured out white wine for the grown-ups and juice for the kids, as Roy and Nicky made their departure with thanks and apologies, and Dennis Savage lip-mimed "We have to discuss this" to me.

Then: "'My Dream Man,'" Virgil read out. "'By Kiwi Brown.'" He looked at us: Dennis Savage and Cosgrove on the sofa, me sitting on the carpet, leaning against the wall with the aid of a pillow. His extended family, as we call it. "Don't be critical," he warned us.

"Just read it," said Dennis Savage.

"'My dream man is gentle but commanding,'" Virgil intoned. "'Sometimes he is rough on me, but I know it is only to make me a better person. And then he always hugs and kisses me to say, "It's all right, and we're still best friends."'"

Dennis Savage and Cosgrove eyed each other suspiciously. Who was rough? *Who* kissed him?

"'My dream man is not very tall, yet he seems treelike to me.'"

Cosgrove, at five-seven, glowed. Dennis Savage, just over six feet, scrunched down on the couch the slightest bit.

"'You may ask, "What color his hair, his eyes?" I say, "It doesn't matter." We two are so close that, however far apart we may be, I can feel what he feels, at the same moment.'"

This bewildered Dennis Savage and Cosgrove. What's going on, *The Corsican Brothers*? They traded a second suspicious look; Cosgrove even made a fist.

"'My dream man loves me not for my special talents but just for myself. I don't have to impress him. But when I do succeed, he is the first to admire me.'"

"Wonderful essay," quoth Dennis Savage.

"I admire you more," said Cosgrove.

"'My dream man has the respect of all who meet him, but no one respects—and loves—him more than I, for he is my very own pop, Seth Brown.'"

Virgil looked at us. "I surprised you, right? You thought it would be just some boy friend."

"Some of us did," I said, getting up. "Now, I have to get some work done and Cosgrove has to do the marketing."

"I'll go, too," said Virgil. "We're fresh out of Puffed Kashi."

Dennis Savage followed me downstairs, eager to settle the case of Roy and Nicky. "Here's the question of the year," he said.

"Why didn't Nicky just tell Roy that he had Schlong Control in the first place?"

"But think of the risk. Getting exploited and patronized on a platonic basis is bad enough—imagine how Nicky would have felt if Roy rejected him *sexually* as well."

"He wouldn't have."

"How do you know? Besides," I added, getting out a notebook, "I think Nicky's worse off now. It's a case of the blind fucking the blind. Okay, Nicky'll get into bed with the man he loves. Right. They may even have a kind of affair. But sooner or later, Roy will tire of Nicky, and he will stun him, scorch him. Why? Because Nicky wants a lover and Roy wants a dream man." I uncapped a pen. "And dream men, by nature, are out of reach. Touch one, and he becomes meaninglessly real."

"What are you writing?"

I shrugged. "Some story."

He looked over my shoulder and read out, " 'The Hunt for—' "

" 'Alice Faye Lobby Cards,' " I finished, my hand covering the truth.

"All right, snarky, I'm on my way out."

Cosgrove got in quite some time later, but then most people can return from a vacation sooner than Cosgrove and Virgil can return from D'Agostino's.

"The most incredible thing!" Cosgrove cried, plopping the groceries onto the kitchen counter. "This guy had set up a little flea market right outside his building. There was a crowd going over, like, these books and clothes and stuff. He was saying, 'Estate sale! Estate sale! Everything must go!' So I just leaned over to see—and guess what?"

"CDs."

"Not just CDs. Rock imports that you can't *get* here! He won't take plastic, so I'm going to rush back and—"

"I thought it was something like that," I told him, turning

around from my desk. "Because, you see, Demento was just here."

Cosgrove froze. "He *who*?"

"Demento came. Something about your having ungratefully passed up rarities that he had placed in your grasp. He unwrapped one of those Klondikes that you're so wild about and rubbed it all over your Rachmaninoff Second. With his awesome power, of course, I could do nothing to intervene. Worse yet, he said that no other copies of that extremely rare and desirable recording will become available till 2001, when a retired mortgage broker in Riverdale will move to Florida and—"

"You didn't," he said quietly. "Are you so heartless?"

"I? *Demento!*"

He marched right over to his collection, snapped open the indicated jewel box, examined the disc—of course it was unharmed—and replaced it.

"That was such a mean joke," he said. "It was the acme of cruelty, and then some."

"Aren't you going to rush back to that one-man flea market and—"

"No. He was asking too much for them, anyway. And now I have a little idea."

I went on working as he unpacked the groceries and returned to his catalogs. Making a quick trip to the bathroom, I wondered if I'd gone too far. But, look, if you can't tease your live-in, whom can you tease?

So I was confident as I came back out. Cosgrove was quiet, deep in catalog and thought. "He was back," he said.

"Who was?"

"Demento." He looked up, cool and resistant. "What a surprise for us to learn that he moonlights as the protector of injured roommates. He set up your Super Mario World on the controller." Responding to the look on my face, he said, "Well, didn't I *tell* him you don't like anyone fussing with your Super Nintendo? I said, 'It took Bud seven months just to reach the Valley of Bowser. Push the wrong button and he'll lose it all.' And you know what Demento

SOME MEN ARE LOOKERS

said? 'I will push the *right* button.' And he erased your entire game."

With that, Cosgrove went back to his catalog.

"You can't fool me," I said as I coolly returned to the desk. (I did take a fleet swipe of a look at the controller. Super Mario was nested there, though I hadn't played it in weeks. Uh-oh.)

I did this and that in my notebook. Then I said, "You would not be so foolhardy as to erase my game. Surely you would not dare."

"But," he observed, "Demento dares all."

"I will not be taken in."

He looked at me.

I said, "Did you do something to that game?"

He was struggling not to smile.

"Did you?"

"Someone is worried, I see."

It was too much to bear. I jumped up, switched the game on, and triggered the playing screen. My game was intact.

"Victorious" does not describe Cosgrove in that moment. "Apocalyptically sated" might do.

"Now who's so great, Mister Smarty?" he asked. "Demento is my dream man."

My voice was low, dangerous, Teutonic. I said, " 'Consida dot a divawss.' "

WHAT A DIFFERENCE MISS FAYE MADE

he first thing Dennis Savage noticed was the "Now I'm *really* worried" look on Cosgrove's face as he scurried through the apartment like Peter Rabbit grocery shopping in Farmer Murder's garden.

"What's going on?" Dennis Savage asked.

"Somebody in this apartment misplaced the TV remote control," I explained, "despite the strict rule that limits its theatre of operation to the couch so we'll always know where it is. And if somebody doesn't *find* the remote control"—Cosgrove raced by, flipping through old magazines, raping the linen chest, nosing into the stove—"he forfeits his birthday visit to Tower Records for any seven CDs of his choice, not to mention the extra two or three he plants by the cash register and then slips in unnoticed—he foolishly believes—by me, his keeper, boss, and mentor."

"I will, I will," Cosgrove promised as he hustled around, dipping into the piano bench and investigating the cappuccino maker.

"It's terrifying," said Dennis Savage.

"It's justice," I told him.

"How sorely it taxes our sweet little Cosgrove," said Dennis Savage, not without gusto, for he is generally one of Cosgrove's most energetic detractors. "But enough of these pleasantries. I have important news to lay on you. I sold my book."

Slowly I turned.

"Yes, I did, too," he went on. "And entirely without your assistance."

"It's bad enough that you brazenly use your closest friends as characters in your fiction. But then to ask me to help you get this grab bag of scrofulous innuendo and betrayal printed is—"

"Well, I *didn't* ask you, did I?" he replied, looking pleased, even all-conquering.

"Who's your publisher?" I asked, hoping it was some feeble independent press, perhaps a vanity outfit.

"Actually, I was rather impressed by an aggressive youngish editor at Grove Weidenfeld, and—"

"I found it!" Crosgrove called out as he ran in from the bathroom with the trophy held in high display. "It was in the hamper, after all. Boy!"

"The TV remote," said Dennis Savage, "was in the laundry hamper?"

"Don't ask," I told him.

"Now I can plan my birthday haul," Cosgrove gloated, settling down with his record guides and magazines. "I've been scouting out the complete Beethoven symphonies, but Miss Faye says, How come we don't have any Janis Paige or Jessica Dragonette?"

Dennis Savage looked at Cosgrove for a moment, then turned back to me. "Meanwhile, the house made a most generous offer—"

"Fiddlesticks," I observed.

"I admit it's in the lower one figure. But everyone starts somewhere."

"Fatty de Pinero started somewhere, in Oxford, Nebraska," said Cosgrove, poring over his folios. "He was just walking. Yet he gradually realized that he would never stop till he came to New York. And here he is even today."

Dennis Savage looked at Cosgrove for a moment, then turned back to me—followed me, in fact, into the kitchen. "The point isn't money," he said. "The point is that now I'll have a book in the stores, a bit of media fuss, and maybe a stalker or two." I was in the fridge; he put a hand on my shoulder and drew me back. "There's more," he said. "I'll also have . . . well, a new friend, so it seems. See, it's this editor. He's this sort of needy guy. I think he bought my stories because he . . . Look, I need your help and can we please be serious?"

"Is this a brew-some-coffee serious or a pour-the-Chiquita-brand-Calypso-Breeze-fruit-juice serious?"

"If we could can the repartee? I've got a delicate problem here. Tweedy, closeted, Ivy League editor hits thirty-three, gazes deep into the mirror, and suddenly senses that just coming out isn't enough. Gay is more than what you are—gay is what you do, and he wants instructions, directions to where, I don't know, the whole handbook. I mean, the first lunch we had, he was so collegiate. We discussed Dante, Hitchcock, origami. Comes the second lunch and he wants to know if they like it better on their stomach or on their back!"

I handed him a Beck's dark—the conversation was definitely taking a man-to-man turn—and we went back to the living room.

"Then," said Dennis Savage, tragically sinking onto the couch, "he asked me about hustler bars!"

"Well, he should consult with Baby Frumkin in that matter," Cosgrove put in. "He has many a dark tale to tell."

"Baby Frumkin is a hustler?" I asked. "Under that name?"

"He would be called 'Nightboy.'"

"You know what it is," said Dennis Savage, not unhappy to be entangled in this wondrous web, this complicated and appetitive yet ultimately intelligible and glamorous Literary World. "He's trying to befriend me! I think he bought the book because he hopes it'll bring him closer to . . . you know, the Life. It's sort of touching, in a way. He wants me to bring him out, socially. He actually thinks I have the key to this . . . this profound sense of camaraderie. Oh, of a shared mission, even. He says my characters are so friendly and fun that you want to meet them. In fact, that's what . . . well, he really does want to . . . ."

"Meet us?" I cried. "Is this a zoo? A parade? I didn't ask to be in your stories in the first place!"

"Look who's talking. At least I have the decency to change everybody's name."

"What's mine?"

"Carlotta. Look, will you please listen? I'm giving a dinner. And please—I beg of you—help me bring it off so that he feels he's seen some truth and joy of gay so he'll shepherd my book through the processes to fame and glory, or whatever it is they do."

"Fatty de Pinero took odd jobs on his walk to New York," said Cosgrove. "This includes shepherding. But the sheep drove him crazy with their frenzied baas. They foretell the weather and comets, you know. They graze in formations duplicating the layout of Stonehenge. They do the hokey-pokey and they turn themselves around."

Dennis Savage not only looked at Cosgrove; he demanded, "Where have you been lately, may I ask?"

Cosgrove grinned. "Miss Faye has been writing some of my latest material."

"Are they real?" Dennis Savage asked me.

"Who?"

"Tubby Lumpkin and Little Grubby and so on."

"Fatty de Pinero and Baby Frumkin," Cosgrove corrected.

"I've heard Miss Faye's messages on the answering machine," I said, "and I've actually spoken to Fatty de Pinero. I'm not sure about Baby Frumkin, though."

"He's as real as I am," said Cosgrove.

"That settles it" was Dennis Savage's opinion.

Then Virgil burst in, very excited about *his* news. "Did you tell them yet?" he asked Cosgrove.

"I couldn't, because I was in trouble."

"Tell us what?" I said.

"Cosgrove and I are going to form a guide service for visitors to New York, where we take them on a tour of the plazas."

"The what?"

"Those big spaces by the new skyscrapers." Tasting now, just a bit, of the air of the carnival barker, he went on, "What does the tourist see in New York, I ask you? The landmarks, the theatres, the hot spots. But what does the tourist *miss,* you ask me? Why, of course, it's our famous plazas, a synonym for mystery and romance."

"That's so true," Cosgrove put in, with feeling.

"Why do I sometimes feel," asked Dennis Savage, "that I am living in a painting by Salvador Dalí?"

"The historic sites!" Virgil enthused.

I said, "The most ancient plaza in New York is like fifteen years old. What historic?"

Now Cosgrove abandoned his charts to take voice in this matter. "We can enlist conspirators to plant Indian arrowheads and strange, dusty coins just before Virgil and I bring our tour group in, which would give us history evidence and dramatic encounters."

"What conspirators?"

"Are you kidding?" said Dennis Savage. "He's got Pushy de Clown and Miss Laye on his payroll. The sky's the limit!"

"Listen, boys," I told them. "Plazas are just plazas. *Things.* Tourists want glamour, color, fame. *Action.* The world isn't about who loves whom. The world is about who's fucking whom. It isn't necessarily the same thing."

"Weren't you saying before that I should get a better job?" Virgil asked Dennis Savage.

"Yes. Just not this job."

"We're entrepreneurs."

"Bud?" Cosgrove asked me, trying to look like something out of Hector Malot.

"Oh, now he's a tearful waif!" Dennis Savage cried in outrage. "But last month he spent an entire week chasing me around with a whoopee cushion!"

"And you fell for it many a time," Cosgrove shot back, darkly.

"We can't forbid them," I told Dennis Savage. "Let them try it. If it works, good. If it fails, they had their chance."

Dennis Savage responded with a grumbling fit. A tiny one.

"Frankly," I said, "this whole project will fall apart before the first group returns to Xenia. That's the profile of the Virgil-Cosgrove business ambition."

Virgil and Cosgrove buoyed each other with "Sez her" looks, and Dennis Savage headed for the door. "I have to go design my autograph for the inscribing of copies of my book at my many signings."

"Cosgrove," Virgil was saying, "we'll be known as the Plaza Kings!"

At the door, in an undertone, Dennis Savage said, "Not that it matters, but when *is* Cosgrove's birthday?"

"Hard to say. He's had three so far this year."

"And it's only April," said Dennis Savage, nearly in awe.

Dennis Savage not only planned a dinner but made me attend strategy sessions. One day, he'd say, "Cold cucumber soup and boeuf bourguignonne. Too fancy?" Next day, it was "Is it too much to ask everyone to be in jacket and tie?" Then I'd hear, "How about stuffed lamb?"

"Doesn't this guy want to look in on our daily routine?" I asked. "Our *real* life? He won't be hoping for Cinderella's ball."

"He hopes to be dazzled," said Dennis Savage, wandering through his place doing those extra little tiny cleaning things, like wiping windowsills and blowing dust off objects.

"Dazzled, right," I said. "By *us*?"

"Listen, after decades of doing the WASP straight rich white-bread thing, he sees people like us as incredibly alluring. The bohemian liberated sexagonzo cruisathon thing."

"Maybe you'd better prepare me for this guy."

"I guarantee you'll like him. Affable, polite, a good listener."

"Name."

"Peter Keene."

"Describe with extreme prejudice."

"Tall, straight dark hair expensively trimmed, old-fashioned dress-up attire with the occasional madcap tie, long-torsoed and probably in very good shape—it's hard to be sure when he's always in a suit. Though, when he takes off his coat, one does notice a shockingly first-rate ass."

"Face."

"Very."

"Huh. So he's eligible."

"He isn't just eligible. In his repressed way, he's a sex monster tugging at the chain."

"Gosh. Am I in love?"

"You're all tied up with our incomparable little Cosgrove," he warned me as he cleaned the TV screen. "Though I have to say you two never act like lovers."

"How do lovers act?" I shot back, brisk and bland.

"You know. With those endearments and touchings and the rueful smiles of resignation at your partner's eccentricities. You and Cosgrove act like shipmates on an aircraft carrier."

"Actually, Cosgrove and I have developed extraordinarily arcane ways of communicating our bond to each other."

"Really? I've never noticed."

"Good, they're working."

"Where are the kids, anyway?" Now he was dusting the bookshelves, pulling the books out in threes to brush the tops. I find this kind of thing fascinating. It's so orderly—like eating spaghetti without getting red bloops on your shirt.

"They're downstairs," I said, "firming up the schedules for the Historic Plazas tour."

That got him; he actually stopped cleaning.

"They're what?" he said. "No," he added, changing tone from incredulous to decisive. "No, they will not prolong this ridiculous—"

"Boy, don't you ever get it?" I said. "They always have a scheme in the works. And it always looks real, but it isn't real. Remember the Spee-D-Lite Messenger Service? The Quiche Я Us Party Caterers? Besides, what do you care if they end up leading a few—"

"Yes, but who are these odious characters they bring into our lives? They're bombs going off, can't you hear them? Miss Faye and . . . who, Flabby Thumbkin?"

"Miss Faye is a drag queen."

After a moment, he asked, "That's all I get? I learn no more?"

"Well, you know drag queens. They come in three kinds. Kind One is sleek and womanly. Marilyn Monroe. Kind Two is facetious and resigned, like Eve Arden. Kind Three is a tornado of sleaze and terror. Think Bette Midler crossed with the Luftwaffe."

Dennis Savage tried to muster the strength to police the area under the cushions on the couch, but he had gone all limp. He knew the answer yet asked the question anyway: "Which is Miss Faye?"

"Kind Three."

"Why . . ." He did one of his helpless gestures. "Why do they have to come here? Why must they pervade?"

"I thought we were bohemians," I said. "Liberated. Remember, your editor wants to see our vitality? Sì?"

"I *hate* drag queens. And so does my editor. He told me it was men in drag—and Danny Kaye—that kept him in the closet all those years. He thought that's what gay *was!*"

"If he's that stupid, I'm not coming to—"

"Oh, for God's sake!" he cried. "Can't a body object to a thing now and then? What are we, a monolithic culture? We all order the same plate in restaurants? We all dance to one song? We all own the same pet with the same name and the same cunning little shoulder harness when we—"

"All right, all right," I said. "Please start cleaning again, so contentment may reign here in Macholand."

He didn't start cleaning again; he stood there looking at me. "That's all it is to you?" he finally got out. "A *man* in a *dress* and *makeup* and a *wig* and you aren't repulsed? Not even in some obscure, hardly comprehended way? Perhaps you think those of us who are repulsed are hypocritical victims of gender panic?"

"I just don't have a problem with it," I said, shrugging. "I call it bohemian and liberated."

"I just . . . Please, *please* don't put these Miss Fayes in my life, okay?"

"I've never met her myself, you know. Cosgrove says she almost never ventures off her turf."

"I rigidly hope so."

He actually shivered.

As always, Virgil and Cosgrove did not go gently into their latest project, but rushed in, complete with motto, pennant, and uni-

forms. The motto was lame ("If you long for times bygone, / Plaza
Tours will lead you on"), the pennant a handkerchief ("Has anyone seen my di Salgo linen square?" Dennis Savage asked, as the
rest of us stared in other directions), and the uniforms were black
T's over black slacks topped by red baseball caps. I thought the two
of them looked great and would probably abandon the whole project in about thirty-five seconds; but no. Worse, Cosgrove made me
come along for a business conference with his "booking manager,"
a travel agent around the corner on Second Avenue.

"Those craziacs!" Dennis Savage cried when I told him. "Can
no one stop them?"

He was racing around preparing the dinner, with a dollop of
horseradish sauce here and a refolding of the napkins there—"No,
Virgil, twist to the left or my literary career lies in tatters!"

"Don't look hungry," I advised him. "People are attracted to
the dégagé, the autonomous, the confident. Think of Yevgyeny
Onyegin, Lord Byron, Jeff Stryker."

"Just be back by six-fifteen at the latest!"

New York hadn't undergone its two days of spring yet, so it
was nippy, and Cosgrove and I had bundled up. High on the promise
of thriving business, Cosgrove was full of piss and vinegar. The
elevator slowed as it neared the fourth floor, and we heard a child's
gladsome "I'm going outside hooray Mommy" noises, whereupon
Cosgrove declaimed, in a cackly manner, "I'm the Furious Witch of
Toscafù and I eat all the cute little children!"

Then the elevator door opened upon a weepy, fearful little girl
and her outraged mother, who glared witheringly at me all the rest
of the way down.

"You think you've got problems," I told her.

"The element we get nowadays," she muttered, shaking her
head in fury.

"Breeder bitch," I said, happily; but by then she was Ignoring Me.

So now, the travel agent. Is Plaza Tours really going to happen? The whole thing isn't a joke?

It wasn't. The guy went on about "re-sign-ups" and "regional favoritism," and I had to speak up.

"I don't understand why tourists who could take in the theatre or poke around in museums would be content with—"

"Patience, my friend," the travel agent told me in a soothing tone. "It is a virtue, patience, yes? Too much life at once can be all so . . . discouraging. Slowly lead to it, yes?" He had a Hispanic accent, though his name was Riordan. "These are people coming out, you see?, from the heartland. Yah, simple people who want a simple trip." His many smiles as he said this. "They cannot use adventures. So what is New York? Robbery within the hotel, scam artists are prowling, everywhere are untrustworthy types casing doorways, windows. It is all cheat, cheat, cheat. Or, in the museums, it is surrealistic paintings, nude statuary, unexpected fountains. Everyone must travel, da? So they have traveled, traveled here—but what do they want?" His head bobbed at every word: "The least amount of challenge we can give them. Harry and Myrna is how I so fondly think of them. Sí, and your two young friends have conjured up a beautiful massage for the Harry and Myrna tour unit. Relaxing. Functional. Inexpensive. And something to take back to their friends in the heartland of Flag Day and the War Memorial. Think of the history! Washington says farewell to his troops in the plaza of the AT&T Building!"

"Actually," I said, "that would have occurred way down in the Wall Street—"

"So what we like about Plaza Tours is the lack of risk. There is no affront to the sensitivities. You show up, you walk and learn, you wonder. Then you go home absolutely untouched. That's what the people want, vershteh?"

"They want surprise, delight," I said.

The travel agent beamed at Cosgrove. "What do they want, my friend?"

"To be safe."

"Yes," the travel agent gushed. "Muy bueno como eso. If you'll sign," he continued, pushing papers at Cosgrove.

"Don't you dare," I said, getting up.

"It is a beautiful tour. Exciting yet healthy. Like knowing about sex without having to have it."

"Cosgrove, we're late for a party."

Cosgrove hadn't moved, and now he said, "As usual, you are not listening to me or Virgil because you think we are just little pandas. You are afraid of what will happen if we have joy and truth."

I looked at the travel agent.

"If someone would sign," he urged.

I grabbed the contract, saying, "We have to think about this." At Cosgrove's protest, I went on, "Virgil has to read this, too, doesn't he? Business is business." I thanked the travel agent for his trouble.

"De nada," he replied, blandly content. As we went out, he added, "Remember, my friend—too much life at once . . ."

Cosgrove sulked and grumbled for a bit, but at the prospect of Dennis Savage's dinner party he brightened and even began pulling ahead of me in eagerness. My suspicions went on instant alert. Cosgrove and Dennis Savage are mortal enemies; as with the mongoose and cobra, the war is ontological, war for war's sake. Many a time have I heard Cosgrove plotting to "fix that Dennis Savage for all the mean things he's done," but when I request a catalog of these sins, Cosgrove clams up. It just is, because it's there. In any case, a quick on-site body search of Cosgrove's overcoat and pants yielded up a whoopee cushion, a joy buzzer, and a small puddle of plastic vomit.

"Where do you even *find* stuff like this?" I cried.

"I have ways," he muttered.

"Look," I said, grasping Cosgrove by the shoulders, "Dennis Savage needs very, very badly for this party to go well. He requires us, his dear friends, to support him on this terribly important turn in his fortunes. Despite our little grievances now and again, we are family—and who else, in the end, can we depend on? You see that, surely?"

Cosgrove slowly nodded his head.

"You realize that disrupting his party with pranks is infantile?"

Cosgrove slowly nodded his head.

"It's a solemn thing. We celebrate ourselves. You see this, right?"

Cosgrove slowly nodded his head.

"Why do I feel that you're setting me up?"

Cosgrove said nothing. We were starting to attract attention as street characters, so I hustled us along.

Our building's elevators used to close too fast, crunching the unwary; now, retuned, they shut only after an interminable waiting period, which makes them run so slowly that there's always a someone or two in the lobby waiting for the next car. Cosgrove and I happened upon a serious-looking man, his overcoat open to reveal one of those really *tailored* pin-stripe suits and a latest-thing tie. Could this be Peter Keene? I tried to frame Dennis Savage's description around him, already editing it—why didn't he mention the devastating green eyes, the affably insolent cheekbones? He was taller than I'd expected, too. I was about to say something when Cosgrove piped up.

"Are you Dennis Savage's editor?"

"Why, yes," the stranger said, after a moment of surprise.

"I'm Cosgrove. This is Bud. We're all in the party."

The elevator door opened, and once we were on our way I made somewhat more elaborate introductions. Peter smiled and said, "Well, you must be Justin." Turning to Cosgrove, he added, "And you're Percival."

Cosgrove said, "You may have to be kneecapped."

Peter glanced at me. I said, "Joke?"

"Yes, of course," he agreed, relaxing. "The nonstop hilarity of the stories."

"I eat pretty children for snacks," said Cosgrove.

"Ah, the eighth floor," I exclaimed, quite immediately after that, "and the gourmet cooking—did you know?—and Little Kiwi is sure to charm, and wait till you see . . ." Cosgrove's features, I noticed, as I ran out of cover material, were set. I told him, "Stop being relentless!" But by then Virgil had opened the door and Dennis Savage was coming out of the kitchen (an entrance that I, personally, had coached him in), his smile slowly growing as he took off his oven mitt and his apartment surged with the scent of French Chef expertise.

"Ah, you've met?" he asked, cooling his anxiety with the gay guy's first weapon: a blasé manner. "Yes, there's our wonderful little Cosgrove, and it's coats into the bedroom, and I'm working on the watercress, orange, and coconut salad for that Balinese effect."

So Peter Keene goes "Balinese salad!" in the tone David Drake uses when Fabio drops in. And no sooner am I back from laying my coat on the bed than I see Cosgrove pulling a *second* whoopee cushion out of his right sock and blowing it up with the cool determination of David facing Goliath. Dennis Savage has gone back into the kitchen, Virgil simply misses this, and Peter Keene is about to drop into the armchair and become Cosgrove's victim when I pull Peter away, crying, "Come see the . . ." We're walking and my mind is racing. Come see? "Oh! Yes! It's Dennis Savage's fabulous collection of Modern Library Giants!"

Actually, it's his pathetic bookcase full of the remainder of his college reading lists; since then he became an enthusiast of the public library. But Peter and I do a little number on the quaint look of the familiar old covers: the gold and red *War and Peace* with the beaten French army straggling homeward, the Lewis Carroll with the Tenniels, the tree-framed country scene for *The Complete Novels of Jane Austen.*

"My parents had this edition," says Peter, just in time for Dennis Savage to join us and blush at the reference to his age. (It isn't fun to be older than your editor; it's like being nineteen in fifth grade.) Drinks were offered and taken, and Dennis Savage slipped off to the kitchen while Peter, Virgil, Cosgrove, and I tried small talk. I always bungle it, Peter seemed shy, Virgil kept running into the kitchen to assist, and Cosgrove was eerily silent, one of his favorite modes.

Suddenly, he jumped up and asked if Peter would like to hear a song. "I have a unique repertory," Cosgrove explained, "so it's sure to be a surprise."

"You mean you lip-synch to records?" Peter asked. "I've heard of that."

"No, I just sing."

"Oh—to karaoke tapes? It's popular, of course, but the selection of titles is—"

"No, I just sing," said Cosgrove, starting to smile.

Peter turned to me. "And you accompany him?"

"No, he just sings."

"Well." Peter turned back to Cosgrove. "What kind of songs do you—"

Peter got no further, for Cosgrove had broken into one of his "country" specialties—more precisely, into the instrumental prelude to the number, which Cosgrove also sings, wordlessly, in imitation of a fiddle tuning up on open fifths with a jazzy upbeat urging it on. The song itself, which Cosgrove rendered in conjunction with an altogether disquieting rustic dance reminiscent of a mule kicking down a barn door, is sung to "Turkey in the Straw":

> Well, the poodle did a dance
> As the chickens pranced and clowned,
> Then along come a farmer,
> But he make no sound.
> He slip into the silo
> Where he petted all the pigs,
> And the crocodile landed in a pile of twigs!
> Life is a barnyard,
> Life, anyhow.
> Farmer is angry,
> Busted his plow.

Chow bell's ringing,
Time to go;
And the goose celebrated with a do-si-do!

Cosgrove posed for the finish, and I noticed that Dennis Savage had come out, his face the very glass of worry. But Peter took it in stride.

"The crocodile landed in . . ." he began. "Who *launched* the crocodile? And what's a crocodile doing on a farm?"

"He escaped from the zoo and found a nice home."

"Awfully cosmopolitan farm" was Peter's view of it.

"What's *he* looking at?" Cosgrove asked, meaning Dennis Savage, who was not too lost in contemplation to signal me with his eyes; but then the buzzer rang.

"Thank God, that's Carlo," said Dennis Savage, returning to the food. But Cosgrove ran to the intercom, passed the guest in, and turned back with a look of do-it-yourself apocalypse.

"That wasn't Carlo, was it?" I asked him.

"You'll soon see."

"Is there some . . ." Peter asked. "Trouble? Young Cosgrove appears to be quite—"

"They have a tiny worm," Cosgrove told him, "that you can bake into a muffin and still it lives. Then you eat such a muffin, so now the worm crawls around in you, nibbling on your heart and kidneys, and it makes more worms out of itself, and soon all these worms are nibbling and you are screaming. First you were quiet, then you're on fire. A freak is loose in you."

Peter looked unhappy, the doorbell rang, Cosgrove answered it, and a drag queen entered, Kind Three. I mean with a Marie Antoinette wig, a nobody-gets-out-of-here-alive bust, makeup by Jackson Pollock, and a walk right out of *Kitten with a Whip*.

"Miss Faye!" Cosgrove cried. "You came!"

"That's *just* what Arnold Schwarzenegger said to me," she replied, "at about two o'clock last night in his—and I do mean— *master* bedroom."

She surveyed the joint, posed, said, "Who's the dearie with the big eyes?"

"That's Virgil. This is Bud, and that's some editor."

Dennis Savage, at the kitchen entryway, was going deeply rose as Miss Faye sashayed (I'd never seen anyone quite *do* that verb before) up to Virgil and stroked his hair, passed me making moue-lips, and parked herself before Peter. She read him up and down *real* slow, then purred out, "I'm a devout Mennonite, you know."

Peter was pretty rose himself. He asked me, "Do I shake hands?"

Cosgrove was looking at Dennis Savage as Iago must have looked at Desdemona; and we all caught the feel of the moment and looked at Dennis Savage ourselves. His ball.

"I'm Dennis Savage," he said. "This is my house. Please honor it." Then he went back into the kitchen.

"Who's the telegram?" Miss Faye asked.

I was shooting daggers at Cosgrove, who glared back defiantly, treacherously, independently. I liked him about as much, that moment, as my parents liked me the day I set fire to the gazebo chairs *and* fed my little brother Tony raw eggs (unshelled), all in one afternoon.

"Let's all sit and be nice," Virgil suggested. "We'll each tell a funny story about childhood."

"Oh, yes," sighed Miss Faye, settling into the armchair. " Getting oh so deeply *shrewed* by Father O'Halloran in the choiry, and he was ever a *hairy* beast, but lean and jazzy." She smiled. "Ah, the blossom time." She turned eagerly to Peter. "Now to you, handsome yet secretly warped type in a suit. Who shrewed you in your teens? The full list, I please, and photographs where possible."

After a moment, Peter said, "I am not warped."

"You're warped and jazzy, 'tis clear to see," Miss Faye rejoined, erasing Peter's resistance with a wave of her hand. "How you long to be shrewd by some rash Viking with a secret soft side. His surprising tenderness will rock you to the core, and ever after you—as I—will dream of this enticing combo of kindness and slaughter, symbolized in the rigid prong that—"

"This is not a funny story about childhood," Virgil pointed out, with a nervous glance at the kitchen, where Dennis Savage was making a racket banging platters around.

"Right," I said, ready to drag out my tired old tale of breaking my mother's antiques in defiance of oppression, or at least early bedtime. It was my personal Stonewall at the age of five. But Peter seemed to light up just then, perhaps feeling he should get over resenting Miss Faye and start making the gay scene. "I've got a story," he said. "I could tell about Brokertoe."

"Yes, let's hear that," said Virgil, looking happily expectant.

"Well, it's . . . it's just this old story," said Peter, in the self-deprecating manner of an amateur who has taken the floor amid a host of pros. "It was a painting I made in school. Kindergarten, I guess. Well, yes, and you see Brokertoe was a robot. And the class voted it the—"

"How did she break her toe?" Miss Faye asked.

"Well, it was . . . it's just a name. I called the robot Brokertoe because . . . well—"

"Isn't someone hungry around here?" said Miss Faye. "Where's the food?" She turned to Peter. "Go on with such a fascinating story, and try to include a footnote on why a pale, dim, square type like you has such big shoulders."

Peter did that silent blinking thing. Then: "Well, so I took my prize painting home, feeling so proud and perky, and I called my family in, all five of them." He smiled. "One brother, two sisters. And I unveiled my—"

"Erect penis," Miss Faye filled in, "sending my sisters into paroxysms and my brother into a bitter tizzy."

Peter was blinking again.

"It would be best not to interrupt the story," Virgil suggested.

"Peter," I said, as soothingly as possible. "Tell."

"Oh, right, then!" he cried, suitably heartened. "It's a terribly vital ghetto party and we're all . . ."

"Out," said Miss Faye, dryly.

". . . living in a musical comedy, I was going to say. Anyway, I announced to them all there assembled that I wanted to see my picture on the wall next to the prize of my parents' art collection, a Renaissance etching, of unknown authorship, depicting Hercules and Coccus."

"Well, how big *was* his coccus?" Miss Faye cried—no, screamed. "Not bigger than yours, I fancy. *Hercules*—the heart flutters. But I go for the deep, silent sort, like you, with a coccus that juts to the side. Or shall it curve, I hope?"

Staring, Miss Faye kissed her lips at Peter so obscenely that he defensively got to his feet; and of course just then Cosgrove came out of the bedroom with the raccoon and threw it right at Peter's head.

Let me explain. Last summer, at a street fair, Cosgrove was captivated by a risible novelty item, a simulation of a raccoon rummaging in a potato chip bag. All you see of the animal is its tail; but with the batteries in place the thing seems remarkably lifelike.

Obviously, Cosgrove had planted it in Dennis Savage's apartment. When Cosgrove came out of the bedroom shouting "Help! The raccoon is loose!" and tossed it at Peter, a certain amount of hell broke out. Dennis Savage came roaring out of the kitchen, Cosgrove cried "Yipes!" and fled to the bathroom, and it took considerable wheedling and begging on both Virgil's and my part to convince Peter to forgive it as a childish stunt.

In fact, once we explained that Cosgrove's true target was Dennis Savage, Peter not only calmed down but became curious.

"You see," he said, "the stories attract me precisely because of their sly undercurrent of dissatisfaction. At first, we see a group of men who enjoy their gayness to the fullest. Not only do they have no wish that they were straight, but . . . Oh, thanks, splendid"—as Dennis Savage passed out refills on the drinks and settled in for Making Peter Feel at Home. "Yes, they seem clearly to be having a more successful life *because* they're gay. It's quite inspiring. And yet." Peter leaned closer to us to Make His Point. "It is the very limitless nature of this paradise that provides extraordinary tensions—the sheer physical competition of who gets whom, the anxiety of losing power through aging—"

"Yes!" cried Miss Faye, who had sat quietly through all the excitement and was now absently petting the raccoon's tail and mouthing up the ice from her drink with insidiously loud crunches. "We must learn to make the fashion sacrifice."

Peter hesitated, then decided to pursue this line of inquiry. "Now, how do you mean that, Miss Faye?"

Preening, Miss Faye made little cooing noises, and I got worried. Old-guard drag queens like Miss Faye are essentially tempestuous, not socialized, and I feared she might be hoaxing him when she spoke, as now, with the delicacy of a schoolmarm trying to slide through the chapter on Reproduction in the sixth graders' biology text.

"The drag queen, you see," Miss Faye began, "was put on earth to symbolize the contradictions of the homosexual. Yes. Yes, true." She's so smiley, so considering. "We are women, yet we are men. We have sexual needs, yet we hide them in banter. Our dreams? Ecstatic. Yet our dialogue is trash. We revel in costume, to your despair—and how do you see us? As spoof. Who led the Stonewall revolution? Drag queens, look it up. Yet we are lowest in the Stonewall pecking order, despised by he-men and feared—yes, I dare to say it—by you university types."

She seemed demure now, dainty, the princess of the Junior Prom; Peter was intrigued. He took up her thoughts, she expounded further, he quizzed her, and Dennis Savage was nearly beaming when he popped out to announce the imminent serving of dinner; so I slipped off to check on Cosgrove.

He was napping in the empty bathtub. I woke and scolded him. "You *promised* to behave," I said.

"Yes, but I didn't say how."

"You'd better come back in now—but *don't* do anything else."

Everything was copacetic (as we used to put it in the 1970s) in the living room. "This is a nice, intellectual discussion," Virgil told me. As Dennis Savage presented the Balinese salad—even to Cosgrove, who kept his eyes down—Peter and Miss Faye were considering the aggressive nature of the queen's performance.

"It seems," said Peter, "so driven by a need to offend."

"It is offense," Miss Faye averred, wreathing herself in Glinda the Good wisdom, "carried to the artistic level."

It was at this moment that Bauhaus chose to make his entrance. He came in dancing on his behind with his paws in the air, barking like a sergeant major on the parade ground and navigating the room in a circular pattern before vanishing back into the bedroom.

"Good heavens," said Miss Faye. "Who's that?"

"That's just Bauhaus," said Virgil.

"I thought it was Laird Cregar trying out for the next revival of *Porgy and Bess.*" To Peter she added, "As Porgy, the singing cripple, of course."

Peter looked dubious, but came then the main course, Dennis Savage's masterly steak-and-mushroom pie, as the conversation proceeded to the intense sexual bent of the queen's patter.

"Some people are unnerved to hear the erotic life so blatantly explored" ran Peter's theme.

"Ah, so," Miss Faye replied, enigmatic as a perfume.

Then the buzzer sounded.

"Uh-oh," said Virgil.

"Who's this going to be," Dennis Savage asked Cosgrove, "Blimpy von—"

"I'll get it," I said. It was Carlo, thank heaven, because nothing welcomes a newcomer like Peter into the gay world better than a friendly hunk. Carlo breezed in like the opening of a window after a cooling rain in a heat wave. Fresh and happy, lightly roughhousing the kids as they told him of the Historic Plaza Tours, Carlo reoriented the party's structure from that of ships passing in the night into that of a regatta, with Carlo as some duke's yacht. Cosgrove stopped scheming, Dennis Savage stopped worrying, and Peter waxed content, interested, wondering. As he shook Carlo's hand, Peter looked like Shelley about to embark upon an ode.

Miss Faye, however, immediately degenerated into her natural state. "Who's this cowboy?" she shouted. "Rope 'em," she growled. Then, in pealing tones last heard when Una Merkel gloated under a parasol in some forgotten western, she laced out, "Why, I do decla-yuh if peace hasn't come to Rainbow City since *you* clea-yuhd the town, Sheriff Clint Kincaid."

Carlo mimed tipping his Stetson to her.

"Now, what say you model some bathin' attire, Sheriff?" Miss Faye went on, her voice tightening up a bit. "For our summer needs."

"Don't model anything," said Dennis Savage.

"We're gettin' to that" was Miss Faye's remark, as she took stage. Her subject, now, was How to Win Oscar, her character was Cloris (Leachman, it eventually developed), and her mode was Drag Queen on the Rampage. She was instructive, nevertheless, going into many a cul-de-sac of Oscar history. For instance, who would have dreamed that Faith Domergue was an Oscar hopeful when making *This Island Earth,* one of the most opulently cheesy sci-fi films ever—the one with Metaluna and the Interossiter and Rex Reason? Who would have dreamed that Faith had her dramatic coach, Ruth Roman, on the set at all times, urging her to throw everything into her screams of terror when an alien monster attacks and thus cop her Academy Award?

"Now it's all quiet on the western front," Miss Faye was telling us—dinner balanced on our knees, Dennis Savage and Virgil re-filling the glasses, and all eyes nervously checking on Peter's reaction. "The monster is coming. Will Faith be clawed, eaten? It's such *delicious.* Ruth signals to Faith—indicate horror, flaunt profile, cringe. But Ruth is all actress, and she becomes *utterly* carried away by the enormous dramatic potential of the scene, and she starts playing Faith's part even as she coaches. 'Yes, the monster. [This was whispered.] It's coming. Scream, Faith. Scream *more*. [This was a bit louder.] Its hideous acid breath, not unlike that of George "Gabby" Hayes!' Then Ruth herself begins to shout, in pride and, strangely, fear—for Ruth knows what waits us all at the Other End. 'Scream, Faith! *Scream for Oscar!*'"

"But surely," Peter put in, "one couldn't receive an Oscar nomination for a B movie fit only for the children's matinée. And why is the dramatic coach screaming during the take?"

"The director immediately ordered Ruth off the set, bien sûr. But Ruth stood proud, true, *thespian*. She knows what she was born to be. We all know it."

Miss Faye looked at Carlo. "Some born to be so splendid that all who clap eyes upon fall instantly, permanently, hopelessly in love."

Miss Faye looked at Cosgrove. "Some born to outfox the fascists, be ever sly, tape the sound of the world to new tones."

"Miss Faye," Cosgrove sighed, utterly entranced.

"And some born to stockpile the inner longing," Miss Faye continued, turning—of course—to Peter. "Oh, scary needs. But needs find their release, do they not? Even degenerate subversive temptationesque fagolust needs. Wherein we divest the self of our smashing suit and tie and cobwebs to be shrewed by some bracing lunk in a tank top."

Miss Faye drew near to Peter with coy little steps.

"Oh, we've seen him, stretching himself at the bus stop. Skin shows between his top and pants. He's unaware. We gaze. Curly hair, strenuous upper torso, loose, surprising, open to suggestion. He's not handsome, so he'll be grateful for the attention. We stare, thinking of how it would feel to be legs high, sighing in the rhythm of delight like a woman."

"Peter, how are you fixed for wine?" Dennis Savage called out; but Peter was riveted by Miss Faye.

"Shrewed and shrewed again, that's my credo," Miss Faye went on. "Craido," she pronounced it. "So many start as tops." Fastidious gestures. "I won't, dear me, don't *make* me take it. I shan't be shrewed, Father O'Halloran, indeed I shan't! I shall retain my manly innocence even unto death."

She was inches away from Peter now, and almost whispered

in his ear, "'In spite of everything, I still believe that people are really good at heart.'" She smiled. "Who said that?"

Peter just stared at her.

"Who said, 'I still believe that people are really good at heart'?"

"Who, Miss Faye?" asked Cosgrove.

"Make *him* ask me," said Miss Faye, not taking her eyes off Peter.

"You better hell ask her, pal," Carlo advised Peter. "She's got you hooked."

Dennis Savage was frantically sending me eye-faxes, so I looked at Carlo, and he yokeled up and took hold of Miss Faye— "Cowboy!" she breathed out, in her heaven—and set her down on the couch with him. There she was silent, though she did take the liberty of running her hands over him every so often in a kind of reverie. There was this lull, and Cosgrove trundled off to the bathroom.

Peter couldn't not watch Miss Faye now, especially while she was fingering Carlo. I thought to myself, this was the wrong dinner party, but not only because of Miss Faye. The trouble with closet cases like Peter is, they don't know what to make of a roomful of gays, because all their lives they've been used to playing the Big Lie: So what do they do when they suddenly can't use it? All their lines and subject matter get blown away; they don't know what to work with. Besides, without any warning, there's all this skin around, muscle and cock. They've trained themselves not to notice. Now not only are they allowed to want it: They're supposed to get it.

Slowly lead to it, yes?

"Where was I?" Miss Faye muttered, during Peter's recollection of how his family, when he was six, packed and fled from Grosse Pointe in their yacht during the 1968 Detroit riots.

"Oh, yes!" Miss Faye went on, back in her Cloris Leachman voice. "How to win Oscar." She let loose an at most mildly compromised smile, waved at a fan or two, looked back while tossing an imaginary scarf over her shoulder, sighed, and began.

"Now, of course, I had Teacup Scene, in *The Last Picture Show*." Miss Faye displayed relish. "You remember, when that beautiful boy was inattentive and then came by for solace, and how I was then seen by rapt millions to *throw* the coffeepot *right* across the *room*—lovely in my rage, as you may imagine—and it strangely became known as Teacup Scene, though . . . *Anyway,* then I grow all tender and fond, as one must when beautiful boys are by. And I say . . . I say, 'Never you mind.' How loving that is, how skillfully forgiving. The diva absorbs our sins, and thus she wins Oscar—because in our belief in her we believe in ourselves. Don't you see that yet, you tiny fools? I am *Cloris!*"

Here she rose.

"I *defy* you! I defied them all: Darryl Zanuck, with his bossy cucumber. L. B. Mayer, who hoped to fuck me with a balalaika while Georgian peasants hummed 'Marche Slave' in some exotic, perhaps Oriental key. And that *querulous,* ever-shrewing Rory Calhoun, costar in my strangely long-forgotten Scottish epic, *The Trial and Kotex of Mary Stuart*." Miss Faye was pacing the room, dramatizing, on exhibition. "Major scenes were shot in Princes Street, Edinburgh, at Flodden Field, in the haystacks near Aberdeen. This was real location work, I say! There we were, eating haggis. And Haggis turned around and said, 'You've got exactly two hours to cut that out.' Then . . . *the rains came!*"

Miss Faye grew tragic and still. Carlo was grinning, as at any good show; Peter was braced for the next helping of Miss Faye; Virgil was trying to look like a guest at the most scintillating soirée since the opening-night cast party for *Private Lives;* and Dennis Savage was mechanically forking up dinner as, I imagine, Napoléon might have taken a little something after Waterloo.

"The *rains!*" Miss Faye wailed, in Faye Dunaway's "wire hangers" mode. "But I showed them all what Cloris *is* and *was!* Didn't I show that Dominique Sanda, with her Lesbian Dance Sequence? Oh, yes, you remember, in Bertolucci's *The Conformist*—and now, on every picture, all she asks the director is 'When do I get Lesbian

Dance Sequence'? Yet *I* never dreamed of repeating Teacup Scene—though I would win Oscar in a second if I did. No, the scene I long for is Rosalind Russell's tear-the-shirt episode from *Picnic,* when the male torso is bared and all stand mute in wild, discordant joy!"

"You speak," Peter began, then clammed up as Miss Faye—well, Cloris, except now she was Rosalind Russell as *Picnic's* Rosemary, the repressed yet erotically greedy schoolteacher denouncing and decreeing—started pacing the room in explosively repressed fury.

"I mean," Peter went on, as Virgil and I nodded in support, "you speak as if life were nothing but the accommodation of sexual hunger."

"All life," Rosemary spat out, "is a yearning for something that just *damn* isn't available! Yes, I said it! Come on and fire me!"

Peter was perplexed.

"Come on, cowboy," Rosemary cried to Carlo. "Dance with me!"

Wondering what had happened to Cosgrove, I slipped off, but he wasn't in the bathroom. I found him in the bedroom; he had thrown the overcoats off the beds and was gleefully stamping up and down on one, and I lost my temper.

"You little idiot," I cried sotto voce, grabbing and tossing him halfway across the room. "It's not enough to humiliate Dennis Savage's editor by sneaking that haunt into the party, you have to mortify his *coat,* too?"

"This isn't his coat," said Cosgrove. "It's your coat."

"How would you like to move into the street?" I said, really angry now and ignoring the uproar that was suddenly cascading out of the living room. "I found you in the gutter and I can throw you back there any time I—"

"*No!* I'll be good!"

"This is too late to be good," I told him, really revved up. "I keep saying *stop* and you keep right on going! My parents are like that—you know what I did to them?"

"Excuse me," said Peter, who had suddenly joined us, anxiously looking for—"Ah, there it is," he said, retrieving his coat from the floor.

"It strangely fell," Cosgrove alibied; but Peter was off and away. "I'm so terribly sorry," he called over his shoulder. Then the front door clicked open and slammed shut.

What happened? Cosgrove and I looked at each other for a bit. Then he warily peered around the corner of the doorway into the living room.

"Carlo has skin," he said.

Joining the others, I found the place in that silently aghast moment just after a bomb has gone off. Everyone except Dennis Savage was standing, a few plates had fallen onto the carpet, Carlo's T-shirt was torn from collar to navel, and his pants were down to his ankles. Miss Faye said, "Beulah—my wrap," mimed throwing a stole tail over her shoulder, and made her exit. "Thanks for the use of the hall," she concluded, posing in the doorway before pulling her curtain down.

Dennis Savage carefully laid his plate aside and rose. He surveyed us all, frozen except for Carlo, who was pulling up his pants.

"He fell in love with my stories because he fell in love with my friends," Dennis Savage began. Believe me, President Wilson at Versailles did not with greater majesty address civilization at large on the Meaning of Democracy Among the Nations. "He fell in love with my *friends*? Because, somebody better tell me, why have I just fallen *out* of love with them?"

"What happened?" I asked.

"A fair question," said Dennis Savage, beginning to pace. "Who knows the answer? Our esoteric little Cosgrove, with his novelty-shop booby traps? Is it our almost biblically redemptive Carlo, so gleaming and undreamed of, who *I was hoping* would intrigue my editor with pastoral fantasia and instead dropped his pants—"

"That drag lady truly shucked them off me before I—"

"And you"—Dennis Savage favored Virgil with a look—"were no help, either."

Virgil, indeed, looked helpless.

"He loves my friends, can you stand it?" Dennis Savage asked, with an operatic laugh, Lily Pons laced with Boris Christoff. "Well, that's all over, now that he's seen you guys up to your jokes." To me he said, "Can he cancel my book?"

"Has he made the offer? The advance and the due date and so on?"

"No."

"Well . . . Then . . . He could . . ."

"Say it!"

"What happened?"

Virgil said, "Miss Faye tried to tear Carlo's shirt off but it didn't all come away, so she pulled down his pants. Then Peter Keene jumped over and was kneeling and held Carlo's thighs and sucked on his—"

"No," I said. "That doesn't occur."

"In this room," Virgil insisted.

I turned to Dennis Savage. "That guy with all the dignity and aplomb just . . ."

"Sat down and ate Carlo's coccus. Yes. Yes. Yes."

"And we all saw," Virgil added.

"It was bigged out when my pants went down," Carlo added, "because that Lady Faye had been working on me, making me all sticky. I couldn't but notice that she wears a cheesy scent, too."

"Miss Faye," Cosgrove hotly contested, "is the world's leading drag artiste!"

"And he really?" I asked Carlo. "Jumped down and? He *really*?"

"Well, my thumper there was pointing to Do It, and that editor guy had this look on him, that he's just got to. I've seen it from time to time. Like years ago, when guys were getting arrested just for staring at something in a tearoom? They knew it was risky, yet they had to. So, imagine, if this guy's coming out and he—"

"Well, *I* came out," said Cosgrove, "and I didn't have to make a fuss at a party and run away. So what's that editor's problem? Everybody's gay now. TV actors are gay. Con Edison is gay."

"We have to be patient with newborns," said Virgil.

"Con Edison is gay?" I asked, mystified.

"Enough with these inessentials," said Dennis Savage. "What happened? One, Miss Faye tore Carlo's shirt like Rosalind Russell in *Picnic.*"

"Two," said Carlo, "she stole kisses."

"Then she, yes, pressed her mouth to his," Dennis Savage went on, "whether to taste of the beauty of love or to outline an arcane satire, we will never be sure. And *then* she, three, opened up his pants. And, of course, he wears no shorts, so—"

"Why should I? They're extra money, and who needs them, anyway?"

"*So,* out flopped the Great American Flagpole, and suddenly the neat and controlled man in the suit goes cock-crazy and blows his self-esteem and marches out of here with my career in a shambles. Thank you *so much,*" he told Cosgrove, "for destroying my dinner. Thank *you,*" he told me, "for knowing this thing in the first place. Thank you," he told Carlo, "for being so wonderful that the center cannot hold when you're in the room. And thank you," he told Virgil—but then the phone rang.

"Ignore it," said Dennis Savage, falling back onto the couch with a sigh of despair. "The tape will take it. I just can't handle any more . . ." He finished the sentence with a fagged-out wave of his hand.

"Come on," I said, over the taped greeting of Virgil promising spiritual advice, romance tips, and information on Plaza Tours, Inc. "He won't cancel the book just because—"

"He *revealed* himself to God and gays," Dennis Savage insisted. "He showed his hunger! My life is rags."

But, lo, it was Peter Keene on the phone; and this was his message:

"Well, I've had a few blocks' walk and some minutes to collect myself, and . . . Yes, okay, I of course am calling to apologize for my, uh, performance, and I hope Carlo isn't too . . . Is anybody there? Or perhaps you've shut the gizmo off. But some gizmos can't really quite *be* shut off, if you take my meaning. It is as if there are parts working away in us like the insides of a watch, whether we admit it or not. And I think that's why I was so drawn to your, uh, characters. Well, your people, really, isn't it? Because they don't pretend that their insides are . . . Are you sure nobody's there?"

(Dennis Savage turned as if to move to the phone and pick up, but I held him back, because then major dish would have been lost in his ear, and I owe it to my readers to stay intimate with all the details of the, uh, characters' comings and goings, in the name of the higher realism.)

"Anyway, I'm very embarrassed, and I hope my rash behavior won't drop me from your guest list, and the contract should be along in a few weeks, but let's have lunch again in the meantime. We can try that place you mentioned, where all the waiters are . . . Well, any old howzle, tell Carlo I hope I didn't make him feel cheap. I guess my alarm went off before I knew what was happening. And, if you'll pardon a word of advice, the little maniac should retire the animal toy, though I must say his vocalism is impressively postmodernist. Again, I'm . . . I'm really sorry. But at the same time I think I have a lot to look forward to—and not the least of it will be assembling my own circle of people as vital and positive as yours. First thing tomorrow, I'm joining a health club. They say Better Bodies is reasonably spiffy, and right in the thick of the . . . the community, so to say. So long, sir, and thank you."

"*What* little maniac?" asked Cosgrove, suspiciously, as the tape machine ran through its clicks and whirrs.

"Oh, my God," said Dennis Savage, his voice low but rising. "It worked. He liked it! He's embarrassed but happy! The contract is coming! I see the galleys, messengered to this very building for me to appraise, amend! I see the dust jacket, one of those . . . oh so deftly understated yet *magnificent* depictions. I see . . . *my book* . . .

in store windows, and I have only to enter one such emporium for crowds of devotees to—"

"Who does he think was a maniac?" Cosgrove pursued. "That's what I should know!"

"I truly think he was referring to Bauhaus," said the conciliatory Carlo.

"Bauhaus doesn't have an animal toy or do vocalism."

"Haven't you had enough?" I asked Cosgrove. "You're already up for certain punishments for your—"

"*No!* What punishments?"

"No birthday CDs this month, for starters."

"Rats," he said, doubtless picking out an alternate birthdate some six weeks hence.

"Not to mention," I went on, "corporal admonishment that may have to be visited upon your person."

"Tonight?" Cosgrove asked, pensively. "With sweet talk, and twisted enchantments whispered into my ear to show how it's really affectionate, to make me a better boy?"

"Can I come, too?" Carlo asked.

"I object," Dennis Savage cried. "That little degenerate *loves* to be spanked! Everyone in this family knows it!"

"What about our Plaza Tours?" said Virgil. "We have to get ready for the new age that begins!"

Dennis Savage sighed, picking up plates and stuff. "Normally, I'd be scratching my eyes on the walls, but I'm so relieved now that I could take on anything. How much do you think Bruce Weber charges for dust jacket photos?"

"A little maniac," Cosgrove was muttering. "I can fix *him!*"

"Who's serving seconds?" Carlo inquired.

"I will," said Dennis Savage, coming out again. "I will, in fact, with gladness, as soon as I catch my breath. All these delicious events going on. This hope. Because—that's it, of course!—the whole secret of la dolce vita is to have something to look forward to."

He was about to plop into a chair; but Cosgrove was ready.

Having snatched another whoopee cushion out of his *left* sock, he'd quickly inflated it and accomplished the placement just as Dennis Savage hit the armchair.

As the great rumor of humiliation rang through the party, Cosgrove triumphed, Virgil considered, Carlo was scarfing up the last of the dinner, and I said, "Life is a barnyard," to view this latest turn of fate philosophically. "Life, anyhow," I explained.

"Life is good sex," said Carlo, munching.

"Life is revenge," said Cosgrove. "And it's coming soon."

"Life is the Plaza Tours," said Virgil. "Where you see how everything happened and where it could go."

"Life," said Dennis Savage, rising above the entire evening, "is getting published."

The one who said that people are really good at heart? That was Anne Frank.

JEOPARDY!

ummer came on strong and so did the Plaza Tours—yes, they signed the contract. I have a sort of contract, too, with the loop that runs around Central Park. April through October, this roadway is closed to cars (except for the southeastern curve) from ten to three every weekday, and I build the season around my bike rides, music pleasantly jamming through my Walkman on my potpourri tapes, in which dance bands and Sophie Tucker interlace with Zandonai, *Louise*, and von Webern. One day in July, I missed my homeward turn onto Fifty-fourth Street and had to cut east on Fifty-second. And, lo, between Sixth and Fifth Avenues I happened past a plaza just as the boys were doing their spiel.

"History rings," Virgil was announcing, "with the names of presidents, senators, and generals who marched through this gilded square."

"Even cabaret artistes have given their all here," Cosgrove added. "Some in mufti."

"To this day," Virgil went on, "the great and near-great mingle freely with the bohemian world in this no-man's-land of power and talent."

I had halted to take it in, and now I saw Miss Faye entering as unto a stage upon hearing her cue; throwing me a sardonic wink, she turned off the street into the plaza with a mighty flounce and passed brazenly before the tour group, many of whom dutifully elevated their cameras. A few passersby stopped to gawk and muse.

"Here comes one now," Cosgrove loudly confided to his charges. "One of the salty habitués of the downtown set. Let us watch as this paragon of the demi-world goes to and fro in our exciting New York plazas."

Miss Faye must be writing his material again, I thought, as Miss Faye paused, struck an attitude, and declaimed, "Oo, tourists! Where are you folks from? Do I smell . . . Ohio? Ashtabula, perhaps?"

The folks, mostly expressionless middle-agers and seniors, just stood there.

"Why, I do believe it's Miss Faye," said Cosgrove, in an aside to the group. "The legend of stage and scream. Why not greet her?"

Miss Faye flourished another pose, but none of the folks uttered so much as a Yo! Virgil was airing out his baseball cap, looking bored, and I trundled on home.

One had the feeling that the Plaza Boys were about to pack it in, and they presently did so, celebrating their freedom by buying fancy cameras and immediately reincorporating as the Photo Snoops, roaming the town in hunt for celebrities to shoot, the pictures to be sold for fabulous profits. Virgil prudently banked the rest of his share of the Plaza Tours income; Cosgrove blew his on CDs and Yoo-hoo.

So it looked like we were in for another of those same-old summers—with one novelty, Peter Keene, who was visiting to consult with us on gay stylistics, sex practices, and parish credenda. I for one have very little patience for people who wait till their thirties to come out. Like, what were they afraid of, that Nancy Reagan would cut their parties? But Dennis Savage of course played the enthusiastic adviser and Carlo enjoyed having someone new to stagger and thrill with the recounting of his exploits.

"Do you know Carlo says he's probably had more sex with straight men than with gay men?" Peter asked me one evening over coffee in my apartment. "He's sort of a natural force, I think. Like Magnetic North. He *uproots* men."

On television, Alex Trebek asked, "What category?"

"Pee-wee Herman for four hundred," Cosgrove replied.

"Political Pundits for one hundred," said the TV contestant.

"Rats," said Cosgrove. "They never like *my* categories."

Cosgrove is a wild *Jeopardy!* buff. Every evening at seven o'clock he parks himself in front of a television and competes with the screen contenders, shouting out answers and berating himself when he misses. But he always misses. First of all, he doesn't realize that players must choose from the categories presented on the show; second, he believes that the quickest answer, rather than the correct one, wins the prize. It's a scattershot, stream-of-consciousness *Jeopardy!* Yet Cosgrove is an addict.

Trebek then put forth his riddle, in that constipated *Jeopardy!* manner that poses the questions in the form of answers: "These essays by Alexander Hamilton, James Madison, and John Jay illuminate the American Constitution."

"Who was George Washington Bridge!" Cosgrove shouted, in a rush.

"What was *The Federalist*," said the contestant.

"Right," Trebek confirmed.

"Famous Candy Bars for three hundred," said Cosgrove.

"Political Pundits for two hundred," said the contestant.

"Shoot!"

"Visiting Soviet Russia in 1919," said Trebek, "he said, 'I have been over into the future, and it works.'"

"Why were they three blind mice!" Cosgrove cried.

The TV contestant was not so quick; nor were his competitors. Finally one pushed the buzzer. "Who was . . . Lytton . . ." He shook his head.

"Who was Lincoln Steffens," said Peter.

Cosgrove shot him a mildly accusing look, as Trebek confirmed Peter's answer.

"Hey," Cosgrove told Peter. "I do a single."

Luckily, the show took a marketing break, and I muted the sound. "Why aren't you upstairs playing *Jeopardy!* with Virgil?" I asked Cosgrove.

"He's in a bad mood."

"About what?"

He shrugged. "Lately he does that sometimes."

"Why don't you show Peter some of your latest Photo Snoops shots?"

Cosgrove considered this, eyeing Peter as if wondering whether to let him even that far into his life.

"Well, maybe," Cosgrove finally conceded, hopping up to fetch his photo album, one of those classy sheer-plastic-over-adhesive-pages numbers that Tiffany's sells for a surprisingly small amount of money. Cosgrove is very proud of the album's felt dust cover, in "Tiffany blue" and fastened with a drawstring, and he invariably makes a big show out of opening it.

I mention these details of fashion because I don't want any of you thinking that gay boys do nothing but talk about the NFL and eat raw beef and piss in the street.

Anyway, Cosgrove presented Peter with the volume and sat with us on the couch to identify the uncaptioned photos.

"We took that one outside the Hard Rock Café," he said. "That's Sly Stallone and his gang."

"It's so dark," said Peter.

"Well, it was night. And a whole bunch of Arab chieftains came in and made me nervous."

"Where's Sly?"

"He's behind the towelheads. And this, now, is Elizabeth Taylor, who had a cold."

"Which one is she?"

"Well, everybody was rushing and yelling, 'Liz! Liz!,' and she hid in a Kleenex. But now *this* is the prize, as you can see."

Peter studied it. " 'The Wounded Stag'?" he guessed.

"It's Michael Stipe, outside the Plaza Hotel."

"What are those blurry things around him?"

"He was laughing and his head moved. *Oh!*" (*Jeopardy!* was back on.) "The Snows of Kilimanjaro, for one hundred!" Cosgrove called out, slipping off the couch, his interest snagged.

It was impossible to talk while Cosgrove played *Jeopardy!* Peter patiently waited it out, though he was not sorry to see Cosgrove march off to D'Agostino's immediately after the show ended.

"Your . . . what do you call him again? Your roommate?"

"My live-in."

"Well, and he's got his fascination, yes, I see that. His . . . energy. He's quite jolly pals with Dennis Savage's . . . live-in?"

I nodded.

"Yes, but the term sounds so neutral!" he protested.

"It's supposed to. It covers almost as many bizarre compromises and perfumed disappointments as the words 'husband' and 'wife' do when heterosexuals use them."

"Point taken. But it does seem odd that both you and Dennis Savage have . . ." He didn't want to offend, so he was choosing his words with care. ". . . well, somewhat youthful live-ins, as opposed to . . ."

"Tired old queens like ourselves?"

"Not at all! How could you think—"

"Look around! Is everyone the same age? Shares everyone the same interests, ho? We're all different, and each relationship is different, and *some* relationships might be *very* different—and suddenly you get one of those keen-to-learn younger man–smart, educational older man duos. Or the protégeur-protégé setup, where they're both musicians, or one's a choreographer and one's a dancer. Or even . . . Bud has just enough money to support a mate, and Cosgrove's homeless and vulnerable and is thus forced to undergo an exploitative degradation such that the Hogarthian brothel madams of Gin Lane would turn from it in—"

"For pity's sake!" he cried, jumping to his feet. "Did I *say* that?"

"More coffee?"

"It just looks—"

"Weird."

" 'Wonderful,' I was heading for, actually. I can see that your live-in is psychologically embattled and feels . . . safe? . . . here."

I nodded, taking our mugs to the kitchen for the second brew. "He can never figure out why people think he's strange. But at this address no one cares, so he thrives. He's supported and protected."

"Yes, surely," Peter agreed, coming after me. "But the usual gay coupling would unite two men of the same . . . No?"

"What's usual about gay coupling in the first place?" I countered, grinding the beans to extra-fine while the water boiled. I use a half-and-half infusion of Medaglia d'Oro decaffeinated espresso and Martinson's Regular, and everyone says I serve the best coffee in town. "Each couple's a mismatch, in fact," I went on. "That's the fun of it."

"But Carlo always goes for men of his own ilk, it would seem."

"Would it?" I asked, laying the filter paper in its holder over my Charles-and-Di mug. Our rituals.

"Well, such . . . such big, virile men doing their . . . that who's-in-charge? tango . . ."

"Rip's a totally out gay guy who likes to date homos so closeted they think they're heterosexuals. Or real heterosexuals who turn to men because they can't get enough from women. You can't call that a union of equals, can you?"

"Well, but his whole vigor is this . . . this *wow*, the way he goes after what he wants. He says we all have it in us to pull down our star. That's his term. Yes, we . . . yes, *snatch* that star close, with the gym and the clothes . . . the right hat, you might say . . ."

Peter might, certainly. Seldom had a man so quickly accommodated himself to the rules of the place, with his " 'Tention, hut!" shoulders and eighty-five-dollar haircut.

" 'The right hat,' " I echoed, pouring the hot water through the filter paper. "Huh."

There are four types of people who come newly into your life: the iffy people who quickly turn out to be no good (usually because they start haranguing you after you refuse to lend them your copy of *Mawrdew Czgowchwz*); the harmlessly unarresting people who will, with the slightest encouragement, drift off in due course; the agreeable people who will be denied your most intimate confidence but may be mentioned in your will; and essential people. Peter was making a strong showing somewhere between the third and fourth grades, and as we talked on about Carlo and pulling down your star and self-transformation, I began to wonder—lazily, with one ear on Peter's elated rap—just how he was going to fit into our lives.

The answer, for the moment, was "constantly": especially in my apartment, because Dennis Savage's ailing mother had suffered one of those turns so pointed that the family had been summoned. So now Peter was taking his after-work Gay Initiation Class with me. Of course, like every fresh adherent to a cause, he was trying to lecture me even as he learned. Oh, he was respectful—but so eager!

One evening, we were in the middle of an intellectually ferocious debate on the value of an extra-big physique.

"Carlo says you've got to overwhelm them," Peter told me. "Make them hungry. That's his—"

"But some of them like a slim-jim look," I told him. "They find heavy muscles tendentious."

He slowly, confidently shook his head and bunched up his right biceps.

"Oh, come on," I said.

"*Feel* it."

Kids, he was big, and I caught him savoring my look of surprise.

"That's my shock value," he said.

"Where did all this happen so fast?"

"Every weekday morning. From eight to nine-thirty. At Better Bodies."

"Jeepers."

"Monday morning, upper torso. Tuesday morning, legs and abs. Wednesday—"

"Stop."

"And, I have to add, I jump out of bed each day almost *on fire* with the devotion. Well? Do you see how serious I . . ."

Cosgrove had come in, bearing an eight-by-ten envelope, and ensconced himself beside me, waiting restlessly for the talk to cease. When Peter, curious, dried up, Cosgrove whispered to me, quite loudly, "Make him go, there's a secret to tell."

"No, that's fine," said Peter, rising. "I have a pile of manuscripts to sift through tonight."

"That's exciting," I replied, taking him to the door while Cosgrove banged his hand against the couch armrest to urge a speedier tempo of farewell upon us. "Think of discovering the next Dostoyefsky."

He gave me an amused look, said, "Somehow that never happens," and left, and I immediately reproached Cosgrove for his brusqueness.

"Yes, but why is he always around?" Cosgrove shot back. "And always *looking* at everyone?"

"Looking?"

"Like he's scoping out our . . ." Wrestling open the envelope, he pulled out more Photo Snoops shots and handed them to me with a look of silent triumph. These were better than the average, well-lit and focused, daylight shots taken down along the West Village piers among the weekend cruising population: bladers and bikers and dog walkers and, in particular, one order of louche to go, a big, bosomy skater in dark glasses and running shorts whom the Snoops had caught leering and winking and staring at all the cute boys, and talking to them in what appeared to be tones as low as the Duncan Hines rating of a hot-sheets motel, and touching them like Ziegfeld auditioning candidates for the *Follies*.

And his name was Pleasure: but also Peter Keene.

"Now, do you see?" said Cosgrove. "He has a *secret life!*"

"Wait a minute. You just *happened* upon him like this?"

Cosgrove made a "Boy, are you dumb" face. "We waited outside his apartment last Saturday and followed him downtown."

"You have nothing better to do than wait out—"

"We're the Photo Snoops, we *have* to wait. We were outside the Hard Rock Café for four hours last week. Remember our motto: 'No star too small, no fee too large.'"

"But why Peter Keene?"

"We're keeping a file on everybody, because *you never know.*"

"Does that include Dennis Savage and Carlo and me as well?"

"'Be afraid,'" he advised me, quoting some movie again. "'Be very afraid.'"

Reviewing the pictures, I had to admire Peter's commitment to the belief that stylish cruising technique is based above all upon a physical makeover. Clearly, he had good genetics, as they say; but clearly he was also Really Going at It. I've seen this before. Guys who took a fast metabolism for granted reach twenty-eight or so, notice that the competition from buffed twenty-four-year-olds is all but running them out of town, and decide to get into shape. The gym turns out to be an inspiring locale, loaded with imitable madeovers, and as the exercise program expands the mirror becomes dazzling. For the first time in their lives, they're starting to look like someone they themselves might want.

"So what if Peter is cruising on weekends?" I asked Cosgrove. "He has a right."

"Virgil told me Dennis Savage says Peter is out of control. And you know if one apple in the barrel goes rotten, they *all* start crabbing. What if Peter becomes crazed and brings tension into the family?"

"What family?"

"This."

It was the first time that Cosgrove had acknowledged that our convivial enclave might be something integral rather than just a bunch of people he knows, and I was thinking, Well, bless his little heart. Then he pulled out another series of pictures.

"Ah, more Photo Snoops," I said, taking in the shots of Peter not only cruising but eagerly coming on: For in these shots he was rifling the shorts of a young man—a shirtless skater, like Peter—then grabbing his head for depth-charge kisses, and at last rolling away with his conquest like movie pals into a sunset.

I said, "Maybe the Photo Snoops should give up celebrity hunting and just shoot porn."

"We may have to," said Cosgrove, collecting his pictures. "Last night we spent the whole evening in the theatre district like those horrible autograph hounds, and all we could find was Dirty Desmond Dilsey."

I was, like, *Who?*

"Some porn star," Cosgrove explained. "He *said* he was, anyway. He was going into Folly City. Are you going to talk to Peter? That he shouldn't do this?"

"It's a free country, Cos."

"But he doesn't know what there could be. Like when they say, Oh, you are such a cutie, I want you to move in and take care of you. So you give them everything, and next morning you say, So what about breakfast? And they go, Get out of my house, sucker!"

There was a pause, and then the phone rang, and it was Dennis Savage from upstate. Cosgrove scooted along and I took the call.

His mother had "gone out like a candle," he said: waning, darkening, throwing off a last momentary shudder, then still.

"Are you okay?" I asked.

"It's better that she is not now, and can never be again, in pain."

"When do they read the will?"

"I knew I could count on your sprightly humor to ease me through the ordeal."

"I hate parents and I'm glad she's dead."

"Yes, keep those droll mots coming."

"Listen," I said, "is there a porn star named Dirty . . . Dickie Something?"

"Come again?"

"The Photo Snoops clocked him at Folly City. Dirty . . ."

"How are they holding up?"

"Fine. Though Virgil's a little crusty with Cosgrove."

"With me, too. He's going through another of his phases. How are you and Peter getting on?"

"Okay."

"I hear a tone."

"Yeah. It's that supergay role he plays. He's like something out of a late-seventies novel. You know: So many men, and it's going to take me maybe till next Tuesday."

"*Oh!* Daniel Daring!"

"Who what?"

"The porn star you were asking about. He did a solo video called *Dirty Daniel Daring* and he dances at Folly City."

"You *are* up on your celebs, aren't you?"

"Remember to go easy on Peter. He has a lot to catch up on. He needs encouragement, and you can give it."

"I will if you give me points in your portion of your mother's will."

"Be good, and I'll be back soon," he said.

I have to admit, the idea of Peter coming into his own legacy as an heir of Stonewall rather intrigued me. I wanted him to recall to me the age in which those who absolutely cultivated themselves as icons of hot could blow open all the locks and screw the world.

There's this, too: On summer weekends, the Park's too crowded, so one has to bike elsewhere. I favor downtown, because of the Strand Bookstore, Footlight Records, and my favorite Polish luncheonette, Teresa's, on Second Avenue.❖ But this day I rode down to the West Village piers, to see what I could see, such as Peter. Nothing much was doing—a few bladers and runners, some posing and taunting. But there was none of the atmosphere of Major Men Seriously Available that once permeated this part of town in the seventies.

This place was a meat rack then; there are no meat racks anymore, because the monolithic sexuality that early Stonewall built so big has dwindled, as Congreve says, into a wife. Sex, today, is a pastime in gay life, like the canasta parties that suburbanites threw in the 1950s: a treat you save for special nights, so it doesn't get in the way of the basic things, like gardening or Burns and Allen.

Or dog owning. For here came a fine and full, tight and trim young lad. Twenty years ago, he would have been lurking in the

❖ It was my father who turned me on to Polish food. He served in the OSS during World War II as a liaison between—do you now see why I'm so twisted, boys and girls?—the Russian army and Polish partisans. Russian he had taken in college, and Polish he mastered in a six-week cram course. I still own his textbook. Anyway, while in Poland, fêted, if that be the word, in country barns and the like, my father developed a taste for Polish cooking. Serious historical study suggests that Polish cooking at this moment in history (roughly 1944) consisted of consommé of tree bark and sautéed rat. At Teresa's, I usually order chicken cutlet with lemon slices. Superb!

area looking studly; today, he was walking a beagle, uninterested in anything else. He wasn't on the make, except for the dog, whom he constantly fondled and purred to. She was Josephine, it turned out, and he was a dreamboat. I guessed his name was Tim.

I'm on my bike, now, immobile, watching.

There's another dog owner around, the kind who owns not a pet but an entire kennel and who believes that New York City's leash law is for other people. One of his dogs decides to investigate Josephine. So he goes trotting up to sniff Josephine's behind in that louche canine etiquette they have. But Josephine doesn't want to be sniffed. She appears quite frightened of this stranger dog's attention, and plants her bum flat against the pavement.

Tim doesn't like this invasion of his pet's personal space. He shouts "Hey!" and tries to chase the intruding dog away. It retreats, briefly, then renews its advances, while Tim uses the hand end of Josephine's leash as a whip in the air to keep it at bay as he angrily calls out, "Who owns this dog? *Call off your dog!*"

The owner has been talking to a Hispanic man, who points out the problem even as the owner has turned at the noise.

Now hear this: Does the owner leap over the concrete divider that he's standing behind and pull his dog away, apologizing to Tim for the harassment?

No. The owner stands there whistling very very lightly at his animal, who of course pays no attention.

Tim is not willing to let his dog be terrorized, so he gives the intruding dog a kick in the ass.

I look at the owner at this point; he's still whistling. The Hispanic man is saying something to him with a look of baleful contentment at the prospect of bloodletting soon.

The marauding dog is not going to be easily discouraged, for despite the kick he comes right around sniffing at the miserable Josephine. This time, Tim kicks the dog in the muzzle, real socko, and the animal yelps but keeps on coming, so Tim kicks it three times in the head as hard as he can.

Finally, the owner of the dog—the thing's still attacking

Josephine, by the way, and still getting kicked—has decided to intervene, but only to assault Tim, jumping the divider and running full-tilt at him.

Next, three things occur at almost exactly the same time: One, Tim intercepts the attack by grabbing his assailant by the hair to use the force of his own charge to slam him head-first into the cement barrier at the water's edge. Two, I note the Hispanic man beaming with delight. Three, the police arrive.

They're all over us *real* quick, separating the combatants and ignoring the dogs. Do you believe that the intruder is *still* trying to whiff Josephine's rump? I presume she was in heat. The cops start piecing it together from onlookers, and one of the cops, taking note of Josephine's barks of distress, grabs the other dog by the collar, slings it over the divider, and tells it, "Stay there or you're dead" in a tone so telling that, finally, the dog desists.

Tim is in handcuffs, an ambulance arrives, and now the Hispanic guy strolls up with "I saw the whole thin', Officer, and this guy [pointing to Tim] started it. He's some piece of trash, Officer. Dissin' everybody, threatenin' me and others I could name like he's some kind of this honcho." The Hispanic guy looks around at all of us, his arms out, nodding at us to encourage him, to chime in with affirmations. "Yeah, they all saw. And this guy—"

"This man is lying," I said, coming forward. "He's a friend of the aggressor in this fight."

"Hey, *you* lyin', you bitch, I never saw any you before. I don't know *any* these guys, lyin' prick."

Ignoring him and concentrating my gaze upon the cop, I calmly went on, "They were talking more or less cordially together when the incident occurred, so they are friends on some level. And everyone standing around here will contradict what this man says. The man who is injured allowed his dog to attack *this* man's dog, and he himself attacked the man when he protected his dog. The injured man committed assault, and the man you have in handcuffs is innocent."

The cop I was addressing, one of those seen-it-all cynics who thinks every citizen is guilty of something, didn't like me, the His-panic, either of the two dog owners, or the dogs. But my outburst energized the community, and suddenly everyone, strangely silent while the Hispanic was selling his lies, was eager to talk. At once, the cops took statements, released Tim, arrested the other guy—he didn't need the ambulance, it developed—and the Hispanic as well, for ob-structing justice, when he started screaming at one of the witnesses.

"Neat," said a voice behind me. "I call that Ivy League con-trol. Master class, my friend."

I had turned and there he was. "Peter Keene's out blading," I observed.

"You're biking. Nice hat."

"It isn't fair to mock helmets. They're not supposed to look hot, they're supposed to protect you."

He smiled, patted my shoulder apologetically, and, with a confiding look, said, "Have you noticed that palling around with lookers means you meet other lookers? As a rule, even?"

"No. I've noticed that palling around with intelligent and stimulating people means you meet other—"

"I'm dividing the whole world into categories, but there's so many of them, you know."

He was grinning, coasting around on his skates, figure-eighting and so on.

"Categories," he sang in a pleasing baritone as he slowed to a stop just behind my left ear. "Like him," he said, nudging me in the direction of a handsome young stoic of a runner in green shorts. "What do you bet he squeaks when he's fucked?"

"You just-came-out guys always act as if sex were some new invention and you owned the patent. This has all been done. It's old news."

"There's a book in it—the categories, I mean. Types. Green squeaky runner. Mambo boy. Hot nerd on ice."

"Listen well," I told him. "There are only five types—evil queen, silly queen, tearful queen, business queen, and dangerous queen."

He sat back on the concrete divider and said, "Pitch it to me."

"The evil queen is enraged and invidious. The silly queen is vapid and contentless, though he can, particularly around the age of twenty, have Looks Control. The tearful queen is dissatisfied, whiny, and always has the wrong boy friend. The business queen has his life in order, his goals identified, his attainment of them in process—"

"That's what you want to be."

"That's what I am."

"Remains to be seen, I suspect. Well, and the dangerous queen?"

"I don't know if I like you or not."

He leaned his head to one side, eyeing me quizzically as a dog does when it hears a quirky noise.

"You keep changing form," I added. "When we meet you, you're this ever-so-*up*-for-it hightown type, with the ties and hesitations. Then you're on your knees before Carlo, throwing dignity to the blust'ring wind or swallowing wave."

He raised an eyebrow at that.

"Lovelace," I said. " 'To Lucasta.' "

He nodded.

"And now," I continued, here you are with seventies muscles and nineties gear, erupting with the confident rap of a veteran."

"Well, perhaps you might think of it as business queen with dangerous queen ambitions and, oh, just a vestige of—"

"Your shorts are too sheer, your nipples are too spiked, and your eyes are too trashy." He was pooling around on his blades again, rolling where they took him. "Stop transforming yourself," I concluded. "Relax!"

"It's the long hot summer," he sang out, sailing away.

I remounted my bike to ride off, but he skated up in front of me, braking to grab my handlebars and block me.

"Okay," I said, letting him. "A few weeks ago, one of my literary protégés came to town from Louisville. We'd known each other for years by mail and phone, but at last we met. Joey was enchanted with New York—his first time, you see—and I showed him Central Park. Then he took me to a party in the deep East Village at which everyone was a zine editor in his early twenties. Except me, right. But I was in tangy shorts, a silk shirt, and dark glasses from our Park walk, so I was not entirely out of fashion. I used the expletive 'way cool' at regular intervals. I never cried out, 'What idiot chose this disgusting music? I want to hear *Flahooley*, or at least Brahms's Second!' I seemed to be, in a narrow way, part of it—and, truth to tell, I did not hear some feckless youth murmur to a friend, 'Who's Grandpa?' But it was a long party, and I drank from nine to something like five A.M., and somewhat later, I awoke in a black apartment stippled with those little red lights that everyone has but me because I don't own the new equipment."

"Dennis Savage says you use a typewriter," he reported, still in charge of my handlebars.

"And balance my checkbook on an abacus. Now, you have to understand that I was very befuddled. From video games, I know that heat-sensing lasers might toom out of the colored light holes—"

"You'd passed out and they'd all gone to bed!"

I nodded. "I felt my way along the walls to the bathroom, took a whizz, then stumbled into someone. I still have my dark glasses on in a dark apartment. I'm still befuddled. So I say Something Key to this gentleman—who I *think* was nude—and then it's later and I'm on the street hailing a cab. I got home in one piece, but the question is, What had I said to whom did I meet?"

He was smiling at me, cruising the place, and drawing conclusions, all at once.

"The next day," I said, "I found out. The guy I'd met was in fact Joey, and what I said was 'I need someone to tell me where I'm supposed to be just now.'"

Peter laughed and said, "That's so nineties."

"Whom does that concept remind you of?"

"I'm immediately due for three weeks off. You want to go biking with me some weekday in the Park? We'll be evil queens checking up on the business queens and the silly queens. Well, and the . . ."

"Tearful queens, a surprisingly common type."

"Yes, but the . . ."

"Torah queens."

". . . No . . ."

"Indignant and enfeebled yet strangely sinister queens."

"Dennis Savage promised that you'd be friendly to me in his stead."

"All right: dangerous queens. Just don't get your hopes up."

"How about Tuesday, eleven A.M., at the Sixtieth Street entrance, by the Zoo? Rain date Thursday. I'll make you like me."

"You're on," I said, and he let me go.

We were both prompt, and the day was so glowing that New York felt like Prince Valiant's castle. It took us two minutes to reach the summit of the hill that gives on to the loop encircling the Park, and already Peter had cruised nine men and a dalmatian.

"Look," I said, as we waited for the light to change, "don't you ever turn it off?"

"Carlo says you get the best sex hot off the street."

The light changed, and we chugged into the roadway. About three pedal revolutions later, Peter was staring at four workers one hundred feet to the east engaged in repaving the pathways. They were shirtless in the heat, and one of them was a looker, but Peter was silent till we reached the Seventy-second Street transverse.

"Can we cut around again?" he asked.

So we bent back along the lower subloop, and when we reached the workers again I led Peter off the road onto the grass so he could fill his eyes—because otherwise I'd know no peace. As we dismounted, I said, "Let me show you how this is done. No, don't look yet. The rules are: One, Don't let him know you're watching him. Two, Don't let *any* of them know you're watching him. Three, Both of us cannot watch at the same time. Four, We have to appear to be in conversation, idly glancing this way and that. Got me? Now, *you* look. Before he senses it and catches you, calmly turn back to me."

Peter was already looking.

"Describe him," I said.

"A little less than average height, straight black hair, slightly exotic features, unbe*liev*able bod. Twenty- . . . six?"

"Now me," I said as Peter turned away. "Nice smile, hair in bangs, I haven't seen that look in . . . Quiet, friendly, extremely excellent V-slope in the torso, just enough hair across the chest to inspire confidence, pinprick navel . . ."

"The jeans ride quite low on his hips," Peter went on, as I pretended to adjust something inside my helmet. "That's a lovely look. Very sweet face . . . Slavic?"

"Czech," I put in, bending down to check the gearshift.

"Marco is his name. Or Anton. He has an enchanting accent, in which he tells impenetrable jokes about life in America."

"Married," I said.

"Don't be too sure."

"What you wish, and what is likely to be true, are not necessarily the same thing."

"How long can we keep cruising?" he asked, turning back to me.

"Provided we don't burn a hole in him with the fire in our contemplation, we could quite naturally lay our bikes on the grass and sit like picnickers, covertly drinking him in. That is, if you haven't had enough."

"I never have enough."

So we did that, taking in our man as he trucked stone blocks in a wheelbarrow. We had ideal vantage, close enough to discern but distant enough to seem uninterested.

"We have to at least pretend to be conversing," I told him, breaking into his reverie.

"Why is it that a man who is half-dressed," Peter offered, "is sexier than a man who is naked?"

"It's the juxtaposition of symbols and the tension of contexts," I answered, missing Dennis Savage. He would love this. "As middle-class observers, we perceive the jeans and clodhopper shoes he's wearing as working-class—virile, iconically uncivilized. Pure sexy. A woman of his own class would say, Gee, he's cute. To us, it's way past cute. It's redemptive. We seek his erotic power to enrich our own paltry sense of ecstasy."

"I don't believe a word of it! And I wish you'd speak for yourself."

"Then there's this thing about hot men going shirtless in the city. All right, we're in the green world—but Fifth Avenue is a minute away by foot. The city is civilization. Civilization is clothes, façades, protection."

Staring at the worker, Peter was listening so hard the tips of his ears were clenched.

"So," I continued, "to go half-dressed in the city is to be half-formed in civilization. Open, uncovered. Natural. Real. On a beach, a man in Speedos is axiomatic. In the city, a man in jeans is incendiary. It's a matter of how one reads the text."

"That is . . . I must say, it's the most—"

"He sees us."

Peter, turning to see, ventriloquisted, "Are you sure he's cruising *us*?"

"I'm not sure he's cruising. But he's definitely got a bead on us."

"He's so beautiful. I want him. How do I get him?"

"You spoke the history of gay life in three sentences."

"What would Carlo do?"

"Oh, Rip would get him. He never fails."

One of the other workers approached our man with some distraction, and the two of them went off to another part of the site.

"But," I warned him, "you have to be Rip-tough to do that. Some of these guys—"

"I need a hook."

"I hope we're joking."

"I'm not . . . maybe . . ."

I shrugged. "Catch him at quitting time. You live nearby—if he wants a shower or a beer . . ."

"Good Lord, am I capable of this? Do . . . well, do you know a lot of men who would . . . try to pick him up?"

"Yes, a lot, over the years. But I feel bound to point out that almost none of them was, like you and me, educated."

"What does that mean?"

"Maybe civilization has a drawback."

We considered our dream man: laughing at a colleague's sally, resting, working his wheelbarrow. At odd moments, he looked at us, but it was never more than a glance.

"I don't know what it is," Peter said. "I've been in the city for over a decade. I must have passed a thousand like him. I scarcely . . . Why is it suddenly . . . Well, I just feel that he could give me some speck of information that I . . . If he could apprise me . . ."

"'I need someone to tell me where I'm supposed to be just now.'"

He said, "Oh. *I'm* the one you think that's about."

About a week later, Virgil and Cosgrove had just got in another load of proofs and were taking inventory when I came in from a downtown run to the Strand Bookstore with a very successful haul: a mint copy of the anthology edition of E. F. Benson's *Lucia* novels (easy to find but almost always in decrepit condition); the sumptuous John Ardoin–Gerry Fitzgerald Callas book (one of the rarest items on the resale circuit—no one voluntarily parts with it, and it's said that the disposition of an owner's copy is a routine feature of the gay will); and a forgotten Patrick Dennis novel that a friend had asked me to pick up for him. I detail the transaction in case some sociology professor wants to know what gay men read.

"Hey, kids," I said.

"Better hide everything," Cosgrove muttered.

"I don't care if he sees," Virgil answered.

"Okay," I said. "What's going on?"

"No, show him," said Virgil.

Cosgrove gave him his "You'll be sorry" look and handed me a series of snaps devoted to Peter and me cruising the road worker.

"Jeepers!" I said. "Where *were* you?"

"We're the Photo Snoops," said Virgil, in the tone that the American lieutenant must have used when he spoke of destroying a Vietnamese village in order to save it.

Then Cosgrove passed me another series, this one closing in on the worker himself, washing up at a fountain, leaving the Park, entering the subway.

"Boy, you're thorough," I said.

Now Cosgrove handed me views of Peter and the worker talking.

So he *did* make a move, the pirate!

Yes, and snaps of Peter and the worker having hot dogs at the cart by the band shell. (It was a different day, because Peter's shorts had changed from blue to red.) And snaps of them sharing a joke. (Yet another day.) And snaps of them walking out of the Park together on the West Side, where Peter lives. And snaps of them on the street. And snaps of them entering Peter's building.

"This cannot be," I said. "It isn't real."

"Virgil," said Cosgrove, "how rich can we get as the Photo Snoops?"

"We'll never be rich," Virgil grumped. "All our pictures come out wrong. We can't even find celebrities. You wasted a whole film on a bunch of high-school girls coming out of the Limelight!"

"I thought they were Madonna," Cosgrove pleaded.

"There's not enough ambition around here!" Virgil went on, as Cosgrove reddened and saddened. "All this lollygagging is getting us nowhere. We keep getting these great ideas, but nothing happens!"

"Maybe they aren't great ideas," I said, gently.

Fuming, Virgil collected his photos and left like an Avignon Pope storming out of a session with the Holy Roman Emperor.

"What's he so jumpy about?" I asked.

"I told you, he's like that sometimes. He's impatient with me." Cosgrove's eyes moistened. "He can be like parents."

I held him for a bit.

"How about we rustle up some BLTs and then I take you to a movie?" I asked.

"Okay," he said, a touch lamely.

We never got out; halfway through the sandwiches, we had a call from Carlo, who'd been arrested for soliciting and had to be bailed out. Anyway, *Jeopardy!* was coming on.

"What's 'soliciting'?" Cosgrove asked as I made ready to leave.

"Saying yes to someone over fifty."

"Cosgrove's Life for four hundred," said Cosgrove, settling in before the television.

"English Literature for a hundred."

And Alex Trebek read out—but who cares? Cosgrove announced the answer as "Virgil," then answered the question as "Who was mean to Cosgrove today."

I headed off to the cash machine for Carlo's bail money, thinking that Virgil was slacking in a quality I especially prize: loyalty.

"He crumbled like Jericho," Peter was telling me. He was cool and happy, but he was pacing my apartment like a cornered bear. Every so often he glanced at Cosgrove, apparently gone from the temporal world as he listened to CDs through his headphones on the far side of the room. "First, he's the young husband and father of two little ones, with those pictures they carry in their wallet. Then . . . he's mine."

"I keep hearing these stories about straight men—or, at any rate, married men—getting fucked, and I don't know where to turn."

"If you could only see him as he lets me lay him out on the bed. The way he sighs as he turns his head, or the incredible stillness as I spread his legs for greasing up, bit by bit, left leg, right leg, slowly, inch by . . . trusting, he is. The slow dividing of his . . ."

"The sages are right," I said. "Women are romantics and men are fetishists. Was he Czech after all?"

"Russian. *Konstantin,*" he uttered, with some baloney concerto of an accent. "His English is very halting and primitive, and that makes him seem dumb, which . . ." He was watching me, to see how violently I might resent this next observation. "Well, it can be very attractive on some men."

"So you just ambled up to him and—"

"Please! It was a painstaking courtship, step by step. A little more each day. And right from the start, it was clear that he knew what this was about. He . . . well, yes, he knew I wanted him, and he let me woo him. Even his buddies seemed to know. They'd laugh and whistle at him when I showed up. Isn't it funny? When you're closeted, most of the world seems straight. When you come out, *everyone* turns out to be gay!"

Coasgrove, I noticed, had quietly taken off the headphones, to listen, though he had not moved or even shifted his gaze.

"He's sweet, though," Peter went on, joining me on the couch. "He . . . depends on you. He needs to learn. Perhaps he regards me as part of his Americanization. Oh, he's so tender and open." Rapt in his fondness, Peter waxed metaphorical. "He has the flavor of an early Diebenkorn."

"Didn't the fact that he's married . . ."

"What? Turn me on in extra ways?"

"'Make you feel guilty?' was what I had in mind. Whatever happens, three innocent people are caught up in this."

Curious, he said, "You. Dennis Savage? And—"

"His wife and kids!"

"Well, you oughtn't be mad at me. It's *society* that—"

"No, it's cowards like your Konstantin who create these problems. No—okay, yes. Societies are tough on gays. But *I* came out without victimizing a woman, and Dennis Savage came out without victimizing—"

"He won't let me use a condom."

I was speechless, and really angry now.

"Most guys won't," he went on.

"And you don't tell them, 'I will use a condom or I won't fuck you'?"

"Of course . . . Well . . . Yes, but how is one to turn down a so very luscious coupling just because—"

"*Just because?* Do you want to die and kill people? Is *that* what? Listen—"

"Yes, it's Skullamask, headmaster of hell," Cosgrove cried as he jumped up to confront Peter with octopus fingers. "His greeting card is love, but his touch is death and fire! He has the flavor of early chicken corn and the color of a South Sea isle, but beware! *Beware Skullamask!*"

Peter, scandalized, possibly because Cosgrove was not only chanting but dancing and creeping, said, "Kindly tell your live-in to chill out."

"The death god lurks and spies, spreading his wicked ways from near, from far. The pumpkin monster distributes sweet candies to the little children, who immediately blow up in a minty shower."

"Cosgrove," I said, "cool it."

"I'm not Cosgrove," he replied, treading fantastical steps as he neared me, "I'm Skullamask, the Pumpkin Lord."

"You're Cosgrove and cut it out," I told him, pulling out my ever-ready X-Men pocket folding comb, a necessary item in my summer of constant bike rides. He stood still, letting me comb his hair. "Apologize to our guest, or at least make some grudging concession."

"'I call myself Phoebe,'" Cosgroved darkly uttered.

"That shows a good heart," I told Peter. "He's willing to meet you halfway."

"I'm willing to feed on his liver," Cosgrove cried, "at casual midnight suppers!"

"Cosgrove," I warned him; and Peter said, "There's something very, very wrong about that—"

"Don't insult him when I'm in the room," I told Peter. "Don't ever do that. Because the young man and I have bonded." I turned to Cosgrove. "Right?"

"I walk between raindrops and spit butterflies of poison at the good little—"

"How would you like no allowance this week?"

He finally melted back into Cosgrove, and went into the kitchen for a cleanup.

Peter said, "I wonder if that's what you mean by the term 'dangerous queen.'"

"You're luring a man away from his wife and children, and you think *Cosgrove's* a—"

"Yes, but *I* don't attack—"

"'Homewrecker,' I believe, is what straights call—"

"If it's this easy to wreck a home, surely there can't be much of a home to—"

"Saved by the bell again!" I said, as the phone rang. It was Dennis Savage. "Everyone's getting arrested or going crazy or degrading the social contract," I informed him. "How are you? Get home quick, because everything's coming apart!"

COULD YOU
PASS IN LOVE?

All stories should have a beginning, a middle, and an end, ideally in that order; but this story has two beginnings, and here's the first one:

I can always tell when fall arrives, because the Quarto Society mails out its annual prospectus. This is my English book club: quite beautifully turned editions of classics and curiosities, from Procopius to *Cold Comfort Farm,* bound now in morocco, now in silk, and often lavishly illustrated. Aquatints! Engravings! *Three Men in a Boat* with map endpapers charting the voyage! An atlas that Gibbon might have consulted while tracing the fall of Rome! Then, too, a quarterly magazine of the Higher Brit Literacy, with the reassuring spellings of "theatre" and "honour" that my high-school English teachers favored, completes the experience.

Each fall, members accept various giveaways and buy four titles from the year's new offerings or from the backlist. Because my library is already pretty extensive, I don't usually want four books—so Cosgrove suggested that he launch his own Quarto library with one volume of my four, and we've been doing that ever since. As with his CDs, he makes a big occasion of it, poring over the club's many brochures and catalogs (plus the magazines), all of which I've saved over the years.

Then come the questions: "How scary is *Nightmare Abbey*?" "How could Gibbon write about the Roman empire a thousand years after it went away?" "Would I like *Love in a Cold Climate*?" "Why would someone be called 'Damon Runyon,' because it sounds like a fish poem?"

Anyway, I know it's fall; and I also know that Virgil and Cosgrove will drop whatever they were doing (such as the Photo Snoops) and take up a new diversion, which, this year, turned out to be the Sex Survey, a question-and-answer poll that they would conduct and then sell to "the networks" for a fortune.

It was Cosgrove's idea; Virgil, at first, balked. But pep talks from Dennis Savage and me—and, especially, my intense warning that Cosgrove was counting on him—persuaded Virgil to sign on, and the two of them cooked up an interview form, which they unveiled at Peter Keene's dinner party.

Here was a first for our new gayomaniac friend: an evening with a guest list drawing exclusively upon homosexual males. I'd been to plenty such parties, of course, but every so often Peter gazed about himself in a perplexed sort of way, like Mother Teresa at a convention of Arian heretics.

"I went to college with most of the men in this room," he whispered to me at one point, "yet suddenly I don't understand half their conversation. For instance, what's the Mineshaft?"

Cosgrove came up to have his hair combed in our new ritual, very useful in soothing him when he goes ballistic.

"How little we know our own friends," Peter went on, as a neatened Cosgrove sauntered off. "Well, I mean, when we're closeted, how little. Because now I see all the fun they were having behind my back. Wait, where is he?—yes, *that* one [he pointed to Greg, a tweedy fellow holding forth at the center of a riotous group] has been here six or seven times, and *every time* he had a date with him! A *girl date!*"

"Deep, deep," I commented, "runs the hoax of the closet."

It was rather a large gathering for a dinner party, but Dennis Savage had given Peter the recipe for Forty Spices Meat Loaf and Bavarian Potato Stew, which, with a Caesar salad and Tiramisù Cake, serves twelve. Peter has one of those weird New York apartments shaped like a drunken corral, but it has a sizable living-room section, so we filled our plates buffet-style and sat around on chairs or the carpet as Virgil and Cosgrove made their presentation. Armed with clipboards and pens perched behind the ear, they were in their suits for that managerial look, Cosgrove sporting my Nicole Miller cartoon tie that everyone mistakes for a Roz Chast and that gives him tremendous confidence.

"Now, each guest will have his own copy to take home and fill out," Virgil announced. "But let us explore some sample questions. If someone in the audience would . . . Ah, you, sir," he said, heading toward Dennis Savage.

"A little too much of the basil and tarragon," Dennis Savage called out to Peter, about the meat loaf. "But masterly on the turmeric." I believe this is called "stalling."

"Yes, if you will, sir," Virgil insisted, as Dennis Savage tried to look as if he were in downtown St. Louis. "We'll start at the top and run through—"

"Why don't you go around the room?" I suggested. "Then everyone gets a chance."

The others, especially Dennis Savage, chorused out yeses, so Cosgrove, happy with his forms at the center of attention, directed a question to Lanning, one of Peter's old college buddies. (Princeton, what else?)

" 'What sex act have you never tried?' "

Hesitating, Lanning lost the floor to Greg, who exclaimed, "I've never rimmed a Martian! No, wait, there was that night in—"

"How about you?" Virgil asked Dennis Savage.

"How about *what* me?"

"Shouldn't you be answering the question, so gently and true?"

Watching the two of them and sensing that something was up, Peter said, "I can't wait to take the test."

"Then *you* answer him" was Dennis Savage's suggestion.

Peter looked expectant, so Virgil turned to him and read out, " 'Would you characterize yourself as (a) monogamous, (b) promiscuous, or (c) a lonely masturbating troll?' "

Lanning let out a low whistle, and Carlo said, "They play for keeps around here."

"Now you," Virgil prompted Dennis Savage.

"I want my own question."

Cosgrove popped up with " 'As the head of a home for wayward boys, you enforce discipline by (a) delegating the responsibility to hall monitors, (b) personally conducting all-nude paddling sessions, (c) choosing the three most lovely—' "

"Stop!" Dennis Savage commanded. "This is not socialized behavior."

"Food's good," said Carlo, and there were general noises of assent.

"Give him a simple one," Virgil told Cosgrove.

"Okay. The first question in the whole form is 'Describe your coupling status.'"

Dennis Savage grumbled, "It'll be 'merry widow' in about two minutes."

"Very funny," said Virgil.

"Why don't we all play at once?" Greg asked. "Just throw the questions out and everyone will take a shot."

Cries of "Yes," and a "Hear, hear" from Peter.

So the kids fired them out. "Name the three most attractive men in history," for instance; and everyone had a bash at that, followed by stimulating little controversies. And there was "You are invited to appear in a porn movie with any partner of your choice. (A) Name your co-star, and (b) What acts do you perform?" That provoked a very cascade of answers. There was an amusing moment when at the question "Have you ever hustled?" everyone looked at Carlo and he said, "Not only hustled, I got busted for it last month. But they dropped the charges." There was a tender moment, when Cosgrove read out "Who was the person you most wanted and never had?" and Peter's Princeton crew sighed, exchanged glances, and, as one man, murmured, "Oakley Enders." This turned out to be the captain of the lacrosse team or something.

Anyway, we continued investigating the questionnaire in a lighthearted manner, though Virgil kept eyeing Dennis Savage with a touch of menace; and then we all went to Peter's piano and sang the Beatles songbook while Peter, Dennis Savage, and Carlo straightened the place up and the kids huddled in a corner discussing our answers to their questions. At length, we'd gone into overtime, and the Princeton group and Carlo left en masse. So the rest of us took a last glass of wine and sat down to dish the event.

"You know," said Peter, "this whole thing is really about the tension between what you get in life and what you really wanted instead."

Dennis Savage, looking at Virgil, quietly sang, to a strain from *Follies:*

> Beavis wants to do what Butt-head does,
> Butt-head wants to be what Beavis was.

"Well, now, what do you fresh young entrepreneurs intend with this survey of yours?" Peter asked them.

"We'll sell it to *Hard Copy,*" said Cosgrove.

"One question we never got to ask," said Virgil, "is 'What do you fear most?'"

"What's that doing in a sex survey?" asked Dennis Savage.

"I knew you'd evade it."

"Oh, but I wonder, though," said Peter. "Well, truly, this tension we speak of. Does it . . . Do straights have the same problem?"

"Speaking of that," I said, "did you consider asking your new boy friend to the party?"

"Yes, wasn't I *dying* to show him off, at least? But I knew Carlo would . . . well, he'd steal Konstantin from me. No—no, he couldn't stop himself."

There was a pause, which Cosgrove enlivened by blowing bubbles in his wine while humming "What I Did for Love." Virgil, who usually sings along, was silent.

"You know, Konstantin is very intrigued by . . . well, how we live. He asks such questions! I took him by the office, and my breakfast place and . . . well, didn't I show him your building?"

"Where we live?" Dennis Savage asked. "Why?"

"What is it?" Peter went on. "A sexual thing? A social thing? Or both? Could he be using sex to . . . become smarter? He wants to know everyone's name. My friends. My boss, even."

"Maybe he's after your job," I said.

"Am I in love with him? How would one know?" He seemed urgent about it. "How would one *know?*"

I said, "That's a question they should put in the sex survey."

Cosgrove was playing with his zipper; Virgil was returning Dennis Savage's stare. I got up to signal everyone that it was time to leave Peter Keene's apartment.

"I know there are questions and answers," said Peter, rising with me. The others ignored us. "It seems so *even,* yes, but then it's so deep and one is wondering, and how would one know?"

That's the story's first beginning. The second beginning, which happened at the same time as the first, took off when Cosgrove returned from the barbershop virtually bald. In my generation, you figured out Your Best Look by about age nineteen, and that style you maintained for life. To Cosgrove's generation, hair is like clothing: part of the fashion statement, ever subject to change. This time, Cosgrove decided on a high-concept buzz cut; in my day, we called it "falling asleep in the barber chair."

Boys and girls, can I let you in on a little fashion tip? *Nobody looks good without hair.*

Besides—as I pointed out to Cosgrove the moment he came in—his near scalping made him extremely vulnerable to remarks from Dennis Savage, who had smarted under Cosgrove's jokes about *his* trendy haircut.

"I forgot about that!" cried Cosgrove, in a panic.

And "Here he comes now," I added: for the doorbell rang to announce a visit I'd been greatly looking forward to, that of Dennis Savage's sister's children, Monica and Alfie, who were staying with their uncle for a week while their parents toured Europe. Cosgrove raced into the bedroom to find a hat as Dennis Savage paraded in with his charges. Monica, age nine, was too hip and contemptuous of everything for my taste, but Alfie, five, was still enchanted and fascinating, a miniature human being who had not yet learned to select what to show of himself and was therefore guileless, trusting, and touchingly vulnerable.

"At first I didn't want to come," Alfie told me. "Because

Gramma Tomjoy is sending me a T-Rex, and it could come any day now. A *real* T-Rex!"

"No, Alfie," said Monica.

"Yes, it is, too, real. Gramma Tomjoy sent it by parcel post!"

With the disgusted patience of a princess correcting a gauche but well-connected courtier, Monica told him, "You can't send animals through the mail even if this *was* a live T-Rex, and this can't be because there *aren't* any!"

"Yes, it *is* coming," Alfie replied, growing unhappy, though Cosgrove's reentrance, in my New York City Opera baseball cap, proved a helpful distraction. Cosgrove and Alfie hit it off immediately, especially when it turned out they shared a passion for Rice Krispies treats, though neither had ever actually eaten or even seen one.

"That's baby food," Monica pointed out, giving Cosgrove a second look. "You cook it off the back of a *cereal* box! Aren't you too old for baby food?"

Cosgrove glanced at me to see how bold he was permitted to get in, uh, debate with Monica, but suddenly Alfie, sensing an ally in Cosgrove, asked him, "Isn't a T-Rex a live animal?"

"Yes," said Cosgrove. "I know several."

"You *do*? I'm getting a T-Rex of my own! From Gramma Tomjoy? I'm going to take it to school with me, so if those big boys try to harm me . . ."

"Be sure he's carefully trained first," Cosgrove advised him. "A T-Rex can get quite rowdy, you know."

Monica said, "There . . . is . . . no . . . such—"

"Eat shit and die, you sluthead," said Cosgrove, which had Monica thunderously silent, Alfie in awe, and Dennis Savage tut-tutting.

"Try to play nice, children," he urged, and I reminded Cosgrove that Monica was, after all, a guest in our home. Mistake: Because Cosgrove, feeling betrayed, whipped the cap off to clock me one with it and Dennis Savage instantly seized upon Cosgrove's haircut with a glad little cry.

"Is someone auditioning for *The Yul Brynner Story,* I wonder?" he asked.

"All right," I said, "no jokes about haircuts, at least till Monica and Alfie leave. And don't give me that whimsical look. We have
to show a united air of authority with all these people of revolutionary age around. No divisiveness."

Dennis Savage made a vaguely concurring gesture as Alfie told
Cosgrove, "I don't trust haircuts, but can I wear your cap now?"
Cosgrove gave it to him, and Alfie beamed. "I'm all grown up," he
said.

In fact, Alfie adopted Cosgrove, even hauling his sleeping bag
downstairs to spend the nights with us. The next morning, I'd find
him and Cosgrove preparing breakfast together, Alfie walking
around in the bag like a manta ray floating through an aquarium.

"It's nice and toasty like this," he explained.

For his part, Cosgrove found himself, for the first time ever,
with an adherent looking up to him, and the experience was a
heady one. They became inseparable, Alfie tagging along on Cosgrove's chores as Cosgrove lectured on matters of both spiritual and
temporal nature. Cosgrove never patronized Alfie or answered a
question with "You're too young to understand" or told him he
couldn't have seconds on Frozfruit pops. Alfie was especially captivated by Cosgrove's whoopee cushion (which I had hid, this time
so ingeniously that it must have taken Cosgrove a whole twenty-
eight seconds before he found it), not least when they passed a slow
morning stalking, and at length bagging, the wary Monica.

Dennis Savage referred to the two children as "i nevodi,"
which is Venetian dialect for a word that English lacks, meaning
"sibling's progeny of either gender." They were the darlings of the
building, Monica becoming the toast of the doormen's lunch room
and Alfie intimately befriending Silver Prince, the Highland White
in 8-C. This was handy, for it meant we could occasionally park i
nevodi with neighbors—as we did, for instance, the night of Peter's
dinner party.

Otherwise, Cosgrove kept Alfie busy and Monica was a constant reader. Still, there were times when Dennis Savage and I had to drop everything and entertain them, particularly on one rainy afternoon when the television was empty and both nevodi rebelled against another of my Oz readings.

"I can see I must tell a story," said Cosgrove, moving in like Johnny Carson for the opening monologue. "Perhaps a tale of the Whistling Candymouse of Summertown."

"The what?" said Dennis Savage.

"There . . . is . . . no . . . such—"

"This would be the episode," Cosgrove went on, as he settled in on the couch between Alfie and Monica, "in which Alfie meets the Candymouse."

"Yes!" cried Alfie. "Was *I* there?"

"It's all so fake," said Monica.

"And yet," said Cosgrove. "One fine day, Alfie went off to school—"

"He doesn't go to school yet," Monica put in.

"I *do* go, to kindergarten!"

"Kindergarten isn't school," retorted Monica, with withering scorn. "Kindergarten is nothing but napping and snacks." She'll make a great Lady Bracknell in fifty years.

"Now," Cosgrove continued, "Alfie's mother warned him, 'Don't *ever* go near the den of the Candymouse.'"

"He's in the *den*?" echoed Alfie, with wonder.

"It's not like our den," Monica explained. "It's his lair."

"I watch *X-Men* in the den."

"But there can be no TV in the Candymouse's den," said Cosgrove. "Instead, we see a table piled to the grim with candy of every kind, and cookies of such sweet liberation, yes, and every sort of caramel cream and Lady Gucci."

"Godiva," Dennis Savage corrected, in a mild manner.

"You can smell the Candymouse's candy horde for miles around. But if that's not enough to draw you in, the Candymouse whistles for you. And once you hear his whistle—"

"What is he like?" asked Alfie.

"Oh, you don't want to know the Candymouse."

"I'm staying home that day."

"But this was the day when Alfie had to pass the Candymouse's den. And Alfie *tried* to be good. But the Candymouse whistled at Alfie, and who can resist?"

Monica gave a sniff of disbelief, and Dennis Savage told her, "Fairy tales are for everyone, Monica."

"It's so made up," she complained.

"All fairy tales are. And they're all true."

Monica, who had long since picked up on (and sternly approved of) Dennis Savage's opposition to Cosgrove, gave her uncle a funny look, even as the storyteller had pressed on:

"Alfie heard the whistle, and he couldn't help but peep into the Candymouse's den. There he saw the treasure trove of candy, so beautiful and tasty. He thought he might grab an exquisite shell candy and slip away. But then he saw a lollipop squirrel and Almond Joy dolls and the most dainty little rim candies, and Alfie began to feast and feast at the Candymouse's table.

"Suddenly, as he was biting the head off a chocolate milkmaid, he sensed something behind him. Alfie turned. And there was the Candymouse."

"That's when I left," said Alfie.

"But Alfie's *couldn't* leave, for the Candymouse had put a spell on him." Here Cosgrove went into a raspy, gnarly Candymouse voice: "'You ate my candy, little one, and now you must pay the bill!'"

"I didn't eat anything," Alfie cried.

"'You will go down the trapdoor to the Zookoo's kitchen and be cooked into delicious candy morsels, like so many children before you. That chocolate milkmaid was Lisa Brownstein of New Rochelle. She blundered into my den, too, and she ended up in the Zookoo's kitchen.'"

"Insipid," said Monica scornfully, bemusing Dennis Savage

and catching Cosgrove, who was ignorant of her meaning, off guard.

"Monica's awfully advanced for nine," I ventured, and Dennis Savage preened with "It's quite genetic, they say."

"I want more story," said Alfie.

"So," Cosgrove went on, "the Candymouse moved closer and closer as Alfie backed away. How could he escape?"

"He calls for his T-Rex!"

"No. He grabbed the edge of the table and said, 'Candymouse, I will throw this table over and destroy all your lovely candy if you don't let me go!' The Candymouse hopped up and down in fury. But even *he* had to admit that there *was* one way out of his den. *One way only*. [The rasping again:] 'You must give up candy *forever*! One lick and you will instantly become a prisoner of the Candymouse!'"

"That does it," said Alfie. "I'm staying."

"In the *Candymouse's den*?"

"I'm not giving up M&M's. And what about Halloween?"

"*This* is the *most* completely *stupid* story I have *ever* heard," Monica declared, with an emphasis that, lest one dare offend one's readers with a failure of verisimilitude, would have to be characterized as "titanic."

"You must forever give up candy," Cosgrove insisted. "Or there's no escape from the Zookoo's kitchen."

"I *won't*!"

"Alfie," said Monica, "it's *just* some dumb *story*!"

"Uncle Cosgrove, please don't make me give up—"

"What did I just hear?" said Dennis Savage, apparently coming out of a trance. "Uncle *what*?"

His expression betokened the destabilizing terror of haircut jokes, so I hustled us all off to the Park for a carousel ride.

"Where's Virgil, anyway?" I asked Dennis Savage as we started off.

He shrugged.

"I thought you were always—"

"We always used to be. Checking in, you mean. 'I'm off to the store.' 'I'll be back in two shakes.' Yes. Yes, we were."

We walked a bit, i nevodi, ahead of us, dancing in and out of the great New York street crowd.

"Yes, we were," he repeated, at Madison and Fifty-eighth. "Lately he's become kind of independent."

All right, now comes the middle; and I'll get right to it. This is a few days later, the last afternoon before i nevodi were to return to Toronto, and I came into the apartment to find a strange man sitting on the couch. He rose expectantly as Cosgrove, doing the dishes in the kitchen, called out, "This guy's a friend of Peter Keene's. He said it was important, so could he wait for you."

The man didn't look like a friend of Peter Keene's. He looked like a construction worker fresh from the site, and of course then I suddenly realized who it was.

Konstantin.

"Cosgrove," I said, "why don't you go upstairs and see what Alfie's up to?"

He came out of the kitchen drying his hands. "Can I take the Risk? I want to teach Alfie how to play."

"He's too young for Risk, but anything, anything."

I turned to our guest as Cosgrove went into the bedroom. "Tak vi Konstantin," I said, offering my hand. You must be Konstantin.

As we shook, he said, "No vi nye govoritye pa-russki?" You speak Russian?

"Ya izuchal Russki yazik v shkolye i v univyersityetye." I took it in school.

Actually, I was only being hostly. My Russian is decrepit these days; besides, I was curious to hear the charmingly lame English that Peter had so often described to me.

"Okay, folks, I'm on my way," Cosgrove called out, heading for the door with the game under his arm.

"A kto on?" Konstantin asked as Cosgrove vanished. Who is he?

How does one explain who Cosgrove is?

"You know," I said, "we'd better speak English, because my Russian is . . . Please sit down. Did Cosgrove offer you . . ."

"He give this," said Konstantin, pointing out an open Beck's dark.

"Khorasho." Fine.

It was interesting seeing him up close for once. Some men are arresting only at a distance, but Konstantin's smart eyes and melting mouth gave him presence; and, too, there was that odd feeling you get when socializing in clothes with someone who is possibly unaware that you've seen him half-naked. You note the pec line in his T-shirt, rising and falling with his breathing, and you think, I know about that.

"Why I visit is, wanting to talk you," Konstantin said, by way of plunging in. "Pityer say you know about this secret thing. He take me before this building, say his friends live here and know. Is whole life for us. Like in Ukraina, Gruziya. Each these place has life different from our great always Russian life. Under the life you see is *other life,* you know?"

I nodded.

"Pityer say, of my family, would I . . ." A gesture of negation. "Ostavlyat?" Abandon.

"Da. Ostavlyat syemyu." Abandon my family.

"He asked you to leave your—"

"Not to do it. Only, do I think of it? This, never. *Never* this." He touched my wrist, asking, "Is permitted? To show pictures? Here is Alyosha i Masha."

"Konyechna." Of course.

His kids were really cute, the boy a feisty four-year-old in a baseball uniform and the girl just walking at a year and a half.

"Here is at wedding," he went on, with more pictures, "perhaps of cousin Syeryozha. Who would go away from loving children, such these? Each day, when I come home, they run up to touch, they hold on so close. They say, 'Oi, I miss you all day till now, Batyushka.' So perfect in love, these children, and I would go? How is it to ask this question?"

I was thinking, *This* is a father? This bundle of tender considerations, barely old enough to drive a car? He's heavy in the chest and tight in the waist and his kids are so lucky.

"You are not pleased I come here? Nye kulturni?" Crass of me?

"No, it's fine," I said, reassuring him with a pat on my favorite hunk terrain, the shoulder caps. "But I feel you want to learn something from me. Something specific."

"Yes. Pityer say how . . . certain people in U.S.A. [which he pronounced as "Oo Ess Ah"] live free. No fake . . . fooling others. No fear of . . . nasyedki?"

I didn't know the word.

"They report on you to authorities," he said.

"Shpioni?" Spies?

"Less than spies, but also everywhere. Going around with tales. No one was safe, that was Russia. Now is Oo Ess Ah, old style no more. Svoboda!" Freedom! "But what is, freedom? Pityer say you, what we do? He say me you know this. Pityer and I, together, alone, safe from nasyedki, in bed?" He was blushing. "He say you?"

I nodded.

"What you think of this, that I permit?"

"If you like it," I offered, "you do it. If you don't like it, you don't do it."

"Oh, yes? But *why* I like? How I answer when Alyosha ask, 'Batyushka, what you do with this man that I do not see? Why you need this?'"

He was looking at me, hard, beseechingly.

"Pityer say you are smart, you know the answers."

"I only know the questions, actually."

"All men do this? Moi father, *he* did? *Your*?"

"Some do, some don't."

"You not help me. Please. To . . . explain it?"

"Konstantin . . . kak vas pa batyushkye?" What's your father's name?

"Ilya."

"Konstantin Ilyitch," I said, going into the formal Russian address, "nobody knows how sex works. The laws of culture"—I shot that into Russian as best I could—"confuse us all. Some *must* have it. Some think they might try it. Some hope they don't need it, the ridiculous fools. Because all of them desperately want it."

"To want it *into* you? To be down-face, ya khachu, you put it to me all full? *Why* I want this?" He seemed bewildered, pleading, accepting of his actions but not of his motivations. "Why a man wants this?"

"You tell me."

"*I* would tell? Does a woman tell? My, wife, these many times? She so enjoy to be . . . you know? Not from behind, as with Pityer and me. Is regular way, as in marriage always of man and woman. From behind would hurt her, I *never* would. So, we are loving, and she say—*says*—'Oh, my Stizha, when you do this! Yes, yes!' With cries out of happiness. I think, what this? Why it so pleases? How would this feel to Konstantin? Then Pityer . . . he *says*, just to try it, why not? I permit him, like woman. Am I ashamed, you ask? How can I help? Do I not also want love, someone to do such yes, yes! to *me*?"

"In the future," I said, "everyone will be fucked for fifteen minutes."

"I should feel shame to say this to you."

"But you don't."

He shook his head with a mildly apologetic smile.

"Well, there's no shame in it. But Peter told me you won't let him use a rubber."

"Shto eta?" What's that?

I explained the condom thing, and he reacted as if I'd suggested leaving the windows open in fourteenth-century Florence during the plague.

"This crazy American . . . *mashini*?"

"It isn't crazy. It is protection from a terrifying disease that you might call down not only upon yourself but upon this family that you love so much."

I was speaking slowly and he was staring at my mouth as one who is deaf and needs visual aid.

"Anyway," I went on, "do you really think you can balance this 'other' life with your family? You can't—and you know why? You're too good-looking to take a sample here and a sample there. Everywhere you turn will be a Peter Keene signaling to you. You will be *widely* wanted, do you understand me? It is hard enough to turn down opportunity when you are closeted, but once you start saying yes, you'll never stop. You know why? Because it's so good. It's not just playful temptation; it is life itself. What do you fear most?"

"What this means?" he asked, startled.

"Shto vy boityes bolshe vsyevo?"

"Da, da . . . anything bad happen to my family. That is great fear."

"Then you must renounce candy forever."

He looked confused, as well he might—but then, who am I to tell people what to do with their lives?

I was trying to restate my position in simpler English when Cosgrove stormed in, his features set. He went into the kitchen and came out brandishing the bread knife.

"Bozhe!" said Konstantin. "Yesli Rasputina zakolili etam nozhom, on pravdiva umyer." If they'd used *that* knife on Rasputin, he'd *really* be dead.

"What's with the cutlery?" I asked Cosgrove, by way of calling him back.

"A certain Dennis Savage has called me 'Auschwitzhead' for the last time. I'll show him who's queen of the meat rack!"

Where does he *get* that stuff? Oh, of course, from Miss Faye. "Let's put down the knife," I said, "because—"

"This your friend?" Konstantin asked me. "Your love friend?"

"I wouldn't put it quite like that, but—"

"Is this Peter's secret guy who's really married?" Cosgrove asked me. "We should give him the sex survey and see what he'll do."

"Who is?" Konstantin asked me.

"This is Cosgrove, but you already met," I said, relieving my love friend of the knife.

"Yes, and what his position?"

"Second, with a demi-plié and a *Nutcracker* turnout," I replied, redepositing the knife in the flatware drawer.

"He gets nervous when people ask about our relationship," said Cosgrove, coming near to Konstantin, who held him by the waist.

"You seem fine young fellow," said Konstantin, taking Cosgrove in. "When you love, what you two are doing?"

"Tower Records," I quickly called out to Cosgrove, "first thing tomorrow, fifty-dollar limit, both ways by cab. All this just for your silence at this dramatically somewhat overladen moment."

"One hundred," Cosgrove demanded. "Not counting the tax."

"Oh, come on!"

He leaned over to Konstantin to whisper in his ear—he actually had his hand cupped—when I said, "All right, one hundred."

"Why you have secret?" Konstantin asked me.

"I never wanted anyone knowing anything about me," I replied. "No matter what it was. Even neutral things. I just—"

"But this fellow," Konstantin insisted, about Cosgrove, "what he *means* to you?"

"Boy, this *is* a sex survey," said Cosgrove.

"Cosgrove," I said, "why don't you tell Konstantin about your work?"

Cosgrove turned to Konstantin, and as they gazed upon each other there passed between them an accepting look such as men, straight or gay, send out when neither feels challenged.

"I'm in the performing arts, mostly," Cosgrove began. "Lately I've been specializing in commercials." Cosgrove sat on the couch next to Konstantin. "I'm starting a postmodernesque repertory company, a band of mystical talents where we do nothing but commercials about imaginary products. That's very postmodernesque, you see. But we take the historical approach, and we refer to the great roles—Hamlet, King Lear, Dumbo. The company already includes such acclaimed talents as Miss Faye and Baby Frumkin, who is sometimes known as Jacky Pete. He spiels in the audience between the acts, because he has a way with the public. He's quite the flatterbox, I dare say."

Konstantin looked inquiringly at me. I shrugged.

"How old are you?" Cosgrove asked Konstantin.

"Twenty-three," said Konstantin, smiling at Cosgrove as if at an adorably frisky four-year-old.

"I'm almost that myself. I can see you're very handsome, but you were worried when you came in. Is everything all right?"

"Perhaps no," Konstantin admitted.

"I'm sorry to hear that. May I ask how you got into this . . ."

"Apartment"? I wondered. "Predicament"? "Story"?

". . . nice costume? As the head of my repertory company, I'm always looking for a new postmodernesque look. Baby Frumkin works in a spiderweb outfit that sets off his white, white skin. I appear in regular clothes. But that's a costume in itself, if you think about it."

Then Alfie came down, because, as he explained, he "thought it was time for make-your-own banana splits."

I said no, that was for after dinner, and Cosgrove got the notion that he and Alfie should perform the commercial for Café de Môte, for Alfie had very nearly mastered the all-important role of the Duke of Kraken.

"Is what?" Konstantin asked; but the players were even then taking stage, and Cosgrove signaled to me to introduce his sketch.

Of course, I had looked on as the piece was conceived, developed, and perfected (if that's not too confidently put); and I devised the spelling. So, as Cosgrove and Alfie moved chairs around, grabbed props, and struck poses, I announced, "We look in on a lavish dinner party among New York's ultrasophisticates. Prince Panizetti demands attention and declares . . ."

"The pâté was sinister," says Cosgrove, as the Prince. "But the Rice-A-Roni was exquisite. We await the coffee."

He and Alfie assumed imperious looks.

"The coffee is poured," I said, watching Konstantin look from me to the players in perplexity. "But consternation ensues!"

"What coffee *is* this?" cried Cosgrove, making a face.

"Mine tastes like throw-up!" said Alfie.

"No, Alfie: 'What a vile-tasting cup!'"

"This vile taste of cup!"

I smoothly put in, "Now the hostess springs her surprise," as Cosgrove jumped up to take another role.

"It's Café de Môte," Cosgrove announced, as the Hostess of the Party. Then he jumped back into the Prince as he and Alfie chorused an "mmm" of delight.

"What heavenly taste," said the Prince.

"Dibs on seconds, I call it," said Alfie.

Jumping up, Cosgrove cried, "The party was *saved*! And all because of Café de Môte! Shouldn't you get some . . . *today*?"

The three of us now looked at Konstantin, who was just sitting there.

"What this?" he finally asked.

"Didn't you like it?" said Cosgrove.

"I was the Duke," said Alfie, coming up to Konstantin. "Did you notice?"

Konstantin, staring at Alfie, asked, "Who this boy?"

I introduced them, and Konstantin said, "This so beautiful a child. So loving. Where his father?"

"France," said Cosgrove.

"London," said Alfie. "The Alps."

"His folks are touring Europe," I began, stopping when Konstantin took Alfie in his arms, petting him and weeping.

"What's *his* problem?" Cosgrove asked me.

"He's been invited to appear in a porn movie with any partner of his choice."

Alfie clearly liked being held by Konstantin. He was sitting in the man's lap now, his head on Konstantin's shoulder, more or less dozing.

"Children is, that you love," said Konstantin, stroking Alfie's hair, "because they always love back to you. Okay. Now we apart," he told Alfie. "Ras, dva, tri!"

Alfie jumped free with a "Yay!" and Cosgrove said, "Now we'll do the commercial for Mamzelle Dainty Self-Me-Wipes."

I said, "I believe Konstantin has a family to get back to, and we have to . . . we . . ." Ah, relief! "What happened to Risk?" I asked.

"It sucked," Alfie replied.

Konstantin got up. "I should go," he said. "Tyepyer ya znayu . . . Nichevo. Spasiba." Now I know . . . Never mind. Thank you.

Konstantin shook hands with us all very firmly, in the Russian style, and left.

"He's cute," said Cosgrove. "Is he hung?"

"Goodness," I remarked, "it's just time for make-your-own banana splits, after all!"

You don't have to repeat that to the likes of Cosgrove and Alfie. They ran into the kitchen and were immediately discussing the contributions of hot fudge sauce, walnut topping, and silver sprinkles to the creation of a perfect banana split.

Good, I thought, as I dialed Peter Keene's office number. They'll be distracted for hours.

Peter was on site and free to speak. He came on with "You told Stizha to go back to his family and forget me, didn't you?"

"How did you—"

"Oh, I sent him to you."

"Fine, but why?"

"Well, didn't I figure out that what you'd say would be what he needed to hear?"

"You sent him to me to show him off."

Two beats. Then: "He's beautiful, isn't he? Almost miraculous. Such love in him! You know what his favorite thing is? Sexually? To be massaged! He loves that more than . . . well, and how he laughs during it! A child at pinball . . ."

"He's not a child and you can't have him anymore. He has to—"

"Go back to his biological role, I know that."

"No! To his first loves!"

"I don't mind. I met this—just a second." He fielded some business from a co-worker. "At the Roxy, last week, I ran into this incredible youth who's a writer, and when I said I was . . . Well, true enough, not a *published* writer. But later that night at his place he showed me some stories. I made him read them aloud in the nude. They need work, but he's been . . . well, you can imagine . . . very . . . accommodating . . ."

"His idea of breaking in is letting you fuck him."

"Not so loud. Anyway, I'm trading expertise for . . . Well, he's no Saint Francis in the first—"

"You're taking the loss of Konstantin quite well. I congratulate you."

"Well, of course he has my number, if he . . . Yes. Quite well. He has that lovely family."

"I am totally shocked, let me tell you, that you fucked him neat. Just because he doesn't understand condoms doesn't—"

"No, no, no, my slightly irksome but so dear fellow. Let's see, *I've* never been fucked, so how can—"

"You don't know what devious routes this evil thing can pave to seep into us," I insisted. "It's brilliant and undying. It'll get into napkins and french toast before it's finished."

"Well . . ."

"Just start rubbering up, will you? Because, let's face it, no one's going to slam out of your apartment just because you want to use a raincoat. Men who want to get fucked will take it any way they can find it."

"You have contempt for bottoms, don't you?"

That was unjust enough to hang up on.

Now we've had the middle. There are three endings—unavoidable, because it was a busy time. First came the departure of Alfie and Monica, whose parents picked them up at our very doorstep, out in front of the building. Alfie raced into their arms, crowing about all the things he'd done and seen. Monica moved more grandly, like a gondola on one of Venice's many festal days, high in the water, untroubled and without need of harbor. Monica's father, Stephen Tomjoy, listened to a few seconds of her complaints and knelt down and held her. Ha! She was limp, silent, and in love. Monica, I know you at last!

"So you're the famous Bud," Dennis Savage's sister told me as we shook hands. Linda. She really did look like him. Same hair and eyes. "I've been hearing one tale or another since the two of you were thrown out of the Boy Scouts."

"They *called* it the Boy Scouts," I said. "But it's really the Hitler Youth, and fair folk everywhere regard separation from it as honorable."

"Oh, Stephen was thrown out, too. It's nothing to worry about."

I turned to Dennis Savage. "You never mentioned this."

Stephen addressed us now. (All right, he's good-looking, but enough with the straights.) "We tipped over a couple of cows," says Stephen, "and they got real strict with us. S'okay."

Stephen has Alfie on his shoulders, feinting in directions as Alfie screams in delight. Monica turns a dour eye upon this, and Linda tells her, "Pride goeth before the fall."

"Everything's so boring, Mother."

Linda sighs—*just* in the manner in which Dennis Savage sighs, and I'll bring that up a bit later. Linda says, to Monica, "Don't ask how Paris was, or anything."

"That's right, I won't."

"How was Paris?" Dennis Savage asks his sister.

She smiles. She holds up her right forefinger. She touches his nose with it. "You should go, big brother. It's way different. You say to yourself, Why don't I live *here*? Then you think, Where would I get a sitter I can trust? What about Kentucky Fried Chicken? Sneakers are too expensive. It's good to be home and see you. Are you okay?"

"Daddy!" Monica calls out, in regard to the shoulder-riding of Alfie. "Take him down! Everyone's staring!"

Linda considers Dennis Savage. It's funny, these two. They really know each other, and he's so quiet now. "You miss Mom?" she asks.

Her husband, Stephen, is rampaging around with Alfie on his back. "I'm the Candymouse of Toronto!" Alfie cries. "Everybody loves me, and I am free for candy!"

I ask Linda, "Did Gramma Tomjoy's T-Rex arrive?"

"Oh, it must have, by now. Of course, he's planning on a real dinosaur, and . . ." She touches Dennis Savage. "Come on, boyo, what ails you?"

"We're always planning on real dinosaurs," he says. "But then we find—"

"Here's a cab!" Stephen calls out, to us all.

Linda holds out her hand to me.

"Nice to meet you," I say, taking it.

"Where's Virgil?" she asks Dennis Savage.

He starts to make a telling gesture, but Stephen is already pushing his family into the cab, and the Tomjoys take off for the north.

"You know," I said, as they vanished around the corner, "I keep thinking of questions that Virgil and Cosgrove left out of their sex survey. Essential ones—like 'How do you hold your lover?'"

He nodded as we went back inside.

"But what's your answer?" I said.

"It depends on the lover. You hold a fine, eager young chap by teaching him. They love that—getting smarter, more powerful.

You hold an older, perhaps more sturdy man by sharing his sorrows and celebrating his victories."

"How do you hold Virgil?"

"I did, for fourteen years, by giving him structure, entertainment, and praise. I was his college, emotionally, psychologically, and culturally."

"Fourteen years is a long college."

"Yet everybody is graduated sooner or later."

We got into the elevator.

"How do you hold Cosgrove, while we're at it?"

"I don't. He has nowhere else to go."

"I knew we weren't going to get a straight answer on that. I just wanted to enjoy hearing you finesse your way around the question for the hundredth time. 'He has nowhere else to go'—as if he were checking into a hotel during a blizzard."

"Ah, here's my floor," I said, doing an exit.

That was ambiguous, indirect. Yes. But the second ending is more elucidating, for in it Peter and I are having a postmortem lunch at the Broadway Diner, my local joint.

"I knew it couldn't continue indefinitely," Peter is telling me. "The way he would go *on* about his family. Besides, I'm too young to settle down. I visualize turning forty and . . . well, the *ideal* man shows up, and *he's* forty, so—"

"Define 'ideal,'" I said.

"Oh, well, isn't that the problem? Some piece of poetry passes the night and you're a convert to Young Energy. A bodybuilder catches your eye and you think, Ah, the Power of Fathers. Then all those supplementary considerations, like straight as opposed to wavy hair, or skin tone, or lip context—"

"Excuse me, *lip context*?"

"Well, there's high context, the full, sensual kind, and then we know of low context, the thin, dangerous, perhaps even executioner's lips that—"

"Jesus!" I said, resting my head on the table. "Over twenty

years after Stonewall, the taxonomy still isn't finished!"

"I think I must love a dark-haired but blond-skinned and not overly chiseled muscleboy with . . . well, not notorious but at least presentable abs and some chest hair, either in T formation or just for emphasis along the pectorals, and a long, long torso and simply no hips at all, but immensely filled-up thighs of the smooth and supple yet thunderous variety that I imagine one would have to be born with, and . . . consider . . . yes. The ass must be high, firm, and round, and I know this is rare but I mean *really and truly* high, because how could you love someone who didn't . . . Well, what are you moaning about down there?"

I raised my head; people were looking. "I have never approved of the concept—in fact, before now I never even heard of it—of considering a man lacking a high, round ass as unlovable."

"Doesn't Carlo have a beautiful ass?"

"Deliriously so. The Museum of Modern Art has a pedestal waiting with his name on it. They plead weekly."

"And Carlo is the *key man*!"

"Yes, and what's wonderful about him is his love and smarts, his cultivation of friends, his passions, so large they—"

"I'll tell you what's large about—"

"Even as a joke this conversation is disreputable," I told him. "Some men are lookers, that's all."

He was grinning at me.

I said, "What happened with that kid from the Roxy? The writer."

Getting back to his food, Peter said, "I have to tell you, he has a *lot* of talent. He's quite, quite the discovery."

"And how's the writing?"

The third ending is Cosgrove and I at sleeping time, when, for some reason he refuses to explain, he insists on being held tightly. If I happen to tire and turn over, he engineers me back and sets it up again.

I asked him, this night, "That question, 'What's your favorite activity with your partner?' Would you mind giving me your answer to that?"

"In winter. When it's so cold out that we have to run the heater all night and be under extra covers. And no one can come in and get mad at me. It's so still that I feel safe. Do you think Alfie just liked me, or did he admire me, too?"

FOR THE LOVE
OF MIKE

I'd like to tell you about a friend of mine, but first I'll have to backtrack a bit—all the way to the early 1980s, a major era for the gay porn industry. First of all, tape had overwhelmed film as the medium for live-action narrative, which meant that badly lit and perfunctorily edited features gave way to technically secure ones. Moreover, tape made possible home viewing, replacing the creepy outlaw theatres of the city tenderloins. The industry's center was moved from New York to Los Angeles, which drew casting preference away from the dark, exotic, and often titanically built hotman toward the fair, Main Streetish, and sleek-limbed stripling. At the same time, print porn had come out of the closet in a myriad of soft-core magazines.

Suddenly, porn had lost all sense of taboo. It had been subcult, dangerous, a thing of the night town. Now it was sitting on the coffee table when Aunt Laura dropped by with your Christmas present. Porn was so acculturated that even Kern Loften, the most prudent man of my acquaintance, began to amass a Collection of Magazines. You know how you never seem to have more than a very few friends who share your particular taste in men—maybe only one friend? Mine was Kern. He and I would spend afternoons going through his library, wondering and speculating. We'd play Anyone You Want: One would show the other photos of more or less naked men, the player to choose the icon of his choice for the date of a lifetime. I could never play this game with anyone else, because only Kern knew what I knew. I'd show Dennis Savage shots of Clint Walker, Richard Egan, Jim Cassidy, and Stutz—and where Kern would cry "Who could choose?" with a comprehending edge of despair in his tone, Dennis Savage would ask, "What is this, Save the Whales?"

"Whales," he says! Because the particular type that Kern and I responded to was, basically, full, big, and huge. Bodybuilders, you could call them, I guess: but with a trashy masculine tilt, the kind of men you saw not in bodybuilders' contests but in dreams. Dirty smiles. Keen eyes. They had "mystos"—a term Kern recalled from

a sitcom that had enthralled him in his youth, *The People's Choice*. I could never quite make out, from Kern's enthusiastically garbled reports, exactly what happened in this show, except that there was a talking dog named Cleo and that in one episode the series star, Jackie Cooper, was unshirted by an eccentric sculptress and cradled in the arms of her blond Amazon assistant. Why? Because he had *mystos*.

Whenever Kern would readduce this dowdy footnote of television history, I'd pass a remark. I mean, Jackie Cooper? But remember, Kern's and my youth was a time starved for homoerotic stimuli; the juxtaposition of virtually any bare torso with a Magic Word, a grown-up's summoning term, fed our imaginations. I could visualize young Kern coming into power in this way, making his first realization of the great world that he must explore. I thought back to my own such moments. That gave us a point of contact, and "mystos" became one of our conjure words. Let someone mention a circuit beauty and we would remark, say, "Mystos 7"—his score on a 1 to 10 scale. Few established media stars could make it past 4; there was something unpredictable, uncontrollable—perhaps threatening to hetero culture—that marginalized anyone with a strong dose of mystos. But gay life was filled with 6's and 7's, and there was one porn firm, which specialized in our type, that regularly produced 8's and 9's. It even had a 10, Vic Astarchos.

I don't know if you recall this guy. He had a certain fame, perhaps, among a certain coterie, but for Kern and me he was absolute, with a face that was intelligent rather than pretty, dark curly hair cut short, and a torso of doom, the abs as articulated as the Rockies and the V of flesh where the waist overhangs the thighs as built up as the Berlin Wall. Everything about him was big; even the navel was not slit but gouged out.

We are talking Major Man. There were local touches of magic within the panorama, too, for instance in the very light dusting of hair along the pectorals, an almost unbearably earthy touch on the statuesque physique.

"Is he available?" Kern would ask as we pored over Vic's pictures. "Is he in town? Is he real?"

In one shot, Vic was standing nude in a doorway, his left arm thrust up, emphasizing the heaviness of the neck and shoulder muscles; his expression was almost angry, as if he'd been surprised by the prying camera. In another shot, he was walking out of the ocean, surf to his waist, hands cupping the water, the whole thing breezy and athletic—yet the face was still serious, deep.

"He's full of himself?" Kern ventured.

"He's revolutionary," I said.

"He's wondering why."

"He's had them all."

We speculated about him endlessly; we even told each other stories about him. "Vic at the Gym." "Vic at the Opera." "Vic Falls in Love"—but that was improbable. Why would anyone this complete need anything as complementary as a lover?

No one else ever became initiate of our cult, but then nobody wanted to. Have you noticed how angry some gay men get when you mention some icon of the day whom they don't happen to fancy? In this one matter, heterosex culture may have achieved a higher stage of evolution: When straight men talk about women, you don't find one of them getting all wounded and defensive if he doesn't share another's enthusiasm; he just chimes in with one of his own favorites. But put six gays at the dinner table, mention . . . oh, Ryan Idol or Lucas Ridgeston, and everybody starts screaming at you. What's their problem?

Anyway, I promised to tell you about someone, and the story starts here, on an evening in late spring, when my phone rang well after midnight. This is never a good sign; but it was Kern, who had just been to the St. Mark's Baths and had a tale to tell, of such elated nature that it could not wait for daylight.

"You went to the baths?" I asked.

"Eric dragged me. You know how cheap he is. It was Buddy Night or something, and there was a discount if you got there by a certain time."

This was indeed news, for Kern was strictly a barfly when he went out at all. "Call me *passéiste,*" he once told me, "but my idea of where you have sex is your bedroom, not a urinal."

"So what happened?"

"Someone was there. Guess."

"I need a hint."

"The ultimate."

I thought, That could be almost anyone, because the gods thoughtfully did not sprinkle but rather inundated life with beauty. It's the only thing that allows no short list. Or wait. "Not . . . Vic Astarchos?"

"*Yes!*"

Now, this was a headline, for though we'd eventually learned that he lived in New York, we had never actually seen him, not even on the Island or at Flamingo.

"Is this just a sighting?" I asked. "Or was there . . . contact?"

"'We are not alone,'" he reminded me. Then, after a deep breath: "So there I was, still trying to get my bearings in this postmodernist brothel—which floor am I on? Where's the coffee bar? Why is that man wearing jeans and mirror glasses and carrying a whip? Suddenly, I see this . . . person coming toward me down a long hall. First glance—it *can't* be! Second glance—it *is* and get ready. We pass, I try my nicest smile, he just nods slightly and moves right on."

"More! More!"

"Was I crushed? Let's face it, a sensory overload like Vic Astarchos doesn't visit the baths to meet a presentable but not incendiary chap like me. He wants artistic meltdown. I figure, I have a job I like, I have a nice apartment, I have stimulating, supportive friends. I'll get over it. *Then* I figure, Run after him, jerk, and offer him money!"

"Holy cow!"

"Well, he's a porn star. They hustle, don't they? The worst that can happen is that he'll get offended and brain me."

"Where's Eric during this?"

"He missed the whole thing. *So.* I catch up with the god one floor down, nosing around in the open doorways."

"He won't find anything there but schmengies. The Talent roves."

"That's what Eric said. Anyway, I'm about to make my pitch when some guy comes up and tries to cop a feel under Vic's towel as he passes. Now, dig this manly style: Vic simply knocks his hand away without even looking at the guy. Vic *negates* him."

"That's our hero—solid, easy, in control."

"*So.* The guy stands there with . . . you won't believe this, with his hand on his hip, and he goes, 'What's *your* problem, Ermintrude?' Vic ignores him, moving on down the hall. Then the guy gets *really* nasty—"

"Meaning *really* rejected, showing no grace, no pride—"

"No smarts, too, because everyone's popping out of the rooms to watch. *So,* completely ignoring the fact that he is gazing upon one of the most splendid backs in the whole gay world, he shouts, 'Hey, muscle faggot!'

"Well," Kern went on, "Vic stopped, turned around—and I told myself, *You're on.* I went, 'Phone call!' like a page boy. 'Call for Vic Astarchos!' and I planted myself in front of him and whispered, 'Two hundred dollars if you come home with me. And he said, 'Let's go.'"

"Kern, my God, that's . . . How did he look?"

"Like the living end."

"You really did this? Just—"

"It was love or die."

"Kern, I'm . . . I'm proud of you."

"Anyone else and I would have shrugged and gone on my way. But *just once,* I thought, I have to know what it's like to touch the godhead."

"Two hundred bucks is awfully high, though."

"This was not the time to hedge. This was a time to gush. Call it acceptance security."

"So what was it like?"

"This man is unbelievable. He's not just hot, he's . . . nice. He's a little rough socially, like those kids from the tough high school who were always in trouble with the cops. But he's funny and even sensitive. He listens. That serious look on his face is what he's marketing, but once the sex is over he's like some old buddy of yours. Get this—his real name's Mike Feinman. He's Jewish! So of course we started comparing pasts, like summer camp color wars and the one aunt you have who figures it out before your parents do. Mine was Aunt Sarah, his was . . . Oh, but, you know, the thing is, *before* that, he was monosyllabic when he talked at all. As if . . . he wants to be able to contain whatever you need, so he doesn't do any personality. When we got to my place, I was about to ask him if he wanted a drink or something, but he was already tugging his clothes off."

"Sounds like he's done this before."

"Oh, he's a pro, all right. He told me. He has this odd background. He dropped out of high school and then had to vanish— just disappear—to avoid the draft. The kids I knew stayed out of Vietnam by joining the Peace Corps or becoming doctors. This guy lives a road movie."

He was talking a bit nervously now, quickly, staving off the lull and the question that was about to confront him. When it came, I moved in quick and deadly.

"What did you do?" I asked. "In bed."

Silence on the phone. Kern knows I want to slurp up his experience, and he hopes to stay dry.

"Well," he finally said. "I can't, really. It's too . . ."

"It's the core of the report," I answered. "It's the true Vic."

"You'll just tell everyone."

"I solemnly swear that I will never speak of this to a soul as long as I live." (Note clever choice of verb, leaving open the possibility of *writing* of this to a soul; as herewith.)

More silence.

"Please?" I begged. "Don't I *have* to know?"

Kern struggles. Yet he *wants* to tell. News is worthless till it's reported. The joy isn't quite real till others appreciate it.

He said, "I told him, 'You take charge. Just do whatever it is to me. Show me what you are. Rape me.'"

Now I was silent.

"I said that," he insisted.

"And how did it go?"

"I'm telling you, the *living* end. By the way, he gave me his number. Do you want it?"

"Why not?" I replied. Casual. Nonchalant. In fact, I had it in the back of my mind that I should avail myself of the opportunity, but then I started stalling. Did I see dishonor in Paying for It? After all, I was into the second year of my gym era, though the elaborate program that the instructor had set up for me when I joined had dwindled into three curls and incessant lurking in the steam room. Did I feel shy about calling a stranger? Well, maybe: You never know what you'll get. And did I fear to encounter the ultimate?

Yes: and that decided me. *No one* should entertain such fear. Enough of this, I say, and I'm dialing the number, still readying my rap when, after one ring, a voice as deep as the Grand Canyon picks up with a *"Yeah?"*

Now it's three months later, high Pines summer, and I'm tooling along the boardwalk when I come upon a man I had met at a dinner party six weekends previously. He was picking berries off a bush right there on the walk, and naturally I stopped to say hello. He was neither unfriendly nor especially forthcoming, and it finally dawned on me that he had no recollection of me whatsoever. What, after six weeks? The fact that he was a looker made it doubly annoying—we all want to have impact, but especially on lookers.

Granted, that dinner hadn't proved one of my more sparkling nights, and I'll be, if not the first, then certainly the eighth or ninth to admit that the moment when I put a lampshade on my head and danced the peabody all along the porch that surrounded the house probably did not enhance my reputation as a soigné raconteur. Still, you expect to be at least recognized after a mere month and a half. So I was not having a good afternoon as I pushed on toward home.

Two walks later, I caught sight of something dazzling heading in my direction from the right. Cautious peripheral investigation through the dark glasses (I feel it's okay to cruise promiscuously as long as no one actually can tell that you're doing it) disclosed Vic Astarchos. Oh yes, it was: Who else had a neck the size of the Trylon? My heart surged—no, wait. What if Vic didn't know me, either? What if he regarded the Pines as sacredly separate from his hustling? Because, I tell you, boys and girls, I was not about to be negated twice in a day.

I played it cool and kept moving, but then I heard "Hey, Bud!" called out behind me. I turned and waited.

He was shirtless in Speedos, carrying a little bag and smiling.

"If you're heading for the gym," I said, "it's about forty miles to the northwest. Just follow the boardwalk and hang a right at Brooklyn."

"They kicked me out," he replied, as we shook hands.

"Who?"

"My host. That fashion designer." He mentioned a Name. "Picked me up in Studio—the rush treatment, big plans for you, ever modeled? You know that stuff." He shrugged. "Okay, I'm no fool. Fashion models don't look like me, huh, do they?"

His chest muscles rose the slightest bit, to bring the point home.

"Still, I figure there'll be something in it. Long-range? Who knows? But yeah. Take the seaplane out and all. So, next thing, this other guy shows up, my host's boy friend. They had a fight, now they're going to make up, Mister Fashion's overjoyed. And suddenly him and his boy friend and all their yeah friends are looking at me like, The hell I need with this piece of trash? Okay. Mister Fashion ups to me and it's 'You—*out!*' "

"Are you kidding?"

He shrugged again, and I marveled. Be there a queen with soul so dead that this if-nothing-else-spectacular-looking fellow was no more than an extra man in a Pines weekend? And Vic was something else in any case. Because, after the first seven minutes, nobody is the living end on mystos alone.

"Yeah," he said. "So I'm going to try tea, see can I cook up something else for tonight."

"Work?" I asked, as we started walking toward the harbor.

"Too competitive to try to sell it out here. I'd as soon settle for a clean bed and a baloney sandwich. Mustard. Shredded lettuce."

"Why don't you stay with us? We've got four bedrooms and only two out this weekend."

"Sounds good to me," he said, I think a little surprised but refusing to show it.

"This way," I said, turning left up the hill.

"You on the ocean?"

"One line back. But it's a neat house. Ultramodern, and on three levels, so the living room's like a theatre with the beach as a stage, and the rooms overlook it but they have privacy, too. We each have our own bathroom."

"Brother, you made a friend. Thing I hate is those little bungalows where there's just one bathroom right in the center of it and you have to take a crap like two inches from whoever's around."

We reached the summit, I pointed, and Vic paused.

"Okay, let me in on the secret," he said. "You loaded, is that it?"

"Actually, I'm just an occasional guest. The other guy in the house is a guest, too. It's the regular tenants who're loaded, but they're all away now."

He nodded. "Just want to know how it stands, right?"

Carlo was in the kitchen, his back to us, cutting up melons, strawberries, mangoes, and the like for the giant bowl of fruit cup he likes to sample on and off throughout the day. As we came in, I said, "Carlo, we have an emergency guest. This is Vic Astarchos. Vic—"

Carlo had turned around, grinning. Losing the knife and wiping his hands on his trunks, he said "Who the damnhell is this, I truly wonder?" and started to advance.

"Yeah, *Rip!*" Vic cried, dropping his valise.

The two of them immediately locked in one of those boisterous bearhug tangos typical of former gringos who have not been fully acculturated into metropolitan gay life. I mean, when Kern and I meet after a longish separation, do we act like goons fanfaronading at a dogfight?

"Cut it *out,* you two!" I said. "You'll *break* something!"

"You old Mike," Carlo was saying as they finally stopped scuffling and barking and pushing and mauling and practicing wrestling holds and grab-assing and being noisy and getting on my nerves. *"Damn,* you look *sweet!"*

"Now the whole place stinks of testosterone," I was grumbling. "Someone fetch the Glade."

"How'd we luck into the temporary ownership of this scoundrel, anyway?" Carlo asked, pounding his fists on Vic's back. "He's some scoundrel kind of guy, I know he is."

"I'll tell you," I said, "as soon as the Wide World of Sports is over."

"Shit, I got thrown out of where I was," said Vic. "Bud found me like a wino in the gutter, handed me a Bible and a dollar, and promised I'd be saved."

"Hot damn," Carlo observed.

I interfered with a résumé of the tale Vic had told me, and Carlo responded, "Well, those famous guys are really rude."

"Yeah, it was more than that," said Vic, as we sat at the bar and Carlo poured the Perriers. (We took it macho-style: no lime.) "I just didn't fit in there—like you're in a T-shirt and they're all in the button kind, open to like two buttons from the bottom. Okay, but *every single one* of them, like they got a costume guy checking before they leave their rooms? And they're all looking at you with this sneer, like, Didn't you get the club shirt?

"Or last night—yeah, put this in the *Guinness Book,* I swear— they got this video camera out, and everybody had to do a drag routine *on tape*. These men putting on dresses and beads and makeup? Took almost all afternoon, okay. Sure. And they're *excited*, like they're booked for Washington's Birthday weekend at the Concord Hotel. Yeah, they're opening for Sammy Davis."

"The fashion designer, too?" I asked.

"Every ass in the place. I just went off to the beach. Dropped in on tea. Visited a few friends. Figured I must have missed the whole thing, right?"

He shook his head.

"They're just getting started! Somebody looks at me, says, 'Hey, Hercules isn't ready.' I go, 'Listen up, you guys.'" He smiled like a drill sergeant about to administer such penalties as a thousand push-ups and midnight marches through snake-infested marshland. "'Dresses and makeup'—I'm telling them this—'are what a woman wears. I'm a man. What I wear is pants and no makeup. I thank you.'"

Carlo was laughing. "You tell 'em, Mike boy."

"Shit, the whole place was like a sorority house, see?"

"You're better off out of there," said Carlo.

"May have missed out on a dividend or two—I mean, those rich guys squeeze you for every last drop of cream, but when they pay they pay big."

"Life's so short," said Carlo.

"I heard that," said Vic, jabbing Carlo's arm. "Yeah, so well at least I didn't drag and scream around like those other queens."

I said, "You should save that for your tombstone."

Vic winked at Carlo and said, of me, "Who's Mister Smart-ass?"

"It's this sad story," said Carlo, "where I'm working sixty-hour weeks to send him through medical school. He's some little brother kind of guy that first you loved, but then he goes weak and decadent and I have to decide to dump him or save him."

"Yeah, and I understand that I'm the wicked brother," Vic put in, "who corrupts everything he touches."

"Paramount, '36," I said. "Carlo's Randolph Scott and Vic's Clark Gable, on loan from Metro."

"Who are you, then?"

I shrugged. "Somebody."

Vic nodded. "Well, somebody did me a turn for the better today. Just want you to know I appreciate it."

He said this looking right at me, and it wasn't easy holding that gaze. Then, abruptly, he rose, saying, "They had me up all night squeezing those drops, and then at eight promptly morning they start in with the dippy Bette Midler records. So how about a nap for me, say?"

"Let's give him Reed's room," said Carlo, as we started upstairs. Reed owns the house, so though all the rooms are the same size, Reed has the View: absolute ocean to the south and total bay to the north.

"Man alive," said Mike, encountering the black-tiled bathroom with the sunken tub. "Who's the guy thinks this stuff up?"

"There's more of the same," said Carlo, "in his other houses. Ready? New York, Paris, St. Moritz, Maine somewhere, and Mexico City."

"What is he, the Great Houdini?"

"No, rich."

"Cripes."

Vic got serious. He told Carlo, "Rip, you're the man," and thrust his hand out so broadly that when Carlo's palm met it, one heard a kind of Hiroshima snap.

Vic didn't take my hand. He fixed me with a look and said, "I'll get even with you, baby."

Huh?

Carlo, seeing my confusion, said, "Be nice, Mike," and Vic grabbed my hand and told me, "I owe you one, and we both know it. Because those guys were kind of a little cold to me. Bump into you, you say, Join us, no questions asked. So you're saving me, and if I tell it in front of Rip here, that is a sacred trust. You ever want the bill paid, you advise me pronto, okay?"

"How far can I go?" I asked.

He said, "I still don't get fucked"; and Carlo almost broke his leg falling down laughing at that one—no, don't assume you know what that means, because I don't tell everything. Anyway, Carlo and I went downstairs to figure out what to do for dinner, traded fifty suggestions, and ended up heading for the Pantry to get the fixings for the inevitable spaghetti carbonara.

Some three hours later, Carlo and I finished off the dishes, poured the coffee, settled on the music (the old Angel *La Bohème* with Maria Callas; accept no substitutes), and readied the game, Chinese checkers, in Carlo's adaptation, in which each player mans three armies and the right to move is governed by the old once-twice-three-shoot duel of fingers. Good shooting luck had given him the freedom of the board. He was advancing every turn; I was paralyzed.

"So," he said. "How'd you meet Mike?"

"From the size of your smirk, I assume you've figured it out."

On the third floor the shower went on, and we both instinctively looked up. "Mike's awake," he said.

We matched hands, I finally won, and I brought up my forward men, frantically trying to devise triple-jumps over his stragglers.

"I'll never make it," I said. "The game's just started and I've already lost. What's the skill to this?"

"You're good at other things," he told me, bringing his armies home after winning the shoot. "Everybody's good at something, I truly believe. The trick is to find what you're good at."

"But how come you keep winning when we shoot fingers? Is it dumb luck, or am I being outwitted?"

"That depends on do you believe in dumb luck."

"Yo, down in the valley!" came Vic's voice overhead. "Did I miss the whole fucking dinner?"

He was standing on the balcony, toweling off from his shower.

"We saved you stuff," Carlo called out. "Including a joint."

"Man, that'll be my appetizer," Vic replied, pulling on his Speedos. "Light it up and let's do it."

"I will say that is one solid guy," Carlo told me as Vic negotiated the stairs. "One of the few you would keep going back to. The night I met him, it took me the damn *longest* time to get him to let me screw him. And that's so pleasing to me, when they don't want to give it up to you, but they do. Especially Mike. Because he's so *man*."

"So what's the food?" said our guest, arriving.

I said, "Spaghetti—which I will now heat up—salad, and blueberries and Grand Marnier over raspberry sherbet."

"Sounds like an Italian bar mitzvah. We going to do the bunny hop later?"

"The what?" Carlo asked, as he passed the lit joint to Vic.

Organizing the dinner, I said, "Vic, do you want to start on the salad or wait till the spaghetti's hot?"

"Call me Mike and pass the salad bowl. Yeah. So what's the music?"

"Bud likes opera," said Carlo.

Vic turned to me, about to say something, maybe make a joke. If Bette Midler is dippy, what's Maria Callas? But he just smiled and said, "Sounds good, pal."

We got him fed and high, and he leaned back and laughed and said, "So who do I have to fuck to get to live like you guys?"

"Live how?" I asked.

"Shit, this great house is how. I got the hots for it. That shower is, man, like—"

"The owner's an old friend," said Carlo, "so he lets me use the place. Bud's my guest. That's all."

We had the dimmers down, candles, and we were up to Mimi's death scene, sitting on the floor and passing another joint, listening to the music.

"This is so great," Vic observed, at length. "Have this bad experience, run into my man here by merest chance, and next thing you know it's this excellent party. Candles, I see, like we're waiting for Liberace. It's a . . . a kind of satisfying thing, like, because I can't figure out how they could just shove me out of there, you know? Thought I had the edge."

La Bohème dropped its curtain as Rodolpho sobbed out "Mimì!" on high G sharp.

"Somebody croak?" Vic asked.

"Hey, Mike," said Carlo, moving closer to him. "What was your first time like?"

"He means today, Vic," I joked, "not in your whole life."

"Hey," he said, touching my arm. "Call me Mike, okay?"

We were smoking again, still on the floor, but now pulled back from the Chinese checkerboard and the dishes, leaning against the furniture in the blackness barely tempered, now, by the denatured light of the guttering candles. Carlo and I had left the windows open, and the frosty Pines night was upon us. The shirtless Vic shivered now and again.

He said, "My first time fucking was with my cousin Harvey. He was twelve and I was fourteen, but he was the one who started it. Like, what did I know?, and this kid's got muscleman porn and a tube of Vaseline. The make-out king of Rego Park."

Inhaling the joint, he then passed it to Carlo and said, "Anyway, how's that matter, where you *started*? What *I'd* ask? It's when did you feel you had the *power*? You know? The first time you realized you could have any guy in the room. Yeah, and it took me some years at the gym, but they were *serious* years, with some great moments, like you see the separations come into your back in the mirror. Your chest ridges out so fine. These fucking abs. My first time? Okay. I went to the West Village on a Sunday afternoon. It was summer, and guys were flooding the streets leading to the piers. Real hot day, so everyone's like out of uniform and going, This is *me!* One's got that wideboy V. One's in those crispy little shorts so his cock's slipping out to say hello. One's a blond. Everybody's got something today, see that?

"Well, I cruised my way through the whole pack, and what I saw was, none of them were up to my level. And they knew it, too.

I could have any of those guys. I could have all of them—line them up and suck the insides out of the first one, kiss the mouth off the second one, pump the ass off the third one. Yeah, the high-school dropout who my parents said I'd never be anything. But this was my world, and look who's the center of it. Me."

Here he looked quizzically at us, wanting help on a mystery.

"Me," he repeated. "So who'll tell me why they were giving me the bum's rush today? If I'm so great, I mean."

"There's always a cuter guy, somehow," Carlo said. "I've been noticing. No matter how you have it stacked. There's always someone new who they could love even more."

"There's a place we can all see," Vic replied, "where it's always someone else who gets into it. No matter how we try, we can't get there. What is that place? You know, Rip?"

Carlo reached over and pulled Vic into his lap. He was going to pet Vic and soothe him, and Vic seemed like a little boy then, perhaps one who had come to some bewildering grief and was being allowed to stay up past his bedtime as a consolation. Vic was a six-footer, yet he folded himself into Carlo's grip as if he always had to be consoled, walked to school, guided in the preparation of fruit-juice ice pops. Carlo stroked Vic's hair, and Vic sighed and slept.

"This guy is so beautiful," Carlo told me, after quite a long time. "You know I have my list based on look, personality, and intelligence, and this boy scores in my favorite half dozen or so. He's what I will always love, and that is a guy who pulls 'em right down and he's already hard and going to."

"Mystos 10," I said.

"What's that?"

"It means that a lot of guys could have a crush on Vic."

Carlo thought that over, and nodded, but he said, "No."

"No?"

"It means," he corrected, running a finger along the crust of muscle in Vic's stomach, "It is not your dumb luck and we are not outwitted. We know what it is, and this boy is good at it, even though his feelings can be hurt when they throw him out of a place. Dibs on him tonight."

"He's all yours," I said, not conceding: reporting.

I do not blush to admit that I hired Vic a few more times after that: when my bank account swelled, when I craved a treat, when I damn well felt like it. You might term it a central course of instruction in my sentimental education, for unlike many gay men, Vic would do just about anything—*just about*—and there were a few practices I'd never tried, at least not with a partner who made it his business to root me on with growly endearments and asides on tactics.

Kern, who had similarly kept in contact with Vic, thoroughly approved. But Dennis Savage expressed alarm.

"You're keeping the sex safe, aren't you?" he asked—warned—me.

"If it's safe, it isn't sex. You mean, are we keeping the sex *safer*, and of course we are."

"For all you know, that guy could be going with fifty clients a week. Do you realize what a network of poison you're biting into every time he walks into your apartment?"

Fair enough. And, yes, I was worried about that. One method of damage control was to pretend that I had suddenly become an aficionado of the homoerotic shower for two, my hidden agenda being to clean off whomever he'd been with before he got to me. I believe Vic saw through the stunt, but he played the sport and went along with me. Besides, showers are fun.

Look, how is any of us to turn down intimacy with what most impells us—to touch, as Kern put it, the godhead? I don't know what straight men want, but certainly gay men need to get close to the spasm of life, whether in images or experientially; through fucking, blowing, or masturbation; with partners acceptable, encouraging, or guaranteed. It is *literally* the living end, no? Combine the choice act with the ultimate partner, and you have something like the absolute ground zero of Stonewall.

So I told Dennis Savage, "I'll never have sex for free again," and I was only partly joking.

Anyway, one afternoon Vic called, not to hustle me but because he had a problem with a letter he had to write.

"This'll got to be impressive, see?" he said. "I don't want the people who read it to think I don't know where the commas are and like that. Spelling and nouns? Perfect score. I want this like a letter Teacher puts on the blackboard."

I said, "Come on over."

He had printed his rough draft in block letters on red-tinted store stationery.

"Don't read it," he told me. "Just correct it."

"I can't correct it without reading it."

"Well, this is private, man."

It began "Dear Parents" and seemed clearly to be an attempt to heal an estrangement between Vic and his folks.

"Pretend I'm a doctor," I suggested. "I'll see everything but it won't count."

"Yeah?" he asked, doubtfully.

"I can already tell you, you wrote this all wrong. It should start 'Dear Mom and Dad.' The whole thing's too formal. It's all in the passive voice."

"Okay, Mister Published, you going to fix it for me?"

"Tell me what you want to say."

Reluctantly, even shamefully, he did tell me: He and his parents hadn't spoken in some years, and this was his . . . well, plea to them to—as we finally decided to phrase it—"reopen the dialogue."

"Could we put a famous saying in there?" he asked me. "Something from the Bible, or the classy poets?"

"How about Lord Byron?" I said, going for the book and quoting:

Oh thou, Parnassus! whom I now survey,
Not in the frenzy of a dreamer's eye,
Not in the fabled landscape of a lay,
But soaring snow-clad through thy native sky,
In the wild pomp of mountain majesty!

"Hey, I don't think my parents should hear about guys getting laid."

"It's not that kind of—here we are. *Childe Harold's Pilgrimage:*

And now I view thee, 'tis, alas, with shame
That I in feeblest accents must adore.
When I recount thy worshippers of yore
I tremble, and can only bend the knee;
Nor raise my voice, nor vainly dare to soar,
But gaze beneath thy cloudy canopy
In silent joy to think at last I look on Thee!

He loved that. "Does it mean anything?" he asked, as if what is beautiful need not be sensible.

"We'll type it up," I told him. "Then you can sign it floridly with two emphatic lines beneath your name, and they'll—"

"You really know this stuff, huh?" he said, clapping his hand on my shoulder.

"It's a skill," I said, deprecating it as an angel or safecracker might downplay his expertise on *Oprah,* because the crowd loves not a showboater.

"Think this'll work?" he asked, looking it over.

"Well . . . do your parents miss you?"

He blushed. "Of course your parents miss you."

"Not of course. There are parents and there are parents."

He looked at me for a bit, then said, "Guess I owe you one again. Come on, I'll buy you a hamburger."

❖   ❖   ❖

He called another time, without a letter, and again, then I called him, and so we got to know each other somewhat. Unlike some hustlers, he never in even the subtlest way tried to edge me into giving him work, even when he was short of cash. He treated me like a friend, not like a john—but then, that's how he treated all his johns. It's why he was so successful.

It was an odd friendship, prone to last-minute rescheduling problems because of his "appointments." Also, he never wanted to do anything. Dennis Savage gave dinner parties. Virgil took up rococo hobbies and planned theatre trips (especially—in fact, only—to *A Chorus Line*). Carlo was always dragging one to the movies. Other friends wanted to go bicycling, play Monopoly, take pointless walks, try out a new restaurant. Vic just wanted to come over and talk; but that was fine with me. It was no fun playing Anyone You Want with him; he could already have anyone he wanted. But he did speak freely about sex, and I was always ready for such chat: Most of my friends felt as naked talking about it as they did having it.

"You know what it's all about?" he would say. "It's about Who Is That Guy? When they cruise you, which, you know, is always going on. They look and they like it, but they want to know who's inside that skin. Not what are his interests, but what's his *power*? Who Is That Guy?, they go, and they mean, Is he this awesome thing that's going to take me over?"

"*Everybody* thinks this?"

"Maybe."

I had made us BLTs and tequila sunrises and had then persuaded him to join me in sampling the late-afternoon air. It was September and chilly; even the runners had bundled up. Sunday in the Park with Vic.

"What about all the tops?" I asked him.

"What tops?"

He's laughing.

"Come on," I say, "that's the conventional gay irony, but it's not that simple."

"Okay, sure. Like me? I see some Mister Slim with the floppy dark hair I love, maybe parted in the center and a little too long in front. Maybe he's tanned up, *real* tight little yeah waist, and there is no question then . . ." He halted, arresting my advance with a hand on my arm, and looked me straight on. "Then," he said, "and no haggling, I'm going to have that young man's butt. I know just what he looks like, see? Got a name picked out for him, too."

"What is the name, Vic?"

"Keep telling you, call me *Mike,* huh? His name is Gareth. Cute, huh? Like from the old legend stories."

Pause.

"Who is that guy?" I asked.

"Gareth? He's the kind don't ask questions a lot. Just gets along with you, rolls with it. He reads comic books jay naked on the bed, stomach downside, and you oil him up and slide in to see how long it takes him to push the comic book away and lay his head down. Cheek down on the bed, and Gareth loves you. Doesn't ask for much, and I'm going to enjoy him from the inside out, like I could take him apart and put him back together with what I do to him."

"Where's he from?" I asked, as we walked on.

"Texas. Foster homes."

"Does he love you passionately?"

"He loves easy. He's not tense, he's sweet. But, see, most gay guys don't want Gareth."

"They want you."

"They want a guy in charge, expert and shameless."

"Is that you?"

"Well . . . it isn't the kid my parents raised, is it?"

"Who cares what you were?" I said. "All gays reinvent themselves. That's what coming out *is.*"

"Thought coming out was where you strip yourself open to the world."

"I don't think anybody does that ever."

"Love'll do that to you, maybe," he said, considering it as he uttered it.

"Have you ever met a guy like that? Someone who just blew you out of the pool with . . . I mean, someone who made you strip yourself—"

"That's enough walk now," he said.

We parted at a subway stop, but I was to ask him about this matter at other times; he would joke, turn the questions back on me, growl at me. But it did happen that I would call and find him depressed because some boy friend had ditched him, and I couldn't compute that. I would ask him, "Who would ditch Vic Astarchos?"

"Man, there is no Vic Astarchos. That's pictures."

"It's you in the pictures, isn't it?"

"What about Mike?" he'd say, pleading with me to see somewhat more—but I *was* seeing. His Mike was a reduction of Vic, wasn't he? Vic is the one with the whole world wired down; Mike is just another struggling slob with rough manners, bad grammar, and an astonishing ability to get his feelings hurt. Gareths could make him weep with frustration; I believe that they wounded him in hopes that some of his extraordinary physical power would bleed out and enrich them, like primitive man eating a fallen warrior's genitals. He would show up unshaved and morose, complaining that at home all he did was stare at the telephone trying to witch it into ringing; and it would, but it was just a client. He would recount, in helplessly fastidious detail, a Gareth's latest outrage—a no-show, or ridiculing Vic . . . *Mike* . . . in front of Gareth's "laughing faggy friends." Then this—I had thought—impregnable man would actually drop a tear or two. To me, leaking eyes on that Stonewall Superman face were, like, they cut Bob Dole open and found a heart.

But this: Mike would always recover. You know how you fall in love maybe once every ten years while some of your friends seem to be able to break up with one boy friend and find another within eight minutes, tops? Mike could rebound like a Spalding, and as soon as his new partner found out how he lived, Mike would introduce him to the business—all his lovers became hustlers, at least for a while.

"So they don't get jealous and all," Mike explained.

I was full ears and Mike was an expansive talker. He welcomed questions from the floor, especially twisted ones.

"Describe your best-looking client ever."

He didn't even have to think about it. "It was a hotel date," he said. "Really *top* hotel. Door opens, guy's in a suit, but you can see that he's in good shape for his age, which is already probably not forty. Clothes off—he's not in *good* shape, he's *true hot* all the way across, really smiling butt and great kisser. Fucked him four times, and when I staggered out of there he'd talked me down to ten bucks. For a whole night's work! But what a lay. Spanish, too."

"Did you ever back out on a gig?"

"Once, yeah. Door opens. Guy's not only eighty, but in a wheelchair. I go, Sorry, no can do."

"Who was the love of your life?"

He looked annoyed. "The fuck kind of question is that to? How should I . . . What are you up to here?"

"I just wondered who would be . . . who would have the power to capture your—"

"Well, nobody's going to capture me, okay?"

"Who would be good enough for you," I finally got out; and he: "Who says they're good enough for anyone? Sure, when you meet them they're all amazing. But then it's after, right?"

"What's after?"

"You come with me. Come on, get your coat now, it's windy out."

He took me way down to his apartment. I'd never been there before: a startlingly small square of space, the bed within inches of the kitchen sink. Out calls only.

"You just look a little at some of this stuff," he said, fishing around under the bed. "It's here somewhere."

It was a box of photographs—studio poses, snaps, four-for-a-buck strips from arcade booths, black-and-white and color.

"I can show you who is good enough," he said, handing me pictures. "How about this guy? Beautiful fuck, even if he had a dictionary of about six words. Dictionary?"

"Vocabulary."

"Here's one. Lovely as hell, right? Stole me day after day. Dipped into my wallet—or here's Claudio. Cute? We admit it."

"Very."

"That long dumbboy look, huh? And the see-through skin. Goes drug-crazy, police come in shoving the world around, you don't want to know."

Pictures, pictures. Everyone's beautiful, and everyone's unfit to be Mike's boy friend. Unworthy.

"Here's all the models," he concluded, spreading the photos out before me. "Lush as lush could be, but why were they so mean to me? Say I'm a dumb ox, but what are they, Oxford professors? Oh, here," he said, pointing out a Polaroid of a working-class man, older and less grandly groomed than the rest of Mike's harem, posed in a celebratory manner by a burgundy Mercedes.

"Jerry," said Mike. "Now, this guy was different. Car isn't his, though. He was a plumber. Drains and leaks, like. Met him one Saturday ringing in for a baseball team. You know, where the Broadway shows play each other in the Park? Think of it, actors and baseball. So they get a few guys like us to come in and show a little class, you might say."

Staring at the photo, Mike smiled—grimly, I thought—showing it to me again and tapping it with his finger.

"Yeah, Jerry," he said. "Him and me spotted each other for like-headed guys by about the second inning, and we're getting friendly, talking pretty straight, I'd say. So he decides to get confidential, tells me about his girl friend Luna, how he likes to donkey-fuck her. *Come again?* Well, it turns out it's ass-fucking when first you really heat her up with kissing and body-tonguing because she doesn't like getting ass-fucked. So you have to work her up, and there's this whole way of greasing up her chute so she gets the donkey flops."

I must have had this look on my face, because Mike said, "What, I'm shitting you or something?"

"How come he's telling *you* all this?"

"Well, that's part of the story, and if you want to come on and grab a burger deluxe, I'll fill you in, because you like a good story and Mike's not a guy to let a pal down."

Burger deluxes were Mike's idea of dining out, along with pizza and, on your birthday, a trip to the Belmore Cafeteria.

We went to the place below the Sheridan Square Gym, claimed a booth, ordered without looking at the menus—who reads greasy-spoon menus?—and Mike kicked into first gear.

"Okay," he began. "Jerry and Luna. Donkey-fucking. That's the topic, Saturday after Saturday. Getting to be good summer buddies, us two, so he's giving me all the details. Like the technique for greasing Luna up. Here, give your hand over."

I thought he was going to read my palm, but instead he pressed my thumb and index finger together in a rude circle, then began sliding his fuck-you finger between them. I started to pull my hand back, but he held it firm, saying, "So what? No one's looking."

"I just don't want to be—"

"See, it starts with the Circle, where you go all around the hole, bit by bit, hotting it up. See that? This is how he showed me, right there in the bleachers while our team's at bat. Then comes the Probe. See? It goes slow and deep, working away till it's sending tingles all through her body. Yeah, see that? Calm down, it's okay. Look up a little, so you can see me. Come on, eyelock. Right. It takes two to do this. Now you work two fingers in there and you rub them together. . . . That's the Wiggle. See?"

"Okay, okay."

"Not yet."

He stopped demonstrating, but still held my hand.

"I want you to see what it was," he said. "I'm watching him and trying to figure this out. Who is this guy? Because now he's going on about how she's got the flops and he's going to flip her onto her back and donkey her . . . and I'm looking at him, right?, and it's like an *alien* took over in him! He's so laid-back before, even playing ball, just loping to first when he cracks a single instead of really running. You know, the grin-and-lazy type. But *now* he's all lit up. Has the oh-yeah eyes and his hands just got real big and he's sitting in a whole new way. Going over and over his secret words. Doing the donkey and, man, she flops tight, and right up her love chute."

Letting my hand go, he said, "Well, by then I'm hypnotized. I want to see those eyes some more. I start encouraging him—you know, share in a few of my own pointers, trade bimbo stories with him. Because somehow I've got to get close to that . . . the thing in him that lights his eyes up. You know what I mean?"

"You wanted to touch the godhead."

"Say what?"

"Wait a minute. Did you tell him that you like men?"

"Huh, no way, buddy. This guy only plays with his own kind. Anyway, *so*. I make it that he's a real show-off, so I joke that we should do a threesome someday, really like to meet that Luna. He *jumps* at it."

The food came, but Mike went right on.

"Says, 'How about tonight?' He's got a date with Luna at nine and she loves surprises. And get this—with those eyes still like coals in a barbecue, he looks me over real slow, yeah, all of me, baby, and he puts his hands on my sides, pulls me close, and whispers in my ear, 'I know she'd dig you extra special, Beautiful.' Then he gets up, takes his turn at the plate, and hits a triple."

"What am I hearing?" I asked. "Is this a closeted—"

"No, leave out the politics. Because guys like that, you can't set categories. See, you and me, we control our sexuality, right? We decide who we're going to go with, for whatever reason. With Jerry, I'd say his sexuality is controlling him. An opportunity comes up and he can't say no. It isn't Is he attracted to his partner—if it's sex, he's attracted. Like, that night, we're at his place waiting for Luna to show, and halfway through the first drink he gets to grinning and, boom!, he's whipped it out and worked it up. Mister Boner, so proud of it he can't wait for the action to start. Not that it's so big or anything—just that it's his and he likes it.

"So you can't have one guy's hard and the other guy's dressed, and now we're two naked guys standing around drinking that stinking booze of his—those straight guys never know what to drink, you know? Of course Luna's going to be a no-show. You knew that already. He's getting drunker by the minute, and I'm steeling myself up for getting fucked, because there is no way Jerry's going to let me top him, no matter how stoned he is. Donkey-fucked, no less—but, I tell you, anything's worth getting my mouth on his while his eyes are crackling like I told you.

"So he's finally up to the rubbing-the-back-of-my-neck phase and his breath stinks and I keep feeding him cue lines that he misses till I say, 'Maybe Luna wouldn't have liked me, anyway.' *Payday.*

"He goes, 'You kidding, guy? She would eat you raw with cherries.' Got his hands on me now, taking a tour, and I say, 'Boy, I sure would have liked watching you do the donkey.' His eyes do that voodoo thing or, I don't know, a pinball machine, and he's halfway to it. I'm reeling him in like working from a script. I'm hustling him, is what it is—letting him think he's getting something special out of me when *I'm* the one who's getting."

"And how was it?"

"The living end."

That gave me pause: Kern's very words.

"Fact, I liked it so much, I tried to set up another date with him. But first he wasn't at the ball games, and second all I get is his phone machine, which he isn't answering my messages, anyway. Finally I run into him playing ball in Prospect Park—like, is he avoiding me? I went up to him, and from word one he is not friendly, this Jerry of mine. Finally he goes, 'Look, man, you're a faggot.' Neat and clean. 'I don't dislike faggots,' he says. 'But I don't neither like them, now, would I?' Both of us know I could deck him with half trying, and he's just . . . with a smile on his . . . The hell makes him think I'm going to take that from him?"

"You dropped him?"

"I dropped him, right there on the diamond. Thinks he's so bitching?"

Mike's left hand felt his right fist as if going over it again for the thousandth time, still outraged and not entirely reassured.

"*He's* so yeah? What, I don't got twice his shoulders, I ask you? Cracked him flat, he's down, I'm sayonara, and that's all she wrote."

"He didn't understand you," I said. "Straights cannot comprehend a Vic Astarchos."

"Don't you get it yet? It's just Mike."

"Okay, but there's a Vic in Mike, isn't there?"

"There's a Mike in *Vic's* how I see it. That's all Vic is—pictures and Mike. *Pictures.* It keeps us going, huh? We see those shots and we . . . Hey."

He got lively then, and dragged me back to his place to see one more photograph.

"This one's special," he said, retrieving it from inside a book he kept sitting on his bed. "See for yourself."

It was a color shot of an unforgivably handsome young man in checked shorts standing on the deck of a house in—it had to be—the Pines. You recall what I said about gays and their discontented rumbles over type? The man in this photo was the bringer of peace to that war, for he transcended type with a slim construction that somehow bore a lot of muscle without losing its grace. Maybe it was the really quite full arms balanced by the chiseled but understated chest, maybe the alarming breadth of the thighs upheld by the sturdy waist. He was a manly boy, a cross of types.

"Harry," said Mike. "Nice? Unh-unh. He'd break your heart for a quarter. Broke mine, many's the day. Had me hating him and begging him at once. Hard time, this one."

"He wasn't Gareth?"

"There is no Gareth, probably. Guys who look like him, they don't have his insides. The pictures keep fooling us, you know?"

"Is Harry still around?"

Staring at the photo, Mike didn't answer immediately. Then: "Lives in Florida, mostly. Or L.A. He maps around a lot. He still calls, sometimes, says he's in New York, how are you, oh I've got to catch a plane."

He tried to smile.

"Maybe I shouldn't have taken this out again," he concluded, placing the photo back in the book. "Did everything I could—gym and all. Try to be nice, generous, hold them strong and loving when they need to feel skin. Treated them a little rough when they wanted it but wouldn't admit they wanted it. What more can I do?"

He was crying.

"You tell me," he went on, not caring that I saw. "What *more* can I fucking do, huh?"

He sat on the bed, wiping his eyes.

"Oh, yeah, I shouldn't have pulled that out of the memory file. Friends'll say, Forget him, he's not worth it. The fuck do *they* know about it? If he's worth it to me? He isn't nice? Shit that, I'll be nice for two. I'll take up the slack."

He was silent for a while.

"That letter," I said. "To your parents. Did it get results?"

Mike slowly shook his head.

"You can't go back to something," he said. "Because you pulled too far away."

We contemplated this.

"Those fucking pictures, man," he said. "They tear you apart."

Mike decided to move to California sometime in the late 1980s. When he called with the news, I reminded him that he still owed me, and now I wanted payback.

"You're entitled," he said. "What'll it be?"

"I'd like one of your model photographs. A souvenir."

"Got plenty of those. Come on down."

Most of his stuff was packed up, but he had no trouble locating a carton of what you might call his press cuttings: countless doubles and triples of Vic Astarchos playing come-hither, soaping up in the shower, floating on pool rafts, beating off.

"Got some real heavy ones," he said, rummaging around. "That famous photographer who . . . yeah, you'd better have your own lab to print up these babies, or they'd call the cops."

He found an envelope and pulled out some eight-by-tens. "You man enough for this?" he asked with a wicked smile, handing them over without waiting for my reply.

It was Mike and someone else in darkness, both naked, Mike's arms virtually holding his partner captive as they kissed. For the next shot, Mike was rubbing the other guy's neck and shoulder muscles, loosening him up for something. Then Mike had him facedown on a bed, straddling him while binding his hands at the wrists. For the fourth shot, Mike had turned him on his back to stroke his hair with a look of strangely threatening tenderness.

"It's Harry," I said.

"Yeah. Told you I always turned my boy friends out."

The next still found Mike gorging himself on Harry's cock; the next after that showed Mike looming over Harry and opening up a pocket knife.

"Jeepers," I said.

"Art studies, they call that," Mike informed me.

In still number seven, Mike was lovingly pulling a pillowcase over Harry's head, and for the finale Mike held Harry down with his left hand as his right bore the knife on high for, unmistakably, an ecstatic plunge into Harry's heart.

"Well, for gosh sakes!"

"Had a feeling you wouldn't go for those," he said, chuckling as he packed them away.

"What did Harry think of all that, may I ask?"

"You kidding? The session got his cream so stirred up we had to go on and fuck right there in the studio. I didn't trim that little bastard easy, either. Stuck it to him wham-style. But he was just laughing. He liked to shout 'hee-haw' when he was about to cream. He'd go crazy."

"Could we find a picture of the real Mike?" I said. "Just, like, how you appear to be?"

"You mean this?" as he whips out a faded snapshot.

"Who's that?"

"Me. In high school."

Boy, was he different then. Slim and smiling in some team uniform and brandishing a baseball bat. Some kid. Gareth?

"Okay, now here's one you should like," he said, diving into the pile as I deftly pocketed the shot, undetected. "Classic Vic Astarchos."

That it was: the brooding Titan of note, standing around in just about nowhere, being himself.

"This'll do," I said.

You know, I didn't realize how much I'd liked Mike till he was gone. I hid the stolen photo of the young Mike in a secret place for considered review at some future date and set the champion porn Mike on the mantel, where Kern and Carlo would, on their visits, pick up on it and favor us with a few words.

"That good old crazy Mike," Carlo would say.

"The indomitable Vic" would be Kern's salute.

He was neither crazy nor indomitable. He was a man, like all men; finer than many in the look of him but equal to all in the rough fashion of his clay and the sheer bloody nature of his coming into and going from this earth. When I first heard that he was dead, I thought it another of those rumors. But this one persisted, and was, at length, confirmed. Mike was over, of the usual reason, at the age of forty in San Francisco.

"You're not going to start mooning about this, are you?" Dennis Savage asked when I told him the news. "You haven't spoken to the guy in ten years."

"He haunts me. He was special. He had something."

"When," he asked me, "are you going to learn that muscle and cock are not the mirror of the soul? You find these . . . these utterly themeless johnny-go-lightlies and you build them into Parsifals! Yet all they had going for them was a three-hours-a-day gym habit! *That's all they are,* at long last. What do you think you're on, some holy quest?"

"What would you call it?"

"Cruising."

"Well, that's what I call gay life. Only we're cruising for more than hot dates. Something of value's at stake. Affirmation, recognition. A warmth that tells us that we don't have to score to connect."

He thought this over, then said, "This is what it's all about: Hearing that this unfortunate man has been struck down as he was about to approach middle age emphasizes the concept of youth. You don't just want him alive again, you want him *young.* Because if he's young, *you're* young. You're not sad for him. You're sad for you. You're mourning your loss of freedom."

"You're wrong."

"Outside, it's another lurid, humid Saturday in the New York summer. All sensible people, like me, are inside with the air-conditioning set to IGLOO. Only zanies and the homeless are on the streets, and that of course includes Virgil and our rudimentary little Cosgrove, who, as we speak, are combing the Upper West Side for respondents to their sex survey. Join them—fill your water bottle, take your ridiculously antique Raleigh three-speed that was trendy among eleven-year-olds thirty years ago, and work this off with a nice hard ride. Because, as I hope you recall, we have a video evening with my editor, Peter Keene, Esquire, at eight o'clock tonight, and I don't want you crushing the proceedings with gloom."

"I couldn't possibly face a party in my present mood."

"Very well, but it's my famous horseradish meatballs and seven-layer cake."

I paused, delicately.

"What's the movie?" I asked.

"*La Dolce Vita*. Peter insisted."

"I'll be there," I said.

I did go out on my bike, riding straight west, turned onto Eleventh Avenue and pedaled down into the West Village, braking at something like the spot where Mike might have stood when he first realized that he had the power. In those days, the Village teemed with punters on summer weekends; today the place is nearly deserted.

I thought of Mike here, and everybody going Who Is That Guy? at him. I thought of Carlo cradling him that night long ago in the Pines, and "You should save that for your tombstone," and how Kern might have felt when he first glimpsed Mike in the baths, the Mystos 10 wolfness heading right for you, touch the godhead. Your Vic. Your Harry.

No, your *Mike,* I kept saying to myself as I started home. The sky had grown black with cloud; it would pour any minute. I ran lights and overpedaled all the way up Third Avenue. Your Mike: because he was the living end and I vainly dare to soar and all of you know I stole his picture, because it's part of life. And it had his insides, so I hid it. But when I got home I started looking and I couldn't find it anywhere.

LET'S CALL THE WHOLE THING OFF

hy shouldn't we have a cabaret act?" Virgil asked Dennis Savage. "Everybody else does."

"I don't have a cabaret act, do I?" answered Dennis Savage, entering upon another coughing fit.

"Some have cabaret acts," said Cosgrove. "And some have bronchus."

"Bronchitis," Dennis Savage corrected, for the hundredth time.

"It's nice when guys have a hobby," observed Carlo, our referee. "So they can get all fulfilled."

"*A* hobby, yes," Dennis Savage agreed. "Not a hobby a minute."

"We had this hobby for four weeks already," said Cosgrove. Whispering to Virgil, he added, "And he has bronchus."

"*Bronchitis!*"

"What's it to you if they want to put an act together?" I asked Dennis Savage.

"Everyone's against me. Great!"

"Anyway, it's not a hobby," said Virgil, priming the tape recorder. One of the many innovations of his and Cosgrove's act was the use of taped piano accompaniment (by our boy, hem-hem) instead of live music. I thought this a little dangerous, given that Virgil has the mechanical expertise of Squirrel Nutkin and Cosgrove can't even master a cock ring. But Virgil has been applying himself, because he wants to take a serious shot at stardom.

"You're just annoyed," he told Dennis Savage, "because we're going to be famous."

"And everyone will be nice to me," said Cosgrove.

"Let's get our costumes on, Cosgrove," said Virgil, briskly, efficiently. He has no time to waste.

"Costumes," Dennis Savage fumed as the kids went into the bedroom to change. "Banjos. Medleys. Vegas lounge patter. 'How you folks doin'? How fine're you today?' This isn't an apartment—it's a variety show." He turned to me. "And where did they get those costumes, or do I guess?"

"I helped them pick the clothes out, as you have dourly surmised," I said. "Virgil paid for them on his plastic."

"I thought he had a limit of fourteen dollars."

"They've been upgrading him for good conduct."

"The sneak."

"Wow," said Carlo when Virgil and Cosgrove trooped on in their finery: charcoal gray slacks, white turtlenecks, and navy blue blazers. "I want to eat them with a spoon."

Cosgrove giggled.

"It won't hurt you," Virgil told Dennis Savage, "to admit we look formidable."

"Who's been teaching him words?" said Dennis Savage.

"Stop grousing," I told him. "They're only trying to find self-affirmation."

"Yes, but for every one who goes up, someone has to go down."

"Carlo," said Virgil, "will you announce us so we can make our entrance?"

Grinning, Carlo broke into it as the kids ran into the bedroom: "And now, the world-famous Paradise Bar and Grill presents that erotic little duet . . . what's the final name of this act, anyway?"

"We don't have one yet," Virgil called out. (The Von Sondheims had been changing their billing by the week.)

"Well, you truly got to take some title to yourselves, don't you? Or how could I announce you?"

"What about Company?" I said. "Just like that."

"How about The Little Fiends from Hell Who Think They Sing and Dance?" Dennis Savage put in.

Virgil, in the doorway, said, "I think the name should be sexy yet suave and just a little fun-filled."

"I could call you The Fire Boys," said Carlo, as Cosgrove joined Virgil at the bedroom door, " 'cause you're so hot that when you turn up, the whole place goes red in flames."

Virgil, thinking that over, said, "I think I would be more of an ice boy, actually."

Cosgrove said, "I want to be The Ice Boy of the Casbah."

"Presenting that internationally acclaimed act," Carlo intoned, as Virgil and Cosgrove scampered back out of sight, "The Ice Boys!"

In the bedroom, Virgil started the tape and he and Cosgrove sauntered out, stepping to the beat. Like everything they do, it looked completely ridiculous yet won you over with its charm. Virgil's projects attract not through expertise—he has none—but through absolute lack of attitude. If the world is a series of interconnecting systems based on accumulations of money, power, fame, or whatever, Virgil operates as if there were no systems, as if there were nothing in the world but the wish. You think of success, then accomplish it. Virgil is wonderful because he acts as if the world were comprehensible, or a miniature golf course, or his life.

The act:

"Here we are, Cosgrove," Virgil proffers, speaking in rhythm. "Here we are, now then."

"Yes, we're there."

"Fine night, Cosgrove."

"Yes, I'd say."

"What'll come next, now?"

"Why don't we toot?"

"Something smashing?"

"Something cute!"

Whereupon, meticulously timed to a piano flourish on the tape, their smiles and body language and hand gestures cliché Las Vegas lounge—even cliché Port Authority Terminal waiting room—but, to be sure, sexy yet suave and just a little fun-filled, The Ice Boys launched their opening number. Virgil sang:

> You say potayta, and I say potahta,

To which Cosgrove replied:

> You say a chickpea, so I say regatta—

"Stop the show!" Dennis Savage thundered. "That's not how it goes!"

Virgil regarded him patiently. "Cosgrove only remembers his own words."

"But it doesn't make sense that way."

"It does to me," said Cosgrove.

The taped piano was noodling on, the act stalled, the joy oozing out as air leaves a blown bicycle tire.

"What will people think of you," Dennis Savage pursued, "if you can't get the lyrics down?"

Carlo said, "They'll think they're pretty nice to see. Did any good-looking guys ever flop in front of a gay audience?"

Dennis Savage had not taken that into account. He was so busy rating the kids for their lack of talent that he forgot to bottom-line the event: Sweet little boys in white turtlenecks and blazers will hit one hundred on the gay entertainment scale. Ed Sullivan wouldn't have hired them. But Chita Rivera would; and Chita knows.

Well, Virgil and Cosgrove got on with the act—a further helping of chickpea and regatta culminating in a *Chorus Line* medley with top hats and a strutting exeunt.

"A couple of visits to Broadway and he's a choreographer," Dennis Savage moaned.

"Seven visits," I reminded him. "By now, he's virtually the show's dance captain."

Carlo was clapping as if Steve Reeves, Richard Locke, and Rick Donovan had just blended the epochs in a marathon three-some, and Virgil asked him if he'd like to be The Ice Boys' business manager, in a three-way split. Carlo said sure, what else did he have to do?

"Carlo will get us booked at various posh nightclubs," Virgil explained to Cosgrove, "and then we perform."

"We get money, too?" Cosgrove asked, his eyes wide as the fantasy enlarged.

"Only if someone is stupid enough to sign this act up," Dennis Savage said; and Virgil replied, "You really should never rain on our parade."

Dennis Savage shrugged. "Except, let's face it, you're terrible."

"Carlo?"

"They've got something," Carlo said.

Now everyone looked at me.

The thing is, you know, that they're so weird that they're sort of fun. A public that knew nothing of their backstory might take them for an extraordinarily high-concept satire. So:

"This is hot stuff," I said.

With a whoop, Virgil and Cosgrove began celebrating their arrival as artistes and invited the rest of us down to my place for refreshments, which of course meant Virgil's famous grilled cheese and tomato sandwiches and Cosgrove's specialty, Sliced Deli Pickles à la Cosgrove.

Dennis Savage begged off, and, sensing something deep coming down, I stayed behind with him.

"Okay, best friend," I said when we were alone. "Now what?"

"A little talk."

"Yes, it's time for one, I can tell."

"Does it bother you, at the multifarious social functions you are privy to, having to introduce our smashing little Cosgrove to your associates as your beau, or your boy friend, or . . . What word *do* you use, besides that pathetically noncommital 'live-in'?"

Though he has been with Virgil for many years now, Dennis Savage never refers to him as his lover. "They were lovers," he will say, or "Was that Name Name's lover, or just some trick?" But it's always They, never We.

"I mean," Dennis Savage went on, "you do have a certain credibility to protect among the cognoscenti, right? They're going to judge you by—"

"Do you think they judged me when I never had anyone in tow all those years. Do you think they pitied me, or presumed I was too awful to love?"

He was silent, as he always is when I reroute one of his conversations.

"You've raised a valid point," I said. "How much are we judged by the company we keep? And, FYI, I don't use any term when I introduce Cosgrove. I just put a proprietary hand on his shoulder and say, 'This is Cosgrove.'"

"All right, think back now. Of all the men you've known or known of. Not movie stars or porn models. Just people in the world, like us. Whom would you most, to the depths of your being, have wanted to claim as yours? Think of who. Think of why. Think not only of what you would have done in bed but what it would be like at breakfast the next morning. Think! Who was your secret ice boy? Not just for Saturday night, but for life."

I thought, but I already knew the answer. I always know it.

"I'll guess," he said. "Give the hints."

"Tall, suits, Voisin, Brahms," I said.

He smiled. He loves to guess. But his tries weren't even coming close.

"More hints," he said.

"WASP. Nice. Strong. The most dazzling butt in the East Sixties."

He couldn't call it.

"One more hint."

"Straight."

"Are you *still* doing that?"

"What me?"

"I ask for the love of your life and you give me—"

"You asked a question and I answered it. Anyway, haven't you had your moments of crossover? And Carlo—"

"But *we* always know what we're doing when we sneak across the border. You always hope to believe in the improbable, don't you?"

"Anyway," I said, "nothing happened."

"Who was it, finally?"

"Bill Upton."

He drew a blank.

"I may never have mentioned him. We met at D'Agostino's."

"Ah, romance!" An interlude as he coughed up some more bronchitis. "For some there's eternal Rome. For others it's Paris in spring. You find it in D'Agostino's!"

"You know those days when you suddenly realize you have to have a sweet or civilization as you know it will dissolve? And you're fresh out of everything—Entenmann's, applesauce, chocolate, ice cream, plums, Grape Nuts—"

"Grape Nuts is a duty, not a sweet."

"So I got myself together and hiked up to the grocery. And then I couldn't decide between a box of animal crackers and whole-wheat doughnuts."

He put a hand on my shoulder and said, "Now, I don't want to hurry you. The tale is Proustian and the teller is Flaubert, I can see that. Every detail shall be comme ça, précisément. But I just wondered how much time this will take, because in three months my taxes are due and—"

"Do you want to hear or not?"

He smiled. "Think of them downstairs. Three little boys of various sizes. One twenty, one thirty, one . . . how old is our Carlo?"

"Forty-something?"

"The two younger ones whipping up those sandwiches like Chef Boyardee preparing a soufflé for crowned heads, then the three of them eating and laughing and holding each other like teddy bears larking in the store after the toy man goes home. Why don't I feel like that? Why didn't I ever feel like that in my life?"

"You've waited thirty years to tell me this?"

"I didn't know about it thirty years ago. Let's go on with your story. You were eating a Hershey bar at the corner of—"

"Why is it every time I turn around you're having another depression? I *knew* something was up with you!"

"I can't help what I feel, can I? Just go on with your saga of beauty and truth in D'Agostino's."

"Okay. I couldn't decide, right? So I got animal crackers *and* doughnuts. And on the way out I added in this and that. When I was unloading it at the checkout, I noticed that it was all desserts and knicknacks. Potato chips, pretzel logs, rice pudding, Pop-Tarts. Because I already had all the real food at home. But it looked kind of silly, and the man ahead of me was looking over this haul and grinning, and he said, 'Well, I guess we're all set for the orphans' picnic.'"

"Is this the good part? Because by this time it's almost next Sunday."

"I'm about to describe him."

"I hope so, because meanwhile I could have performed a matinée of *Show Boat*."

"He was the handsomest man I'd ever seen. He must have come from work, because he had an attaché. He was six feet two of class and kindness and reason, and I fell hopelessly in love with him at sight. Now, you must remember, this was years ago, and I was young and fit. Quand'ero paggio. You may not believe it, but I was once very, very young. I was a sliver and a smile."

"This must have been sometime around the Lisbon earthquake."

"I took to haunting D'Agostino's at that hour, hoping to bump into him again. And I did. We performed a little chat here, a little joke there, and finally a walk-out-of-the-store together. What did I have to offer, you ask? What did I have on him? Just that I was twenty-three and he was . . . I don't know. A bit older. I started walking around the neighborhood a lot on weekends. You know, to happen upon him on a free afternoon? Finally I did, one spring Saturday. No crowds, no bad New York; even the streets were clean. Jesus, what a day that was! He was so stalwart and I was . . . I. But I started picking up on certain things he said. Even the way he moved. We were walking to Yorkville and back, and—"

"You never do it right. The Village would have been more apropos."

"No, that's just it. He wasn't Village. He wasn't *gay*. We had dinner, and by the end of it I knew for certain. No closet. No bi.

Somehow he just felt at ease with gays. He dated women, he socialized with any man he liked, and he doted on numerous god-
children born to his old college pals. Everyone adored him because
he was so nice. No, admirable. Strong . . . and . . ."

"Profession."

"The law."

"Address."

"That high-rise across from the Catholic school on First Avenue.

"Dress."

"Labels, but not noticeably so. A lot of gray crew-neck
sweaters. Very upscale in shoes, but any old khaki shorts in summer."

"Music."

"Classical standards. Mahler's Fourth, but never Mahler's
Sixth."

"Movies."

"Not so much. He never saw *Bonnie and Clyde,* but he knew
what *Citizen Kane* was."

He pondered. "Princeton?"

"Amherst. You were close."

More bronchitis, then: "How come you never mentioned this
to me before?"

"First, it was too exciting to share and, then, it was too hu-
miliating. He was so wonderful in his sensitive, husky way that you
kept dreading the moment when you would let him down. It was
a heavy wager in self-esteem."

"Wait now. How straight was he?"

"So straight that he would say things like 'I wish I could be
gay sometimes, because I've felt so close to my men friends that I
want to hug them and—'"

He had put a hand over my mouth. "*That* is the most closeted—"

"You had to be there," I got out. "He was on the level. He *was.*
A flawlessly honest and secure man."

"Not married, I'll guess. Right?"

"Divorced."

"What a shock."

"You think every divorced man is a repressed gay? Oh, there's always that fantasy. But if it had been an act, he'd have given himself away. You know: 'Where do you . . . people . . . go?' Endless jive about masturbation. Pseudo-idle comments about men he finds attractive. He did none of it. Bill was pure. So. Did I drift away? No—and you'll like this part: I misbehaved at a party."

He would *love* this part. He beamed like a gay Saint George at the outing of the dragon.

I said, "You remember that little era when I was very political and always getting into fights? Fights about anything?"

He nodded. "You were throwing drinks in so many people's faces, we had to hire a man to follow you around bearing glasses and a decanter of vodka. Some nights I'd see crowds coming down Third Avenue with cocktail onions and ice all over them and I'd say, 'Bud's been to a party again.' That's what I'd say."

"I felt *terrible* about it. Bill was so generous it was catching. You wanted him to admire your style as you admired his. Well, he gave this wingding where all his friends of different kinds would meet and love each other just as he loved them. The babies were cute, and the parents were okay, and the women were smart and fast. But the gays were . . . I don't know how he did it, but except for me, they were all dreary, vicious, left-out queens."

"Except for you."

"They called you Denise at the Valley Forge Jamboree. I was going to take it to my grave, but provocation this fierce demands absolute honesty."

He smiled, the crocodile. "Story, please. I'll even up with you later."

"Story's over."

"Come, come. You'll feel better after you unburden yourself."

"Cosgrove's right. You're Mr. Fee Fo Fum."

"He calls me *that*?"

Another coughing fit.

"Good," I said.

"Tell."

"Full party, and I arrive, dressed to the nth. I am in form, and my style is ready. Everyone at the party will call the next day: 'Who was that marvelous boy who played the piano and knew theatre and opera and, oh, just charmed our tails off?' Okay, so he won't need me physically. He'll need me for who I am, which is even better."

"That isn't better."

"Trouble begins when I am introduced to these two queens who start in on Maria Callas."

"No wonder you got into fights. That's such a personal matter. Anyone would destroy himself socially for Maria Callas."

"It wasn't the subject. It was the manner. They were so supercilious yet so ignorant. Why do these creatures always feel free to expound on subjects of which they know *nothing*? It was like 'Who does she think she is?' in this queen gabble. 'Born in Brooklyn and suddenly she's singing *Le Trovitata*'!"

"Surely you—"

"Look, she wasn't born in Brooklyn—and so what if she *had* been? Jesus, these stupid, pushy freaks. Are these what Bill had in mind when he wished he were gay? Take *them* as far as they need to go? They move through life knowing nothing and claiming everything. . . . So why did I stay on talking to them, going into my slow burn? Why don't I know when to leave?"

"You threw a drink? Two drinks?"

"One of those jerks decided to emphasize a remark by blowing cigarette smoke in my face, so I grabbed his hand and stubbed out the butt on his right cheek."

He shook his head with a crooked smile. "If only they'd had you in Italy when the Visigoths arrived. Rome would never have fallen. We'd be speaking Latin." He sang, "Dixis potetus et dixi potatus."

"I've reformed now, as we both know."

"Ipse."

"Wasn't there something on your mind?" I asked. "Something you wanted to say?"

"First tell me how Bill Upton handled your faux pas."

"There was quite a to-do. Both the queens were shouting and people were trying to help the cigarette guy. Some vigilante cried out, 'Look at him!' to all and sundry, about me. 'He shows no remorse whatsoever!' It was total no-win, so I decided to split. Poor Bill looked so bewildered. He just couldn't figure out what this *was,* you know? I mean, it's something about Maria Callas, then somebody's lying on his carpet having convulsions. Bill is the most perfect man in the East Fifties and such things simply don't occur at his parties. Anyway, it wasn't about Maria Callas. It was about I got fed up with the assholes of the world at the wrong place and time."

"You went home. Now let's guess. You wait a few days, then write a letter of apology."

"I write several, and never send a one. No matter how I explained it, it seemed unforgivable. Bad *style.* The only crime in Bill Upton's code of law. And it kept reminding me how much more work I had to put in on my own sense of stalwart. So I thought, The hell with it. Time will pass and we'll bump into each other and then we can start over."

"And you never did meet, did you?"

"Never."

"Do you miss him?"

"I have done, at times. Terribly. Then I would think, What am I doing with a crush on a straight man? Free yourself! Move on out of there!"

"I quit my job today," he said.

Big pause.

"In the middle of the school year? Aren't you—"

"I told them I was in ill health and could not foresee a secure recovery, and they were happy to let me out of my contract. They think it's AIDS, of course. Let them. They fear the disruption of the PTA and whatever, and I'm afraid that one more day in a classroom and I'll bloody murder those fucking assheads. Ye gods,

I've spent my *life* in a classroom. And I know when to leave."

"Well, well."

"Yeah."

"What," I asked, "are you going to do for cake?"

He shrugged. "I've got savings. And the money from my mother's will. Now I'm going to take it easy. And who knows? Maybe . . . royalties?"

He was looking at me, to see what I thought of that, but I stayed pretty blank; and just in time, the rest of us banged in, cheering and shouting.

"Carlo got us an audition!" cried Virgil.

"Our name in lights!" Cosgrove uttered.

"Gave a call down to Cash Westman at the Nine O'Clock Song on Spring Street," Carlo explained. "He still likes me. Says, 'Any act you're managing has got to be prime.' "

"Well, we are," said Virgil.

Dennis Savage started coughing again.

"Guess who still has bronchus," said Cosgrove.

Dennis Savage looked at him for some time. "What did I tell you this condition is properly called?"

"Fee Fo Fum Disease," said Cosgrove, getting behind Carlo.

Dennis Savage turned to me. "You know, bronchitis can lead to pneumonia. It isn't a joking matter."

Cosgrove chanted, "*Bron*chus, *bron*chus, they *say* that you have *bron*chus!"

Without a word Dennis Savage went into the bedroom and slammed the door.

"He's pretty sore," said Carlo.

"He quit his job today."

"He quit his teaching?" said Carlo, baffled. "Why?"

"He got bored and gave it up. He knows when to leave."

"We know when to enter," Virgil put in, collecting his tape equipment. "Because the Ice Boys have the look and sound of the nineties." He seemed efficient, even brusque, as he got his stuff together, sure of where he's headed.

"The Ice Boys," Cosgrove gloated. "You can run, you can hide—"

"We have to rehearse," Virgil nearly barked. "Carlo, you should work the tapes, and Cosgrove, you're not turning fast enough on the twirls in 'Roses of Picardy.'"

"I will, though."

Virgil surveys his crew. "Men, in two days we're going to face the business end of the playbill. It's every performer's nightmare. Yes: the audition. But I know we can pull together and win the cup." He focused on Cosgrove. "Think of it as a performance, as our debut."

"Everything's coming up Cosgrove," Cosgrove hopefully offered. "Okay, Virgil?"

"We're the Ice Boys, and we're going to move like today. We're going to show them the steps of the age. The citywalk, Cosgrove."

"By ourselves?" Cosgrove fearfully asked, suddenly aware of the strain, the challenge, between the ego and the audience.

"Carlo will be there," Virgil replied. He's military, then he's airy, then he's reassuring. What does this mean, and who does he think he is becoming?

They were looking at me, Cosgrove pleading, Carlo inviting, and Virgil tolerant.

"Me come too?" I said. "Sure."

I should have realized that Cash Westman would turn out to be one of Carlo's old tricks and thus a maddeningly bracing hunk; but who would have guessed that Cash was wild for kids? He welcomed Virgil and Cosgrove to his SoHo club, deserted in the dead afternoon, as Boswell drank in the chatter at Child's Coffee-house. Never, I think, have I seen a man so erotically playful with strangers, not just flirting but pervasively seductive. Carlo diplomatically explained that Cosgrove was "hooked up with Bud here." I don't think Cash was listening, as he was busy tracing the lines and planes of Virgil's face with a long, lean finger. He told Virgil, "I want to call you 'Skyman.'"

Virgil was reserved and Cosgrove was staring. I looked at Carlo, signaling, Do Something.

"The Ice Boys are truly New Wave," Carlo said. "You're going to like them."

Cash, still fascinated with Virgil, nodded.

Now Cosgrove tried to Do Something. "Some boys are easy," he said. "I know one boy who has to be paddywhacked and doggy-fucked as hard as can be."

"This boy?" Cash murmured, his eyes on Virgil's.

Then Virgil finally Did Something. He put his arms around Cash and rested his head against Cash's chest. Cash held him close and stroked the back of his neck. It was very unpleasant, a splendid moment that gives no joy.

"Virgil," said Cosgrove, "will you help me fix the handkerchief in my jacket pocket? It's all fluffing out."

Virgil slowly nuzzled Cash's chest, ignoring Cosgrove and their new act and some outstanding responsibilities.

"We have to to do the citydance," said Cosgrove. "Please."

Virgil let go of Cash, took half a step back, then stuck a finger inside Cash's belt, pulled him close, grabbed him by the shoulders, and kissed him.

"Who's he supposed to be?" I whispered to Carlo.

"That little Virgil's always got a surprise for us," replied Carlo, not smiling.

Cash and Virgil broke apart, staring at each other.

Cosgrove coughed lavishly. "I wonder if I have bronchus," he said, watching Virgil.

Cash finally noticed us, and smiled. "Let's hear the act."

I was repositioning Cosgrove's handkerchief and Carlo was setting out the tape equipment. Virgil pointed Cosgrove to the banjo cases, and they took out their axes, Cosgrove nervously fumbling and Virgil pensive, distant, his ear on new music. I had seen flashes of this developing Virgil, in sudden confidences in strange places or impatience with those he should treat gently. But I hadn't seen him throw it all on at once like this. Had he no thought of what

Cosgrove was feeling at this moment, or what I might need to say to Dennis Savage when he asked about the audition?

It went fine, by the way. Cash was dazzled—yes; yes, we know that, but I mean he really liked the act. Perhaps he realized that the Ice Boys' charm lay in a magnificent lack of perspective. "'You say a chickpea'?" he echoed, at the end.

"It's The Ice Boys' version," said Virgil.

"Wild. And you're the pianist?" he asked me. "Why don't you play live?"

"Virgil wouldn't let me."

Cash grinned at Virgil. "You're really in charge, huh?"

Cosgrove said, "He has the lock and key to my inner soul."

I think it was at that moment in particular that Cash and Virgil fell in love. Virgil was standing on the stage, ten feet from Cash, who was down near the first line of tables. They were simply looking at each other. But it had the atmosphere of fucking.

Cosgrove started to cry, and Virgil said, "Cosgrove, I told you not to be nervous for the audition."

"That's not why," said Cosgrove. Virgil at least took him in his arms—which was the least he could do, I thought—and Carlo pulled Cash off to the side to explain choice details about our beveled ménage.

Anyway, we collected ourselves, and The Ice Boys were offered an engagement, and Carlo and Cash talked business—Carlo, I'm thrilled to say, driving an advantageous bargain for our side, with all sorts of perks about flyers and free entrée for friends of the act, and so on. In the cab going home, the four of us indulged in some victory cheers, but, let's face it, this wasn't a happy outing.

You know what I did? I called Bill Upton. Term it impulse; we all have such from time to time. It was much later that evening, and I was well advanced upon the splendor of my cups. I shot high.

It was a nice call, real citywalk, a little brandy with your chocolate. Bill was right there, no tape, and he responded warmly to my name, and we went over those days when I was twenty-three and had nothing to lose. I was blitzed enough to tell him that the second greatest thing about him was the way he looked when he'd take off his suit jacket, because he had such wide shoulders and such a tight belt line and such a dreamy butt; and that the greatest thing about him was he didn't get upset when you told him.

He asked if I was still "a caution," and I explained that I have retired from the field of battle. So he invited me to a party, on the same night as the Ice Boys' opening. Bill Upton's parties run late, so that was neat and I said yes.

Dennis Savage managed to shake his bronchitis and suffer a relapse a few weeks later, so he was unable to attend the Boys' debut. I can't say that he expressed more than perfunctory regret, and I told him that boycotting Virgil's project would drive a wedge between them.

"Oh, there are so many wedges already," he replied. "A wedge of age. A wedge of energy. A wedge of adventure. It's such hard work trying to be an ice boy at my age."

"He needs—"

"Encouragement? Were you going to?"

I nodded.

"Say? Yes. Encouragement. How we all need it. But he gets all he wants from inside himself. One day I looked in the mirror, and you know what I saw? He was a young thirty and I wasn't there at all."

"Can't you just wish him—"

"Of course I can. I *won't*."

So the rest of us went off to the Nine O'Clock Song, Cosgrove excited because this was the third time in a week he'd been in a cab. Virgil was composed, and Carlo, turning around in the front seat, was studying him. When we reached the club, the kids went in with their banjos, and Carlo, bearing the tape machine, loitered while I paid the driver.

"Want to hear a news?" Carlo said as I turned around. "That kid's been sleeping out."

"Virgil?"

He nodded. "And I don't mean a little East Side nooky. He's been doing it slow-mo, and rough-me-up-style, and standing-in-the-window, and the whole rest of the all-the-way handbook. You see his eyes? They look like the moon."

"He seemed very quiet."

"Sure he's quiet. A boy is quiet because he's thinking about it. How great it was and how great it's going to be. Tell you something else. He's taking heavy chances. I know Cash."

"Virgil's been seeing Cash? But when? He works in the day-time and he rehearses at night."

"What do you want to bet?"

Cosgrove met us at the door, proudly showing off The Ice Boys' PR photograph. It was posted in front of the club, too, along with those of the other acts on the bill: the usual chorus boys brimming with Broadway, a rather attractive woman comic, and one quasi–drag queen. (He worked in pants, but the kind of pants Carmen Miranda might have worn to a lambada contest.) Cash ran a smart and friendly place: The food was decent, the service admirably functional and attitude-free, and the entertainment organized around the notion that if you don't like this act, a few minutes later you'll like *that* one.

The talent dressed in one big room at the back, and Cosgrove immediately befriended the drag queen and spent the spare minutes telling him about Miss Faye. Virgil was testing the tape equipment. Carlo was talking business with Cash. I went out front, where tables were filling with the performers' friends. Lionel was there with his latest—he never runs out—and Kenny Reeves had brought Rick Conradi, who was now writing a cabaret column for one of those neighborhood giveaways that pile up in your mail room and that nobody reads. Carlo came out and table-hopped. I wondered what Bill Upton would think of this place. He was an enthusiastic theatre- and concertgoer and he loved a party. But did straight men, even wonderful ones, ever truly make the scene? Why do gays always have to invent the arts?

One of the chorus boys opened, followed by the comedienne, then another chorus boy. I haven't heard so much Jerry Herman since the summer of 1979, when someone I was after told me the story of his life in a piano bar.

Then Cash brought on the Ice Boys, to cheers from our crowd and a welcoming buzz from the others. Virgil had drilled Cosgrove ruthlessly to ensure a flawless performance, but that was all run-throughs in an apartment, the two of them alone or buoyed up by family. Suddenly Cosgrove was onstage, playing to strangers, and he clearly had no idea how to treat the assembly. Look over their heads? Look through them? He chose to stare right at them as if looking for someone in particular, and whenever he spotted a familiar face, he said hello.

That was odd, but the whole act is. Nobody knew how to take it, not even our confederates. Well, how would you take it?: It must be a spoof, but it isn't acting like one. There were Cosgrove's bizarre emendations on Ira Gershwin in "Let's Call the Whole Thing Off," what we might describe as the Chickpea Effect. Ah, but on the line "If we had to part then that might break my heart," there was Virgil's tender enfolding of Cosgrove, to show the pain of parting, what we might describe as the Two Chickpeas Hotting Up the Stage Effect. I mean, even Carlo—who has seen this act many, many times—was so taken by that moment that he turned to me and whispered, "Sweet *damn* it all!"

So was it one thing or the other thing? No one knew how to handle the Ice Boys until they got to the Opera Medley. I had begged them to drop this, partly because they accompany the selections on their banjos but mainly because I think it's the sole part of the act that is witless rather than piquant. But they insisted. "I wrote some of these lyrics myself!" Cosgrove wailed. You can tell. At least it's short, snatches of familiar operatic excerpts sung to English words, mostly hoary parodies. For instance, Virgil doles out the F Major strain of Escamillo's aria as:

> Toreadora, don't spit on the floor!
> Use the cuspidor;
> That's what it's for!

while Cosgrove delineates the Wedding Chorus from *Lohengrin* as:

> Here comes the bride!
> All dressed in white!
> Stepped on a turtle
> And down came her girdle!

Well, at this the entire audience, freed from indecision as to what this act meant as a Platonic concept, began to laugh and roar and shout for joy. So I was wrong about the Opera Medley. It's so clearly idiotic that it centers—defines—the act, tells the audience what to do.

The Ice Boys were a big hit. There were calls for an encore, and Cash had trouble working his public down to announce the next performer. Backstage, after the revue was over, I found Cosgrove running around the room like a puppy with a red rubber ball. But I couldn't find Virgil.

"In the office," the drag queen told me, with an odd look.

The office, where Cash shuffles his papers, has a window in its door. The door was closed, but through the window I saw Virgil and Cash, both in the nude, going at it hungry and wild. So Carlo was right; but maybe this was temporary, like just one of those things or let's call the whole thing off and I ran away and visited with our friends out front but I didn't want this new information interfering with Bill Upton's party so I jumped into a cab and there I was at Bill Upton's where I didn't have to think about anything except Can I finally be an ice boy and behave myself?

Bill Upton's: and nothing had changed, including Bill. He had aged maybe three months; I looked like The Picture of Dorian Gray's great-uncle. The piano, the steamship prints, the robust leather couch. The smooth, straight, upright host who liked you no matter what. Everything as it was—including the same angry, stupid queens. Only instead of fighting about Maria Callas, now I get to fight about politics.

Jesus, was he friendly when I walked in! I wondered, If I played handball, would I look like this at his age? He grabbed me like Apollo dating Hyacinthus. Turning me around, showing me off, dazzling me. Great, remind me what I've missed all these years.

Do I have to outline the fight I got into with the queens on the subject of censorship? Except it wasn't about censorship, and I know I'm repeating myself, but it's *never* about the immediate topic, do you realize that, boys and girls? It's always about the rage of the inferior intelligence confronted by an idea. Rich minds like to be challenged; it gives them a chance to rethink their worldview. Empty minds are threatened by challenge, because they don't want to think: They want to be petted. They're like beggars. They insatiably need to be given.

I have to admit, my mind wasn't on the conversation, as I was busy rehearsing what I would say to Virgil when I got home. I do recall saying that MTV should ban all performers who make gay-bashing statements, because "music television" has become so integrated into the rock industry that no singer or group whose videos were dropped from rotation could be called major, not to mention personal appearances on the various specials. The notorious Shabba Ranks had, not long before, announced on British television that all gays should be killed—I happened to have been in England at the time and caught the moment, though it was difficult to understand what Ranks was saying through his loathsome accent. Yet Ranks was allowed to do a guest shot in MTV's annual spring break show. I was so disgusted that I turned the set off, despite the skin festival that MTV's beach programming provides.

Think of the potential of my proposed social experiment. MTV is probably the single greatest influence on the minds of American youth. What a message it could send to them on the morality of tolerance!

Of course, MTV could never ban rock's homophobes—nor

rock's anti-Semites, its racists, or its exploiters of women. Haters—even evilly reveling haters, dancers in blood, Farrakhans so hopped up on murderous anger that their eyeballs balloon—are part of the System. How could they possibly be isolated, marginalized? Disgusting, even alien, as he is, Shabba Ranks is more "American" than a gay man or woman. Hatred isn't unique to America, but only in America is it a business. Televangelists, "family-values" groups, rap: Hatred is capitalism.

And so I was saying to the usual enraged queens, and one of them said, "Banning videos is censorship."

"No," I said. "Censorship is the silencing of ideas by state force. Throwing bigots into prison is censorship. Throwing bigots off a television channel is free and democratic, as long as the channel and not the state makes that choice. They can go elsewhere. They can still sell their records. They can go on *Arsenio;* he drooled over Louis Farrakhan."

"Who are *you* to judge?" cried the other queen. Remember, we're talking about demonizing homophobia—yet *gay men* are rolling their eyes and going red. Am *I* wrong or are *they* filth?

I decided to turn on the charm. I said, "You two must have pathetically unintegrated ego structures. You're ugly, you're old, you're fat, and you scream at anything you don't agree with."

"I'm not screaming!" one of them screamed.

"Yes, you are," I replied. I felt so tired then, so aware of how sides can slip in even the best protected house of cards. Virgil. I thought we were safe. I knew he was growing, but I figured he was content. You know, I felt miscast in my own play? I turned away from the screaming queens to admire the Bill Upton refreshment table, crowned with an elaborate birthday cake frosted in the design of the logo of the Lincoln Center musical *Hello Again*—Bill must have been saluting an actor friend's anniversary.

Remember the argument? The screaming queen counters with "Well, you're screaming, too!"

"No, I'm not," I said, laughing at him. Everyone was looking at us, but still I grabbed the guy by the hair and ducked him in the birthday cake, logo and all, long and hard, all the while enjoying the noise he made, like a walrus buffeted by ice floes.

"More! *More!*" I cried, obliterating the cake with his brainless head. So our boy had another of those scenes at another of Bill Upton's soirées, and this time I marched out without waiting for the crowd to unite against me or for some schmengie to bleat out "He shows no remorse whatsoever" or for Bill to be his stalwart, disappointed self. I told him "I'm not fit to know you" as I passed. He tried to follow, but friends held him back. "I don't have the style," I told them.

I ran the four blocks home, barged into my own apartment, and asked Carlo and Cosgrove to go upstairs so Virgil and I could have a talk.

"Where's Dennis Savage?" I asked him.

"In bed. He's still sick, you know."

"I saw you and Cash in the office tonight."

"I saw you, too."

He showed no remorse whatsoever.

"All right," I said. "What's next?"

Sitting on the couch, he swung his feet up, took it nice and easy.

"I'm moving in with Cash. Tomorrow."

"You don't know anything about him. How—"

"You're wrong. I've been with him every day for three weeks now."

"When?"

"In the days. I quit my job, and I didn't tell Dennis Savage or anyone. I knew what you would say if I told you. So when I left in the morning, instead of going to the magazine, I went to Cash's. Then I helped him run the club in the afternoons. And then I would come back to Dennis Savage's."

"You blindsided him!"

"I secretly knew you would blame me for this. But I had to see what it would be like with Cash. He calls me Skyman, and he whispers whole stories in my ear about the adventures of Skyman.

And when he comes to the door in the morning, all he's wearing is a T-shirt, and I just go ape for the way he is."

"Don't tell me any more."

"It's no one's fault. And you would like Cash, regardless of a certain look on your face. He is very, very nice, mostly. And he never laughs at me, unlike some people I could imagine."

"Will you stay with Dennis Savage if we promise not to laugh? You could have Cash on the side, opening his door in the morning. You don't have to break up the household. Who'll take care of Cosgrove if you—"

"Cosgrove has to grow up now. I couldn't always be taking care of him. Besides, I'm planning that he will visit me. I'm going to take him for steak dinners at Tad's with long bread, onions on the side, and potato-in-the-jacket. That's Cosgrove's favorite treat. If he's a good boy, I let him have an extra salad."

"Virgil, you're the center of his life. His sunlight. He's only content when you're around. If you desert him—"

"I'm *not* deserting him, you rascal man." He sat up. "You . . . guilt-trip man. I am only moving across town, and there will always be room in my life for Cosgrove!"

"Orphan abandoned on East Fifty-third Street. Teacher in shock. Friends downcast. Film at eleven."

"You can *not* hope to blackmail me with that!" he said, weeping. "I know what it is," wiping his eyes. "And you won't make me sad. I took Cosgrove off the street and got him a home. I made him safe, whatever you say. How long do you look after someone before it's his turn to go out to the world? I kept saying that he could go to Tad's by himself, but he wouldn't go without me. The man who cooks the steaks knows us so well he calls Cosgrove Chico, and says 'Chopped steak well done, sí.' He says, 'Special for you.' When he serves Cosgrove, he says, 'Como eso, sí? You like it like this?' I told Cosgrove he can go there anytime he wants."

"He needs you."

"Oh, this is what you say parents always do. They try to get you to do things because it's supposed to be for everybody's good.

And it's just because that's what *they* want. Then they say you're mean when you won't . . . What's that word you use?"

"Placate them."

"Yes." He got up. "I better go upstairs and tell Dennis Savage what it is. He doesn't suspect anything, does he?"

"I don't believe so. Virgil."

He paused.

"I hope you're going to be very gentle with Cosgrove about this. You know it'll dismay him."

"Look who's talking. The big meanie who laughed and laughed at Cosgrove."

"I didn't know him then."

As to what then transpired between Virgil and the usual suspects, I can say nothing—not because I have at long last been seized by a respect for the privacy of my friends' feelings, but because they were too glum to talk about it.

The next day, Virgil left us. You might say that, like Dennis Savage, he quit his job. He decided to move sparely, quickly; he had never had much in the way of clothes and he decided to leave his eleven years' worth of hobbycrafts to Cosgrove. He packed a valise and the attaché case I gave him several Christmases ago, and of course there was the aged, withered, and infinitely stale Bauhaus to lead off. Down came Skyman to render his farewells, giving each of us a warm hug—long ones, I must admit, reconciliatory with me, apologetic with Carlo, and profound with Cosgrove.

What did Dennis Savage get? I never asked, and he never told.

Carlo set a tone for the house by adopting a "Let's see" attitude, keeping open the possibility that this was nothing more than an aberrant junket on Virgil's part and that he would be home in a few weeks. Cosgrove, who lives for the day and doesn't know how to believe in possibilities, spent the afternoon that Virgil left alternately weeping in the armchair and stamping up and down on Virgil's discarded toys.

Dennis Savage behaved impeccably, philosophically, and practically, immediately placing an ad for a houseboy—as if that were all that Virgil had been. Dennis Savage's attitude could be summed up in the ad's headline: "LOOKS COUNT." Carlo thought the whole thing premature. I call it reckless. Cosgrove wondered how "we could get a new Virgil." We were going to get *something,* because Dennis Savage was offering very attractive terms. He even joined a gym and went on a crash diet, in order to facilitate employer-applicant rapport for the interviewing period.

"We have to look on the happy side," he told me. "After all, I've been virtually monogamous for eleven years. Now I can catch up on all the new erotic practices. There's a whole next generation out there."

"The smart ones haven't been doing much."

"So who needs smart?"

As the weeks rolled by, Virgil pursued his honeymoon with Cash Westman and was not seen, except of course onstage at the Nine O'Clock Song. Cosgrove would return from these gigs emotionally depleted, having made, I imagine, overtures of every conceivable kind to Virgil, all of them, surely, sorrowfully, patiently rebuffed. Surely.

"He isn't as nice as before," Cosgrove told me when I asked how it was going. "He's not mean to me, but he's always like his mind is somewhere in the occult. But then I said I wouldn't go on as The Ice Boys unless he gave me a hug and a little kiss each time. And that's better than no Virgil at all."

It was, at least, until the act's booking was up and Virgil declined to seek further engagements. That night, Cosgrove came home, climbed into bed, and cried all night.

But Dennis Savage was rejuvenated. I've never seen anyone lose weight so easily—or, rather, so quickly; but then he was hitting the gym like a neophyte bodybuilder, living on lettuce and solid white tuna, forked up raw from the can.

One night he strode in to show off, and what he had to show was his packet of answers to his houseboy ad. Cosgrove was working on a jigsaw puzzle—one of Virgil's bequests—and Carlo was watching a Clint Walker movie.

"Here comes The Man of a Thousand Salads," I announced, letting Dennis Savage in.

"Turn the TV off," he suggested, "and I'll show you some *real* skin."

He read from the letters and passed round the pictures, and all I could think was, Is this happening? Has Little Kiwi abandoned us without a glance behind him? Cosgrove was staring at the pictures like Columbus in mid-Atlantic, examining the horizon for a sight of the thing that saves you. I didn't say so, but it seemed to me that the person who might save Cosgrove wouldn't be answering an ad for a live-in whore.

"What's *his* name?" Cosgrove asked, looking over an applicant who sent in a coy nude, "artistically" lit and posed, a shot in the dark.

"He calls himself Hardin," said Dennis Savage, examining the accompanying letter.

"How can anyone even see him like this?" said Cosgrove plaintively. "How will we *know*?"

"I like this one," said Dennis Savage, handing me another snap. This kid, smirking in running shorts and Reeboks, was hardly the successor to Virgil whom Cosgrove hoped for. But in another part of the forest he could prove useful. The look was pure hustler, absolutely guaranteed do-everything hotness and no strings attached.

"Billy," Dennis Savage said.

"He looks mean," Cosgrove observed.

I asked, "Didn't you once treat me to an endless spiel about what you wanted was personality along with the sex?"

Dennis Savage shrugged. "Maybe that's how I felt that week," he replied, gathering his mail. "This week—"

"You tell me this," I insisted. "To the depths of your being, whom would you most have wanted to claim as yours?"

"Oh . . ." He tilted his head and thought about it. "The one I had, I suppose. But we may have gone as far as we needed to go.

The occasional setback, while temporarily painful, often has a stimulating effect upon the system as a whole."

"Listen, he's Doctor of Philosophy," said Carlo.

"He's Doctor Pompous von Fruiter," I said.

"He had bronchus," said Cosgrove.

So Dennis Savage went upstairs to give Billy a call; and Cosgrove, woebegone at his puzzle, feeling each piece as if it might put him in touch with Virgil, perhaps by astral projection, asked Carlo, "Mr. Smith, will you please help me with this puzzle?"

Carlo said, "No, just climb into my lap and I'll hold you for a spell." Whereupon Carlo stroked the boy till he fell asleep, exhausted by apprehension.

Then Carlo said, "He's afraid that with Virgil gone he'll be thrown out on the street."

"He knows better than that."

Carlo shook his head. "Virgil was his magic. Magic's gone now, so anything can happen. It doesn't have to make sense."

"I'll have a talk with him tonight."

"Be better if you could get that Virgil back where he belongs. I know Cash's scene. That's not our Virgil boy, no way."

I sat next to Carlo on the couch. I said, "They invited me to dinner, he and Cash. Next Sunday. Skyman called me this afternoon. He said they want to take us one at a time. I suppose they figured I'm the easiest of the family."

Carlo gave that an ironic chuckle.

"I mean," I went on, "in the sense that Dennis Savage and Cosgrove are Virgil's castoffs, and you've had some history with Cash. I'm the neutral party."

"Don't be too neutral," he told me, pulling Cosgrove closer. "This hurts."

I've been to dinner for all sorts of reasons other than pleasure, but I really grumbled about this one. First of all, Carlo and Cosgrove regarded me as The Man in Charge of Getting Virgil Back, and nothing would dissuade them. They even horned in on how I should dress. Anything I chose they rejected. "That looks too hungry," said Carlo; or "Isn't that a flashy style?" Cosgrove worried.

Carlo wanted me in cords and a white T-shirt, his go-everywhere ensemble since he'd hit New York, but outside it was the coldest day of the year.

"Hey!" Carlo cried. "You'll wear your school coat on top, with the crest!"

"That blazer is from ninth grade," I protested. "I can't get into it anymore. Cosgrove wears it now."

"I spilled just a little tiny bit of Coke inside the pocket," said Cosgrove. "But it's good as new."

"This is ridiculous," I told them, but they were already bundling me into my overcoat. "It's too dressy. And I need a sweater."

"Cash won't be impressed by a sweater," said Carlo, winding a scarf around my neck. "He likes his men tough and plain."

"Like Little Kiwi?"

"That proves they're wrong for each other," he said, pushing me out the door. "Be firm with Cash and extra nice to Virgil."

"And don't come back without him!" Cosgrove added; but I said, "Wait," because Dennis Savage had just stepped out of the elevator and was regarding us wryly. Someone was with him: Billy, the new houseboy.

"Going calling?" Dennis Savage asked me. "Anyone I know?"

"Perfect stranger, if you ask me."

Dennis Savage introduced Billy to us all at once. He was taller than we thought from his picture and, if possible, even hotter, with nervy, cool facial expressions and fast-operator tones, so turned-on by his own sexuality that he could do a marathon with Jeff Stryker and it would still be masturbation. The ideal ice boy, Mystos 10.

"How come he's dressed so ritzy?" Billy asked Dennis Savage, of me, as we shook hands. "Is he richer than you?"

Carlo instinctively put a hand on Cosgrove's shoulder, but Cosgrove pushed forward wonderingly and helplessly. "I'm Cosgrove," he said. "Will you please be my new friend?"

"Who's the faggot?" said Billy.

"I don't like that talk," said Carlo.

"*Hey,* big guy, like it's . . . Come on, it's no offense. I'll be everyone's new friend, watch. I'm moving in with the moneyman here. There's plenty of time to get acquainted." He patted Cosgrove's head. "Sure I'm your friend. You call me Billy, get it?"

"Please be nice."

Billy snickered. "I'm the nicest. Watch."

"Oh, they'll be watching," said Dennis Savage, as I signaled the elevator. The door opened immediately.

"Yeah, Billy the wonder boy, they call me. In and out, slow and deep. Get it?"

"The moneyman, huh?" I said to Dennis Savage.

He smiled. "All things can be worked out."

"Yeah," said Billy.

I got into the elevator.

One flaw in life in New York is The Cab Ride from Hell, which you get approximately every fortieth trip—a speed demon barreling wildly through the streets, a cokehead drifting across the lane markings, a smoker with no visible driver license. I got a combination of all three on my ride to dinner with Virgil and Cash, but it was so cold I was reluctant to get out. After we took the Seventy-ninth Street Park transverse in seven seconds, however, I erupted from the cab and started walking to the address, on Eighty-fifth Street near Columbus. But one long block of Arctic weather and I stopped to hail another cab.

They were all occupied, the few that were out. It must have been the coldest day of the century. The ice caps were expanding, glaciers had advanced as far as Darien, and the population had been evacuated. Only a few stragglers were left, like the man heading toward me, a rakish hat pulled down over his eyes, his hands in his pockets, a well-dressed man checking the street in search of rescue, like me. Soon a cab would come and we would fight for it, every man for himself, New York–style.

He saw me, stopped, then came up, perhaps to suggest we share it—which sometimes happens, even in New York—when he pulled off his hat with a broad smile and treated me to the stupendous handshake that has passed into legend on Sutton Place.

Bill Upton.

"What are you doing here?" I said. "This is the West Side."

"I just had late brunch and I forgot my gloves and it's the end of the world."

"I've got to get to Eighty-fifth Street."

"I'll drop you, if we can—"

"No, you take it."

"Don't be absurd," he replied, looking down Columbus Avenue for a sign of life.

"Everything's going wrong," I said. "Some lose gloves and some lose friends, and I probably shouldn't say that to you, but you don't know what's been happening to me. And to my . . . my people. I don't do flawless as automatically as you do, but I usually try to be fair. Not impartial, maybe, but generous."

I was moving too fast, blurting things out, making allusions to taboo material, his and mine, that I myself didn't catch till I had uttered them. I tried to slow down and catch up the reins, but there are times when the things that absolutely must not be said are the things you have to say. Even violence has feelings, boys and girls.

So I brought up his latest party and how badly I had, once again, behaved. I ran through the action with tactless exactness, as if I had only heard tell of it and were rehearsing a column, recounting the doings of strangers. Ice, sheets of it, engulfing my life. Or *fire*. Ice boys and fire boys: Who will you be?

Ah, but here came a cab, and I hailed it. I thought of a

debonair smile and put it on, as I said, in conclusion, "He still feels no remorse whatsoever."

I gulped as I said it. I lost it, kids—I almost sobbed.

And my stalwart, endlessly forgiving friend reached out a large hand and stroked my hair.

CHE SARÀ, SARÀ

My parents never explained why we were suddenly moving to Venice; but when did they ever explain? We kids were chattel, walk-on parts. "What's for dinner?" we would call out, entering the kitchen like David and Ricky Nelson. But my mother, adjusting the drape of her shapeless black gown and repositioning her black peaked hat, would scream "You'll see when you get it!" as her cauldron bubbled.

Years later, we reckoned that my father, a building contractor, had got into trouble with the Boys (as they're known in the building trade) and sent us off while he renegotiated. Friends ask, "Surely not to *Italy*?" But the Mafia is empowered only in the western half of Sicily. Venice is as safe as Nairobi.

"Take only essentials," my mother warned. "Leave all hope behind." My father, already fluent in Italian because of his war experiences, bought a Berlitz hear-it-repeat-it record course for family use, but nobody went near it except me. As a born record buff, I officially collected the discs (meaning I took physical possession of them and, when anyone asked, denied all knowledge of their whereabouts). I also used them, not realizing that Berlitz "Italian" was in fact the Tuscan dialect of the area around Florence. Venetians spoke their own dialect, different enough to be impenetrable to the outlander sporting tourist Berlitz. I still remember crowds of locals gathered in the cafés to watch television of an evening, the Venetians howling with derision at the Roman, Tuscan, or Milanese inflections they heard.

There are no intercontinental flights to Venice because of the tidy dimensions of Marco Polo Airport. We landed in Rome, took the Rapido up the boot, and had pretty much the same experience that Katharine Hepburn has in the movie *Summertime,* surging out of the railroad station to see, with one's uncompromising personal take, the last thing one was ready to believe: The city is really built on water!

We took the vaporetto—the city bus—down the Grand Canal to the Salute stop, just one short of San Marco, at the round Baroque church that has been a symbol of Venice for over three hundred years. My father (who was to settle us in, then fly home) sped on to handle the business side of our arrival while the rest of us straggled along with the luggage. As we neared the address, my father, who had doubled back to meet us, warned my mother that she would not be pleased. We had taken the house by description only; the building we presently pulled up in front of was a lugubrious pile of Wailing Wall stone.

But when we passed through the street door, we found ourselves in a little courtyard giving directly onto a beautiful garden. And the garden led, around a turn, to a trim, fresh two-story villa. These were to be our house and garden for the next fourteen months, and their proximity to the decayed façade that had so jarred us typifies the Venetian scene: the slum opening up upon the green world, the outrageous juxtaposition. Venice, after all, was the police-state democracy, the city that once had countless sumptuary laws but eleven thousand six hundred fifty-four prostitutes, the least anti-Semitic state in the Catholic world yet the inventor of the ghetto, an impregnable power in the fifteenth century and a joke by the seventeenth.

The very new shoved up against the very old *is* Venice, I was to learn; a teenager from one neighborhood may harbor, against the folk of another neighborhood, grievances dating back a thousand years. We had a teenager in our courtyard, one Zulian, and he did not bear a grudge against anyone. He was fifteen, two years older than I, a crucial difference among adolescents, who traditionally honeycomb only with their immediate coevals. But Zulian and I clicked instantly, partly because my family had a TV set but mainly because he was fascinated with the U.S. and I was the only one of my brothers who could converse with him—in bits and pieces, true, and with him constantly redirecting my tongue from Berlitz, improving, for instance, "Ella è sua moglie" (when I was explaining who a certain Mrs. O'Toole was) to "La xe so mujer." It sounded like Spanish to me. But that was Venetian.

I'm not going to pretend that this was some idle good-neighbor policy. I was in the stewing-hormones stage, and he was an Aristotelian compound of a very telling type, all eyes and hands. When he wanted to get serious, he held you like a pickpocket. He was my first love, but so was Venice and its men in general. Italian life prepared me for the essential fact of gay culture: Beautiful males get away with everything.

Zulian was my point of contact with that philosophy. I saw how frustrated his mother would get when berating him for some infraction, because she and he both knew she was already forgiving him unconditionally even as she chastised. That's mother love in Italy, a no-win combat. I've seen them weep in helpless fury. In other places, "Boys will be boys" is an excuse. In Italy, it is a religion.

Boys will be Zulian was my religion. As the months passed, we grew closer, as he graduated me from Zulio, his all-purpose nickname, to Zulì, for friends only, then to Zuleto, as his family called him. We played calcio (soccer) in the street. We kept each other company on his messenger routes, an after-school job that took him into offices with a mysteriously fly-by-night air where people looked up startled and guilty when we entered. Zuleto was magic, Zuleto was cool, and Zuleto was a map: Tagging along on his deliveries, I got the city down cold.

Zuleto was a language lab as well: He taught me Venetian. I was flailing till I found a grammar in a pawnshop that specialized in used books and suddenly realized how consistently Venetian simply scaled down Tuscan in both syntax and spelling. That freed Zuleto and me actually to enjoy halting conversations, especially about sex. I learned an entire subvocabulary that the Berlitz discs had blandly omitted, including twenty-six synonyms for "chiavere" ("to key": to fuck).

I was so stupid that I thought I had a chance. Well, why not, when the guy can't say ciao without feeling you up and giving you a kiss? When the words for "I like you" are the same as for "I love you"? Italian boys flirt with everyone; it's partly why the country is so wonderful, but it's mainly why the country is so confusing.

For the warm months, my family took a cabana at the *Death in Venice* hotel on the Lido, and my mother, brothers, and I went there every day. There was a lot of skin—a lot of men wearing very little—and coming from the ascetic American culture of the early 1960s, I was taking in a lot of information, particularly from the Swedish body gods who changed in the inexpensive by-the-day cabanas at the rear of the beach. I don't mean that I actually spoke to them. I mean I was lurking and watching and figuring out how the entire world worked philosophically and ontologically—what gay culture, I later learned, terms "cruising."

Back in town, as we passed through the courtyard, Zuleto would come running down to pull me away from the others to narrate some exploit. A fight, an encounter, a possible new job. We would walk along the Zattere, the long straightaway overlooking the huge Giudecca Canal, and I would pretend to listen while drinking him in and thinking, All I want in the world is to touch this . . . well, "unbelievably beautiful boy" is how we put it now. There were no such terms in those days, no modes for romantic expression of any kind. Not for a thirteen-year-old American gay kid who was still a good decade ahead of his first Parade.

I schemed. I scenarioed. I what if?ed. A bolder soul would have been able to flourish a more imposing report than I can, for nothing occurred between Zuleto and me. Oh, sure, I should have staged one of those . . . you know: Alone together in my bedroom, my family at the beach, we talk of girls, we get excited. Then the famous One Thing Led To Another.

Except one day, when I did in fact skip the beach, I happened to look out of my window to catch Zuleto and some girl in the garden. (I had given him a blanket permission.) I couldn't hear them, but there was no mistaking her practiced look of alarm as he tried to lock her eyes with his, dared a caress, another, held his finger to his mouth only to touch her mouth with it in turn, presto, prestissimo, pulling out his smile that reads "I'm too marvelous to be guilty," leaning forward to whisper, his fingers reaching for her sides, cheek, breasts. I'm watching, the hidden me. Yes, as his eyes turn on to full, and he'll take her this way, because his looks move to yes, and, thus captivated, because now she's so yes, that girl took that boy in with the longing of Juliet for keen Romeo.

There it is. My hopes amounted to no more than a pathetic hunger: And I gave them up.

Zuleto and I stayed friends, though on a less elated level. In fact, I believe I maintained a very healthy relationship with him—as many gay men have to, where one is Barkis and the other isn't willin'. Sex is everything; but on the other hand it isn't. Fourteen months after we hit Italy, we returned home—again, without a word of explanation—this time to a new start in the New York suburbs. Zuleto and I exchanged letters every once in a long while. He even telephoned—when he got engaged, when his wife became pregnant, when she died in childbirth. And, most recently, when his son, Candio, began seeing a girl Zuleto did not approve of and refused to break it off.

"Co se fa?" he moaned. What do I do now? "With all our fighting, the whole sestiere will learn of our shame. Guai, un scandolo de piazza!" It'll be a public scandal!

"But what's wrong with the girl?" I kept saying. "Xela bela?" Is she pretty, at least?

He sighed. "Amico mio, is it not enough that I say she is unworthy? You want her papers to look over?"

"But what's the problem?"

He sighed again. "La xe una tedesca." She's German. "A guide for the hotels. You know. In this palazzo died famous English poet Robert Browning. In that palazzo my beloved German soldiers tortured Venetian patriots. Ma, bene! I love Italians! I date Italians. I kill Italians. *Now* you see? This trash that my boy picks out, of all Venice, to be loving?"

"Maybe it's only an episode."

"They want to marry," he said, as doleful as a broken old church bell. "He tells me this."

We had a rule, in these calls, that at some point or other the one who had been phoned would offer to call the other back after both had hung up, to equalize the bill. But Zuleto was so unhappy that he couldn't tear himself away from his text, basically that of every father about every son: *He won't take orders!*

Well, he shouldn't. And gay men and women, I proudly note, are the pioneers in the case. We weren't put on earth to placate the furies of the father. His disapproval is his problem.

So I wasn't much help. But Zuleto thought this the ideal opportunity for me to revisit the home of my youth and meanwhile "talk reason" into Candio, who respected all American ideas.

For a moment, I was tempted. I mean: Venice again! But wait.

"Zuleto, there's no 'American idea' about whom your son chooses to date. What could I possibly say about it?"

"Ma, amico, no gastu el don de parlantina?" Don't you have the silver tongue? "Talk him into circles till he doesn't know what he wants."

I couldn't believe it—I had actually reached the age of the domineering parent. And here was one such inviting me to become his confederate in manipulation.

No way. I put Zuleto off, to his quite formally delivered disappointment. But it's hard to concentrate on someone else's domestic troubles when your own family is exploding.

I mean, *Gakk!* That dinner with Cash and Virgil, the one so coolly hot, so suavely trashy, Ledermeister doing Noël Coward; and the other in the uniform of his new life, rape-me-quick mesh pants topped by no shirt, a colorful tie, and a black leather vest. (This despite the Arctic weather that day; what dedication.) All right, I enjoy a hot look on a kid. But not when it's your nephew, or whoever he was. Then getting grilled by Carlo and Cosgrove, enduring Dennis Savage's fastidious ignoring of the event, and having to field questions from our many bewildered friends. How did Goethe put it? "Life's a bitch and then your boy friend splits."

Listen to this bit of whimsy from the front: Entranced with an electric pasta-maker I saw on an infomercial, I tried Bloomingdale's, found the very model "as seen on TV," and brought it home, to Cosgrove's immense delight. Like all Americans, he loves gadgets, and suddenly we were swimming in vermicelli, macaroni, tagliatelle, angel hair, fettuccine, linguini, penne, manicotti, pappardelle, rotini, shells, and so on. With my help, the little chef devised his very own dish, Rigatoni à la Cosgrove, in which the pasta is stirred up with sautéed shrimp, mushrooms, red pepper, peas, onion, raisins, and cashews. Top with, as we put it chez nous, "a little fresh grated." But Cosgrove insisted on adding a "secret ingredient" to it all: "which we would never tell anyone," he explained, "so it's always our magic thing." The secret, after some trial, turned out to be Pickapeppa Sauce, which bites tartly on the tongue and lends a handsome dark color to the plate.

We were so proud of ourselves that I invited our own master of the kitchen, Dennis Savage, to sample and judge. Billy elected to pass, which was fine with Dennis Savage. "I must say, I prefer the less overwhelming kind of romance," he blithely explained as we headed downstairs. "These really so *devouring* affairs, where everyone's always on top of everyone else. No privacy, no independence. It's a *fascism* of love." He shook his head like an animal lover at a bullfight.

I said nothing.

"See, what holds Billy and me together is, he gives me sex and I give him money. We don't try to flourish on pretenses."

As I unlocked my door, he looked me dead in the eye, daring me to haggle. I kept my counsel.

As we entered, I could hear the roar of the pasta machine, and I led Dennis Savage to the kitchen, where Cosgrove was, as he sometimes does, keeping house in jockey shorts. He shot a house-proud smile at Dennis Savage. But the latter suddenly recalled a childhood rhyme, and chanted,

> I see London,
> I see France,
> I see Cosgrove's underpants.

For a moment, Cosgrove stood frozen in outrage, his eyes on overload. Then he grabbed the usual bread knife and went after Dennis Savage, who ran into and locked himself within the bedroom.

"Get him off me!" Dennis Savage called out, as Cosgrove banged on the door and cried, *"I will chop you into messes!"*

I took the knife from Cosgrove, and order was restored in a grudging sort of way. We ate mostly in silence, so I put on every intelligent person's favorite opera, Verdi's *Don Carlos* in the original French version with all the extra music, so we could pretend there was some good reason why we weren't talking.

"Can we have the cordon bleu report on the house special?" I finally asked Dennis Savage.

"Indescribable" was all he would give.

"Maybe we should go to a movie."

"We've got one right here," he replied, looking at Cosgrove, "and its title is *Deadly Friend*."

"And I," said Cosgrove, "look forward to seeing you in *Last Ride on the Elevator from Hell*. In the title role."

"Boys, boys," I said.

Silence.

"This would never have happened," was my view of it, "if Virgil were still here."

"Piffle," said Dennis Savage, forking a shrimp around in the sauce. "What do you use for flavoring, may I ask?"

"That's the secret ingredient," Cosgrove informed him.

"And it is . . . ?"

"Secret."

"Oh, for heaven's sake!"

It occurred to me just then that I could use a vacation. Not just time off but a trip away from here. Like maybe to Europe. Like maybe to Venice. Zuleto and his problems were looking more attractive by the minute.

Good old British Airways had an off-season book-six-weeks-in-advance hotel-and-airfare tie-in at bargain prices. I figured six days in London doing theatre and opera and six days in Venice would fortify me for the playing out of "this Virgil stuff."

There was one snag: Cosgrove wanted to come, too. Look, I know he's sensitive and greatly given to self-doubt and helpless furies, but I needed a getaway, solo. I argued with him for a while, guiltily noting his increasingly deflated air. Then a brainstorm: He didn't have a passport and probably couldn't get one in six weeks. Probably? Certainly.

"But I do have one," he said quietly.

"How . . . You've never been abroad."

He was already hunting around in my old toy box, where he keeps his stash. As my heart sank, he brought out the familiar blue booklet. I opened it and discovered a photograph of Cosgrove at some absurdly early age.

"Where on earth did this come from?"

"This guy took me to Bermuda. To this fancy hotel with scuba diving and caviar dinners."

"You weren't even legal then."

"Yeah, that guy liked cream of chicken. On the floor under you, pulling on your legs, and he looks up as he slurps. It's real cute."

"What else don't I know about you?" I asked.

"He drank me dry, because that's what he likes, over and over. The people in charge of me were so freaked when I got back! The man? He got into a coughing fit, flopping all around till the woman was worried. So I said, 'Fatty get a heart attack.'"

That's how Cosgrove refers to his former parents: "the people in charge of me."

"So that's why I have a passport. Now can I come?"

Cosgrove's hair lies flat on his skull without a parting, but it curls out slightly at the forehead. People have been known to reach out and smooth him down there, and he bears it stoically.

"I don't think I should be left out of everything," he went on. "I'm not so great at the various social techniques but I always treat you with respect, don't I?"

One can at times be very aware of his skin, which is startlingly white, especially at winter's end. I have been careful not to let him learn what I love about him, but he knows, he knows.

"Can I whisper to you?" he asked.

I nodded. He carefully put his hands on the sides of my torso just below the shoulders, leaning forward to lick my ear with "I know that Cosgrove would find luscious new ways to make your day complete."

"Fatty get a heart attack," I predicted.

"I would really be nice to you," he continued, still whispering. "I would be Cosgrove the Unknown."

"You've been holding back on me."

"Just till now. *Please*?"

Cosgrove turned out to be the ideal travel companion. He didn't want to shop, feast, or inspect the indicated shrines. All he did was explore. He was especially eager to discover what he called "secret routes," clocking himself ever more speedily in foot trips from, say, Oxford Circus to our hotel in the Strand, or from the Tower of London to St. Paul's.

"There is a secret route to almost everywhere," he told me in the hotel dining room at our second London breakfast, while comparing his travel times on a chart he had devised. "Finding that route is the mission in life."

"You know," I said, "my brothers and I used to hold secret-route races in Venice. We'd start at this bench in the Public Gardens way to the east in Castello. The first one to get to the railroad station won."

"What did he win?"

"He won self-esteem. He won true delight in his resourcefulness in discovering new and vital passages through the maze. No dead ends of the kind we so often find ourselves in. No bridges to nowhere. No walking endlessly about within sight of the bell tower we somehow cannot reach. The winner's choices were pure and he gloried in them."

He regarded me with interest. "Say more," he urged.

"The oldest of us, Ned, had taken advantage of the move to Venice to elude the hard law of my evil mother and vanish forever. So there was Jim, my other older brother. He favored an at first direct route from the bench to St. Mark's, except that was clogged with tourists most of the year—and, in winter, the whole Piazza was usually underwater because of the floods. Anyway, there he'd cut north along the Merceria, even more clogged, till he crossed the Grand Canal at the Rialto and then abandoned himself in the contortions of Santa Croce, the most twisted sestiere in all Venice. He was in quest of the perfect route, but he never found it."

Cosgrove spooned up the last of the marmalade from one of those little individual jars they give you, blotted his lips with a napkin, and smiled in that way he has when he really likes what he's hearing.

"Who else was in this?"

"Just my younger brothers, Andrew and Tony. They used to straggle in hours late, till they hit upon the expedient of taking the vaporetto, which would have worked if they'd once tried the express instead of the local."

Cosgrove considered. "How big is Venice?"

"Very big for an old European city that hasn't really grown in area for a thousand years. But not big in the modern sense. From end to end the long way it can't be much more than from Fifty-third Street to the Brooklyn Bridge."

"What was your route?" he asked, taking up his handmade fruit compote with sour cream dressing. The Strand Palace offers an eat-all-you-want buffet breakfast, and Cosgrove was probably the most appreciative customer in the hotel's history. You could have fed Hannibal's elephants on Cosgrove's breakfasts.

"My route was . . . secret, of course. And I always came in first."

"Tell me your route," he suggested, "or I'll kill you."

Clamping some of that crazy uncooked-looking English bacon

between two toast triangles, I asked, "What happens when you reveal your secret route?"

"You instantly go into dust and blow away to nowhere."

"Then I'll tell you never."

"I challenge you," he said, so excited at the prospect that he actually stopped eating for a moment. "We'll hold a championship when we get to Venice. I'm going to buy a map now, and then you'll see."

I suppressed his arrogance with a stately sarcasm, but I was thinking, *Good,* because any vital project not involving Virgil is healthy for Cosgrove. That's my job: seeing him safely off to his secret routes.

The London-to-Venice plane trip is a breeze—little more than lunch, and you're there. Cosgrove ostentatiously spent the time poring over his map of Venice, marking out determinations, possibilities, choices.

"Consider the complication of foot traffic," I warned him. "Some streets are crowded, others empty. It makes all the difference on your time."

"Like Oxford Street is so filled with people while no one's on Great Marlborough Street, which is just one block to the south!"

"Right—but in Venice the streets change every thirty feet or so. Nothing's parallel to anything. It's all alleys, like the life you lead. They dwindle, turn, collide. A map is nothing. Venice is a mystery never solved, a lady of countless lovers, a place of reverent pagans. Do you dare?"

Cosgrove loves fancy talk. "I yes dare." As an afterthought, he added in a spectral voice, "'Redrum,'" another of his Great Moments of Movie Cinema, as the loudspeaker advised of our descent.

Zuleto had promised that we'd be met at the airport's little harbor in one of his motorboats. He owns a small fleet catering to the upmarket tourist trade. Heading to the water, I glimpsed my name on a sign and, with a shock, saw all time fall away to nothing. Still fifteen, so hot and too wonderful, Zuleto stood before me. The same wild eyes, those arms coming out of the shirt despite the brisk weather, the light and heart and weight of him. Impossible.

"Signor Mordden? I am Candio, and welcome to Venezia. My father—"

"Oh, of course," shaking hands. "Candio, who else?" Zounds, my heart was beating. "Bon zorno."

He smiled at my sally into the local tongue, then ordered his crew to load up our bags in, I noticed, irreproachable Tuscan.

"We're going in a motorboat?" Cosgrove cried.

"Yes, this is—"

"Tutti pronti?"

"A *motorboat*! That's what I call service!"

"I am Candio."

Cosgrove bowed.

"Su, forza! Everyone hold on. We depart!"

Ropes flying, motor chugging, some shouting. And we stormed away.

"Wow!" said Cosgrove, so excited that he beat his hands on the gunwale, or whatever it was.

Satisfied with our takeoff, Candio returned to the etiquette of the trip. "My family is happily expecting your arrival, Signore, especially my doubting father."

"It's thrilling to return. To see it all again."

Cosgrove was staring at the distant view, a riotous murmur of light and shadow bobbing in the lagoon directly before us. No, we were doing the bobbing. The past is still.

"What's all that?" asked Cosgrove, pointing to it.

Candio smiled, and I was thirteen again, because, once more, I saw his father.

"All that," said Candio, "is Venice."

Cosgrove was staring, as all first-timers must, in thrilled disbelief. Houses, walls, towers, in the middle of a tiny sea. A floating city, floating like choices. When we steamed into the very *there* of it, through the canal that passes the Church of the Jesuits, Cosgrove could not contain himself. He did a little cakewalk around the deck, calling out, "Cosgrove is here! Cosgrove is coming to town!"

We docked at the Salute just as my family did all those years ago. Candio's men saw us to our pensione, two or three doors down from where we all had lived, and no sooner had we checked in than Cosgrove ran off to discover his routes and I, after a fast phone call, went out into the street to meet Zuleto.

This time it really was he, surprisingly trim and youthful nonetheless. He gave me the operatic hug typical of an Italian male greeting a long-lost brother and led me to a café on the Zattere, new to me, where we each ordered un macchiato—coffee with a blip of milk. Then he launched into a tirade about la tedesca.

Italians are the least racist people in Europe and very tolerant of the quirks they perceive in other nationalities. But Venetians have very, very long memories. They speak of Napoléon (one of their very few conquerors) as if they'd seen him last Thursday. So the German presence in Italy during the Second World War— especially after 1943, when the Italians vaulted Mussolini and tried to surrender, and the Nazis invaded to make war as much upon the native population as on the Allies—remains an extraordinarily bitter experience. It is so not only for the Italians who lived through it but also for their children, raised on tales of German atrocities.

Zuleto didn't mind Candio's dating the girl. But to *marry* her? Bring her into the family? Corrupt his biological line with Angst, Weltanschauung, and Verfremdungseffekt?

"He is young, he is stupid, he is stubborn," Zuleto complained. "Ostinato, eh?" he added, banging his left wrist against the side of his head to portray inflexibility. "When you are young, you want to marry every girl you make love to."

"Did you?"

"Doesn't everyone? Didn't you?"

I'd never come out to Zuleto, by the way. Was I supposed to? Such as now? But this wasn't about me: I'm the listener.

"Tell me," I said, "are you against this because you think the girl's no good for him? Have you actually met her?"

He sighed, held his right hand up, palm in and fingers extended. "One," he said, waving his thumb, "she is older than Candio. That is never good for a man. Two," waving the index finger, "she is bossy and that is worse for a man. Three," at the middle finger, "she does not even speak Italian."

He said this in the tone you'd expect for "She does not even wear clothes when she enters a church."

"Well," I said, "she isn't Italian."

"She speaks *English,* doesn't she? That's how she and Candio converse. He's dating a woman in English! And why, amico mio of the old days? Why?"

He leaned over for a field goal.

"So *I can't understand what they're saying!*"

A sip of coffee.

He got his hand up again and said, "Four, she is too tall for him. And, five, la xe una mozzina."

"She's a what?"

"You don't know this word? It means . . ." He paused, to render it in the simplest Tuscan: "Ella fa la civetta con tutti."

"Oh, a flirt."

Zuleto rested his case with a look: the eternal father, so utterly disappointed.

Then he smiled, sanded my hand upon the table, and said, "Amico, you are here again. It is so amazing."

I nodded. It *was.*

"Except," I said, "if I'm going to be any help, I have to ask this—if she weren't dating Candio, would you find her attractive?"

Out poured a torrent of denials, protestations of injured honor, appeals to our lifelong friendship, exclamations of innocence, and mai, mai, mai, mai, mai, mai. *Never.* Two beats. Then he said, "Ma già, I'd fuck her if she wanted to, but she isn't my model."

Type. "Ste picole bele scagazzere forestiere," he added, trying to look blasé. These cute little foreign know-it-alls.

But even though it's not about me, maybe it's cowardly not to confront my old friend with my old truth. He'll be wondering about my relationship with Cosgrove, anyway, won't he?

"Aimò," he breathed out, a meaningless expression of despair. "But surely you will help?"

"Come, let's take a walk so I can scope out this incredible place, and we'll discuss possibilities."

"Alla Piazza?" To St. Mark's Square?

"Bene," I agreed.

We walked in silence at first, down the Zattere to Rio Terà Antonio Foscarini, one of Venice's many streets that was a canal centuries ago, when you couldn't get around without a boat. We were heading for the Accademia Bridge, one of only three ways on foot over the Grand Canal. In some cities, you are hardly aware of geography—London, Rome, Paris, Moscow, and many other places are really just a collection of districts on either side of a river. But in San Francisco you have hills and the omnipresent bay, in Petersburg you have the ever-threatening sea, and in Venice you have the canals and bridges and the tiny, ever-surprising walkways. Add to this the boats, the weird old architecture, and the realization that the town was raised not on islands but, mostly, upon wooden pilings driven into the watery mud, and you have a city that never stops telling that you are *somewhere*. Yes, the façade is man-made, but the substance is nature. Venice isn't a clearing in the woods. Venice is a lake.

"So, my friend?" Zuleto at length asked me, as we scaled the big bridge.

"I will say three things. One, Candio is extremely good-looking and will have a lot of access to women."

"And is also very heavy in the pants, like me."

That gave me pause for all of a microsecond. You have to go along with these salty confessions if you pal around with Italians.

"Two," I went on, "you cannot tell someone with the need not to have the need."

"Long and thick, with a big head that is always slightly pointed and continually dripping."

"Three, no parent can assume that his offspring have signed a contract to put up with him for life. You can alienate your own flesh and blood, you know."

"Oh, this *never*! Candio will be furious, but he must always forgive."

We broke off, ambling through Campo Morosini.

"They don't always forgive," I finally said.

"Ma," he said. "In casa, comando *mi.*" In my house, *I'm* the boss.

The next day, at the crack of noon, both Zuleto and Candio whisked Cosgrove and me off to tour the western half of the lagoon, at my request.

"No, to the east," Zuleto had protested. "Mazorbo, Burano, history, amazement, as you will see."

"I've done that already," I said. "I want to see the crazy parts."

"Yes!" Cosgrove agreed.

"La Laguna Morta," I said. The Dead Lagoon, an alternate Venice that never happened, all seaweed and slimy, deserted mud-flats. "And Chioza!"

"Not Chioza!" Zuleto and Candio said together, throwing up their hands.

"Sì, Chioza."

They exchanged a look, and Candio gave his dad an encouraging or perhaps commiserating slap on the shoulder as they set about launching the boat, and I thought, They really are incredibly close, like best friends. None shall part them, including la tedesca.

Chioza ("Chioggia" in map Italian) is much older than Venice. It is rectangular and orderly in its structure, unlike the fish-shaped, chaotically fashioned Venice. Seniority leads the Chiozoti to arrogance; Venetians in retaliation look upon Chioggians as underpeople. "Sti pizoti," Venetians call them: They even piss funny.

We made a stop in the Dead Lagoon, the boat's motor cut to lull as we contemplated sullen clumps of clay just below the water's surface, desiccated greens, and ooze.

"It's Venice taboo," said Cosgrove.

"So Venice itself must have seemed," said Zuleto, "in the very olden days. The terror of barbarians? Subito, presto, an escape into the lagoon! We live in the open on islands, like birds. We evade the German hordes."

Candio pulled down his right cheek below the eye in that universal Italian gesture meaning, "Yeah, right."

"So next what?" asked Cosgrove.

On we sped to Chioza. An Italian city without an opera house is a nowhere indeed, and that's Chioza: boats and fish, not music lovers.

Cosgrove adored it. "They finally have cars here!" he noted. Automobiles are, indeed, one of the few distinguishing features of the place. It's a dreary Venice, without landmarks or, apparently, any sort of public life. I don't think I saw a single café. They do boast one oddity, a type of boat that is very colorfully painted up with emblematic designs.

"Sì, el bragozo," Zuleto explained, nodding at one as we pulled up and Candio saw to the rope. "In fifteen hundred years, Venice has given the world painting, music, democracy, double-entry bookkeeping, printing, the carnival, the gondola. If Venice didn't invent it, Venice perfected it. In the same time, this is what Chioza gave the world—the bragozo." He gestured as one glided past us. "A fishing boat with funny pictures."

As Zuleto and I spoke in Venetian, Candio simultaneously translated every line into English for Cosgrove, adding his own ironic commentary. Irked at his son's tone, certain he was being mocked, Zuleto constantly hectored the boy with comebacks and challenges. Yet it was clear that the two adored and accepted each other lock, stock, and barrel. Zuleto must have passed thirty cracks, minimum, about la tedesca. But Candio laughed or shrugged at every one. They weren't like father and son. They were like lovers who are perfectly suited but for one trivial yet recurring problem. Like one's always on time and one's always late.

Cosgrove was fascinated with all their byplay. When we left Chioza, he caught me while our hosts were deep in a nautical discussion and asked, "Do they know about us yet?"

"*I* don't know about us; what do you want from *them*?"

"I just mean, can we say gay things?"

"Say whatever you want. This is Italy. There are no language police here. And if someone's homophobic, that's *his* problem."

We had pulled well north into the lagoon, and Candio, driving, had opened her up. Cosgrove leaned over the rail into the spray, enjoying the speed, the freedom. He was shouting for joy, in fact, and Zuleto came over, probably wondering, finally, exactly what transaction the two of us represented.

"Ti piase sta Chioza?" Zuleto asked Cosgrove.

I translated: "Did you like Chioza?"

"Oh, it was the worst place ever," Cosgrove reported enthusiastically. "What a freak."

I translated.

"El xe un bravo puto," said Zuleto, riffling Cosgrove's hair. Good boy. "Xelo . . . un cuzino?" Is he your cousin or something?

"No," I said.

"Ma no el fio?" Not your son, surely?

"No."

I guess it's now. I got my mouth halfway open when Candio called over to Cosgrove: "Ask my father to tell you his Malamoco story. It is always his favorite, and you will be friends for the whole life."

"Tell me how to do that," Cosgrove asked me, his eyes on Zuleto.

I realized that Cosgrove really liked Zuleto (in the "thought he was hot" sense), and for some strange reason I was glad. Maybe because . . . Anyway, I said, "Tell him, 'La me diga, sta bela storia de Malamoco.'"

Cosgrove did as told, to Candio's laughing "Ausgezeichnet!" Excellent!

Zuleto, ignoring the German, pointed over the water to the Lido, on our right.

"It was there, imagine it, that Venice built her capital, Malamoco. Out in the sea, as far as possible from the barbarians invading the mainland. Then came a vicious conqueror to destroy Venice: Pepino, the son of the terrible emperor Carlo Mango." Charlemagne. To his son's back he added, volume knob up, "A German."

"Francese," Candio laughed. French.

"He was born in Aachen," Zuleto countered, emphasizing a German pronunciation. "Does that sound French?"

"Forza, pare," Candio replied, still laughing. Go on, Dad.

"Pepino, he arrives by sea and takes Malamoco. Now comes la cria. Take hostages! Prisoners will be killed! Like all Germans, they want to crush everyone, this is known."

"That was a thousand years ago, of course," Candio put in.

"But everyone has run from Malamoco, before Pepino comes. They are all al Rialto, in the center of the lagoon. Safe from Germans. Only one person is left in all Malamoco to greet Pepino, a woman so old that she couldn't manage the trip of escape and so ugly that no one would bother to hurt her. Una popolana! Un' eroina!"

Cosgrove, fascinated, said, "She will find the secret way out!"

"La deve!" She must! "But you should know about our wonderful Venetian lagoon that it's mostly very shallow, with just a few channels deep enough for boats. These are clearly marked by posts, *but!* When everyone abandons Malamoco, he takes with him all the posts. Now it is nothing but lagoon, quiet and waiting. What will happen? What is Venice? What is Pepino?"

"How he loves to tell this," Candio noted.

"So the ugly old woman is brought before Pepino, shoved

roughly in the German manner, of course. We hear Pepino's famous words: 'Dove il Rialto?'" Which way to Venice?

"Now her pungent reply. Turning to point to the glorious towers of the great city of Saint Mark evangelista himself, the old woman cries, 'Sempre drito!'"

Cosgrove turned to me for a translation, for I'd taken over from Candio throughout this recitation.

"Straight ahead!" I told him.

"And so Pepino and his army sailed straight ahead, and there upon the mudflats of the lagoon they were wrecked to pieces. And Venice lived and is always here. Look! Where we are? This is where it happened, just here a thousand years ago."

Then Cosgrove threw his arms around Zuleto and pressed his cheek against Zuleto's, and loved Zuleto. They were at one in this way for quite some little time, then broke apart.

"Grazie," said Cosgrove, pronouncing it Venetian-style: "Grassye."

Zuleto looked at me and . . . well, what would *you* have done? I nodded, that's all.

I wasn't off the hook about applying my silver tongue to Zuleto's family problems. As we docked in Venice, he gestured to me behind Candio's back that Now Was the Time. To be sure that I would perform, Zuleto took Cosgrove hostage. Well, just out to dinner. Still, I was expected to make some sort of dent in Candio's marriage plans, and I hated that. Who am I to interfere? Who, even, is Zuleto to? It's Candio's life, so it's Candio's choice to make, to his profit or pain.

Besides, wasn't it ridiculous for me to have an opinion about this girl without even having met her?

Candio was affable about it all, especially once I assured him that he had the right to diagnose his own condition without reference to a second opinion.

"It is always this," he told me, as we ordered "ombre" ("shadows," denoting late-afternoon white wines) at a café near the Accademia. "Your family is telling you what it is, what you should do. The old, they think they know everything. Mostly. I believe they are jealous because you are young and can do anything. For him, now, it is all . . . how you say 'un zoco da puti'?"

" 'Downhill all the way.' "

"I am sympathetic to him, you know this. It was shipping in evil water for him, raising a child without the mother. He is grouchy but kind. And against others, always on my side. That is a rule with us. But now, when he is to beat sullo stesso chiodo senza fin . . ." When he hammers on one nail incessantly . . .

"Has he met her?"

Candio laughed ironically. "When he learns that she is German, the stadium collapses and the game is surrendered. No more football shall be played today. But what?" He shrugged. "Do you, for example, tell your young friend how to live?"

"Yes, but he wants to be told. He's not a former motherless child. He's a current orphan. So he feels desperately in need of parenting."

Candio thought that over for a minute, then said, "What?"

"Cosgrove never really had a childhood, as far as I can make out. He's undergoing it now. Under my supervision."

Candio nodded. "This is strange American thing. In Italy, everything has been the same for two thousand years. In America, everything changes every five or six years. *That* is place to be young!"

One day of exploring later, and Cosgrove officially challenged me to a race through the town. We took the bus to the Public Gardens stop, and, at the bench, I laid down the rules.

"No transport of any kind, if you are a serious contestant. On foot, from here to the station."

"Can I use my map?"

"Those who need to crib will never win. The race is to the fantasist who carries all the data in his head."

"Can I use my map?"

"If you like."

"When do we start?"

I was backing away from him, slow and smiling, hands in my pockets, heading for the Naval Museum on my way north to the first leg of my secret route, along the Fondamente Nuove, which run virtually opposite to the Zattere: along the *north* edge of the place. Life would be seen to be filled with opposites, if only we noticed them.

"When do we start?" Cosgrove repeated, following me.

"We have started, fio mio. And I'm ahead. I'm winning already."

I waved at him, and instantly he took off down the Riva dei Sette Martiri while I nipped up the Viale Garibaldi. Some seventy-five minutes later, sitting on another bench, this one in the Papadopoli Gardens across the Grand Canal from the station, I saw Cosgrove stagger in from San Simeone Piccolo. I had a bottle of water for him and a salami sandwich, which he tore into. Now that we were on the Continent, breakfast consisted of coffee and rolls, and Cosgrove ravened all day.

"This is the greatest place ever," he announced after a while of eating. "I'm never going back. I expect I would have to be pathetically grateful to you if I didn't suspect a hidden motive."

"There's none."

"But Virgil told me that everyone is selfish all the time. He said some appear generous and others sly, but if you *really* know . . ."

"Do you think that's true?"

After a bit, he said, "It could be. But would that mean Virgil is selfish, too? I owe everything to him, for saving me from the desperate life of the streets. Is he now saying that he did it for his own good reason, and not out of tender love and compassion for Cosgrove?"

"There was once a composer of great symphonies, German and total, as symphonies should be. Fear overtook him after his Eighth, for both Beethoven and Schubert died once they'd composed their Ninth. It seemed, to this composer, a barrier beyond which Death beckoned."

"But what about all those Haydn symphonies?" Cosgrove asked, scarfing up the last of his sandwich. "They go past a hundred."

"Haydn was guacamole to this composer. He dealt in *profound*."

"Next stop," said Cosgrove, napkining off, "a gelato stand."

"The composer thought of a trick to play. He would *entitle* his Ninth Symphony. So it wouldn't be his Ninth at all. It would be . . . *The Song of the Earth*. Then he would write a Ninth, having got through the terror."

I paused, feeding Cosgrove's interest. "So he what?" he asked.

"So he made very public this new symphony. And he thought he had fooled his fate."

Now Cosgrove was interested. "Then somebody stabbed him?"

"Then he wrote his Ninth Symphony."

"And?"

"And he promptly died. Because *nobody* fools his fate."

Almost delicately, Cosgrove asked, "Is this another of those little tales to tell that are really about what's happening now?"

"Let's start back," I said, rising. "We're having dinner with Zuleto's family tonight."

"I like Zuleto," said Cosgrove, following me across the bridge to the bus stop.

"So I notice."

"What was he like before?"

"Exactly like Candio, physically."

"Yum."

"But very intense. Everything a do-or-die proposition."

"Did you ever fuck with him?"

"No."

"Did you want to?"

"Ah, here's our boat."

It was an express, and we charged on amid a heavy taste of tourists of many nations, all first-timers going Wow! As we took

274

off, to the clicking of many cameras and the silent turning of video machines, Cosgrove jumped up and cried, "Mi son Cosgrove, el fio de Venezia!" I'm Cosgrove, the boy of Venice!

Then, to sounds of appreciation, the cameras turned to catch Cosgrove in his guiltlessly elated tumult. "We're going to move here," he told them, while executing poses.

About Zuleto's dinner in famiglia I was somewhat apprehensive. Wouldn't *somebody* wonder about Cosgrove and me and pipe up with a Troublesome Question? I didn't know the Venetian for what Cosgrove and I are, and, besides, I enthusiastically resent and habitually reject questions of a personal nature from people I hardly know.

(Boys and girls, let me share my list of the Five Forbidden Questions:

How much money do you earn?
Are you a top or a bottom?
Did one of your female ancestors mate with an animal?
Is that your boy friend?
How old are you?

The reason why these questions are forbidden is that if the subject wanted you to have this information, he would have volunteered it himself. Remember, too, that none of us enjoys letting someone else set the limits of our privacy. It may seem hypocritical of me in view of how ruthlessly I have detailed the lives of my friends; but any reader who has reached this late stage of the fourth volume in this series must have noticed that there are a lot of Interior Contradictions in these stories. I dream that that's their charm.)

Back to the tale at hand: No one in the whole dinner party paid the slightest attention to the, uh, income-tax status of Cosgrove and me, and Zuleto had thoughtfully invited a few English speakers: a woman reporter for some French magazine who only wanted to know about Sylvester Stallone, and an English academic émigré researching some arcane bit of Byroniana for a monograph.

Cosgrove, next to the magazine woman, was in his element. "You know the Limelight story, of course," he said. "The Night of the Big-Hung Contest?"

"Tell me *everything*," she breathed out, conspiratorially.

I was stuck with the academic, but at least he quoted Byron more than himself. He was working on translating *Don Juan* into Toscano, which boggled the mind—isn't *Don Juan* the most untranslatable of works because it uses language to summon up a culture yet at the same time uses that culture to summon up the entire world?

So the academic and I had quite a nice chat about all of that. And the food was great, and the wine was tangy, and the feelings were warm. But I did notice a sense of challenge and defiance from Zuleto and Candio, the one's more relentless *no* calling up the other's now more organized and determined *yes*.

This was not good. I saw Zuleto leaning across the table, pointing and certain. I saw Candio looking less bemused than offended. There were ructions. At times, the aunts, uncles, and cousins got into the debate. "Sta tedesca!" some were saying. That German girl! Again and again, tempers would flare *almost* to the danger zone, someone would cajole and soothe, and then it would start anew.

Meanwhile, I would hear Cosgrove saying, "They called Sly's name, and of course he was kissing up his harem to get ready," and "So then he dropped his pants . . ." Also meanwhile, the academic was fluting out his Byron, complete with spoken footnotes such as "But be warned, this particular usage went decadent in the sixteenth century in all regions north of Cremona and was almost entirely suppressed in the Veneto at that singular time."

I was woozy on wine and not entirely clear on the next order of events. I remember Candio and his father in a shouting match. They were standing. Others were standing, too, I think. Candio was stalking out, and someone was . . . You know? Fights. All I remember is Cosgrove telling the magazine woman, "Then they learned that Arnold was there, and the crowd went *absolutely wild.*"

"Do you want a job with our publication?" the woman asked him. "We pay well for this information."

"I make most of mine up."

"Then we pay better."

After that shambles of a banquet, Cosgrove and I enjoyed a quiet day, climaxed by a rematch of the race. I won again. This time I got him a miniature pizza for the post-Olympics snack.

That night we went to la Fenice, Venice's historic opera house. Cosgrove has been to the Met a few times, but never to anything like this "little jewel," famously known, until arsonists took it out in 1995, as the most beautiful theatre in the world.

Mingling with the jazzy crowd in his beloved suit, Cosgrove felt like Gene Kelly in the title number of *Singin' in the Rain:* truly carefree. At one point, someone said something to him that he couldn't catch, and Cos simply nodded and replied, "Figurarse," the Venetian "nichevo."

The opera was Puccini's *Manon Lescaut,* in which young love is destroyed by an old man's jealousy. The audience sided almost from the start with the tenor, wooden but very full-voiced, though the soprano was, if shrill, very personable. American audiences are good sports, splitting the difference between the best and worst and clapping for all; Italian audiences play favorites.

"That lady was nice" was Cosgrove's review of Act One. She may have reminded him of Dianne Wiest, his favorite movie star, because—I believe—he wants the mother in *Edward Scissorhands* to have been his mother. Too late now.

Anyway, we all trooped outside for the first intermission and had pizza at the taverna. Some years ago, my brother Andrew was almost burned to death in this place, a story Cosgrove never tires of hearing. I'm his Scheherazade, maybe; could that be the secret of our success?

Manon Lescaut, Act Two: Cosgrove is getting involved. There is a moment when the old guy's denunciation of the heroine to the police hangs in balance. She could run—but she is paralyzed by the luxury she must, yet cannot, abandon.

"The geezer's coming!" Cosgrove called out. Nobody noticed; there's a lot of commentary from an Italian audience during opera performances, so no one minded. Still, she *was* diddling around, losing escape time while singing.

"Move it!" Cosgrove cried.

She didn't, the geezer led the police in, and the rest was torment and death.

Cosgrove couldn't stop talking about it. "Why didn't they run when they could?" he asked, back in our pensione. "Everything you get from old guys is bad news, right? It's about control."

"Depends on the old guy, maybe."

Then Cosgrove went into my favorite of his expressions, bespeaking contentment, confidence, and anticipation. "Thank you for this trip," he said.

The phone rang. It was Zuleto. Urgent, we must talk.

"Hold the fort," I told Cosgrove, who had stretched out on the bed to page through *Oggi* magazine. "I'll be back in time for the climax."

I found Zuleto, as agreed, on the Zattere end of our old street, anxiously pacing. "Miseria," he said. "What can I? Is there no justice for fathers?"

"Well, *what?*"

"But no. To behave so, whining on the street like some immigrant from the south. Come!"

We had to walk some to find a place open that late, and, like all Italians, Zuleto would not begin his lamento until we'd settled ourselves at a table. It's called Being Civilized.

"That son of mine!" I heard at last. "Ungrateful! Arrogant! Good for nothing! I finally told him that no one living in my house will sing an antiphon with una de ste tedesche. It's so simple—he will move out tonight or he will give up sto sono annoiato." This irritating dream.

I said, "I love you only as long as you do what I want?"

"Ma che?"

"I do not accept you if you defy my taboos?"

"Dai!"

"Live within my rules or I kill you?"

"Then so *what* is that which you say?" he cried, in utter bewilderment.

I was thinking, Tell him? Don't tell him?

Tell him. "All my life," I said, "I have been sexually attracted to men. Teachers. Counselors at summer camp. You. And another eight or nine hundred thousand, many of whose names are unknown to me."

He got this look on his face: the weary guy getting wearier. "Bravo mio, can we do this some other time, when my life is not falling apart?"

"I have to be honest with you."

"My life is turning into an opera, and you want *honesty*?" Reaching across the table, he grabbed me at the sides of my head and planted one on my mouth, deep, long, and angry. "Cussì for your honesty!" he spat out. "Now can I have your help?"

After a bit, as suavely as possible, I said, "Okay, you're not shocked."

"Tell me *what do I do with my son*!"

"Nothing."

"Benone!" he replied, utterly exasperated.

"Calm down and listen. Remember the Three Rules of the Happy Life. One: Always check the mirror before going out, even if you're only off to the kiosk for a paper."

"Sì, sì," impatiently.

"Two: Go on a white diet✣ at least once a year, whether you need to or not."

✣ Limited to foods supposedly good for the liver: veal, fish, pasta in bianco (without sauce). Italians believe that a smoothly functioning liver is the key to an effective existence.

"Bene, mi so." I know that.

"Three: Never do anything irrevocable, unless you're *absolutely sure you want it over.*"

"Why to speak of 'over'?" he asked me, suddenly saddened, almost tearful. "Why must I know this?"

"Your kiss packs a wallop. Your life force is overwhelming. Europe was invented in this country. Rome was a metropolis when the French were making mystic passes at oak trees and Austrians made Wiener Schnitzel by locking a calf in a barn and burning down the barn. Be magnificent in your power: Give it up. If you're right, he'll learn the hard way, soon enough. If you're wrong, he'll be happy. You want him happy, right?"

Head in his hands, he more or less nodded.

"It could have been worse," I said. "She might have been from Chioza. Imagine the in-laws."

"Arùf!" he cried.

"Let's go back."

"I am not happy," he announced, as we walked along the Zattere. "It is not resolved. You say, it is so. I do not feel that it is so."

We had reached Zuleto's street, and he suddenly pulled me back into the shadows.

"It's those two," he whispered. "Why must they always be out in the road at night, like robbers?"

I stealthily leaned out to see: It was indeed Candio and his tedesca, gamboling about, laughing, shushing each other, and wrestling the way kids do when they're drunk on the genuinely guiltless high of youth at its freest and most beautiful.

Hey, do you remember that? Your First Symphony?

La tedesca was not the hard-faced taker whom Zuleto had described but a spirited little doll, stacked and ready, a fresh breeze from the north. Of course Candio was wild for her.

"She's lovely," I whispered.

"No, that is her mask," Zuleto assured me sotto voce. "Then comes the stiletto."

He leaned out to have another look, then jumped back against the wall, flattening me along with him, for the two were right at the end of the street, at the drinking fountain. (Not to worry—it's not canal water, but pure stuff, piped in from the mountains.) Pranking around, Candio pulled a long and bizarrely thin black comb out of his pocket, stuck his head under the stream of water for a while, then parted his dark hair way to one side and held the comb above his upper lip.

"Now he's Hitler!" la tedesca cried, in English, collapsing in giggles.

"I am your Führer," Candio told her, mildly enough and also in English. "You must undergo my orders."

"But I am the Resistance," she answered, gently taking the comb from him.

"There is none," he said, all eyes and holding on; oh, I know how those Italian guys hold on, and you know. It's in the gay file, this knowledge. Then comes the kiss, and caresses. I had seldom seen so exalted a delineation of what the term "feeling her up" means since . . . well, since that day, long before, when I saw his father and that girl in the garden. When I saw what yes wants when a boy is straight. It's just yes and total, desire in its truest sense, unstoppable because the white goo is life to all the generations.

The two eventually took themselves off up the street, and I told Zuleto, "Now you saw and now you know. Can you fight that? You had other plans, okay. But now these two are very yes and you must give your plans up. This is not about *your* hard-on. This is about *his* hard-on. (My Venetian went a little sketchy here, but Zuleto got the point.)

"I am not happy," Zuleto told me, thoroughly deflated. He shook his head and repeated the sentence. "He jokes about Nazis."

"Do we have to keep on hiding behind the corner? I think they're gone."

Zuleto peeled himself off the wall, still shaking his head.

"But you're not shocked at my revelation," I said. "Omosessuale, frocio, gay . . . That's something, anyway."

Mourning his lost authority, Zuleto sent me that Italian gesture of the fingers bunched together and banging on the chest: Will you *please*?

"Okay, okay," I said. But I learned something, didn't I? The best time to come out to someone is when his life is falling apart.

The next day was our last full one in Venice, and Cosgrove challenged me to a second rematch, this time from the station to Castello, the precise reverse of the classic course.

"It's only sporting," he explained. "This way, we'll both be new to it, instead of just me."

"Fine," I said.

But Candio called and invited us to a motorboat tour to, and lunch at, Torcello, a famed near–ghost town in a silted-up corner of the lagoon. "I would like you to meet my sweetheart," Candio added. "She is called Brenda and is always more pleased to meet Americans and learn the slang."

"Sounds great," I said.

"My wonderful father of course does not want to come. Maybe this is grouching day. But I am charging this most expensive lunch at Cipriani to the business, so he pays for it, anyway."

"I pay for nothing," Zuleto cried, off-mike.

"Maybe he would come," Candio went on, "if you ask personally."

"All right, I come," came Zuleto's voice. "Only don't expect to have a nice time."

We had a great time, though Zuleto did some minor sulking. Cosgrove was fascinated with Torcello, a thriving metropolis a thousand years ago, when Venice was still on the rise, but eventually a malarial backwater as the young new Venice became Europe's superior naval power. Brenda told us the tale, in her flawless tour-guide spiel. Cosgrove liked it so much that she did the whole thing over for him in German and Spanish.

It was a lovely visit and a sad leave-taking. Zuleto gave me a luxurious hug and joked that I should make it a habit and return *every* thirty years.

"It can't have been that long," I said. "Seeing you brings me back so surely that I must be thirteen again."

"Candio's still thirteen," Brenda observed. "It is part of his cleverness, ja?"

"We call that 'jailbait,'" said Cosgrove.

Brenda expressed interest in collecting this term, and while Cosgrove explained it Zuleto took me aside.

"What do you really think, eh?" he asked me. "The two of them."

Brenda was listening to Cosgrove, and Candio was standing behind her, gently rubbing the back of her neck with two fingers.

"I think they're terrific together."

He winced, then mimed wiping a tear, wrapping it in a box, and throwing it away.

"Vediam' un po," I said. Wait and see.

"I wanted other advice."

"I haven't any."

We hugged again, and I was thinking, Next time let's not wait thirty years.

Cosgrove and I ran our race after dinner; it was twilight before we'd barely started. He took off south of the Grand Canal into Santa Croce, but I held to my usual track along the Strada Nuova through Canaregio, north after the Misericordia Canal, then along the Fondamente Nuove to the Arsenale. That was always my secret, and why I generally won: I kept to unfrequented straightaways and let the others get tangled in the maze. It's funny, though, how different it all looks when you're going from end to beginning. I actually took a couple of wrong turns. Then I really started blundering in the last section, in Castello, and finally reached the bench to find Cosgrove nonchalantly eating a gelato. ("My third," he told me, emphasizing how much I'd lost by.)

"So," I said, joining him on the bench of my youth and accepting the offer of a bottle of water. "It's come to this."

"You were in control before," he said. "But the next generation is taking over."

"What was your route?"

"Secret, of course. It can never be told, despite your many blackmail attempts to come."

"I think that, sometimes, when you tell your secret, nothing happens to you at all."

"I still won't tell."

It was quite dark by now, in that majestically personal Venetian night with the big spaces and little spaces. The everything all mixed up. We were sitting before quite an expanse of water, the Mola, as it's called, where the Grand Canal opens up into the lagoon. Where the indomitable Venetian fleet would embark or return. What history had happened here! How much *ago* lies in the past, life after life, one generation making another out of . . . goo.

"You know," I told Cosgrove, "you're so much more self-reliant when you're away from your sidekicks. Virgil, Miss Faye. There are these uproars in life from time to time, but we have to . . . Someone cheats you. Someone dishonors you. Someone eats your candy. You don't chase him with a bread knife. You *ignore* him. You don't let him into your day. You show him that he has no impact. When I was growing up, there was no celebrity in being a victim, as there is today. Whatever happened to you, you were expected to get over it. Nowadays, we've lost the concept of pride, and of shame, and of responsibility. Nobody's guilty of choosing blameful acts—a rap tape made him do it. He saw a movie. Folks appear on afternoon talk shows and parade their shame. Everyone wants to be a victim. It's the way ignorant idiots call attention to themselves. It's chic to claim to be a victim now, screaming for a spot on *Oprah* and a book deal. They've even started a support group for men who've tested HIV-*negative*!"

"Why do you take care of me?"

"Because I like you."

"That's not why," he said.

We sat for a bit, gazing about us in the amazing Venice night. Singing, gondolas, an idyll.

"What would happen about Candio and Brenda?" he asked.

"Probably all great things, as Zuleto gnashes his teeth. He'll be especially fond of the grandchildren, though, just to be vexing."

"He'll never give in about Brenda?"

"Never."

"Why do you take care of me?" he repeated.

This time I thought it over. "Because I reached a certain age and figured—"

"That's not why."

Again we sat there silently. Cosgrove offered me the remaining bit of a pouch of potato chips, but Europeans can't do junk food the way we can, because Europe isn't junk. It's history, art, and kitsch, but it doesn't understand about turning something beautiful or interesting or useful into trash in order to make money. "Horrible chips," I said.

"They taste too healthy," he agreed. "So why do you take care of me?"

"Because you make me feel young."

"Yes." He yawned. "That must be it. My favorite thing is how you got rid of your parents eight years ago, and that could give them heart attacks even now, this second. They're falling around on the floor and can't get up. Their hair turns white, and green slime drools out of their ears."

I put an arm around his shoulder.

"You little sweetheart," I said.

EVERYBODY
LEAVES YOU

A four-year-old boy, holding his mother's hand as they crossed Madison Avenue, had a system of walking whereby he put his feet down toes first, like an Indian in a First Grade Culture project, or a Gilbert and Sullivan pirate. Or a sissy. His mother, annoyed, yanked his arm so he would lose his footing, and as he dangled, she screamed, "What are you *doing*? *What are you doing*?" He didn't answer. He seemed, in fact, to take no notice whatsoever of her fury. Perhaps that was his solution to the problem of spending forever with someone who hates what you are. He even took a few more Indian steps before abandoning the expensive game.

Don't think Cosgrove missed a single integer in this bioemotional equation. But he said nothing. Sometimes he keeps his counsel, and worries, and eventually he tells you what that was.

But he was chipper this day. We were heading for FAO Schwarz to buy him a treat to take the sting off "this Virgil stuff." Telling Cosgrove he can have anything he wants (within reason) gives him great pause. It's too late to ask for "parents who liked me"; and who would have thought that "having Virgil around" was something you would have to ask for? Cosgrove knows he'll be given only a thing, not a new set of feelings. But it must be *the* thing. Then there'd be feelings in it.

He found his thing in a television commercial for a new Super Nintendo game, The Legend of Zelda. This turned out to be what is called an RPG—a role-playing game, in which one taps his name into the program at the outset, then sets out on a sword-and-jerkin adventure. Zelda more or less drops the player into an Oz in which he fights battles and discovers things. Each battle, if he prevails, makes him fitter, stronger, righter.

The game "pak," as Nintendo spells it (abandon the globe, civilization is doomed), can compute three different role-players at once, so Cosgrove and I punched in separate games, I under my own name; Cosgrove, for some reason he kept as mysterious as possible, as "Fook."

"If you knew life on the underside," he hinted darkly, "you wouldn't ask."

Zelda was a sensation in our house, a genuine epic, with its desert, forest, lake, mountain, castle, and village sections, its ingeniously elaborate dungeons in which one snatches last-minute victory from near-certain defeat.

"This is how life should be," Cosgrove averred. "Instead of just D'Agostino's and the laundry. It's like having Venice in your own home."

Two cannot play at once, of course, so he and I waged a sub-battle over screen time, as I would send him off on trumped-up errands or barter game tips and secrets in exchange for portions of Cosgrove's time allotment. Then, too, we were constantly on the hot line to the Nintendo office in Seattle, where experts stand by from four A.M. (why so early?) to midnight, their time, to field frustrated players' questions.

Well, the house was in an uproar: *stimulated*. And so it should be. I kept thanking the gods for letting me live into the era of video games. Never before Zelda did I in such concentrated doses get so much work done (game rush had me so tanked up that I would hit the desk running), and never did Cosgrove bound out of bed mornings with such determination.

"Today I defeat Mothula!" he would cry, so eager that he was brushing his teeth at the controller.

Finally, I called a two-day moratorium. We were getting hyper, talking Zelda till Dennis Savage was shooting me worried yet sarcastic looks and friends were all but hanging up on me.

I proposed that Cos and I spend the two days collecting ourselves—and we tried. Yet we were feverish, hot for our . . . hobby? Is that all it is? Cosgrove spent the two days wandering around in a daze with his Gameboy in hand, and I got no work done. We listened to irrelevant music and picked at our food and stared at the empty screen.

Came then Dennis Savage's knock, and I told Cosgrove, "Act natural. No one must know."

He nodded, flopped onto the sofa, and turned on the Game-boy. I got the typewriter going and clattered for a bit, to suggest work-in-progress. Then I opened the door.

Dennis Savage took one look about and said, "Something's going on."

"Nothing," I said.

"You think you're so great," Cosgrove told Dennis Savage in a meandering, unaddicted way; bless his heart. "But I have Game-boy by Nintendo."

"You *are* Gameboy by Nintendo," Dennis Savage replied, nos-ing around the place as if he were Inspector Fortescue and we had hidden a body.

"I'm playing The Bugs Bunny Crazy Castle."

Dennis Savage shot me his "Can we please?" look, so I re-minded Cosgrove about resting his eyes when he uses the hand-held, and he went into the bedroom to sing to himself.

"After all this time," Dennis Savage asked, "what do you see in that?"

"Me, without the advantages."

"Pardon me, but I hadn't noticed any."

"First," I said, "there was *Mutoid from Hell,* your greatest role. Then *Mutoid 2: The Mutoid Positively Returns,* your greatest se-quel. Now we have the greatest performance ever told, in *Mutoid 3: Mutoid Versus Swamp Thing, Megalon, Spawn of the Slithis,* and *Renata Scotto.* The industry, agog, is talking of an Oscar."

"For you in the title role of *The Lady Vanishes*—and the sooner, the better."

"Yes, with your special credit: 'Gowns and accessories from the closet of—'"

"Enough, I'm too old for this!" Flopping into a chair, Dennis Savage. Exhausted, he is. Aghast. But calm. Through the bedroom door we could hear Cosgrove rendering one of his latest numbers:

> Puppy had to play,
> So Puppy ran away;

He went to the town,
Now he's barking up and down. . . .

"How's Billy working out?" I asked.

"Settling in. Not much of a housekeeper, okay. But he runs the errands well. He listens. He types over my pages like a pro."

"Billy *types*?"

"He's slow but he's sort of perfect. If you, uh, get my drift."

"I thought Billy was another Cute but Dumb thing."

Dennis Savage was miffed. "He isn't dumb. He isn't *dumb*. That's just his way of playing cool."

Cosgrove was singing: "'So Puppy was the one' . . . No. 'If Puppy could be there' . . . Wait . . ."

Dennis Savage put a hand over his eyes. "Talk about *dumb*? Anyway, about Saturday—"

"You're going and that's it."

"Didn't I *say* I'm going?"

Carlo had suddenly got worried about Cosgrove, and planned for us to spend a Saturday at an amusement park in New Jersey. "We have to cheer that Cosgrove up," Carlo said.

"'Puppy had to play . . .'" Cosgrove sang, in the bedroom.

"What is he *doing*?" asked Dennis Savage.

"He's creating 'The Ballad of Puppy,' just as Virgil created so many golden oldies of our past. Do you recall 'The Ballad of Fauntleroy'? Or—"

"Well, I don't want to hear about him, okay? I just want to clear it with the family that Billy can come with us."

"Of course he can."

"I don't want anyone giving him a hard time, either. He's been very shy about fitting into . . . the scene here."

"I've noticed how shy he is. I mean, Madonna is shy. Howard Stern is shy. But Billy's shyer."

Dennis Savage smiled sadly. "Yet I'll be patient. Because you don't know him. All you see is street trash."

"What do you see, Snow White?"

"Right this moment I see the Wicked Queen."

" 'Puppy wants a friend' . . . Yes," Cosgrove sang as he composed. " 'His troubles seemed at end . . .' "

"Just go easy on Billy," Dennis Savage went on. "He'll work in nicely here if you guys just give him a chance."

"Well, he didn't exactly extend himself in making a first impression, did he? That obnoxious know-it-all smirk—"

"Don't you see how naked he felt? All of you looking him over, judging him. Naturally, he needed to put on . . . what?"

"A negligee?"

"*Bravado,* I was going to say! Jesus. Just stop *looking* at him, will you? Stop scoring his points, and let him be. He's worthy in ways you don't yet know."

"Fine. I will. Fine."

A pause, and Dennis Savage listens to silence in the bedroom. "What's he doing now?"

I shrugged, but then we heard Cosgrove break into a vamp suggestive of lurid bongo drums and reckless woodblocks, a back-alley *Création du Monde.*

"What on earth *is* that?" Dennis Savage asked.

"That's Cosgrove's Nintendo song."

Out of the darkness
Gameboy creeps,

Cosgrove began, but Dennis Savage leaped up, saying, "Oh, that's it for me."

"If only you listened," I told him, "you might hear things."

"What, 'Puppy had to play'?"

"You're missing the point. Who's Puppy?"

"Who else around here 'had to play'? He's singing about himself."

" 'So Puppy *ran away*'?"

Finally catching on, Dennis Savage froze.

"You speak so lightly," he finally said, "of something so close and tense?"

"I'm trying to show you how adequately Cosgrove describes the human comedy. His art is cruel but just. He could teach you, if you stopped treating him as a punk and listened."

"Oh, and what would he teach? Do I dare imagine? How to dance a lurid coranto around the fairy ring, perhaps, as thug pandas and man-eating bunny rabbits clap the measure?"

"Ridiculous. We only ask macrobiotic bunny rabbits."

> Gameboy, Gameboy, where will you go?
> What do you see
> Deep in Gameboy's eyes?

"I'm walking," Dennis Savage said, heading for the door. "I'm asking for consideration and I'm leaving the room. Be nice to Billy."

"Be nice to Cosgrove."

I was alone, then Gameboy came out.

"Can I play some more?" he asked.

"Fuck it—let's get Zelda on."

Our Saturday in New Jersey was a test of some kind: people who don't entirely belong together in a place no one believes in. Imagine a benignly fumbling gay tour guide (Carlo), a testy gay Dido (Dennis Savage), his gay Aeneas replacement (Billy), the gay Gameboy (Cosgrove), and me (gay), set down among straight families and dating couples and the usual mischievous strays. It felt queer; know what I'm saying?

Yet Carlo was going to make us jolly if it killed us. "Look at all the rides you can go on," he kept saying. Every now and then a group of teenage boys would pass and Carlo would get pensive. Then he'd be egging us on again.

We came to the bumper cars, and Dennis Savage grew fond.

"Oh, remember this?" he asked me.

"Pure violence," I said.

"No, it's . . . to work off your frustrations. An energy container."

He looked happily at the children riding around and crashing into one another, squealing and shrieking.

Dennis Savage sighed. "They should settle territorial disputes and religious controversies like this. No more war: just diplomats in bumper cars. Think of Khomeini and Salman Rushdie tooling around in there, and Rushdie wins, and the fatwa is canceled."

"That's great," said Carlo. "Then we burn Khomeini alive."

The five of us stood watching as the ride ended and the kids hopped out of the cars.

"Well, I'm going to take a little trip around the ring," said Dennis Savage, and he paid up and took his place in a bumper car.

Cosgrove, Billy, and I watched him patiently waiting for the power to turn on as kids of all kinds rampaged in and took their places. Carlo was staring at a shifty-looking blond boy who grinned and shot Carlo with a water pistol. Carlo grinned, too, as the youth vanished into the throng.

"You can see that Dennis Savage is the one, true grown-up around here," Carlo told me.

"I don't think of him like this," said Billy. "Doing bumper cars. Do you like them, Cosgrove?"

Carlo smiled. He's glad when anyone is nice to Cosgrove.

"I don't see the point of all that bumping," said Cosgrove. "Doesn't it hurt?"

"No, it's just fun."

Dennis Savage waved at us.

"Everyone gets bumped," Billy went on, "and they have a good time."

Cosgrove, looking at the bumper cars, suddenly cried, "I'm going on that," and he pulled out his wallet, grabbed a ticket, and rushed into the ring.

"That kid is so rad," said Billy. "Look at him sitting in the little ride-a-car thing."

We looked; and Cosgrove did seem unusual. I mean, unusual even for Cosgrove. Impatiently working the steering wheel, loudly singing the Shark Theme from *Jaws,* and banging his feet on the car floor, he looked like . . . well, like someone about to lead that coranto around the fairy ring with the pandas.

"Something's going to happen," said Carlo, who always knows.

Then the electricity pumped in and the cars shuddered into motion. Cosgrove screamed, *"Get out of my way I'm going to kill him!"* and he tore after Dennis Savage, still singing *Jaws* as he maneuvered among his fellow players to smash into Dennis Savage's car.

"What are you *doing*?" Dennis Savage shouted, looking over his shoulder as he tried to steer away.

Billy was bemused.

Cosgrove rammed Dennis Savage again and again, screaming and singing and even gesturing at the overhead sparks as if they were friends of his.

Carlo was frowning and Billy just watching as the ride went on, the other drivers spinning out of Cosgrove's way as he sallied forth.

"I'm going to bump him off!" Cosgrove cried as he bore down on Dennis Savage.

Gslamm!

"Get him off me!" Dennis Savage called out. "Make him—"

Tchbyoing!

"Cosgrove," I called out. *"Stop!"*

But Cosgrove was singing the *Jaws* music and cascading all over Dennis Savage once again.

"They can't get hurt," Billy pointed out.

"Except their feelings," said Carlo.

"Gangway!"

"Somebody stop him!"

Schmathrumm!

"You *lunatic*!"

"Now I'll get even! You threw me out! You made me cry and be alone! You wouldn't let Virgil take me to love!"

"A lot of good that did us," Dennis Savage reasoned, desperately driving out of Cosgrove's way, "since now he's—"

Dadasplong!

"Get that murderous zany out of this—"

"Cosgrove, you now will *cut it out!*" Carlo called out, and that is a call that Cosgrove must heed.

"I was only playing," said Cosgrove, slowing down.

"*Stop* playing."

Cosgrove did. Another minute or so ran by, of nothing: kids laughing, the odd crash, the sparks, a few faces quizzing the participants in the drama.

Dennis Savage and Cosgrove came out of the bumpadrome, or whatever it is, rather sedately.

"That lurid little—" Dennis Savage began.

"Some fun he turned out to be," said Cosgrove.

"Listen," I began, but Carlo went right to Cosgrove and held him extra tight. But what he said was "You have to stop doing this."

"Except I'm the one who got assaulted," said Dennis Savage. "I had contemplated moseying around the circus minimus in a thoughtful nostalgia. Oh, but how wrong I was! Just as I was wrong to think that a first-class face and a lot of gym would get me through the 1970s. Or that I could skate through the rest of natural time on a profound and boundless love for the most handsome young lad in Stonewall. Everything I believed was wrong, *wrong*. Now here I am, sliding off the end of the big spoon. And who supports me? No one. There's a demon at my back singing strange music—"

"*Jaws,*" said Billy. "Yeah."

"What is?"

"The music the little kid was singing. That's *Jaws*, the movie. Get it?"

"As opposed," said Dennis Savage, *just* keeping his poise, "to *Jaws* the musical? *Jaws* the underpants?"

"I want to go on the bumper cars again," said Cosgrove.

Carlo said, "There are other rides for you."

"I don't want children's rides. I'm twenty-two."

"He's a dead horror," Dennis Savage muttered. So that was our Great Adventure. Disaster: because everyone's feelings were stale.

As Billy explained it, "Nothing's forever. Get it?"

I was painting. I'd ordered a new black leather couch from Bloomingdale's—no, you're wrong; it had been reduced down to nothing, which tells us that it's not the name of the store but simply what day you happen into it that matters—and I had the old one carted off, and I moved a few things around. Suddenly I had an almost nice living room. It had always looked like a record store. Now it looked like a record store with a black leather couch.

Anyway, having changed the layout, I had to paint over newly exposed bits of wall. Cosgrove was out running errands. Dennis Savage was writing. And Billy came down to talk.

"I've been in and out of these places," Billy was saying. "Don't ask how many. And there I am, and this guy'll be, like, 'Oh, Billy.' You know, during it. And, like, 'This is incredible. Oh, Billy.' Like sighing. The way chicks do, right? Or they'll whistle real high like an alarm. Because I know I've got the Big Thing, and that's what the deal's about. Surely now, I wouldn't bluff you. I'm Billy Boy, and they know me. At the clubs. On the street, even. Those glitter parties, too, and all that. 'Hey, there's Billy Boy.' Do my act or something. Sure. That's cool."

I was behind the armchair—also new, also black leather—catching up the wainscoting on the new look.

"Cos says you're real nice to him," Billy said.

I wasn't sure what he meant by that, so I kept it loose. "I take care of him," I said.

"So you like the slendy type, huh? Some guys like heftos. A real heaviness. Eyes that . . . you know, can really look at you. They're an armful, really fuctious. I don't mind knowing about them, I can tell you."

Painting.

"Everybody leaves you, though, sooner or later, don't they? That's what I keep noticing."

"Everybody—"

"Leaves you. Nothing's forever. There's always some new thing in your life. Some glitter party to check out. Who knows who you could meet there? Going home after that, see? A little . . . you do me, I do you. I mean, it's *okay* if they're fuctious. You can really get off. But aren't you always thinking of someone else? Someone you really liked before? Do you find that? Is that what happened to you, too? Because I notice you stopped painting.

"See, I know this guy," he went on, right on. "Of the lawyer type, or something associated with that—with those cases you carry along with you? Everywhere they go, they open up the case, and there's what they need. Folders and printouts. A *fax* kind of guy. Stripes on his suits and excellent shoulders from the gym and a beautiful ass like nothing else on earth. And if you stare at him long enough, you could tell his asshole is tingling and he knows what you know. All this in a striped suit and the briefcase, and this, like, really *handsome guy* kind of thing. Oh, you like this, right?"

Because I had put down the brush and was sitting on the toy box in which Cosgrove keeps "all my worthly possessions," especially including the Gameboy, the game paks, my old ice skates, my father's collection of miniature hotel soaps, and the forty-two crisping sleeves from fourteen boxes of Belgian Chef frozen waffles. If Cosgrove ever leaves, it'll be an easy move.

"We were all in this building," Billy is telling me. "I'm a guest there, you understand. But this lawyer is a tenant, all by himself. And a cop lives there, too, also by himself. Two single guys. So just imagine the elevator. Because the lawyer is hot like I told you, but now the cop is so beautiful he's freaky. Only you can tell his asshole doesn't tingle when you cruise him. He doesn't like that, right? Heftos and slendys. You take your choice. And there's me, surely, Billy Boy. And every so often"—he pronounces the "t," by the way—"here comes some guy saying, 'Well, you're this kind of Huckleberry Finn.' You know who that is, right?"

I nodded.

"Me, too. I know they tingle for a slendy like me with the Big Thing. That's all they can think about. But I don't want them, certainly. I don't even want the lawyer or the cop. I want them with each other. And guess what else?"

"The cop wants the lawyer," I said.

"You're smart. That was years ago. I was a little kid in the elevator then. But they're together, those two. Can you imagine? All this time? And the cop is looking at the lawyer, and the lawyer's asshole is tingling like the Liberty Bell. And when they're in the elevator, riding up and riding down, the lawyer has to grip his briefcase tight to keep from throwing his arms around this guy who loves him so deep he's never going to leave him. They're going to stay and stay and stay. I'm not going to cry in front of you, even though my voice . . . I don't want you to hear that part of me. Just listen to these words. Because how come *I* don't get that? I'm thoughtful, aren't I? I'm friendly. I fit in anywhere you put me down. I've got the Big Thing."

I was painting again.

"Don't I?"

"That's for sure. If Pasolini had seen you, he'd have wanted to remake *Salò*."

"So why . . . I don't get it. What kind of score do you have with Cos? Heavy stuff?"

"You don't see rope in here, do you?"

"I mean, do you—"

"I take care of him."

"Right. Cops take care of lawyers. The guy with the eyes reaches out for the guy with the stuff inside . . . the feelings. That always works out somehow. The cops screw the lawyers. The guy with the piece takes hold of the guy who understands. You know what I mean? Taking care of Cosgrove. I hear that. He's the lawyer. It's just . . . sometimes you don't know who's the lawyer and who's the cop? You can't guess who needs . . . I mean, just by looking . . . Listen, do you want to fuck with me now?"

I kept on painting.

"Everybody does, usually," he said. "I don't mind. Cops and lawyers. And I'm going up and down in the elevator. Cosgrove and you, yeah. He's happy here, surely now. He told me how bad it was for him before. Take care of him—aren't those funny words? 'Take care'?"

I was eyeing the toy box. Paint it white?

"So why don't we fuck?" said Billy.

"Thanks for the flattery. But there's too much agenda going on here."

"Just being neighborly."

I stood back and inspected my work.

"One way to stop them from leaving is to make them laugh. You notice that, ever? Everybody wants to laugh and feel good. Oh, they want the Big Thing—but if you can joke with them it kind of soothes them down from their daily troubles, you know? I believe I'm talking about someone who's great to be with even after you screw. Some cop, I may have to suppose. The six-footer kind of guy who says how much he likes you. He doesn't care if you cry, because it doesn't make you nothing in his eyes."

I found a thin spot to touch up.

"Some big friendly hefto cop who holds you all night because of who you are. He doesn't need anything else."

Done.

"So how come you don't want to fuck with me?"

There was a knock at the door. I let Carlo in; he took one look at us, immediately sensed what was happening, and said, to Billy, "I was starting to like you, so don't screw up."

"What's the word?" I asked.

"I spoke to Cash. I told him he can't have Virgil anymore."

"You actually said that?"

"That's what it is, isn't it?"

"He went off of his own free will, though," I said.

"That little boy belongs to us," Carlo replied. "We know what's right for him, and Cash doesn't."

I closed up the paint can.

"I want him back," said Carlo. "I truly could treat him rough for doing this to us."

"Boy, what a cop," said Billy, admiring Carlo. "Yeah."

"Say what?"

"How did Cash respond to all this?" I said, putting the paint things and newspaper in the kitchen. "He didn't strike me as the sort who takes orders on whom to include in his romantic life."

"Oh, he made territory noises, 'Who're you pushing?' and such. But way in the deep of it, he doesn't care. You know: If it's Sunday, this must be Virgil. Come Monday . . . well, there's always someone heading around the corner in Cash's way of life."

"Something else," I said, washing green apples, my favorite afternoon snack. The most freckled ones are the tartest. "Even if Virgil *wants* to come back, where's he to come back to? Dennis Savage won't have him."

Carlo glanced at Billy, who—despite a gift for speaking his heart even when the moment direly needs discretion—was silent.

"You don't know how fiercely Dennis Savage was hurt by all this," I said, washing and then handing the apples around. Billy held his. Carlo bit right in, like a horse. "He feels demoted to nothing, from root to tip. You have to remember, it wasn't some insoluble problem that grew and grew. They always got on fine. Then, suddenly, Virgil left him for someone he preferred, and that can be hard to take."

Carlo looked at me. "So what do you suggest?"

"That we don't yet know what this is. And that more feelings are mixed up in it than you may suppose."

Carlo glanced again at Billy, who decided to eat his apple.

"Maybe everybody walks sooner or later," I went on. "Maybe that's the way of the world and we'll just have to—"

"Well, *damn!*" said Carlo. "We got us a problem here, do you not see that?"

"You're going to do the right thing," Billy observed, of Carlo. "I would look up to you in the elevator."

Carlo gave this a bit of thought, then asked me, "What's he saying?"

Billy was filling in nicely, and we were all starting to like him. He was a hustler with generous instincts. As the warm weather cut into New York's clipped, useless spring, and the sun came out, and the Park closed off the loop to cars, Billy's duties took in taking Cosgrove bike-riding every weekday. Dennis Savage and I even chipped in to buy Billy a bike.

I had warned Billy to be very protective of Cosgrove, and Cosgrove reported that Billy was indeed "pretty guardian about it," though Cosgrove's approach to lapping the Park mystified Billy.

"He doesn't do laps, exactly," Billy told me. "He does these rest periods with a little pedaling in the middle."

"Well," says Cosgrove, "there's that awful big hill after Seventy-second Street. It takes forever. So then I have to sit on a bench to recover, and sometimes I try a Frozade for refreshment."

"What do you mean, 'try a Frozade'?" I said. "You've been living on them. That's like Salome trying a veil."

"This guy comes up to us," said Billy. "In a raincoat, you know?, and his hair was, like, it got plugged into a radio? And he was looking at Cosgrove and he sang a weird song and then he beat off."

I said, "What?"

Billy nodded and shrugged. Whatcha gonna do?

"He sang a weird song?"

"He stood there and . . . yeah. It was like 'Love them but leave them, and . . . and now they're all lonely' or something. Some kind of song. Then Cosgrove shot him up with the water gun."

"I *knew* he had funny pants on," said Cosgrove. "I could tell how weird he was. *Normally,* I use my water pistol on those pesky blade runners for taking up too much room. But this guy was asking for it."

"All those Frozades," said Billy, trying to joke, "will make you fat, Cos. Who's going to like you then?"

"Biking is good exercise," Cosgrove replied.

"What about crunches?"

"I try to eat at least two a day."

While Cosgrove would run through his vocal repertoire in the shower, Billy would recount the afternoon's events: dead rats and squirrels in the roadway, accidents they'd happened upon, an altercation near the merry-go-round.

"Just watch out for him," I said. "I don't want anyone running into him or anything."

"Be the cop for him, yeah. I will, because he's a sweet guy. How come the boss doesn't dig him?"

"Oh . . . it happened at a performance of Verdi's music-theatre piece, *The Strayed One*. Dennis Savage took a Jungian view of the action, but Cosgrove held to the hard Freudian line and there was a riot of professors screaming and huffing as ivy crumbled and syllabuses puffed into balls of smoke . . ."

"Yeah. That's your joke, huh."

"*The Strayed One*," I repeated, tasting it. How it feels when they leave you.

Billy said, "That Cosgrove, he notices things. Like in Sheep Meadow, because we rest there sometimes. I like to watch the straight boys play Frisbee and stretch their whole bodies. They appear unconcerned. It's a really hot thing, because you know how loose they are at that age, and you can do just about anything to them if you catch them alone and they're sure no one else'll find out."

"What's Cosgrove doing while you're cruising the Frisbee boys?"

"He watches the mothers."

"Say what?"

"With little kids. Like this one he always looks at, four- or five-year-old. Stumbling around with his shirt out of his shorts. You know, with those little stomachs they have sticking out? A tyke who's running all over. He had one of those kazoos he was playing. And he showed his mom how, but she couldn't do it. Or that was what she pretended. They kept passing it back and forth, and Cosgrove was looking and looking at this little kid, who then plays this jump game where he falls down and gets up and runs around a tree and falls down again. And Cosgrove keeps watching."

"Does he say anything?"

"He said, like, 'That boy doesn't need toys. He just plays.'"

"'What are you *doing*?'" I murmured.

"What are you saying?" Cosgrove asked as he came out of the bedroom, showered and dressed. Sometimes he stands in a doorway and listens; he wants to learn what people know.

Billy grabbed Cosgrove and mussed his hair and threw him around a little, and Cosgrove laughed. He loves that—unlike Virgil, who suffers himself only to be delicately and lovingly held, like ribbon candy.

The phone rang, once. Cosgrove froze. After a bit, the phone rang again, twice. Another bit, and Cosgrove made *shh* fingers at us. Next the phone rang nine times, cutting off in the middle of the tenth ring.

"It's Virgil!" Cosgrove cried. "That's the secret code!"

He rushed to the phone, stood over it hungrily, and snatched up the receiver on the next ring like a suitor choosing among caskets in a fairy tale.

"Yes," he said tensely.

He listened.

"Yes," he repeated.

After more listening and yeses, he hung up.

I said, "So you've been in contact."

"That's the miraculous Virgil I keep hearing about," said Billy. "The one who left. Carlo said everything is rotten with him gone."

"We all miss his fun-filled ways," said Cosgrove.

"I don't know if I'm his replacement or what," said Billy. "I mean, there were auditions, and I got the part. But I'm not . . . like him. Am I?"

"Would you throw your family away for a date?" I asked. "Would you turn into Roaring Dick and kick a whole world off its axis? Fare you well to the folk who comprehend and sustain you? Because that's what he did."

"Who knows? I might," Billy replied. "But first you'd have to translate some of that for me."

"He didn't throw us away," said Cosgrove. "How could you say that? If you know Virgil, then you realize that there is some secret message hidden in it. Virgil always seems to know what it *is*."

"He went out fucking," I said.

"You don't understand. He is under surveillance all around the clock. They have made him a slave to passion."

"They?"

"If only you knew," said Cosgrove, shuddering.

"I have to type," I said. "Why don't you two screen something till dinnertime?"

"*Alien*," said Cosgrove.

"Yes, I should think so. The monster among us." That sounds rude of me, but I was thinking of Virgil, actually.

"All the monsters are outside," said Cosgrove, helping Billy hunt through the pile of tapes.

"Why can't we keep those things in some kind of order?" I said.

"That wouldn't help," said Billy, "because halfway through them, like, Pee-wee Herman is suddenly there, or cartoons come on."

"Monsters say everything about you is wrong," Cosgrove observed.

"Here it is."

"Monsters say, '*What are you doing?*'"

"All right, now," I said, "just put it on and let me get some work done."

Billy fiddled with the machine, and the tape rode into play.

"*Alien,*" Billy announced. He put an arm around Cosgrove's shoulder. "See, Cos? All the monsters are make-believe in a movie."

"Not all of them," said Cosgrove.

"I was just wondering," said Billy. "If Virgil came back, you know, and he was going to move in with the boss . . . I mean, what happens to Billy?"

He and Cosgrove were staring at the screen, watching *Alien* heave its vast, stupendously slow outer space into view. So whom was he talking to?

"Everything's up in the air," Billy said, still watching the movie.

Cosgrove leaned his head against Billy, and Billy put his arms around Cosgrove; and now they were ignoring the movie and just sitting like that, holding each other.

"We're the two," Billy murmured.

LOOK WHO'S
TALKING

his is somewhat revelatory. Because someone who spent his twenties fucking all over town, then settled up at thirty for ten years, and then got abandoned, has written a story about a man who could never stay with anybody for more than an hour."

Dennis Savage said, "It's fiction."

"I'll say it is. And look at this title. 'Knowing When to Leave.' It's so sharp, so clipped. It's so——"

"There are such people, you know."

"You're not one of them."

"I *said* it's——"

"Fiction, but why write first fiction about somebody else? This isn't you."

He uncrossed and recrossed his legs. "I'm saying," he said, "does the story work or doesn't it?"

"It lacks despair."

We have these reading sessions. Whenever I finish a story—and now that Dennis Savage is writing, too, whenever *he* finishes a story—the other guy reads the text aloud to the author. It's professional and useful. You hear the dialogue as dialogue, catch word repetitions the eye missed, listen to the story breathing. These are sacred times; one waits till Cosgrove is out running his errands and turns off the phone. One must not be disturbed.

I hope you noticed that I now have an answering machine. I was New York's holdout, but after a decade or so it ceased to be picturesque and became irritating, even to me. And, I admit, having a screening system is an advantage, and makes me think fondly upon the space helmet I got for Christmas when I was nine: You can see out; they can't see in. Cosgrove adores this screening feature, though for some reason he thinks you're supposed to freeze during the operation, as if to move a step would blow your cover, tell "them" who you really are.

Messages are essential, he believes. If you don't get them, you don't matter. So, to buoy him up, Carlo and I took to phoning in miscellaneous advices and queries in arcane voices. That fooled him for about three days. Now Cosgrove leaves his own messages, dallying at a pay phone to check in as Lord Pembroke Wintermonk with a message for a certain Cosgrove Replevin, Esquire.

"This story," Dennis Savage was saying, "is about a man who doesn't know what he needs."

"No. It's about a man who thinks he can get away with everything."

"Look who's talking."

Cosgrove burst in, crying, "Quick! Let's check the phone machine to see if there are messages!"

Dennis Savage said, "Doubtless there are one or two from that fabled gadabouttown, Sir Percival Ravenbat, or however that goes."

"Lord Pembroke Wintermonk," Cosgrove corrected, savoring it as he put the machine into action.

"We're not done," I protested as Dennis Savage tried to pry "Knowing When to Leave" out of my hands.

"Oh, I bet we are, for now."

The first message was from my dentist's office, asking how come I hadn't made an appointment to have my broken filling redrilled. This is called Knowing When Not To Arrive. The second message was from Lord Pembroke, inviting Cosgrove to a weekend on the island of Samedi (I don't know where he gets this stuff; could he be reading?) next July, as Cosgrove clasped his hands together at his throat like a diva ready for her high note.

"I may be free then," Cosgrove told us.

The third message was from Lionel, who's got *I Lombardi* on his Met subscription; and which recording and background book should he buy to Prepare? The fourth message was from Virgil, and ran, "Please listen. I'm running away and I'm going to come there now. Last night he punish-fucked me for no reason at all, and Bauhaus is dead, because of Cash. He took my money away."

He was sobbing. This was real.

"Please be there. It's just through the Park and I'll be quick. Please can I come back? Please, did I do the . . . the wrong thing?

But don't be mean to me. I have been punish-fucked enough."

We heard the beep; message completed.

Then there was this pause.

"Punish-fucked?" I said.

Cosgrove was so stunned by the message that he had to pull himself together—I mean literally, wrapping his arms around his chest and hiking up his socks and smoothing down his hair.

"Now you see what has happened," he was saying. "The rough ways of Cash and his friends."

"Which friends are these?" I asked.

"One's named Gordon, and there's a leather guy known as Whambo. He isn't even gay, mostly. And someone's Rex."

I glanced at Dennis Savage, who was calmly sorting through his papers, quite unavailable.

"Gordon Markey," I noted. "And Rex Don. Jesus, the seventies are . . ."

Dennis Savage was examining a typo.

"Earth calling Dennis Savage."

"Yes, I hear," he said. "Gordon and Rex. Didn't they have some scene with britches and haymows where Daddy directs his boys in disciplinary games . . . ?" He sighed. "Who would have supposed they're still doing those things?"

"Especially to one of us."

Dennis Savage shrugged, perusing his text. "If sex bliss is what he needs, he must pay the penalty."

"Look who's talking."

Dennis Savage looked at me. "Sex bliss? *Moi?*"

"Or what is Billy for?"

Cosgrove came nearer. "He was going to take me to *Creeplies 2.*"

"*Gremlins,* first of all," said Dennis Savage, neatening everything up, as always. "And Billy may, at first regard, appear to be an erotic icon. But you know how it *goes on*? It goes on as something warm to grasp at night. Go ahead and take away my membership card in the South of Fourteenth Street Jackoff Gemeinschaft, if you must. But there it is. All I ask for is a good guy, you know?"

"So of course you wrote a story about someone who becomes promiscuous because he's terrified of hooking up with a—"

"He is *not*—"

"Besides, you already know good guys," I insisted. "You know plenty."

Then Billy ambled in.

"Now, Billy," Cosgrove began, "here are two very important things. First, will you take me to *Gremlies 2,* and second, we have to rescue Virgil any minute now."

"Rescue him?" Dennis Savage echoed.

"Somehow I'm always in the wrong place," said Billy. "Waking up after a cute little nap, and where is everybody? Down here, shooting the breeze, that's surely true. So you're going to be coming down, catching the action. Then you slip into the john for a fast piss-up. Come out and, whoa!, everybody's back upstairs again eating the boss's fancy meat loaf. I don't get my timing right around here."

"There's a two o'clock show," Cosgrove went on, "but we can't go yet because Virgil's coming over to be rescued."

"Rescued?" said Dennis Savage. "No one has to rescue him. If he wants to come home, he can, anytime. Just not to my house."

Cosgrove said, "You wear five-day derodeant pads, and this is the sixth day."

"That is so stupid," Dennis Savage rumbled.

"Easy," I said, as Billy, on an agenda of his own, wandered off somewhere.

It went on like that for a while, till Virgil burst in, his gala return, his first time in the house since he had hooked up with Cash. Our Virgil, weeping.

"I ran all the way," he cried. "Mostly."

Dennis Savage ran, too. He walked out of the room without a word—though he *did* hang around till Virgil showed up, you notice—as Cosgrove and Virgil embraced and whimpered.

"Don't answer the buzzer," Virgil begged me, one eye on Dennis Savage as he split. "Don't let anyone in at all. You don't know what this is. And I will say that you cannot imagine what he'll do."

"Virgil escaped with the clothes on his back," Cosgrove pointed out.

"I still have some stuff upstairs."

"Are you back to stay?" I asked. "Because there've been some changes heareabouts."

Virgil did something strange then: He put out his arms and wandered around in a circle with his eyes closed. I get it: sleep-walking. And Cosgrove performed a touch of boogie, like a devotee at a rock concert when the band performs its hit single.

"What changes?" asked Virgil, coming to rest.

"You're a bad little boy, you know," I said. "You're a piece of trash, in fact."

"I'm back," said Virgil. "I made a mistake and I want to come home now."

"That sounds so simple to do," I said.

"This is the start of the new segment of my life."

"Yes!" Cosgrove agreed.

"From now on, I will be known as James Fenimore Castaway."

"Oh!" said Cosgrove. "And I could be Hopalong Castaway." His look darkled. "Or perhaps Lord Pembroke Winter—"

"You're not anything," I told Virgil. "You're not even a homeboy here. You got yourself written out of the stories."

Virgil began to cry, and the buzzer rang.

"Please," he begged. "It's Cash and his friends. Please don't let them."

"This is ridiculous," I said, answering the summons. "We're not going to—Yes, hello?"

It was Steve the doorman, announcing a messenger. I told him to keep the package for me. When I turned back to the room, Cosgrove and Virgil were holding each other, lightly swaying to the rhythm of Virgil's snuffling.

"All right, you two. Break it up, and let's deal the cards. First," I asked Virgil, "who the hell are you?"

"What do you mean?"

"What I said. Because one day you were this affectionate young man whom I loved, and the day after that you were all serious and self-important and throwing poor Cosgrove around till—"

"He *never*!" Cosgrove cried.

"Yes, he did, all right. He dumped you like—"

"I am *James Fenimore Castaway*! And if you think—"

"And *I* am Hopalong—"

"Both of you *shut up* and *eat* it for *breakfast*! And I am *not* calling anyone James Fenimore Castaway!"

"A simple Mister J. Fenimore will suffice."

"Let me ask you something. Were you planning to just march upstairs and move in again?"

Virgil—all right, J. (which is as much as I can manage)—turned a few colors. "I know there's someone else up there," he said. "And . . . changed feelings of a somewhat kind."

"Would you buy me a puppy?" Cosgrove suddenly asked me. *"Now?"*

He shrugged. "Or a little later."

"No."

"Please!"

"Speaking of that," I asked J., "where's Bauhaus?"

"He died. It was so sad. Cash kept saying he would throw him right out the window, but in the whole truth of fact he just let him run loose in the street and I know it was deliberately. Because Bauhaus really never quite knew what a car was."

"He was run over? Bauhaus?"

J. nodded.

"Bauhaus is dead," I said, taking it in.

"Did he go squush?" Cosgrove asked fearfully.

J. nodded.

Cosgrove exhaled audibly in horror.

J. nodded.

"Although I never really liked him," Cosgrove went on. "He was a little grotesque in certain ways."

"He was a stray," J. reminded us. "And we took him in and tried to be kind to him."

Cosgrove, a stray himself, got very quiet.

"Anyway, I'm back. I missed everybody, whether you believe that or not, and I had a very strange time, which I will someday tell of."

J. and Cosgrove hugged again, more joyously this time. Now he's J.; do you believe that?

"But I have to ask if you could put me up on your couch for a while. Because I don't know where else I can live."

"I want a puppy," said Cosgrove.

"One addition at a time," I told him.

Well, I staved off the question of the puppy, but, with J. moved in, my life became complicated in odd little ways. True, J. and Cosgrove immediately became as inseparable as of old, and could be counted on to turn even the simplest errands into the work of six or seven hours, minimum—which gave me plenty of free time to work in. But J.'s presence stiffened Dennis Savage, got him all prickled up. Conditions were tense in every direction: The elevators were no-man's-land, and the mail room felt like the crush bar at Drury Lane during the feud of Alexander Pope and Colley Cibber.

J. and Cosgrove never took the opportunity to get to Cosgrove's movie. They *talked* about going; mainly, they went birdwatching. This is J.'s latest craze, which Cosgrove seized upon (using my old opera glasses; J. has giant binoculars). Neither of them really has the authentic commitment of the bird lover. Or maybe I misapprehend the scene. But I always thought the idea was to spot specific birds—to "watch" them—and thus collect some sort of meaningful experience. J. thinks all you have to do is peer around in your binoculars and call out the various phyla (or whatever they are) of any bird at all.

So Billy and I are out in the Park with our two bird-watchers.

J. says, "Ah, the scarlet tanager."

"Hm," Cosgrove responds. "The Arctic tern."

"A cardinal."

"Various robins."

"Look at how pumped up that kid is," says Billy, referring to J. "Lats and delts poking around inside a dress shirt in the Park with those binoculars; that's really something. Pointing at the birds, and his whole upper body does this and that. There's a hot class of something, now surely."

"Ah, a flock of swallows," J. observed.

Cosgrove was ranked out, but only momentarily. "Uh-oh!" he called out. "A pelican!"

Billy and I are ensconced on a bench, the two of them wandering now near us and now some distance away: rather as J. himself has been for a while. Billy's watching them, J. especially, for Billy fears that J. is not only his predecessor but his successor as well.

"Shit, that kid is hot," Billy tells me. "Pretending he doesn't know he's cute, and all the time . . . What does he like to do, anyway?" Billy meant in bed.

"I don't know what he likes," I say. "He used to enjoy just being a very-well-taken-care-of young man, secure in the indulgence of a lover and doting uncles. Suddenly he went off like a Roman candle."

"I could enjoy him." Billy is nodding, intent.

"Just leave Cosgrove alone, okay?"

"What about the other one, huh?"

"You can push him under a trolley car."

A pause as Billy takes this in.

"Yeah, I know he's not too popular around about, right?"

"Right."

"What'd he do?"

What's the answer? He did what we all do: got hungry and browsed. He needed to rack up a few while he was in his prime and the sun was out.

"He took the rest of us for granted," I said.

"Now he's back," says Billy.

"Yes."

"The boss won't let me mention him, you know? Can't ask about him, don't know about him. It's *final,* get it?" He laughed. "I'm just asking you this one thing, okay? How final is it?"

"Love that deep is infinite. I don't know if they'll ever get back together . . . even if they'll speak. But I know that their feelings will run deep forever. It's funny about why folks couple." Watching J. and Cosgrove ranging the greensward with their game, and their birds' names, and their love. "I've seen it for hot sex. I've seen it out of empathy. As in *Othello.*"

I had paused. Billy said, "Go on."

"I've seen it for sociopolitical reasons. And out of affection. Out of a need to be understood. Out of wonder. Out of ambivalence. Out of fashion. And of course there's the well-off older man and the penniless kid."

Billy, also watching the kids, shot me a look.

"Look who's talking?" I said.

"No offense."

"But of all these bonds, the simplest is just 'We fit.' That's love at first look, of course, and it generally lasts as long as the two men live."

"So?"

"So Dennis Savage and J. are the fit. But something went wrong, and I don't—"

A crash and yelling turned our attention to the roadway, where one of those ridiculous surrey contraptions worked by pedals had run into a rollerblader and fallen over. No one was badly hurt, and everyone was yelling.

J. and Cosgrove examined the altercation through their glasses, like aficionados at the opera. I had jumped up at first, but now I settled back on the bench, and before Billy and I had got out three sentences between us the police arrived.

Billy said to me, "Did that kid really think his new boy friend was going to come after him? Like sex cops? Arresting you for re-fusing to be, like, punish-fucked?"

"Punish-fucked," I echoed. "Jesus, our sex is complicated. One thing you have to say for straights . . . and I think, on balance, it's the only thing . . . when they have sex, they always know what it's going to be. He'll be on top, and she'll say, 'Ooh, yes,' and every-body's happy."

"Think so, huh?"

"Will you look at that? Or am I in a movie?"

I meant the accident, and Billy looked: at J. and Cosgrove, ap-parently explaining the whole thing to the police, who were tak-ing their statements.

"They'll get in the papers at last," said Billy.

The two of them then came running over to us, thrilled to the eyeballs, all birds forgot.

"Did you see us telling those policemen how—"

"'I am James Fenimore Castaway,' I explained," J. told us, "'and I happen to have seen the whole thing. And this is my asso-ciate, Mr. Replevin.'"

At which Cosgrove bowed.

"I said, 'Officers—'"

"Now can I have a puppy, because I'm responsible and a pub-lic citizen?"

"It is a matter of becoming important," J. observed, and I'm not sure whom he was talking to. He's been beyond us for some time now. "It is a matter of being respected as a man of power. Of knowledge, even."

"'What did I stop being?' is what he says to me," said Billy, looking at J. "I can't help but mention this. What Dennis Savage says. He goes, 'What did I stop being, huh?'"

"He didn't stop," said J.

"Then *you* stopped," said Billy.

"I didn't stop being anything."

Cosgrove was looking through the opera glasses. "Ha!" he

cried. "A flock of ravens, black as the night of the prom!"

"That isn't how it happens," J. sadly added.

So what does happen? Billy and I talked it over after we got back, as the kids showered. Billy paced as we spoke, but slowly, not restlessly: as if he might be concentrating not only on our talk but on some deep through-line of the mind that would tell him of his fate.

"'What did I stop being?'" Billy echoes, a shaman uttering a summons. "You think that kid is going back in, like?"

"I don't know."

"Does he want to, I mean?"

"I imagine so. If only because he has nowhere else to land. But I don't believe it will content him to be Dennis Savage's little hound dog all over again. He's been rebelling for years without knowing it. Used to be, his projects were all private acts, things that Dennis Savage and I would giggle at in his living room. Then he started getting all these ideas for things he could do *outside*. Jobs, and his cabaret act with Cosgrove, and travel . . ."

"Should I split?"

I said nothing.

"I mean, it'd make it easier on everybody, wouldn't it?"

"Not necessarily."

"I got places to go to, you know, me. I'm not just some street kid. Got my black book of clients, certainly. Lonely nights, Billy calls with that Big Thing. Ask me over, flip me two bills. You can believe that, right?"

I nodded.

"Even got my family. I suppose they'll always take me back." He looked at me. "Brooklyn. Yeah, Red Hook. Imagine. You know where that is?"

I pointed east.

He laughed. "Yeah, that's . . . Yeah. If I could take that birthday-wedding-funeral jazz they're always playing . . . You get born in a family like mine, your social calendar is very full from birth. Man, you're eight years old and Great-aunt Teresa is picking out the hat she's gonna wear to your high school graduation ceremonies. Cousin Daniela has reserved the hall for your wedding reception. Her husband, Dominic, knows this girl in Bay Ridge. And she's somebody's cousin, too, right? I mean, who can live like that, with, like, a history on top of you? Those straight guys think they're so macho, but they let their relatives fuck them around for life. They get told what to do, right?, and the thing is, they do it. Slaves is what they are. Then they strut around like they're Jerry Lewis."

"Maybe that's why they strut," I said. "To rid themselves of the . . ."

Billy was listening to something.

"What?" I said.

"Are those two fucking in there?"

"Probably."

"*Yeah*. Really?"

"You have to understand that the personal and sexual relationships in this family are so mixed up that a few of us aren't sure who belongs to whom anymore. Besides, they're probably just holding on."

"Kissing each other?"

I shrugged.

"Kissing leads to cumming," he said.

"Look, I don't know—"

"You sure you don't want to let me move in here with you and Cosgrove? Because I could take care of him, too, you know? Ease up on your time, take him to *Gobblers* . . ."

Then the kids burst in, totally nude and toweling off. They do that sometimes. Billy watched them. For a flash of time I thought he might grab one of them, or slap them with the towel, or dance around them. Billy is very smooth-skinned but for a line of hair that slithers up to his navel; it's the kind of thing one is rather conscious of.

Billy left us. He said, "I got to . . ." and he gestured.

Something.

"I have thought about it," Cosgrove began, "and I absolutely have to have a puppy dog."

"Which we will now name," said J.

"How about Fala?" I said.

"So I *can* have one?" Cosgrove cried.

"All right—but only a Highland White Scottie."

"Well, of course," Cosgrove rejoined. "Just what kind is that?"

"Those little white dogs, very trim and intelligent."

"I want a little faithful dog with a cute nose that he pushes against you because he doesn't know what will become of him."

"Cosgrove," said J., "you may call him Billy Monday."

"No."

J. looked challenged, not congenially.

"It has to be a name that *I* would give," Cosgrove explained.

"Well, at least I'll make spaghetti carbonara for dinner, I expect," J. told us as he rose above it.

"That was the Pines dish of the 1970s," I said. "Cash taught you it, right?"

"So what, who taught me?"

"So gays are becoming like straights. One enters and all follow."

"Oh, that is such a platitude," said J.

Then Dennis Savage came in and everyone froze.

"This is the seventh day," Cosgrove muttered.

Dennis Savage and J. were staring at each other.

"Well, well, well," I said. You keep it moving, like a sitcom. You don't want anyone's feelings exposed.

But J. was fearless. He strode up to Dennis Savage and, looking him spang in the eye, extended his hand.

Dennis Savage looked past him, at me. "Actually," he said, "I came down to discuss my story with you. There are crucial changes I am determined to make in the way it feels to the reader. I have thought about these changes very carefully and I want to make them irrevocably."

J. said, "Aren't you going to shake hands with me?"

Now Dennis Savage looked at him. "No," he said. Then, to me: "If you could drop in later on, I would appreciate the—"

"Please," J. urged him.

"No." And Dennis Savage left.

J. glanced at Cosgrove and me and gave a little shrug and sat on the couch.

"You can crash with us," I said. "Until . . . well—"

"Until what?" J. asked, eyes round, a totally unknowing young man now, the J. I used to know.

"James Fenimore," said Cosgrove, coming over to him, "we still have to name my Highland White puppy who licks my face and loves me."

"I just didn't expect . . ." J. began, then stopped. "There's hardly some good reason not to shake hands."

"Don't worry about it," Cosgrove urged, sitting next to him. "He's just a platypus."

"Is what I did so wrong?" J. asked me.

"No," I said. "You had the right. But it messed everything up, and we're being angry and selfish about it."

"I don't know who my friends are," he said.

"Look who's talking."

And lo, there was another entrée, that of Carlo. He'd brought a bag of red Delicious apples, because now that he's working again (as a bartender; he says the customers tip like crazy) he likes to play the sport.

J. didn't jump up at the sight of Carlo the way he used to, but we aren't getting much jumping from him on any count nowadays. Carlo saw him and said, "I ought to pound you for walking," and J. got up and held out his hand, and Carlo just grabbed him. But as he held him tight he said, "I'm going to scold you, you watch. I'm going to make you understand about something here."

"His name's James Fenimore Castaway now," Cosgrove told Carlo as he released J.

"His . . . did *what*?"

"I call him J.," I said.

"Think I'll just call him Sparky" was Carlo's solution. "Had a dog by that name some years back. Follow me to school and like that. Wait for me all day. Walk me home. You're going to search far and wide for faithfulness on that level, I can say that to you."

Cosgrove said, "I could call my new puppy Sparky."

Carlo looked at me.

"I said he could have a dog."

"Or wait," Cosgrove went on. "Maybe I would call him Fleabiscuit, because he's just about the weirdest little puppy in the town."

"Is he going to stay like this?" J. asked. "Forever? Because, all right, I went away, but does that mean I can't ever come back? They teased me and tormented me and they killed my dog. This was real life, and doesn't anyone feel sorry for me about that?"

"You dumped him," I said. "What do you want from him now?"

"He wouldn't even shake my hand!"

"Everybody leaves you," I said.

"Huh?" Carlo put in.

"I didn't leave," said J. "I just went visiting."

"When can I buy Fleabiscuit?" said Cosgrove. "Now, or in a half hour?"

"Do you swear to buy a Highland White and *only* a Highland White?" I said.

"I will only buy Fleabiscuit."

"That's not the right answer."

So I sorted him out and, with misgivings—the perennial state of life in these parts, it seems—handed him the plastic. One of Cosgrove's quirkiest talents is the ability to imitate any signature on sight, and lending him one of my cards is easier than taking one out in his name—even admitting that, gods know, the card companies continually pester you with opportunities to bless your loved ones with their very own credit power. I wonder if they realize how many of these go to gay boy friends.

"J.'s not wearing socks," Carlo observed.

"I don't even have any. I'm a refugee now."

"Yeah, you got big. What's all that muscle there?" Stepping up, Carlo examined J.'s upper torso. "There's lean and mean all over you, suddenly," Carlo said, running his hands up and down J.'s sides. "Where've you been, now?"

"Cash made me go to the gym with him."

"Shit, scope those delts on a kid!"

J. fought loose and backed away, furious. "I'm not a kid anymore," he cried. "When do you find that out, at last? I'm thirty years old!" Soothing his shoulder joints as if Carlo had hurt them, he went on, "I'm not your doll to play with—you and Cash and his friends. I have feelings more than you know."

Carlo was still, looking at J.; then Carlo said, "I would slam-fuck you for a photographer I know, on your back, hands tied at the wrists. I'd get two, three hundred, and you would definitely have feelings then, my boyo."

Well, I figured this was the right time to hustle Cosgrove and J. out to buy the dog—"A Highland White or I'll kill you," I warned them—and then I washed apples for Carlo and me and played him some music. He likes César Franck's Symphony in d minor.

Then:

"Guess I been all pressured up without knowing it, and I unloaded on . . . what's his name today?"

"James Fenimore Castaway."

He laughed without quite laughing. "He was so sweet and truly loving. He was so responsive and interested. What happened to him?"

"You know," I said, flashing on Zuleto and Candio, "you could be any father alive, saying that, any father in the world."

"He isn't fun anymore."

Filing the record back in the symphony shelf, I said, "No, actually, he's not."

"So what happened?"

"I guess he finally grew up. All kids are amusing, but some adults aren't, and I guess we got one of the duds."

"That's hard to work with."

"Maybe Cash did this to him?"

Carlo shook his head. "He was like this sometime before." Suddenly he chuckled. "Fleabiscuit?"

I shrugged.

"That Cosgrove's the real Little Kiwi now," he said.

"What's 'punish-fucking'?"

Carlo bit a chunk of apple, chewed, and swallowed it before answering. When he turned to me his eyes were lit up, guarded. He's wary of me sometimes.

"How come you ask?" he says.

"It's part of J.'s litany of abuses under the regime of Cash. 'Blow-fucking' is another. Are these arcane practices, or am I really just up in my balloon?"

He thought it over, half-smiling. "Well," he finally said, "your punish-fucking is a San Francisco practice. Doggy position, bottom on his knees. Top guy spanks him while he pumps. Clunk. Clunk. Clunk. It's popular S&M because you can do it without . . . you know . . ."

"Pulleys, a vast crucifix, and six dwarfs?"

"Blow-fucking, that's a table for three. Guy on his face, top slides in, they fuck for a bit so the sap starts rising. Then the top turns on his back so the fucked guy is facing up, and the third man slips right in there and starts slurping. If you remember to sizzle up the fucked guy beforehand, the whole show can get really hot."

"Wow."

"But let's not credit Cash with this. It's been happening all over for decades, right?"

"Not to Virgil."

"You sorry for him or what?"

"Well, whose side are *you* on?"

"I don't know who I like anymore, except you and Cosgrove. People aren't always as nice to me as they might be."

"Maybe everyone's tired of trying to live up to your idea of a noble young man. Maybe everyone's exhausted."

He heard that and he didn't like it. "What are you saying again?"

"We tried, my brave lad, and we failed, is what I'm saying. Stonewall wasn't perfectable. Men took a scope at you and said, Oh, I think I'll do that, too. I want that body, and that smile, and that tall, and that . . . Everyone can be gorgeous, right? Just say yes. Gaze in the mirror, looks to kill. Who's that, *me*? With those triceps and that smile that appears at one fell swoop to be dangerous yet kind, not to mention the sleek black hair with the Superman wave just there at the—"

He had lurched up and grabbed me, and I said, "You have no right to hurt me for saying that."

"I'm not going to hurt you, but you just stop now."

"It's my fault, too."

"Stop talking," he said, holding me. "Be my friend."

"I wrote about it. I glamorized it and made it believable. I invented it. This is all fiction, and I lied." I held on to him and I said, "Save me."

"Big Steve died a year ago this week," he told me. "That says why I'm in a state, yelling at The Kid Himself, who I do nothing but adore. My old buddy Steve took it quietly, hid away. Didn't want anyone to see him all wrecked. But I was in on it. I kept the secret for him, because he was one of my favorite guys. He was so great. So loving and fine, Big Steve. You remember. A stunning guy. So stunning to see. Some big monster man that you dreamed about when you were ten. Right?"

"Yes."

"Sure you do. We'll all remember him."

We had broken apart, very upset, reaching for each other's hands, looking away. There's no protocol for this.

"I intend to stick around," I finally got out, "and I'm remembering everything."

"Yeah, you will." He smiled. "I know that's your style."

"Rip."

"Come on, Bud, or we're getting all glum around here. Come on."

"How'd you get so tall, anyway? Why couldn't I do that?"

"It's some Dakota thing."

"No, I mean . . . I mean, who made you so nice? Every son of a bitch in town has been busting himself to be as like you as possible, and you just got it all, and yet . . . what is this?"

"Big Steve is gone and I was tough on Little Kiwi, and that's two bad things in my day."

"No, what am I saying here? How come . . ."

"Maybe you would square it for me with The Kid Himself—"

Pounding at the door. As I turned, Carlo grabbed me again and said, "Would you do that for me?"

"Sure."

He still would not let me go. "I have to say this first," he explained. "He matters to me even the way he is now."

"Okay."

"Promise?"

I promised; and it was Dennis Savage, with a letter. From Billy. A farewell note. Short and sweet. He felt extra, so he walked.

Dennis Savage said, "I know for certain this is someone's fault, but I don't know whom to get mad at."

"Look how he knows about 'whom,'" said Carlo. "Class."

"Oh, *you*."

"Everyone's down on me today."

"At a time like this," Dennis Savage fussed; but he was calming down. He may have been, in part, relieved at this Turn of the Wheel. Just a guess.

"What if he begged and pleaded?" I asked Dennis Savage. "Would you fit him back in?"

He was cautious. "What if *who*—"

"Virgil."

He just waved that away with his hand: Oh, no. He had his time. He made his move. He must abide by the consequences of his act.

"Billy left a letter," Carlo said, just beginning to comprehend the sequence of events, "and then he vanished?"

"Poof" is how Dennis Savage described it.

"Billy is gone because why?"

"Because that fucking renegade walked back in here as if he *owned* the place, and everybody was treating him like the prodigal son. So Billy hitched up his pride and walked out rather than be pushed!"

"Glory," said Carlo, amazed.

Then the kids came in, bearing a doggy portage cage, a doggy basket, a red rubber ball, seven boxes of Milk-Bone biscuits, a doggy blanket, a shoulder harness, a doggy coat, seven wind-up doggy fascinator toys, a chew bone, and Fleabiscuit, a male Highland White puppy so shy that as soon as they put him on the floor he ran yipping into the bedroom and hid under the bed.

In the excitement of our unloading the props and coaxing Fleabiscuit out, Dennis Savage slipped away.

So we have a dog. He remains shy and stays, for the most part, under the bed, though Cosgrove says he comes out and frolics when no one else is around. I said, "You're house-training him, aren't you?"; and Cosgrove said, "Of course," with immense decision; but I could tell by the look he gave J. that he didn't know what I was talking about.

He is devoted to the dog, and has set up a tiny apartment for him under the bed, with a blanket and a toy tray. Still, though I see Fleabiscuit when he and Cosgrove go out for and return from their walks, and though late at night when I can't sleep I occasionally hear the crunching of biscuits, the dog is fundamentally invisible company.

This has its exasperating side. One day I came in to an empty house with an air of a Presence in it. Could something be lurking in a closet?

In the bedroom, on a hunch, I called out, "Cosgrove!"

"I'm right here," he announced from under the bed, "visiting with Fleabiscuit."

"All right, that's *it*! From now on——"

"No, I just wanted to see what it's like," he cried, squirming out. "Please be nice."

"Some dog you picked out. Tell him to come forth."

"Fleabiscuit! Appear!"

Fleabiscuit yipped but stayed put.

"This is not a fit dog for a gay household," I said. "He should be bold, emotive, Stonewallesque."

"Fleabiscuit," Cosgrove wheedled, "come on, now."

Fleabiscuit snuffled but did not move.

"I know," said Cosgrove, running to the kitchen. He came back with a Milk-Bone. "Watch this," he said, then whispered, "He thinks they're cookies."

Cosgrove left the biscuit on the floor in front of the bed and began calling Fleabiscuit again. After a while a little nose appeared, then two paws—then the dog darted out to snap up the biscuit and Cosgrove caught him, shouting, "It's Fleabiscuit the Great!"

"I don't see what's so great about him," I said, as the dog tried to lick Cosgrove's face while eating the biscuit.

"James Fenimore wants to train him to chase Dennis Savage and mow him down."

Did I mention that J. is spending nights on our living room couch? That's where Carlo usually stays, so Carlo dug up a sleeping bag somewhere and now he sleeps on the floor near the piano. Except sometimes, during the night, J. creeps into the bedroom and joins Cosgrove and me—"Because he's quite worried about things," Cosgrove explained—and Carlo usually drags his bag in, too. I know they're all family, but it's beginning to feel like a bunkhouse at Camp Mudgekeewiss in there.

(If you're wondering when Cosgrove and I fit It in, we've always been afternooners. Just because breeders equate sex with night doesn't mean we have to. So huh?)

I like having everyone on hand, actually, as long as I can count on a few private hours in the noontime, when Carlo is at the gym and J. hunting for a job or taking Cosgrove to the Park to get into some mischief or other. One good thing about us is: Sooner or later we've all got something to do.

Dennis Savage never comes down anymore, for the obvious reason; but I talked him into making us dinner. I said we hadn't had a decent meal in weeks, and anyway, he likes to cook, and of course the idea was to warm him with amity (and scotch) so we could finally say something like "Poor J.'s all alone downstairs, so could we ask him up?" Who would say no?

"We just got to handle it right," Carlo kept saying. "We should truly watch our timing, you know."

"Don't worry about me," J. told us. "I have very choice titles cued up on the video. Pee-wee Herman and a selection of Looney Tunes. And for dinner it's a fresh green pepper and teddy bear macaroni."

He said this calmly, reportorially. Oh, J. is calm, but he can't figure anything out now, because he believes he is the sinless being punished for his sins. He just doesn't know what he is at this point. Carlo knows, but he and J. are keeping some distance in a polite way because of their set-to, so Carlo isn't saying anything.

"*Normalize* this dinner," I urged Carlo and Cosgrove as we went upstairs. "That's the key. Remind him of the good old days and maybe he'll want them back."

Why is it that people change? Dennis Savage was always grouchy but he was also always reachable, even if you had to implore a little, or at least threaten to bite his knee. And Virgil Brown was sweet and curious and devoted and now he's a self-important, dreary load. What happens to people?

Dennis Savage had made one of his greatest dishes, veal scalloppine all'Anna, with these incredibly thin slices of prosciutto cooked onto the veal, and black olives and artichoke hearts, and he whips up this stunning fetuccine with sun-dried tomatoes, some weird sort of mushroom, and beer. I know he thinks we're unworthy of such gourmet prep—what he really wants at his table, impressed and hoping, is some naïve hustler who'll get drunk on la dolce vita and stay over and do everything.

Dennis Savage looks tired and unwilling, but he puts a decent face on it. He's even nice to Cosgrove.

Carlo and Cosgrove carefully simulate an atmosphere of Merry Friends at Festive Table, exclaiming at things they took for granted years ago: the framed Chairmen of the Board LP, with Dennis Savage's and my favorite seventies dancing cut, "Finders Keepers"; his collection of Doctor Dolittle books, including all the original Stokes editions and some foreign translations; his impressive home-entertainment-center breakfront with its orderly little rows of CDs (though for some reason Cosgrove decided to teethe for a bit on Dennis Savage's jewel box of the EMI *Anything Goes* and Dennis Savage got truculent).

Boys and girls, it just wasn't the same. Are Dennis Savage and we even friends anymore, in the real, deeply felt, desperately Stonewall sense? It's not only that we are fresh out of the delight that comes with getting next to intimate acquaintances and feeling one's skin, so to say. It's that we're tired of one another. These visits used to be relief.

Now they're a chore.

Dinner was slow: great eats and nothing to say till Carlo idly asked, "What kind of animal *is* a veal? Don't recall ever seeing any such thing."

"It's beef," said Dennis Savage. "Baby beef. Calf."

"What?" Cosgrove cried.

"Veal is—"

"A *baby*? Who didn't even live yet? I'm not eating a baby!"

"I worked all afternoon on that veal, buster, and you are, too, eating it!"

Cosgrove sorrowfully eyed his plate. "It was a little calf named Juniper," he said, "who frolicked in the dell."

Carlo comforted him (and ate his veal), but another wedge thus got driven between the two sides, and relations did not advance with the hours. Trying to urge it all along, I said, "Have you heard from Billy?"

Dennis Savage looked so weary then. So unable to deal with it all.

"I mean," I added, "maybe he—"

"And maybe he didn't."

We never had an opening to bring J. into; we left the same people we had arrived as. We had failed, you see, and we came home to find Fleabiscuit barking at us, leading us to J., who had fallen asleep in front of the working television; and suddenly he looked thirty years old.

"We can't go on just like so," Cosgrove told me one afternoon when the rest of us were away. "There are pains in the heart."

"Whose heart?" I asked.

"Everybody's. It isn't right anymore. Carlo was mean to James Fenimore. And Dennis Savage is lonely. Why can't we fix it up?"

He and I were working on a thousand-piece jigsaw puzzle, which has replaced bird-watching. J. usually joins us, but today he was out beating the streets in search of employment. Cosgrove loves doing puzzles so much that he has almost abandoned Zelda, and he plumes himself on choosing the music we listen to as we solve the puzzle. Today it was *Parsifal,* Wagner's opera about the utterly uncorrupted spirit whose ability to empathize redeems the world.

If only Stonewall had a hero like like that, I was thinking; at the same time, I realized that if I said that aloud one of my friends would reply, "We *have* a hero like that: Jeff Stryker."

Why can't we fix it up? Because there's a shortage of hot and an excess of hunger.

"I'm sorry for Billy," Cosgrove said, trying a piece everywhere he found an opening; this is what I call "needle in a haystack" puzzling. It's like looking for a lover. "He really occurred to be nice."

Fleabiscuit came running out, looking at us as if he'd just had crucial news and wasn't sure how to convey it. Then he ran into the kitchen to consult his water dish and see if there was any Mighty Dog in his food bowl. (There always is: Cosgrove is a soft touch.)

"Just a little while ago," I said, finding and placing the last piece missing from the puzzle frame, "everyone in the stories was almost content. Did we all have what we want?"

"As far as I know," Cosgrove replied, studying a piece shaped like a revolver.

"It's just that I'm getting tired of those Boy Scout Jamborees in the bedroom every night. All that talking keeps me up."

"James Fenimore talks to work things out. He will chat at night."

I'll say. About four in the morning, you stir awake to a heavy three-way discussion on how to assert yourself, or what gay really means, or the other armchair therapies that Carlo and J. like to administer.

Well, this one night I got a little sharp, and Carlo got sharp in reply, and J. chimed in, so I said the whole thing was we were waiting for Dennis Savage to take him back. And, like, when was this going to happen, may I ask? So Carlo did a little something on that matter, and J. will have his riposte, and then Cosgrove piped up. All this natter is going on, and I am getting irritated.

So I put it out that J. is maybe a stranger in our midst.

"Look who's talking," says he.

"No," says Carlo, moving in quick, because this touches upon something he has had in mind for a bit. "No, you *are* the stranger," he tells J. "Because one day you are so cute and the next you are the icicle from hell."

"I never," says J.

Carlo squirms out of his sleeping bag to confront J., and pull him off the bed, and look deeply into him, and have his effect.

"No," says J., leaning against Carlo and holding him; but Carlo doesn't hold back, and that can be dangerous.

"Yes," says Carlo, opening J.'s pajama jacket. "It was like now you had had us all, so we didn't matter to you." Pushing the jacket back off his shoulders. "Got your Cash muscles by then, you're moving on." Tracing the ridge of the right pectoral, thumbing the nipple. "I had him. Clunk. Oh, I had that one, too. Clunk." Smoothing his hair down, and J. standing there. I don't know what he's thinking. "Clunk, I had them all, right? The chesty blond with the big buttons, and the good old dark-haired boy with the shoulders who suddenly gets shy, and this one, and them. Clunk. Clunk. I'm ready for anything now, right?" Unbuttoning J.'s pajama bottoms and letting them drop to his ankles. "Except by now you are truly not The Kid Himself anymore. You're some guy scoring up clunk."

"I have to admit that's somewhat true," said Cosgrove, who can bear a grudge.

Shivering as he stepped out of his pants, J. said, "I am loving and nice," in a tone I had never heard out of him before.

Carlo ran his hands over J.'s skin, around his waist, and up and down the sides of his torso, and J. rubbed his cheek against Carlo's.

"I know the kind of nice you are, boy," said Carlo.

"Actually, he is usually a very loyal boy," said Cosgrove, no doubt repenting of his momentary lack of camaraderie. He was petting Fleabiscuit and seemed a little apprehensive.

"What did you want from Cash that we don't give you?" Carlo went on. "Why didn't you ask me? I could do that hot stuff for you."

"I was wrong," said J., reaching up to Carlo's shoulders as Carlo worked on J.'s neck and shoulders like a masseur.

"You were selfish, so I'm going to punish you now."

"No," said Cosgrove.

"Some say it's a shame to give a heavy spanking to a nice little boy like you. But who says you're nice now, huh?"

"He's particularly nice," Cosgrove offered.

"I'll give it to you Daddy-style, bare-bottom across my knee." Carlo was holding J. close, rubbing his back and moving against him; and J. was moving along with Carlo. "You like that, pal?"

"I didn't mean to make anyone sad."

They were kissing now, as Cosgrove stared, his head shaking. Fleabiscuit shook his head, too.

"Yeah, you did."

". . . no . . ."

"You got to be spanked, and I wish I could tell you how truly glad I am to be the one who's going to do it. What do you think—light, medium, or heavy?"

J., still on Carlo's mouth, breathed out, "Extra heavy," and Carlo said, "Sizzle you up first for this," and they went at it, kissing and feeling like porn in 1969, reel one . . . or no, like maybe reel four, after we had figured it all out. Carlo was giving J. that mouth-to-mouth wherein the aggressor's lips kind of overlap the victim's, as if the top guy is eating up the bottom's face. "Why'd you do it, Virgil?" Carlo kept asking him. "How come you did that?" Taking the boy by the middle and bending him around, turning him, lifting him. "Why'd you walk out and put on these big lats? Why'd you stop being cute?"

I had to speak. "He has the right to be what he wants to be. And he doesn't owe explanations to—"

"I want to eat your cock," J. told Carlo.

Cosgrove and Fleabiscuit looked at me in horror.

"You're going to lay across my knee is all you're going to do."

J. dove down, tongue at the ready, but Carlo pulled him up.

"Hot you up till you're all set for it," Carlo told him, "and you're going to work real well."

Justice and caprice is who they were then. The man who invented sex and the kid who could only love had traded responsibilities. That's how I know that Stonewall is over. But what's the next era?

"A kiss and fuck," said J. "So we can get acquainted."

"You little bitch."

"I want to see how you come, Carlo man. I want to feel you inside me. I've got real good suction."

Carlo guided J. by the waist and, sitting on the edge of the bed, thrust the kid onto his lap.

"Yes," said J. "Now. Yes. Carlo is king, and I'm going to give it up for Daddy."

He rubbed to and fro against Carlo, murmuring "Yes, Daddy" over and over.

Cosgrove pressed his head against me, hiding his eyes. Fleabiscuit did, too.

"All set now?" said Carlo, feeling the boy, running his left hand through J.'s hair and his right over his butt, clamping his right leg over J.'s legs and grabbing J.'s neck with his left hand. "You ready for me, boy?"

"Spank me right up the shit," said J., and Carlo obliged, extra heavy. Cosgrove groaned and Fleabiscuit yipped. It took a long while, and it must have been the real thing, because when Carlo let him up, J. was crying.

"Now we're going upstairs," said Carlo.

"*No!*"

"You want more?" Carlo turned to me. "Where's his clothes? No, fuck it." He turned to the closet. "We'll take pot luck."

"I'm *not* going up there!"

The two of them standing in my bedroom, their hard-ons just starting to die down. Sex in your house. We can see out; we can't see *in*.

"Boy," said Carlo, "you are going where you have to go. Or how else will we ever know?"

"He won't even shake my hand!"

"I'll be with you."

"He'll just—"

Carlo grabbed J. and held him so tight I thought the boy would cry out. But he whispered, "More. More."

"Another damnhell freak like the rest of us," Carlo muttered, turning on a lamp. "That's what we got now."

He was poking in the closet.

"It's just suits in there," I said.

"Well, where's the sex clothes?"

"In the dresser."

"*Sex* clothes?" Cosgrove echoed.

"Shh," I told him.

Carlo sought, and found, some things to satisfy his sense of occasion. He threw them at J.

"Get dressed, street boy."

"They're going upstairs," Cosgrove lamented to Fleabiscuit.

Fleabiscuit whined. He doesn't like it there, either.

Carlo helped J. dress: in a tight black T, reading "Fire Island Pines" in a circle on the left breast, and baggy white shorts. He smoothed down J.'s hair. Then he struggled into a pair of old jeans and, for some reason, put on my Blue Max medallion.

"This is me," Carlo said, facing us all.

Then he extended his hand to J., who took it, quiet now. I tried to see Little Kiwi there, but J. has made himself over too well.

"This could take a while of talking, I truly believe," Carlo told me, "so give me some keys."

I got into the drawer and tossed him the spare set.

"I'll be back," he shot out, imitating Arnold Schwarzenegger.

"You hero," I told him.

Carlo took J. in his arms. "You're all wet and warm from that, and that's just right. Did I hurt you?"

"Everyone's been hurting me for years now. I didn't say anything till recently."

"Come on."

With a hand on the back of J.'s neck, Carlo gently propelled him out of the apartment.

Fleabiscuit looked at Cosgrove, and Cosgrove looked at me. "Now what?" he said.

"You mean," I said, "who's going to squire you to *Monstlies II*?"

"I don't mean that. I mean, will Dennis Savage take James Fenimore back and save the family?"

He was settling under the covers. I turned the lamp out. Fleabiscuit stretched and smoothed out a place for himself.

"Will he?"

In the darkness, I saw Fleabiscuit lift his head and regard me quizzically, because this is a key question.

I made no remark, because, for the first time in this series, I haven't the vaguest idea what happens next.